Praise for Injustice

A journey into the heart of suspense ... ...ith.
Robin Caroll scores again with *Injustice for All*.
— James Scott Bell, award-winning, best-selling author

The undeniable bonds of love carries through generations in this timeless Southern story. As thick as the bayou, corruption and injustice smother the lives of the innocent in this compelling first installment of the Justice Seekers! Robin Caroll once again pens a masterpiece of Southern charm, mystery, and suspense. This is by far one of my favorite books from Caroll! I anxiously await the next Justice Seeker book!
— Ronie Kendig, author of *Nightshade*,
Digitalis, and *Wolfsbane*

Incredible stakes, unbalanced odds, fearless storytelling, and unforgettable characters . . . Robin Caroll knows how to deliver and she does it again with *Injustice for All*. Don't even try to put this book down."
— Tosca Lee, author of *Demon: A Memoir* and coauthor of
The Books of Mortals series (with Ted Dekker)

If you're a fan of convoluted plotlines and complex characters, you want to read *Injustice for All*. Just sit back and enjoy as Robin Caroll takes you on all the twists and turns of this fun roller coaster.
— Gayle Roper, author of *Shadows on the Sand*

In *Injustice for All*, Robin Caroll crafts a riveting romantic suspense with a hint of political intrigue. Filled with heroes, questions, and the search for truth, I couldn't turn the pages fast enough as the plot tightened into a spiraling noose. I loved these characters and hated to reach the end. Robin Caroll has joined the list of my must-read authors.
— Cara C. Putman, author of *Stars in the Night*

The tension begins on page one and builds from there as Caroll leads us through a labyrinth of suspense to a satisfying and unexpected conclusion. A great start for the Justice Seekers series.

—Richard L. Mabry, MD, author of the Prescription for Trouble series

Gripping and heart-stopping, *Injustice for All* may well be my favorite Robin Caroll book yet. Even after the last page, the characters are still lingering in my mind. My only regret . . . to reach the end. Can't wait for the next book!

—Dineen Miller, author of *Winning Him Without Words* and *The Soul Saver*

Once again Robin Caroll grabbed me from page one and didn't let up till I read the final word. Vivid characters, a compelling story and twists that made me stay up late makes *Injustice for All* Caroll's strongest work yet.

—Jim Rubart, award-winning and best-selling author of *Rooms*, *Book of Days*, and *The Chair*

Injustice for All starts off with a pulse-pounding scene and the suspense doesn't let up. Caroll is a top-notch storyteller with a knack for drawing the reader into the story. Highly recommended!

—Colleen Coble, author of *Lonestar Angel* and other Lonestar novels

Oh-my-stars! Robin Caroll just keeps getting better. I couldn't put the book down. *Injustice for All* is fast paced, with characters to fall in love with. Pick this book up at the first opportunity. It will make a great addition to your keeper shelf.

—Lynette Eason, author of *A Killer Among Us* and *Threat of Exposure*

Absolutely riveting! Meticulously plotted with characters I rooted for, this book was impossible to put down. Robin Caroll is lethal to my to-do list!

—Susan May Warren, award-winning, best-selling author of *My Foolish Heart*

Clear your calendar before starting *Injustice for All*. Once you begin this gripping tale of murder and redemption, you won't be able to put it down.

—Rick Acker, author of *When the Devil Whistles* and *Dead Man's Rule*

Injustice for All is a great read full of suspense, twists, and turns, as it races back and forth toward it's unexpected but satisfying ending. Very enjoyable!

—Linda Hall, author of *Dark Water* and *Black Ice*

INJUSTICE
FOR ALL

Other Novels by Robin Caroll

Evil Series
Deliver Us from Evil
Fear No Evil
In the Shadow of Evil

Bayou Series
Bayou Justice
Bayou Corruption
Bayou Judgment
Bayou Paradox
Bayou Betrayal
Blackmail

Framed!

Dead Air

RobinCaroll

InJustice For All

Nashville, Tennesseee

To MY Remington and Isabella . . .

You girls light up my life in more ways than I ever thought humanly possible. What an honor it is to be your mom.
I love you so much.

Acknowledgments

As always, I'm amazed by so many talented people at B&H who work extremely hard behind the scenes to bring my books to print. I offer my deepest thanks to the whole Pure Enjoyment team, but especially those I'm honored to work with closely: Julie Gwinn, Robin Patterson, Kim Stanford, Greg Pope, Haverly Pennington, and Diana Lawrence. For everyone at B&H, thank you for being part of my publishing "family." I truly appreciate each and every one of you extending your talent and skill on my behalf.

No amount of thanks is enough to my editor, Julee Schwarzburg, who continues to teach me and makes me smile while I learn. You are so amazing, Julee, and I thank you from the bottom of my heart for not only being an awesome editor, but a true friend.

This book dealt with minute details of our legal system. Huge thanks to Rick Acker and Cara Putman for sharing their knowledge with me. Any mistakes in the representation of legal issues is mine, where I twisted in the best interest of my story.

Thanks to Brandt Dodson, who answered my tedious questions regarding the "hierarchy" of the FBI with an enormous amount of patience and kindness. The "adjustments" I made were deliberate for fictional purposes.

A LOT of the research for this novel was garnered by sitting in a federal court, observing in three different trials. I've logged more hours on the hard, wooden bench in the Arkansas Federal Courthouse than I care to remember. Special thanks to the fine men serving as courthouse marshals who went out of their way to be extremely nice and courteous.

Special thanks to the GREAT ONES, for their help in plotting on a scary road trip with someone (ahem) frightening behind the wheel, and for such wonderful memories.

As always, there are many in the writing community who help me in so many ways I can't even begin to list. My heartfelt thanks to: Karen Ball, Colleen Coble, Pam Hillman, Ronie Kendig, Tosca Lee, Dineen Miller, Cara Putman, Jim Rubart, Heather Diane Tipton, Cheryl Wyatt, and my wonderful agent Steve Laube.

My extended family members are my biggest fans and greatest cheerleaders. Thank you for being in my corner: Mom and Papa, BB and Robert, Bek and Krys, Bubba and Lisa, Brandon, Rachel, and Aunt Millicent. Special thanks for all the support to Stephanie Mallett and Scott and Ashley Vailes.

My deep gratitude for the feedback of first readers Lisa Burroughs and Tracey Justice. Whatever would I do without your questions and comments!

I couldn't do what I do without my girls—Emily Carol, Remington Case, and Isabella Co-Ceaux. I love each of you so much! And my precious grandsons, Benton Alexander Miller Forgy and Zayden Brody Forgy—you are joys in my life.

My most heartfelt thanks to my best friend, brainstorming partner, idea-maker, love of my life, husband . . . Case. You make my days brighter and fill my heart with love every day. Thank you for loving me as I am. I adore you.

Finally, all glory to my Lord and Savior, Jesus Christ. I can do all things through Him who gives me strength.

*"I do not understand what I do.
For what I want to do I do not do,
but what I hate I do."*

ROMANS 7:15

Prologue

"The hour of departure has arrived, and we go our ways. I go to die, and you to live. Which is the better, God only knows."

—SOCRATES

Cha-chk.

Every muscle in my body stiffened, and my mouth went spitless. Chambering a round was a distinct sound, unmistakable.

My hand gripped the railing as questions swarmed my mind. A gun? In Daniel's house? He'd been opposed to firearms ever since my father was murdered.

I took a step off the second-story landing. My palm itched to grip my own handgun at the moment, but knowing how Daniel felt, I'd never bring it over. Even when I spent the night.

"Put that gun away." My godfather's voice held a tremble as it drifted up to me. Never, ever, had I heard Daniel's voice be anything but commanding.

My heart pounded harder than before—my ribs felt the punishment. My knees weakened.

"Not hardly. You just couldn't leave well enough alone, could you, Daniel?"

I broke out into a cold sweat, recognizing that voice. And the angry tone. I should have—sure had heard it enough times. Was this real? Not *him*. I had to be mistaken. Because if he's the one with the gun . . .

I descended, my feet making no sound on the plush stair runner. Reaching the first floor, I glanced at the alarm system control panel by the front door. No indicator lights ablaze. My throat and gut flipped places. Why have the security feature if Daniel wouldn't use it? I padded across the cold marble floor of the darkened foyer and activated the silent alarm. The gated community security would arrive.

Would it be soon enough?

"When government witnesses come to me after a trial and confess your team pressured and bullied them to fabricate their testimony, what am I supposed to do? Look the other way?" Indignation rose above the wobbling of Daniel's voice. "That's not who I am."

A boulder slammed sideways in my throat. I froze. This couldn't be happening.

A lone siren howled in the night. Shivers took over my self-control. I peeked down the hall. Light spilled from Daniel's office.

I quickened my pace down the hallway, careful not to bump into the entry table with the lamp that had crystals hanging from it.

"Too bad. It could have saved your life."

"Get out of my house or I'll call the authorities." Daniel's voice, once again strong . . . authoritative.

Hope warmed my chest.

"As if that would do any good? We're acting on orders here. Orders from higher than our pay grade. We've always been acting on orders. You're the one who is dispensable, Daniel."

Daniel's gasp was barely audible. Unlike my pulse pounding in my head.

Thwap. Thwap.

No mistaking that sound either—shots fired with a silencer. Daniel!

Bile burned the back of my throat as my feet took root in the hardwoods. Instinct pushed me forward, but experience—and knowing the owner of the voice—held me in place. I had to help Daniel, but my muscles wouldn't budge. If I was seen . . .

The siren filtered up the long driveway. Flashing blue lights spun against the stained-glass window in the front door.

"Let's get out of here. He must've hit a silent alarm."

I had to move. If I didn't, I'd be as good as dead. Where? I glanced to the hall . . . the foyer . . . the closet. I had to hide—now! If they killed me, how could I help Daniel?

My body trembled.

"Let me make sure the good judge doesn't have a pulse. I've had someone return from the dead before."

Bam! Bam! Bam! The front door was about to explode.

"Mr. Tate? Security. Is everything okay?"

I held my breath.

"Leave him. The rent-a-cop will ask questions we don't want to explain." Footsteps thumped against the wood floor.

No time to debate. Moving into action, my socked feet slipped on the waxed floor as I slid to the dining room. I ducked next to the antique hutch and flattened myself in the dark shadows.

Thump-thump-thump.

A metallic taste was sharp against my tongue.

More banging on the door. "Mr. Tate? I've called the police."

"Quick, out the back door."

I recognized both men's voices. Knew them well. Too well. My stomach churned. How could they . . . ? I felt sick.

The two men rushed past the dining room, neither looking inside. Just enough light lingered in the hallway to illuminate them. Even if I didn't recognize their voices, there was no disputing who shot Daniel now.

Everything I believed in, fought for . . . fled at the positive identification.

The echo of the back door clicking shut sounded above the pounding of my heart.

The cement block anchoring my feet in place broke free. I scrambled toward the foyer, slipping against the smooth floor. I reached for the knob, couldn't turn the dead bolt fast enough, and swung open the front door. "My godfather has been shot. Call an ambulance." I didn't wait for a response from the security guard, just turned and raced into Daniel's study.

He lay facedown across his massive mahogany desk.

Oh-my-stars-oh-my-stars-oh-my-stars. No!

I rolled him over and pulled him to me. He was heavy, like dead weight. I held him tight as I sank to the floor. Two bright circles of red stained the crisp white cotton of his shirt, spreading in diameter. "Oh, Daniel." I could but breathe the words. Not Daniel. Not him too.

"S-Safe. In. My. Safe."

"Shh. It's okay. Help is on the way." I snatched a jacket from the back of Daniel's chair and pressed it against the growing red stains.

"Get. O-out. Of. M-my. S-safe." Daniel's face paled whiter than his shirt.

I cradled him in my arms, my pulse threatening to explode. Not like this. He was all I had left.

Oh-my-stars-oh-my-stars-oh-my-stars. I couldn't lose Daniel.

"P-prom-ise. Me. Get. Out. O-of. S-safe." Daniel's eyes dimmed. "I-important."

Tears streaked my cheeks as I rocked him, keeping pressure on the jacket. "Okay, I will. You be still and quiet now. Help will be here soon." *Don't die. Please, don't die.*

The security guard hovered in the doorway of the office. "Ms. Wyatt, the ambulance is on its way. Do you need help?"

"No. Wait for them outside and direct them in here." And he'd better make it quick—Daniel was fading fast. Too fast.

He spun and sped out. Sirens wailed in the distance.

I couldn't handle this. I planted a kiss on my godfather's forehead. He'd been my rock, my foundation. "It'll be all right."

But Daniel's eyes fluttered. A gurgling stuttered through his lips. He went limp, his head rolling against my chest.

My breathing hiccupped and the tears soaked my face.

Daniel Tate had just died in my arms.

The truth hit me with the full force of a 9mm slug. I had no choice—I had to run.

Or be killed.

The security guard saw me, knew me. If I stayed, it'd only be a matter of time before the men who murdered Daniel would come after me. I couldn't chance that.

These . . . men . . . they wouldn't stop. This was what they did. They'd never give up on silencing me if someone higher than these two were calling the shots and ordered this . . . hit— that's what it was. Not just murder, but a hit.

Oh, Daniel. My body trembled, but I couldn't stop to think about how I felt. I had to act.

Even protective custody couldn't save me.

I ran up the stairs, slipped on jeans and a tee, then raced back down.

The sirens drew closer.

Daniel's safe.

He'd been so adamant I get the contents. His dying words had made me promise. What could be so important?

I shoved aside the framed print, exposing the metal wall safe. Tears blurred my vision as I spun the dial to the right, then left, then back to the right. My date of birth. The safe clicked as the lock disengaged. My hands shook as I opened the door.

Two envelopes and an expandable folder sat inside.

A siren wailed in the driveway.

"They're here," the security guard yelled.

No time.

I grabbed the contents and jammed them into Daniel's briefcase. I shut the safe and secured the framed photograph back into
place. My mind couldn't process anything. Not right then.

Taking the moment I shouldn't spare, I dropped to my knees
and kissed my godfather's temple for the last time. "I'm so sorry,
Daniel. They'll pay for this." One day. I'd make sure. My voice
hitched on the tears clogging my throat.

I stood and lifted the briefcase. Funny how heavy it suddenly
was.

This was it—the point of no return. Fleeing now would save
my life, for however long I stay buried, but Daniel's murderers
would go free.

Could I do it? I swallowed against a dry mouth. I could hide,
knew how. I'd been a consulting psychologist for the FBI for
years. Had contacts and could change my identity with a single
call. Knowing what they'd look for, I would do the exact opposite. The unanticipated could keep me alive.

Would keep me alive.

If I told the truth, no one would believe me. Not without
proof. And they'd kill me before I could find the evidence I'd
need.

Car doors slammed.

"In here. Down the hallway," the security guard barked.

I crossed to the office's patio door and turned the lock. With
a final glance over my shoulder, I left behind who I was. What
I stood for.

Remington Wyatt disappeared without a trace.

Forever.

Chapter One

"A lie cannot live."

DR. MARTIN LUTHER KING JR.

 "Going somewhere, Kingston?" Agent Rafe Baxter leveled his gun at the man he'd had in his proverbial crosshairs for what felt like forever.

Connor halted in his tracks, his gaze affixed on the barrel of the 9mm. Gauging whether Rafe was serious, or if he could make a run for it.

Please, give me the opportunity. Rafe had spent every waking moment for the past eighteen months building the case against master embezzler, CEO of Freedom Investing and greedy scum-of-the-earth, Connor Kingston. The paper trail had been tedious, the gathering of evidence extensive, but they'd finally gotten a grand jury indictment and appeared at his office to arrest him.

Funny thing about that arrest, Rafe had a sneaky suspicion the snake would try to slink out the back door and disappear. It wasn't too much of a reach to think someone would run who'd stolen over 4.6 million dollars. Too bad for Kingston that Rafe stood between the back door and the parking garage where Kingston's Mercedes waited.

Kingston glanced toward the entrance to the garage, then back to Rafe. He slowly raised his hands into the air. "Agent Baxter, what are you doing out here?"

"Enjoying the weather, of course."

Lightning flashed high in the sky. Thunder rumbled in the distance.

The back door to the corporate building swung open, banging against the wall. Rafe's partner, Darren, emerged, his face red.

Kingston spun, dropping his hands as well as lowering his head.

Rafe grinned and jutted his chin toward Mr. Greedy. "Look who stepped outside to get a breath of fresh air."

Darren cuffed Kingston none too gently. "You have the right to remain silent. Anything you say can and will . . ."

Holstering his gun, Rafe approached the backup team arriving from around the front of the building. "Nice of y'all to show up. What were you waiting for, an engraved invitation?" His ready grin took the sting out of his words.

Mumbling ensued, but Rafe ignored them all as he fell in step beside his partner. Darren put Kingston in the back of the designated car, slammed the door, then double-slapped the roof. The car pulled out of the lot and onto the street without a siren, lights, or any other fanfare. Fitting not to do anything special for Kingston.

"And another case closed." Darren held up his palm.

Rafe gave the customary high five, but his gut tightened. At least they'd made the arrest now so Darren wouldn't have to finish the case on his own. It was little consolation, but Rafe would take what he could get at this point. His decision had already been made, and there was no turning back now.

Darren clapped Rafe's shoulder, snatching back his attention. "You coming by the house? Savannah should still be up. You can read her a bedtime story. I'm a little sick of *Green Eggs and Ham* myself."

The fact hit Rafe hard—she'd grow up without him being

there. Throat closing, he shook his head. "I can't. I promised Riley I'd run by her apartment and move some of her boxes down to her storage basement."

Why his baby sister couldn't fit all four seasons' clothes in her closet was beyond him, but he'd given up trying to figure out women a long time ago.

"See you tomorrow, then." Darren headed off to his own car.

Rafe slipped behind the wheel of his unmarked bureau vehicle. He'd miss this, all of this. Sure, it'd be the same, basically. But . . . different. He shook his head and started the car. Riley would be waiting.

If there was one thing Rafe was positive about, his sister didn't like to be kept waiting. Patience was so far removed from her vocabulary it wasn't even funny.

Moments later he whipped into the apartment complex parking lot. He drove past the first two sets of buildings, the Dumpster, then the next two sets of buildings until he came to the last building in the back of the complex. He parked in an empty space down from Riley's little hybrid.

Raised voices greeted him as he shut the car door. Angry voices. Riley's voice.

"I don't care, Garrison. Omission is a form of lying."

His sister arguing with her boyfriend . . . maybe he should just get back into the car and wait it out.

Rafe couldn't make out Garrison's reply. Didn't matter. He couldn't stand the punk. Garrison was as arrogant as the day was long, and Rafe just didn't have tolerance for that type of person, but he bit his tongue because his sister told him over and over that who she dated was none of his business.

"Is that a threat?"

Every muscle in Rafe's body tensed. How many times had he seen such a scene escalate to murder?

He still couldn't make out Garrison's words, but the gruffness and tone reached him just fine. Rafe strode toward Riley's apartment.

"You don't scare me."

As Rafe drew closer, he could clearly make out what Garrison said. Words and names that his baby sister should never even hear, much less be called. He rounded the corner, hands curled into fists.

Garrison's insults would make a sailor blush.

Rafe reacted without thinking—he shoved Garrison against the outer wall of the apartment building. He pushed his forearm against Garrison's throat and got in his face. "That's no way to speak to a lady, now is it?"

"Who's a lady?" Garrison's voice cracked. A sheen of sweat glistened on his upper lip in the setting sun.

This guy was either very brave or very stupid. Rafe applied more pressure with his arm. "I think you owe my sister an apology."

"Rafe, don't."

He ignored Riley, focusing on Garrison's now-red face. "Don't you want to say you're sorry for calling her such names?"

Garrison's eyes bugged as he scowled. "You think you're a big man 'cuz you're with the FBI, don't you?"

Rafe shoved harder against his throat. "Yeah, I do."

The punk slacked against the brick wall.

He released the pressure enough so Garrison could swallow. His Adam's apple bobbed against Rafe's forearm. "I said, don't you want to apologize to Riley for your language?"

"Y-yeah."

Rafe took a step back and crossed his arms over his chest. "I'm waiting." The punk needed a good stomping and with the mood Rafe was in, he was just the person to administer said stomping.

Garrison bent and coughed. Hacked. Gagged.

"Enough!" Riley shoved around him, throwing her arm over the louse's shoulders. "Are you okay?"

Garrison could only cough more.

Riley glared at him. "Are you happy now? You've hurt him."

What? She was mad at *Rafe*? For defending and protecting her? "You gotta be kidding me, Ril. He called you a—"

"He didn't mean it. We were arguing, you brute."

He was the bad guy now? "He's nothing more than—"

"Just go. Leave."

"But you wanted me to—"

"Go, Rafe. Get out of here." She kept rubbing Garrison's back.

The punk snuck a glance at Rafe from beneath that messy mop of hair. And smirked.

Rafe clenched his fists and took a step toward him.

"I said, leave." Her eyes met his. "Please. Just go. I'm fine."

Rafe shook his head, then turned and headed to his car. Nope, he'd never understand women, especially not his sister.

Day 2

How was I going to do this?

Tears burned my eyes, but I shoved them aside. Now wasn't the time for emotional release. I had to focus. Had to concentrate.

The motel room stank like urine. I'd sprayed it with the perfume I found in the outer pocket of my purse, but the stench remained. I had no intention of spending the night in this dive again. I just needed to clear my head and sleep last night. Now I was ready.

First, I had to make Remington Wyatt disappear. I had almost thirty thousand dollars on me that I'd stockpiled for a rainy day. Well, the storm clouds were hovering over my head now as I sat in the motel room. The curtains were drawn, the air turned off so I could listen.

I sat on the edge of the bed, taking sick pleasure as I cut up my credit cards, American Express the only one with a balance. Only a couple of hundred dollars, but still a balance. I couldn't chance making a payment. Even if the authorities didn't consciously consider me a suspect yet, they would be watching my bank accounts.

Good thing I had my cash. More than enough for me to get out of town . . . out of state . . . start over. But where? My backup plan was to get far away, go north where I knew no one.

I stared at Daniel's briefcase. What had been so important he'd use his last breath to tell me to get? Time to find out.

With trembling hands, I opened the briefcase and lifted out two big, manila envelopes. They weren't sealed shut, only the clasp held them closed. I opened one and peered inside.

Cash. A *lot* of cash.

I dumped the contents on the bed. All hundred dollar bills, nonsequential. I turned several over. Unmarked.

The second envelope contained the same thing. Money, money, money. I couldn't help it, I had to count it.

Two hours and a horrendous backache later, I knew each envelope had contained approximately twenty-five thousand dollars. Un-oh-my-stars-believable.

Daniel was just a wealth of surprises, which made me more curious about what was in the expandable folder. I pulled it to me and peeled back the cover. Papers, newspaper clippings, pictures, and more were shoved into the folder. What had Daniel been keeping?

A siren wailed just outside the motel room. My heart and gut swapped places as I rushed to the window and peeked past the gaudy orange curtains. A whiff of a disgusting odor snagged my sense of smell and nearly made me vomit.

The police car, lights flashing, faced the opposite side of the building. Still, it was too close. I couldn't stay here.

I shoved the money back into the envelopes, then crammed them into my bag. The expandable folder went back into Daniel's briefcase. I paused at the door, barely cracking it open.

The cruiser was in the same place, only one silhouette was visible from the dashboard lights. It was dark out. I had to chance it.

I crept to the parking lot, keeping my head down as much as I could. Tossing my duffel into the backseat of the clunker I'd bought off the guy just outside of North Little Rock, I steered toward the downtown area.

I'd find a place to hunker down and regroup. A place where I could think . . . make a game plan. No, a survival plan.

Chapter Two

"Wisdom consists of the anticipation of consequences."
NORMAN COUSINS

Tension, thick as sorghum molasses, seeped into the Memphis field office but wasn't anywhere near sweet. Just heavy. And suffocating.

"Are you sure you want to do this?" Special Agent in Charge Nick Hagar leaned back in his chair and peered over the desk. His dark eyes were holes in his frowning face. "We haven't signed the final paperwork. It's not a done deal yet."

Rafe Baxter swallowed. Again. He stared out the window behind his boss. Gloom hung in the air. Depression cut the gentle breeze. Tennessee experienced an uncommonly early autumn.

No, he wasn't sure he wanted to do this. Matter of fact, he *didn't* want to do this. But needing and wanting were two entirely different things. Images of Savannah's smiling face flitted across his mind. He slumped in his chair, his shoulders aching under the burdens only he understood, and met his boss's stare. "I have to."

"You don't." Nick planted his elbows into the imitation leather armrests. They creaked in response.

Rafe snorted. They'd already had this argument a week ago.

14

And the week before that. He'd won them then and would win them now.

Because he didn't have a choice.

"I can always refuse your request for the transfer."

"But you won't." Although Rafe's life would be easier. The decision taken out of his hands, beyond his control . . .

Nick shoved forward, tenting his hands over his desk. "I understand why you feel compelled to take this drastic step, and I admire you for it, but I really wish you'd reconsider. You're one of my best agents." He slapped his palms against the desk. "Probably one of the most insightful I've seen. Ever."

"And Darren isn't?"

Nick sighed. "It's not that he isn't good—he is. But you have the killer instinct. The drive. The determination. The desire to claw your way up."

"It only seems that way because Darren can't put in longer hours. He's a good man. A good agent." And the best friend and partner Rafe could ever hope to have. Darren could follow a disconnected paper trail like nobody else.

"Stay here, Rafe. Maybe it'll be good for Darren to go to a new office. Give him a chance to see what he can do out from under your shadow."

"But Savannah's doctors are here. You know that. He can't leave." And as much as it hurt to admit it, Rafe *could*. "I don't have a choice."

"You aren't his keeper." Nick's expression and voice had softened, carrying not a hint of accusation, but a volume of experience. It was hard to believe the man was only a couple of years older than Rafe.

No, he wasn't Darren's keeper. But he *was* a man of his word. A man with a traitorous, sinful heart, but one of his word.

"I promised him. Promised Savannah." Rafe's voice cracked. He swallowed. Hard. "I stood before God the day she was dedicated and vowed I would protect her to the best of my ability."

"But . . . Arkansas? Seriously, Rafe, that's the armpit of the United States. The Razorbacks? You're a die-hard Volunteer. The BCS is just around the corner."

The Bowl Championship Series . . . yeah, Rafe loved it. He responded with a weak smile and casual shrug. It was only football, right? At least he'd still be in the Southeast Conference.

"What if I really *did* refuse the transfer? We need you here." Nick cleared his throat. "I need you here."

Nick wouldn't . . . Rafe narrowed his eyes and clenched his jaw. "If you refuse, I'll have to quit."

"No way you'd throw away your career just like that. You have serious ambitions with the bureau." Nick sank back in his chair, his face twisted into a scowl. "Come on. I know you're loyal and all, but that's pushing it."

"I'm serious. The bureau says cutbacks are mandatory and this office is one agent too heavy." There wasn't any other option. "Little Rock's office is an agent short."

"You realize you're probably tossing out any chance at promotion by transferring, right?"

Rafe smiled even though the muscles in his stomach curled into a tight ball. "If I'm really as good as you say I am, then I should have no problem impressing the Arkansas SAC and moving to the front of the line for promotion."

If only he could believe that. It'd taken him almost a decade to get himself in position where he was . . . building trust in the office, gaining commendations on cases he'd worked . . . all in hopes of catching the attention of the higher-ups.

Nick shook his head and grabbed the transfer paper. He slapped it in front of Rafe. "I hope Darren appreciates your friendship."

"Let it go, Nick." Rafe lifted the pen, hovering the ink over the signature block.

Oh, God, give me the strength to go through with this. It was the right thing to do—the only thing—but Rafe felt the prospect of his career advancement slipping from his grip.

Images of *her* bright smile flashed across his mind's eye. Guilty heat spawned in his veins as he drew in a shaky breath, then scrawled his name on the line before passing the sheet back across the desk.

His boss took the transfer paperwork, glowered, tossed it onto a stack, and let out a heavy sigh. "I guess that's done then."

Rafe stood, his legs weaker than when he'd stormed into the SAC's office. "Thanks, Nick." He thrust his hand across the desk. "For everything." His voice thickened heavier than the tension.

"I hate to lose you. Especially like this." But Nick's timbre shook along with his hand.

Rafe couldn't let himself get too emotional. Wouldn't. This was a job. Wasn't like he was changing careers. He was still FBI. Still doing what he loved and what he was gifted to do.

He'd just do it in Little Rock instead of Memphis, and probably never be promoted.

Clenching his jaw, he gave Nick a curt nod and hustled out of the office before he changed his mind and ripped up the transfer request.

Back at his desk, he resumed packing his personal effects into a box. Framed snapshots of Darren and him in the academy. At their graduation. Darren's wedding. Rafe's certificate of commendation went in, followed by the paperweight of Savannah's handprint at age two.

Niggles of doubt poked at Rafe's conscience. He ignored them and closed the box. Hoisting it, he took a final glance over the space he'd called his second home for eight years, then turned and marched away.

His stride didn't falter until he reached his truck. His muscles bunched as he placed the box in the passenger's seat. Every fiber of his being screamed for him to run back and tell Nick it'd all been a mistake. A huge mistake.

But he couldn't.

Wouldn't. He'd sacrifice his own dreams because of his promise. His vow.

His guilt.

Rafe forced himself to slide behind the steering wheel and turn over the engine. The truck roared to life. He stared at his reflection in the rearview mirror. How had he aged so much in mere weeks? Even the gray strands at his temples had multiplied.

He slammed the truck into gear. Frustration pushed his foot harder on the accelerator. The tires spun on the loose rocks in the parking lot. Rubber squealed against pavement.

Less than twenty minutes later found Rafe whipping into his driveway. His neighbor had placed three more political signs in his front yard, bringing the total to eleven. There should be a property owners' association rule on how many signs could litter a yard.

His lawn, on the other hand, had a more formidable presence. The forlorn FOR SALE sign flapped in the wind. The Realtor said it might take several months for the house to sell, considering the economy. Probably a good thing. He could do the paperwork from another state. Would make it easier on him. Signing away the home he'd come to love would make his moving all too real.

Too permanent. Too final.

No, he'd made up his mind and wouldn't look back. This could be an adventure. The start of a whole new beginning. It'd be fine. It'd be great.

Once inside the house, he finished packing the last of the boxes. He capped the permanent marker after labeling, then stood back and glanced around his home. Everything was set for the movers tomorrow morning. Eight o'clock sharp, the salesman had warned.

The house already had the stuffy smell of empty.

The doorbell chimed.

He maneuvered around stacks of boxes and wrapped furniture to the door and swung it open.

"So, when were you planning on telling us you were moving?" Riley stood with her hands on her hips.

He sighed. "I told you weeks ago that it was a possibility."

She pushed her slight form past him, barging into the house. "A possibility doesn't put your house up for sale." She spun in the middle of the living room. "A possibility doesn't have all your possessions packed in moving boxes."

He shut the door, then leaned against the back of the couch. Yeah, he should've told Riley and Maddie, but the image of his sisters' faces had stopped him cold.

"Well? Don't you have anything to say? Were you just going to leave without saying good-bye?" Her penetrating blue eyes undid him.

"Oh, Ri."

In an instant she was in his arms, clinging to him as if to root him in Tennessee. Her sobs ripped apart his conscience. "Shhh."

"But . . . but you can't move. You can't leave us." Her voice was so much like Mom's: hoarse, throaty. Her words clawed against his heart.

"I have to." The words inched past the lump of emotion clogging his throat. "I don't have a choice."

"What about me and Maddie?"

"Y'all will be fine. Better than that." He gave her a final squeeze, then shifted to put about a foot between them. "Just think of how much trouble you can stir up without me breathing down your neck." He forced a smile.

She sniffled and gave a snort. "I like you breathing down my neck."

He laughed. "No, you don't."

Riley grinned up at him. "You're right. I don't." Her smile faltered. "But that doesn't mean I want you to leave."

"It's the right decision, Riley. It was down to me or Darren, and you know he can't move. Not until Savannah is older."

"You don't have to be so noble all the time, you know." She threw a soft punch that grazed off his arm.

He raked a hand across his stubble. If she only knew the truth. "It's not a matter of being noble—it's about keeping my promises." Even the ones no one else in the world knew about.

Riley's eyes filled with moisture again. "I'll miss you."

"Hey, it's Arkansas. That's not exactly a foreign country." At least he prayed it wasn't. "It's not that far of a drive. I'll even start texting."

"No, you won't." Her smile returned, lifting some of the weight from him.

"I will. And you'll have to come help me decorate my place."

"True."

He held open his arms again. She stepped back into his embrace. Rafe hugged her, inhaling the pure, innocent scent that was his baby sister alone.

"I love you, Rafe."

His throat closed over his response.

Day 3

I heaved air in and out, letting the steam from the shower cloud my lungs. What was the big deal? It was just a change of hair color. Considering the more permanent, and definitely more painful, steps I'd taken to change my appearance, the hair color was nothing.

It wasn't that I was vain—I'd never paid much thought to my looks. In all of my thirty-two years, I never did the whole makeup thing, the tailored clothes.

So why was I so hesitant to take this last step? What did it matter what color my hair was? It was such a minor thing . . . petty. Silly to have tears building over something so meaningless in the big scheme of things. Women changed their hair color all the time. Why was this hitting me so hard?

Because something deep inside me screamed it would be the final step in erasing who I was. Just another form of death . . .

No . . . my *former* self. I could no longer be that person.

I liked who I was. Not many people can say that, but
I could. Honestly. I enjoyed my life. And now I had to change
everything.

Like I'd had a choice? This wasn't some random decision
I made just for kicks. Something to do because I was bored.
This change could save my life.

Would save my life.

I tightened the belt of my robe although it wasn't loose and
exhaled, keeping my eyes closed. My hands trembled as
I reached for the thick towel covering my hair. I yanked it off
but refused to look.

The wet terry cloth hit the hotel bathroom's polished floor
with a muffled thud. It seemed to echo off the walls decorated
with modern-art paintings. I sucked in another breath.

Touching my hair, I noticed it wasn't as soft as normal.
Yeah, it was wet, so how could I really tell? Maybe it was only
my imagination. Maybe I was freaking out over the menial
stuff so I wouldn't have to deal with reality.

Oh-my-stars. Quit being a baby. Just deal with it.

I opened my eyes, and my breath caught in the back of
my throat. Gone were the golden blonde tresses I'd stared
at for thirty-two years. I swallowed. Stupid tears burned my
eyes.

No! I was disappearing. My bottom lip quivered.

Stop it. I was alive for the time being and had to do this to
stay that way. I was rather partial to breathing.

Licking my lips, I surveyed my hair with a critical eye.
It wasn't bad. Just different. But no more drastic than the
changes I'd made to my face.

I wiped the ornate mirror over the bathroom sink and
took stock. The Botox injections had caused some redness and
swelling, but that disappeared yesterday. My lips were left
fuller, my cheekbones less pronounced. Now that I'd gotten
used to wearing the green-tinted contacts covering the natural
blue, my eyes took the color of a bright aqua. I leaned closer

to the mirror. The caramel hair dye with coppery highlights brought out the freckles sprinkling the bridge of my nose.

All in all, not too bad.

I'd been blessed with good bone structure, or so my father always claimed. I couldn't do much about my slight build at the moment, but I'd start eating food to add on empty pounds even though that went against my natural grain. To actually eat meat—gag. But being a vegan was too telling.

And telling could get me dead.

Grabbing the comb from the counter, I pulled it through my hair. They would expect me to change its color, but I had to. The blond was too recognizable. Too distinct. But they'd also expect me to cut my long hair, so I wouldn't. Not yet, anyway.

So much to keep track of. All the little particulars. But those minuscule details were what they'd find most telling.

And I didn't want to be heard. Couldn't afford to be.

I set the comb back onto the counter, slipped the 9mm into the pocket of my robe, and crossed the carpet of the suite to the bed. As I passed the hall door, I checked to make sure the security latch was engaged. I glanced under the door—no shadows from someone standing on the other side.

If they followed protocol, and I was pretty certain they would, the airport and bus station would be swarming with agents on the lookout for me. They'd check all the places I was known to frequent. Then they'd check every dive hotel in a hundred-mile radius. When there was no sign of me, they'd assume I'd slipped right past them before they got the word out.

I felt pretty safe in the downtown Peabody Hotel. But that didn't mean I wouldn't keep my firearm with me at all times.

Reaching the window, I yanked the curtains shut. Unless someone was Spider-Man, I was safe on the twentieth floor. But I didn't want to gaze at the darkening sky. An Arkansas January was about as bleak as my life at the moment. Cold and depressing.

Letting out a sigh, I set the gun on the bedside table and sat on the edge of the luxurious down comforter, clenching and unclenching my fists. The situation I found myself in was deplorable. Horrible.

With shaking hands, I lit a cigarette. I held the smoke in my lungs. Wasn't certain, but after many years of smoking, I thought I could feel my anxiety dissipating like the steam in the bathroom. I exhaled as slow as I could, letting the enjoyment linger. I'd really miss smoking.

Visions of my godfather tiptoed across my mind. I pinched my eyes shut, refusing the tears access. I couldn't afford to wallow in grief or anger. Or confusion.

But what I'd found in his safe befuddled me. I thought I'd known Daniel. He'd been my guardian since my own father had been murdered when I was a little girl. I'd loved him without condition. All but hero-worshipped him. Yet, if what I suspected from the documents I'd taken were true, I hadn't known him at all. And that ripped me to the core.

Staring at the attaché case on the room's desk brought me no comfort. The documents I'd taken from the safe sat inside, tormenting me with their secrets. Along with a lot of cash and an atlas.

I took another long drag off the menthol. The coolness soothed my throat.

I had a plan. Something Daniel had taught me—always have a backup. For years I'd followed his example and kept a good sum of cash on hand in the event of emergency. Nothing like what he'd kept in his safe—over fifty thousand—but plenty to run. Combining both stacks of cash would let me start over with ease.

But I'd rather have Daniel to laugh with me. To toss me his special sneer when I said something he found amusing. To give me a hug when I needed it most.

I took a final puff off the cigarette before crushing it into the ashtray. Maybe now my fingernails would whiten up.

Falling back across the bed, my fingers automatically scraped against the comforter. The scratching sound echoed in the silent room. Once again tears threatened to overtake me. I'd had to leave Whiskers behind. I missed her. Missed her tickling my nose. Missed her rough tongue bathing my fingers. Missed her purring. Someone would take care of her. No matter how much I longed to have her feline self with me, I'd have to get a dog.

Every single action I took would have to be weighed. Considered. Even down to what pet I owned and what type of soft drink I consumed. I couldn't take the risk of some minor detail outing me.

I rolled onto my stomach and buried my face in the pillow, everything inside me screaming. In rage. In mourning. In fear.

Curling into the fetal position, I allowed myself to . . . feel. The tears washed over me. Poured out of me. Ripped from my heart.

I'd pull it together and get on with what I had to. In a minute, I'd dress and get ready to meet Smitty to pick up my new identity. From there, I'd embark on this new life of mine. I'd follow the paper trail Daniel had left in his safe to a state I'd never visited. Unfortunately my godfather had failed to leave direction of what he wanted me to do with the information. I'd have to play that by ear.

But, for now, I'd just let myself feel.

And mourn what was, and what could never be again.

Chapter Three

"All mankind is divided into three classes: those who are immovable, those who are movable, and those who move."
BENJAMIN FRANKLIN

"You come highly regarded from SAC Hagar." Alphonse Jackson pinned Rafe to the hard-back chair with a penetrating stare. "Says he hated to lose you." He arched his brows, creasing wrinkles across his forehead. "Says you were one of the best agents he'd ever worked with."

The clear invitation to explain why he'd requested the transfer, which obviously the paperwork stated had been a request, stood gaping like a wide yawn. But Rafe didn't want to go there. Not yet. Instead, he cleared his throat. "I'm excited about the opportunity to work in this office."

Jackson narrowed his black eyes, then laughed. "That's a diplomatic reply if I ever heard one." He crossed his designer suit-covered arms over his massive chest.

"Yes, sir." Rafe dared not smile.

The Special Agent in Charge of the Little Rock field office stopped laughing and cocked his head. The man was, in a word, intimidating. Built like a middle linebacker, Jackson had hard lines etched deep into his face like a stone wall. Unmovable.

"I hope you understand we didn't request any transfers. Our unit is doing just fine. The bureau is leveling out the number of agents based upon jurisdictional coverage."

The SAC didn't want him here—Rafe got the message loud and clear. But what could he do? "Yes, sir."

Silence ricocheted off the walls adorned with certificates of achievement and merits of commendation. Rafe's racing pulse echoed inside his head as the hint of his new boss's cologne wafted in the closed office.

Jackson clapped his hands together. Rafe sat rigid, refusing to show his unease to his new boss.

"Well, let me get my ASAC in here and introduce you. He'll show you around." Jackson lifted the receiver, growled out an order, then slammed it to its cradle. "We're a tight group. Like family."

"I understand, sir." Rafe's hope plummeted to his knees. He knew it'd be hard to fit in but hadn't expected such animosity. Especially from the boss. Everyone else would look to Jackson as an example of how to treat the new guy.

Rafe was sunk.

The door swung open before Jackson could finish his lecture.

"Good, good." Jackson stood. "This is our new field agent, Rafe Baxter."

The fifty-something man who stood about two inches shorter than Rafe's own five foot ten extended his hand. His suit, while not designer, was clean and crisp and draped appropriately over the agent's bulky frame. "Lars Hartlock." His husky voice indicated many years of smoking.

Rafe rose to accept the offered palm. The man's handshake was firm, oozing confidence. "Nice to meet you," he managed to mumble.

Jackson grunted. "Hartlock's been around this office for a couple of decades. Hope to keep him around for at least one more."

The Assistant Special Agent in Charge grinned at Rafe.

"Don't let Alphonse fool you—he knows I'm itching to take the bureau's offer for early retirement."

"Don't blame you. The incentives the bureau's offering makes a man sit up and take notice." Especially with an ASAC rank. Made the difference of several thousand on the retirement package.

Jackson grunted again. "Show Baxter to his desk. Give him the grand tour." He plopped back down to his chair, an obvious dismissal.

Hartlock headed over the threshold. Rafe hesitated. "Thank you, sir."

Jackson gave a quick nod.

Rafe turned and followed the ASAC down the hall. Their footsteps were muffled by the carpet as they headed toward a large room filled with cubicles.

"Pay no attention to Alphonse. He thinks he's a grizzly when really he's nothing more than a teddy bear."

Yeah. Sure. Right.

"And call me Lars, by the way. Never really got into the whole last name thing." Hartlock turned into the room and stopped at the first cubicle.

Two desks sat together, forming a big square. One side was empty. The other housed a dumpy-looking, balding man. How long had it been since he'd qualified on the physical?

"This is Jack Devane, my partner."

Rafe extended his hand. "Rafe Baxter, new kid on the block."

Devane stood and shook hands. Not a firm one like his partner's. And his hands were beefier and sweaty. "Pleased to meet you. Welcome to our humble abode." Shorter than both Rafe and Hartlock, he wore his cheap black suit without flair or style. He had to be a couple of years older than Hartlock, maybe even Jackson.

"Come on, I'll show you to your work space before I introduce you to the rest of the crew." Hartlock walked at a fast clip to the cubicle in the corner. "Here you go."

If Rafe had entertained any thoughts about being accepted from the get-go, his fantasy shattered right now. The cubicle he'd call his office was less than half the size of the others they'd passed. A lone desk sat pushed against one wall, with just enough room to squeeze around to sit. The lighting over the cubicle was shadowy, at best. He'd have to get a desk lamp to be able to read. Winter seemed to have crept into the corner, making the small space even gloomier.

Rafe stepped into the cramped cubicle.

"Human Resources already set you up in the computer. Same system as what you're used to. Your login and initial password is taped there to the monitor." Hartlock leaned against the cubicle's opening. His cell phone filled the stale air with chirping.

While Hartlock took his call, Rafe lowered himself onto the ripped chair and spied the yellow scrap of paper on the screen.

Hartlock slipped his cell back into its holder and addressed Rafe. "Alphonse said we should let you work some cold cases . . . just to get your feet wet with the new location and all." He pushed off the opening and pointed to the dented in-box on the corner of the desk. "There's a listing of all this office's cold cases. Pick any you want to work. Maybe a fresh set of eyes will blow open a case. The files are in the record room, right off this main hall. It's got a sign on the door."

So much for the grand tour.

"I'll hook up with you later to introduce you around. Just got a call that Jack and I have a witness to interrogate, or I'd do it now."

An excuse or the truth? Didn't matter. Either way, Rafe was on his own. "Thanks for showing me around." He reached for the list.

"Let me know if I can help you with anything." With that, Hartlock smiled and disappeared.

Rafe heaved a sigh and let the list slip from his fingers. It slid to the desk, sending particles of dust dancing into the air.

The bit he'd seen of Little Rock over the last few days wasn't so different from Memphis. The efficiency apartment he'd rented was nice enough, as was the neighborhood to the west of the city, but he already missed his coworkers back home. And his sisters. And Darren and Savannah. The memory of telling them good-bye almost shattered his resolve.

What was he doing here? Was the sacrificing of his personal dreams going to be enough? Would it restore his relationship with God? Would it make up for his breaking of one of *the Big Ten*?

He sat straighter in the chair. It squeaked as he inched closer to the desk and lifted the list again. Maybe if he solved a couple of these cold cases, he'd earn the respect of the agents here.

A grunt of laughter boomed outside his cubicle. Maybe he should make the first move. Careful not to slam his chair into the wall, Rafe stood and stepped into the hall.

Two agents stopped in their tracks. One was about twenty-five or so—had to be a rookie—with wild, scraggly hair, scrawny at no more than five eight or nine. The other man looked to be at least ten years the rookie's senior and stood at least six one or two.

Rafe smiled and extended his hand. "Rafe Baxter, new to the office."

Neither man moved at first. Then, after the longest pregnant pause Rafe had ever experienced, the rookie took his hand. "Ed Major. Undercover." That explained the grunge look.

"Jay Snead." The agent beside Ed didn't bother extending his hand before moving on down the hall.

Ed hesitated a moment, offered Rafe a quick shrug, then hurried after Jay.

Rafe stared at their retreating backs. He was about as welcome here as a severe case of shingles.

Day 24

Oh-my-stars, I was officially on the run now, with an illegal identity.

I glanced at my new driver's license, the third one I'd had made since the original fake identification Smitty had procured for me. Didn't matter the name, as long as they were different. It wasn't that I didn't trust Smitty . . . or Mike . . . or Brian, it was all a matter of burying myself under many layers.

Layers that would keep me alive.

Completing my inspection of the documents, I nodded at the man, keeping my eyes from darting from his stare. "This all looks satisfactory." I forced myself not to tighten my slouch.

"That'll be fifteen hundred." Brian glanced over his shoulder, then slid his focus back at me.

Textbook indicator of nervousness and deception.

I paid the man cash, then hopped into my new-to-me truck. Man, if only I could've bought another little hybrid—I'd adored mine—but the point was to do what a normal person on the run wouldn't. And that meant, for me, forsaking cute, energy-saving cars in lieu of a big diesel truck. I couldn't even get blue. Had to settle for a white one.

The sun dipped behind the trees. I snuggled into my leather coat. Snow wouldn't hit Arkansas again until February. This was my window of opportunity to escape. But the gloominess of the weather tugged at me. I turned over the engine and welcomed the heat from the vents. On instinct alone, I glanced around the parking lot of the hotel.

My hands trembled and I could almost taste nicotine. I cracked the truck window, letting the fresh air fill my lungs.

Wasn't as satisfying.

I had no excuse not to head toward my destination. As I pulled out of the lot in North Little Rock, emotion clogged my throat. I gripped the steering wheel tighter as I drove, willing determination to put a dam on the waterworks threatening to erupt. I couldn't afford to let my guard down, not even an inch.

Right now, everything in me screamed to do something about Daniel's murder. I'd watched the news as they reported the murder, including the BOLO for me. Yeah, the feds were on the lookout for me all right. They just assumed I'd act like everyone else and try to get as far away as fast as possible.

Stupid of them, really, knowing what I did. I'd taught them, for pity's sake. I'd instructed them for years on what to expect from someone on the run. Did it never occur to them I'd do the exact opposite?

Obviously not.

Perhaps local could get involved. Ask the right questions. Look at what the feds would ignore. I sure couldn't trust anyone with what I'd witnessed, but maybe an anonymous tip.

I couldn't do *nothing*.

I whipped the truck into a convenience store's parking lot in Pine Bluff and pulled alongside the pay phone. Harder to find than most people realized these days. Everyone had a cell. I glanced at my shiny new Go-phone in the console. No one could track it back to me, but I didn't want any law enforcement to have the number.

Silly to have a phone when I had no one to call, but I needed a number for reference when I tried to rent a place, or anything else. Most people were suspicious of folks who stood out from their perception of normal—paying for everything with cash, having no telephone number and the likes. Now so many people didn't bother with landlines, so only having a cell was the norm rather than something that would raise questions.

I slipped out of the truck, handgun in my coat pocket, and lifted the pay-phone receiver. Fighting the urge to jerk my head in every direction, I let my gaze roam the area. No one paid any interest to the brunette at the pay phone at dusk. The parking lot was a bustle of activity as people stopped to pick up last-minute items on their way home from work. As per the pattern of human nature, busy people paid attention to very little outside their own world.

My fingers trembled a bit as I punched 911 and cleared my throat. I couldn't just blurt out the truth. They'd know I was alive in a nanosecond and come after me. I was still too close, the murder too high profile. I could only hint, and not too obvious at that.

"What is the nature of your emergency?"

"I have information about the murder of Daniel Tate." I glanced at my watch. No way could I allow them to trace the call to this phone. I sped up my information, struggling to keep from telling all. "They need to look at his recent cases. That's the connection."

"May I have your name?"

My heart pounded and I knew I exhibited a million nervous nuances that anyone with a little training could detect. "My name isn't important. Just listen to what I'm telling you. Have the police check Judge Tate's most recent cases. The murderers are a direct connection to one of those cases."

I hung up the phone and let out a long breath. First dry run with law enforcement, and I hadn't done so hot. I'd have to work harder.

Or go with my gut instinct and avoid cops at all costs from here on out.

⚖️

Now what?

Hayden Simpson held his breath as his younger sister marched into the Hopewell police station. By her quick pace and scowled face, there was no mistaking she was ticked off about something. And it had to do with him, no doubt. Didn't it always these days?

She approached his desk, hands on her hips. "Why did you give Boyd a DUI?"

Glancing at his day officer's interested stare, Hayden rose and shut the office door before addressing Emily. "Why do you think? Because he was driving under the influence." He returned to his chair, gauging her reaction.

"He wasn't drunk. He'd only had two beers." She blew her wispy blonde bangs from her forehead. "You pulled him over because you don't approve of our dating." Emily crossed her arms over her chest and glared. "Admit it."

"I pulled him over because he was weaving all over the road. I gave him a DUI because he failed the field sobriety test. It had nothing to do with you." But that it'd been Boyd Keller had made him enjoy his job.

Emily huffed, much like she'd done as a spoiled toddler. "You don't approve of me and Boyd."

Of course not—the man was *married*! Hayden selected his words very carefully. "Em, I only want you to be happy. I just don't think being involved with a married man is going to give you happiness in the long run." If only he could tell his sister what he *really* thought. But he'd learned the hard way—Em was stubborn enough to do the exact opposite of any lecture he gave her. He had to slip little bits of truth in when he could.

"He's getting a divorce."

"Does MaryBeth know that?"

Emily's face fell. He was lower than pond scum for hurting his sister. Especially considering her illness. But someone had to be the voice of reason. And since Dad died . . . the duty fell to him.

Standing, Hayden rounded his desk and put an arm around her. "I don't mean to be unkind, but just last week MaryBeth was telling some of the young ladies at church she and Boyd were looking for a house to buy. Doesn't sound like someone getting a divorce, does it?" Why couldn't Emily see the truth about Boyd? Was she that naive or delusional? Could it be her bipolar disorder?

Shrugging out of his embrace, Emily narrowed her eyes. "Lies. She's trying to turn the town against Boyd. She knows he doesn't love her anymore but doesn't want him to leave." Emily stomped her foot, firming up Hayden's memories of her terrible childhood tantrums. "He loves me. He's going to divorce MaryBeth and marry me. You'll see."

If only his sister wasn't so fanciful. Or was she still acting out, pulling her rebellious routine? It'd gotten old already. He could never know for sure if it was her disorder or just plain old rebellion. "I hope it works out for the best."

She cocked her head as if to wonder if he meant that best for her or best for MaryBeth.

He kept his expression neutral as he went back to sit behind his desk. *Small steps.*

"So, can you drop that DUI charge?"

His jaw fell. His sister actually believed he'd let it go? "I can't do that, Em. This is my job, and he failed the field test. And the test here at the station."

"Please, Hay." Her voice tipped to whining, and she used his long-abandoned pet name. "Boyd's a good man. He's just under a lot of stress because of everything going on with MaryBeth. He can't have another DUI on his record. His insurance company will drop him."

So sad, so sorry. Hayden had to concentrate on keeping his expression in place. "I can't, even if I wanted to. The report's been filed, his insurance company already notified."

Her face scrunched. And turned red. Really red. "I knew you wouldn't help us. You hate the idea of me and Boyd. Offends your *Christian* sensibilities."

So she was back to personal slams on his faith. He wouldn't take the offense.

"You'll be sorry one day, Hayden. Sorry you didn't listen to me."

He cleared his throat. "Hey, Bella and I are going fishing next week. Want to come with us?"

She opened her mouth, hesitated, then clamped it shut. Without another word, she spun around and stomped from his office, slamming the door in her wake.

Lord, why did You make women so confounding? His baby sister included. No, his baby sister especially.

He'd take her exit as a *no* on the fishing invitation.

Chapter Four

"Things do not change; we change."
HENRY DAVID THOREAU

Day 28

The twanginess of the country western singer's voice spilled from the truck's radio speakers as I crossed the Arkansas state line into Louisiana.

I grinded my teeth. Oh-my-stars, how did people listen to this stuff? And like it? I reached over and turned the volume louder. The grating on my nerves didn't improve.

A record of purchases I'd made in the past was being scoured over by the FBI. They would try to track me from new purchases in the same items. Human nature demanded people re-create their comfort zones, even when they shouldn't.

It was why so many in the Witness Security Program failed. They couldn't go against what was ingrained in them. Dog lovers got canine pets. People who loved certain country singers would continue to buy the same artist's CDs. Lovers of a certain brand of coffee or soft drink would keep to their drinking preferences. And these little telling signs often outed people trying to hide.

Not me. I knew the score. Was trained to look for and track
these trends. Had taught many agents to do the same.
I wouldn't make a mistake.

But, man . . . this music . . .

A forlorn diner sat off the road, its neon sign in the window
lit up the word OPEN, calling to me. Nestled against a dark,
wooded backdrop, the eatery was perfect.

I hit my brakes and whipped into the deserted lot and
parked. Darkness surrounded me. I grabbed my purse and
flipped open my wallet, gazing at my new license.

Once sure I wouldn't slip up on my identity, I headed inside.
Even though no one would probably ask my name, it never
hurt to be prepared. A little bell over the door announced
my arrival. The strong aroma of coffee wrapped around me
like a down comforter. My stomach growled as I took in the
surroundings.

Small, a little on the shabby side, but at least the diner
didn't look like they'd gotten many warnings from the health
department. A single man sat at a corner booth, his face
buried in the latest hardback best seller.

"Sit anywhere you want, honey." A skinny woman in a
seventies waitress outfit appeared behind the counter. She
lifted a carafe. "Just made a fresh pot of coffee."

My taste buds tingled as I dropped into the vinyl booth
closest to the door.

She hovered tableside, her from-a-bottle red hair pulled a
little too severely from her face with a band and bounced with
her movements. "Coffee?"

I salivated and reached to turn over the cup on the saucer
she'd put before me. I froze, swallowing before clearing my
throat. "No, thank you. Just water, please."

The woman's arched brows went up a good half inch.
"Water?"

"Yes, ma'am. Please." I lifted the stained menu from behind
the napkin dispenser before I snatched the pot from her hand

and downed the scalding liquid. I *so* needed a cigarette right now.

"Suit yourself." She went back behind the counter, her slippers shuffling against the dirty linoleum floor.

Now, to figure out what I wanted. While I'd love a fresh salad, I didn't think the word *fresh* and *salad* should be used in the same sentence in such a place. One of the reasons I'd pulled in—I'd never eaten at a real diner before.

I'd stomached a piece of pepperoni yesterday and it hadn't made me hurl. Not like the first beef hamburger last week. The stomach cramps were the worst. Over time my body would get used to the nastiness stuffed into it, but I doubted I'd ever learn to truly enjoy the taste of dead animal.

Skimming farther down the menu, I tried to find something that wouldn't upset my stomach. I still had many miles to drive before dawn, and getting sick would mean I'd have to go ahead and snag a hotel room for the night.

The meatloaf special was probably way past its hot-and-fresh claim by now. More than not, dried out and harder than a shotgun shell. Ick. What else? Hmm. A crawfish po'boy didn't sound too bad. But it was probably made with spices I wasn't accustomed to, which could give my already-stressed stomach misery.

The waitress's shuffling announced her impending arrival. I had to make a decision posthaste.

She plunked the glass onto the table. "Have you made up your mind?"

So much for Southern hospitality. "I'd like the hot ham and cheese with fries, please." I offered up the sweetest smile I could muster as I returned the menu to its rightful place, careful not to disturb the salt and pepper shakers.

"Anything else?"

Yeah, a gallon of hot coffee and a salad using a whole head of lettuce. "A glass of tea with my meal, please."

"Sweet or unsweet?"

"Sweet, please." My teeth would hurt for sure. Could fugitives get dental insurance?

She smiled and headed back to the counter. Apparently I'd made the right choice. And if anyone came in later, asking about a lady alone, the waitress would be sure to remember I'd passed on coffee but ordered sweet tea. And meat. Anybody looking would feel assured it wasn't me.

While I waited for my meal, I pretended to text on my GoPhone but really thought about all the tips I'd made to the police over the past couple of days. Five anonymous calls to the Arkansas state police, six to 911, and three to the Little Rock police. I'd even gone to various Internet cafés and sent tips in via e-mail, paying cash for the service. As far as I could tell, which was based on news reports and newspaper articles, the feds were still looking for me as a person of interest wanted for questioning.

Someone was plugging the cork on the truth.

One day, Daniel, I'll see justice served.

⚖

Case status: unsolved/open.

Rafe glanced at the date on the folder. Three years ago? He'd read the brief, knew this was a murder case. But not just any murder—that of a federal judge.

Solving this particular cold case would make Alphonse Jackson sit up and take notice. Might even earn Rafe some respect. Earn his *place*.

He loosened his tie as he scanned the case notes a final time. Because the victim had been a federal judge, all stops had been pulled out to investigate the murder, but nothing had come of the investigation.

Was he beating a dead horse and setting himself up for failure? None of the other files had such high visibility. Sure, he could solve a couple of the white-collar cases, but that wouldn't impress Jackson. Or anybody else.

Rafe left his dank space and headed to Lars's cubicle. He smiled as both agents glanced up. A thought struck him—both Lars Hartlock and Jack Devane had a foot in the bureau's early retirement plan. Maybe there could be room for promotion after all.

He turned the corner and ran smack into Agent Ed Major. The man shoved him against the wall.

"Whoa. Sorry."

"Watch where you're going." Major didn't merely growl, he snarled. "Nobody wants you here, Tennessee. Why don't you just leave?" He jabbed Rafe in the bicep, then pushed past him down the hall.

Rafe grabbed the file he'd dropped.

Major's partner, the rookie Snead, gave a little shrug. "Ed's just . . . well, he, uh . . ."

"Don't sweat it, kid." Rafe shook his head.

Snead nodded, then fled in the trail of his partner.

Ed Major was going to be a pain in Rafe's heel, that was for sure. What was his game? Why did he seem to hate Rafe, personally? He'd have to figure it out. Later.

He wiped his palm on his slacks and gripped the case file tighter as he entered Hartlock and Devane's cubicle. "I was wondering if you could answer a few questions for me about a specific case on the list. It was one the two of you handled."

Caution flickered in their eyes. He could understand. They had to feel like he was about to question the way they did their jobs, and they had at least ten more years in the bureau than he did.

"What can we help you with?" Hartlock asked.

"Right now, I'm only reviewing a file." Rafe shifted his weight from one foot to the other. "Verifying the information."

Devane raised a single brow. They didn't want him here—none of them did. They'd made that abundantly clear yesterday when the rest of the agents gave him the cold shoulder. But what choice did he have?

He was doing the best he could.

"Which file?" Devane's bald spot had snatched more space than hair follicles.

Rafe opened the folder and flipped through its contents. "The Tate file. Do either of you remember the case?" His presence meant the boundaries had been set, and he had to proceed with caution or he'd alienate the two people who knew most about the case.

Both men sat straighter. They made eye contact. For a fleeting second. If Rafe hadn't been looking for it, he would've missed it. These two knew he'd chosen the one case that would draw attention if he solved it.

"I do." Hartlock scratched the back of his head. "Hard case."

Rafe pulled out a report and glanced over it, even though he'd all but memorized the file. "I wondered if there's anything additional in the search for the prime suspect. There's been no update for more than two years."

Hartlock shook his head. The blend of gray through his dark hair gave the impression of distinction, maturity. "We did what we could at the time—put out a BOLO . . . have an alert on the social security number . . . staked out the home address and that of known friends. Suspect has no family. Those measures are still in effect as far as I know."

"You seem to recall the case very well." Rafe hated the way they stared at him like a nasty bug needing to be squashed under their shoes.

"Of course we remember it. A federal judge was murdered. Not likely to forget much of that case." Devane leaned back in his chair.

"There've been no hits? No leads on the person of interest? Not even a wild-goose chase?" Hard to believe. A quack or two always called in a sighting.

Hartlock laughed. "Did you read her file? See what she did for a living?"

Rafe nodded but pulled the sheet anyway. "Psychology. Freelanced for us. Gave several training seminars." A real smart cookie. He'd attended one of her seminars on profiling years ago. From what he recalled, she was good. And attractive with that almost-white blonde hair and slim figure. They'd even shared a cup of coffee afterward. Perhaps that was another reason Rafe was drawn to this particular case.

"Right." Hartlock lifted a shoulder and brushed lint from his jacket. "She knows how to hide. If she doesn't want to be found, we ain't gonna find her."

True. "What about this?" He lifted the document he'd found shoved in the bottom of the evidence box. Was listed as trash from the scene.

Devane took the document, glanced it over, then handed it to Hartlock. "Never saw this before. Where'd you get it?"

"Found it in the evidence box. So, y'all didn't follow up on this?"

Hartlock studied the single piece of evidence before passing it back to Rafe. "Nope. Never saw it. Probably not even connected to the murder."

Maybe not, but Rafe's curiosity was piqued. It'd been easy enough to run the name through an Internet search, determine the legitimacy of the person and his current status. Rafe had and discovered Hayden Simpson was the police commissioner of Hopewell, Louisiana. That fact alone warranted further investigation.

Hartlock continued. "It could've been missed. We handled the case hard for a couple of weeks, then the attempted murder of the governor happened. We were assigned that case, and since the governor was alive, that took top priority."

Rafe swallowed, understanding. "Look, I'm sorry. I don't mean to imply you took shortcuts." They hadn't. It was yet another piece of evidence of being overworked and under-manned. And now the bureau was cutting again.

Maybe he *was* grasping the impossible. He stabbed his fingers through his hair. "I didn't know you were assigned to the attempt on the governor." Talk about high-profile cases hitting at the same time.

Devane smiled. "We know it's tough on you to come into an office where you don't know anybody and have to do follow-up. Nobody wants that duty."

"I don't mind it at all. It's okay. I just want to pull my weight around here."

"I get that." Hartlock bobbed his head. "Respect it."

"So I'm following up every possible lead I can find. Even the extremely remote ones."

"Bad deal you picked this case right off the bat." Devane scratched his head. "We did everything we could with the information we had, and nothing's come up since. It was too smooth. Too professional."

Professional. Like someone who knew how to leave a clean crime scene.

"Do you think this goddaughter could've really shot him?" He couldn't quite match the confident woman he'd met years ago with a cold-blooded murderer.

Hartlock steepled his hands over his desk. "I think so. I worked with her on a couple of cases. She was always a bit of a loner . . . Tate raised her. She knew how to handle a firearm. Knew how we'd investigate." He dropped his palms flat to his desk. "If she didn't kill him, why'd she flee the scene?"

The same question had plagued Rafe from the moment he'd read the file. Innocent people didn't run. Guilty ones did. "If she shot him, why did the security guard's statement reflect that, in his opinion, she was devastated by the shooting?"

Hartlock snorted. "You know as well as I do that a rent-a-cop's opinion doesn't matter a hill of beans. He wasn't trained in observation. But most important maybe she was actually showing guilt and the guy thought she was devastated. She does have a master's degree."

Another good point. Rafe smiled. "Thanks for the info."

"If we can help you in any way . . ." Devane pushed to his feet. Hartlock did as well.

"I appreciate that." Rafe closed the folder and moved to exit. "I'm sorry if I sounded accusatory before."

"No problem. We understand the stress." Hartlock clapped him on the shoulder. "So, where do you go from here?"

Rafe smiled and waved the trash document. "Hopewell, Louisiana."

⚖

The sun filtered through the cypress trees, casting prisms of light over the bayou. Louisiana experienced a nice October afternoon. A little overcast, cooler than average. A perfect day for fishing.

Hayden made another cast. A glimmer of light to his right turned his head.

Bella, his best friend, adjusted the camera lens, then smiled.

He waved her over to the pier.

"Any bites?" She plopped onto the pier beside him, set her camera in its case, and nodded toward the red-and-white bobber lazing atop the water.

The hint of fish hung over the bayou, mixing with the clean smell of dirt. Hayden hauled in a deep breath, letting the soothing scent of home wash over him. "Nah. I think I'm just feeding the fish." He squinted at her. The afternoon sun caught the reddish hues of her short hair. "Get any good pictures?"

"I think so. We'll see how they turn out." She grabbed a Diet Coke from the cooler and took a swig. "I think these should finish out my 'Seasons' series."

"That's good. Sun's about to go down and the temp will drop pretty fast. We should head back." He stood and pulled in his line. "Can't wait to see your shots." He meant it. Bella was one talented photographer, that was certain.

She shoved to her feet, dusted off her jeans, and lifted her camera case. She slung the strap over her shoulder and reached for the soft-side cooler. "Hope it turns out like I see it in my mind." She stuck two fingers in her mouth and whistled.

He laughed as he reached for the tackle box. "You creative types . . . always seeing stuff in your head."

Her black Labrador, Chubbers, bounded up to them, tail wagging.

"Hey, don't knock it, buddy." She rubbed Chubbers behind the ears before leading the way up the path to his cabin. "Speaking of knocking, have you heard from Emily?"

His steps faltered. "Not a word. She still isn't speaking to me."

"She'll come around. Give her time."

"Yeah, so you keep saying. At least she calls Mom every day or so."

"There is that." She kicked a stone from the path, rounding the curve to his storage shed.

He hadn't spoken to Emily since she'd left his office days ago. "She doesn't appreciate me taking over for Dad. And with her being bipolar . . ." Shaking his head, Hayden shoved open the shed door and slipped the tackle box inside on the shelf. "I think she keeps seeing Boyd just to tick me off." He set his rod in its reserved space.

"Could be." Bella handed him the cooler. "Why don't you try acting as if you like him for a while and see what she does?"

"Are you kidding me? You know how he is. The guy's a drunk . . . a loser . . . a troublemaker with a capital *T*."

"I didn't say you had to really like him, just give Emily the impression you do." She shrugged.

"I'm the police commissioner. How would it look if I start hanging out with the hoodlum? That'd do wonders for my new contract negotiations."

Bella reached out a hand and stopped him. "Are you really worried about having your contract renewed?"

He wanted to shrug it off but couldn't. "Marshall's been making noise about wanting my job. He's talked with the city council and put a bug in their ear."

"You've got to be kidding me. Marshall Abernathy is the definition of *good ole boy*. He has no law enforcement experience."

"He was in the ROTC. An officer."

Bella rolled her eyes. "Oh, yeah, that's such a great background for being police commissioner."

"Heard he completed a criminal-justice course."

"Let me guess . . . online."

"Either way, he'll have the degree." Despite his best attempts not to, Hayden sweated the situation.

"And you have ten years of experience."

"You know what people say—time for new blood. Fresh ideas, welcoming technology, and all that."

"That's ridiculous." She wrapped an arm around his waist and tugged him toward his cabin. "You're the most amazing thing that ever happened to this town."

"I'm doing my level best to keep my nose clean. Everything I do is under scrutiny now that Marshall's in the game."

"You'll be fine." They stopped at the steps. "Everybody knows you're an awesome commissioner."

He concentrated on Chubbers nosing the hedge. "Maybe so, but you know how Marshall is. He'll dig and dig to find something I've done that'll make me look bad, and he won't hesitate to tell everybody and his brother. There are a few on the council who'd love a reason to replace me." Like Caleb Montgomery, who thought because of his placement on the council, Hayden should ignore Mrs. Montgomery's habit of speeding.

He reached for the railing, one foot on the bottom step. "So I can't be seen hanging out with Boyd for any reason. Even if I could, I wouldn't. He's married, and it's plain wrong of him and Em to be involved. I've prayed and prayed that she'd see the light."

"In your praying, did you remember the Scripture about not judging?"

Not for the first time, Hayden wondered about his best friend's spiritual background. "Well, yes, but I also know 1 Timothy 4, which basically says to point things out to our brothers and sisters in Christ."

"Just read James 5:19 when you get a chance." She squeezed his arm. "But it'll all work out. You'll see. Emily will come to her senses and dump Boyd, and the council will see Marshall for the idiot he is."

She knew the exact Scripture? She'd told him years ago she was mad at God, but he hadn't realized she was so well versed. There was hope she'd see the light. He grinned. "Spoken like a true friend. But I hope you're right." He nodded toward her Jeep. "You coming to Mom's for supper tonight? She's frying catfish."

She smacked her lips. "Wouldn't miss it."

"Didn't think so."

She laughed. "I do so hate to be a foregone conclusion, but when it comes to Ardy's cooking, I'm hooked."

"Then we'll see you around five-ish."

He gave a final wave as Bella climbed into her truck.

Lord, please let her be right about my contract being renewed and Emily coming to her senses. And please let it be soon. Real soon.

Chapter Five

Day 33

This was way too easy.

I sat in the chair facing the new account officer at the bank. He smiled a wide, Cheshire-cat smile as he explained all the benefits of my checking and savings accounts. While he had nice eyes and a normal nose, his smile stretched clear across his face, revealing a row of perfectly straight, white teeth. It was because of this single feature that I couldn't stop staring. Those had to be Lumineers or something. Nobody had such perfect teeth without help.

"And here's the information on our online banking, just like you asked about." He passed me more papers.

I smirked back at Mr. Big Smile and took the folder, nodding as if I were paying attention. I wasn't anymore. I'd already taken note of his body language when he'd returned from pulling whatever check the bank ran. No sign of nervousness. Nothing indicated he'd seen something amiss and called the authorities.

I was *so* in the clear.

Oh, this bank wasn't in my final destination. It was about four towns over. But it was a national chain, and where I was going had a branch. I needed to establish my credentials before I arrived. Someone showing up with a large amount of money in a Podunk town would raise questions.

Small-town residents talked, which was why witness security tried to move people to large cities. Easier to stay under the radar.

But I didn't have a choice. And besides, doing what I shouldn't was what this game was all about.

Except it wasn't a game—I was gambling with my life.

"Where did you say you were from?" Mr. Teeth asked.

I plastered on a wide, plastic smile. "California."

"And you have no family here?"

"Nope. This is my adventure." California was such a smorgasbord of people that my accent wasn't uncommon. And most people in the South assumed all Californians were kind of bohemian-odd. I dressed the part today with my flowing skirt of odd design and oversized blouse that billowed around my waist. It made me look about ten pounds heavier than I was, but that suited my purpose.

He just smiled wider.

"Daddy gave me this inheritance and let me go on my year abroad before I settled down to find a husband." I winked.

Maybe he'd been trapped in an early marriage. Maybe he'd always wanted to travel like a free bird. Either way, a glimmer of jealousy blinked in his eyes. "Well, I hope to see you around town."

I stood and shook his hand, picked up the folder, then made my exit without any further conversation. I headed to the little guesthouse I'd rented.

The afternoon sun filled the southern sky. Big, puffy clouds dominated the air, but held no menace. The drive across town took less than five minutes.

Mrs. Cox, my landlady, was sweeping off the porch when
I pulled the truck into my designated parking place. She
glanced over at me. "Hi, there. You gettin' settled in okay?"

She wore a housedress with a worn wool coat and completed
her fashion statement with large rubber boots. The woman
might be losing her vision and hearing, but her eccentricities
made me smile.

"Yes, ma'am. Just fine. Brought my knickknacks from
storage." I yanked out the first box I'd filled from the local flea
market. Stale dust almost choked me.

"Good. Do you need any help?"

"No, ma'am. Like I told you, I don't have much. The fire got
most of what I had." Man, my stomach flipped to lie to the
kind if odd lady, but I'd needed a story.

"Honey, I'm so sorry. So young to be a widow." She shook
her head. "I understand you requiring a change. You just holler
if you need anything."

"Thank you, ma'am." I balanced the box on my hip as
I unlocked the door.

My chest ached as the lies piled up, the trail of deception
grating against the moral code I'd lived by all my life. I'd been
raised to honor and cherish the truth . . . respect it. Now,
I had to reject it.

Trample it to death just so I could survive.

⚖️

"You aren't eating much." His mother peered at him over her
glass. "Is something wrong with the catfish?"

Hayden took a sip of his iced tea and cut his gaze to Bella
sitting beside him. Thank goodness she was present for the conversation about to take place. He shifted his attention back to his
mother. "No, it's great, as usual." That was true. The light beer
batter with just the right amount of cayenne and spices was melt-
in-your-mouth good.

"Then what's wrong?"

The street's security light filtered in through the great window in the open floor plan of the home he'd shared with his parents and sister. A hint of burning leaves drifted on the air stirred by the ceiling fan set on low.

He set down his glass. "Mom, have you heard from Emily today?"

"No, why?"

If only he didn't have to explain. But Ardy Simpson was inquisitive as well as downright nosy. "MaryBeth Keller's car was vandalized. Keyed, windows and lights smashed, and slit tires."

"And you think Emily might know something about this . . . why?" Mom's eyes narrowed, and she gave a little tilt of her head.

The same quizzical look she'd displayed many a-time when he'd come in late for curfew as a teen.

Hayden groaned inside. "Come on. You know about Emily and Boyd." *Everybody* in Hopewell had heard about Boyd chasing a skirt almost ten years his junior. And the police commissioner's little sister . . . a home wrecker.

His mother flicked her hand through the air in a dismissive fashion. "Just a passing fling is all."

"Mom, she's seeing a married man. Everybody in town knows and is talking about it." He wadded his paper napkin and tossed it on his plate. "A fling isn't something to be dismissed. It's seedy."

"She's just going through a stage. She's just twenty-two. All young girls that age go through stages." Mom glanced at Bella. "Right?"

"Um." Bella shoved another french fry in her mouth and chewed with precision and intent.

Chicken.

He spared her a glare, then struggled to keep his voice void of emotion. "It's not some silly stage, Mom. She honest-to-goodness believes Boyd is going to leave MaryBeth and marry her."

Why couldn't his mother see his sister's faults? Sure, she was the baby of the family, but it was hard to ignore the facts when they were slammed in your face, day after day.

"Perhaps she's right and Boyd *is* going to leave MaryBeth."

He snorted. "That's not even the point. What matters is she's involved with a married man. It's indecent, immoral, and against God's will."

Mom traced the lip of her glass. "You can't know the matters of someone else's heart, Hayden. And you're going to sit there and tell me that *you* know the will of God? Really?"

He looked at Bella, imploring her to chime in and help his mother see how serious the situation was.

She obliged after wiping her mouth with a paper napkin. "Well, I won't claim to have all the answers, but if Boyd really did love Emily, then he would've left MaryBeth by now." Bella reached for her glass. "And MaryBeth's been telling everyone who'll listen that she and Boyd are house hunting."

"Right." *Thank you, Bella.* "I told Emily that the other day. Of course, she refused to listen. And now MaryBeth's car has been vandalized."

His mother's eyes widened and she dropped her hands into her lap. "You think Emily was involved in such an act?"

"The officer who took the call reports Emily was the one person MaryBeth said she could think of who would do such a thing." And deep inside, Hayden knew his sister was just stupid and vindictive enough to act on her warped sense of justice.

"And you believe this woman over your own sister?"

"I can't find her to get her side of the story, which was why I asked you if you'd spoken to her."

"I haven't spoken with her since last night, but she isn't responsible. She wouldn't do something like that."

Hayden sighed. "Look at the facts, Mom."

"I can't believe you'd even think such a thing for one second."

Bella cleared her throat. "Is Emily still taking her medication, Ardy? I mean, I've heard that sometimes if people just stop taking their bipolar medication, they can do some strange things."

"Emily knows to take her medication." His mother shot from her seat and snatched her dishes. The fork clattered against the plate. "I'm not going to sit here and listen to you smear your sister's good name." She turned and marched into the kitchen.

He stared at her retreating back. Was his mother as delusional as his sister?

Dishes rattled. Pots and pans clanged. Cabinets slammed.

"Hey, she'll get over it. You know she never stays angry for long." Bella's words were soft.

Hayden shook his head, every knot in his stomach tightening. "Why does she defend Em over and over?"

"Because she's her mother, that's why. One of the things I love about Ardy—right, wrong, or indifferent, she's behind you and Emily 100 percent."

Meeting Bella's stare, he shrugged. "She thinks Emily has a good name? She can believe that? She has to hear the rumors. All the talk." Which oftentimes made him blush. But what could he do? He couldn't fight every guy who repeated lewd things about his sister. Especially not when they were true.

"It's a mother's job to believe the best in her children."

True. "But how can Emily be so . . . for lack of a better word, stupid?"

"C'mon, Hay. She's a kid. Yes, she's making some obvious bad choices, but she'll learn. She'll grow up. And remember she does have an illness." Bella reached over and scraped the remains of her supper onto his plate.

"Which the medication takes care of."

Bella sighed. "Didn't you ever do anything stupid in your youth?"

"Never got involved with someone married." He handed her his fork, which she piled on top of the stacked plates. "Never beat up somebody's car."

Bella smiled, loosening his irritation. "But something you aren't quite proud of now, looking back?" She rested her chin in her hands, probing him with those odd aqua-colored eyes of hers.

"I guess." Visions of broken knuckles and black eyes stormed into his mind. He met Bella's gaze. "Okay, okay. I got into some fights because I hadn't learned to walk away. One or two."

"See, you weren't perfect." Bella straightened and waggled her brows. "I would've liked to have seen that. Mr. Calm, Cool, and Collected punching somebody."

He couldn't stop the grin. "Hey, I admitted it was something I wasn't proud of."

"People grow up and learn their lessons. Some just take longer than others. Emily will come around. She always does."

"That's the point—she isn't learning from her mistakes. She keeps creating bigger and worse ones." And he hadn't a clue what to do. Her antics had put him in a precarious position on more than one occasion. Now, with his contract about to come up . . .

"It could be the disorder."

"Others who have it don't act like she does."

Bella sighed again. "So, what helped you?"

"What?"

"What helped you see the error of your ways and put you on the right path?"

Grief swirled. Four years hadn't diminished the ache of loss. "Dad. He wouldn't put up with any crap."

Bella smiled a half smile and put her hand over his. "I'm sorry. I know it still hurts."

And she wasn't just giving him lip service. Her parents had died in a car accident the year before his father. He couldn't imagine the pain she suffered, losing both parents at the same time. No wonder she'd packed up and moved. Sometimes he wished he could've done the same. Started over someplace new.

But he was the head of his family now, responsible for watching over his mother and sister.

Lord help him, it was up to him to figure out a way to reach Emily. Before it was too late.

If looks could turn someone to stone, Rafe would be a statue.

Alphonse Jackson didn't blink. Didn't move. Rafe couldn't even be sure the SAC was still focused on the here-and-now.

Rafe held his breath, waiting. For what, he wasn't sure. He hadn't known his boss long enough to read the man.

After forever, Jackson let out a long sigh. He leaned back in his chair, lacing his fingers and resting them on his chest. "Let me get this straight, you want me to authorize a little field trip to Louisiana based upon a piece of trash?"

"An investigation follow-up to an unsolved case."

"And you can't do that from here?"

Rafe swallowed. "I could, but I believe the interview would be better suited to the case in person."

"Why not bring him here to be questioned?"

"I believe the element of surprise will garner more information for the case." Rafe sat as straight and still as the statue his boss's stare could turn him into. "The body language and response to the questions is often more telling than the answers the person gives."

"I know basic interrogation, Agent Baxter." Jackson glanced at his computer screen.

"Yes, sir."

"With budget cuts on the horizon, I just don't know if this is worth the expense. And we don't have a spare vehicle for you yet."

"I'll drive, sir. My own vehicle." He swallowed.

Jackson peered at him from over his reading glasses and spiked a brow. "You think this is that important of a person of interest?"

Rafe paused. "Yes, sir. I think this is the only clue the original agents didn't follow up on. It's our one opportunity to possibly get a real lead in the case."

"And you think you should be the agent going and doing the questioning? Might I remind you that you've only been here a week?"

So Jackson would just hand his clue over to someone else? Someone who'd missed it all this time? "I do, sir. I realize the reason new-to-the-office agents are given cold cases, per se, is because they often have a fresh perspective. I think my perspective makes me uniquely the one to go and conduct the interview."

"Fine. But I expect you back in the office ASAP, with a full report. And keep in constant contact with both me and Hartlock. E-mail and call in updates. If you need information, Hartlock will help work this end of the case. Keep us abreast of the situation. I want daily updates from you."

Rafe struggled to stand. "Thank you, sir." He moved to leave before Jackson changed his mind.

"And Baxter?"

Rafe turned back to face his boss. "Yes, sir?"

"You better get a solid lead from this."

"Of course, sir." Rafe scrambled from the office and headed back to his cubicle.

After pulling up MapQuest on the Internet, he printed driving directions to the small town. If he left right away, he could drive to Louisiana tonight, stay at some roadside motel, then finish the drive and arrive in Hopewell before lunch tomorrow.

And maybe, just maybe, he'd score a definite lead before nightfall tomorrow.

Chapter Six

"Never give in. Never. Never. Never. Never."
Sir Winston Churchill

Day 72

My nerves were tangled to the point my stomach turned. I was determined to meet the man in Daniel's documents today.

Oh-my-stars. Could I do this?

I'd scoured all the papers from the safe. If what I believed to be the truth actually was, I hadn't a clue what I was going to do. It would prove I never knew my godfather at all. That he kept such an important secret from me . . . for so long . . . well, I just didn't know how I felt about everything. But I first had to meet this man and determine if my suspicions were true or not.

I had to be wrong. *Please, let me be wrong.*

Sitting before my computer, I accessed the *Arkansas Democrat-Gazette*'s online edition. Nothing about the murder. Again. It was as if no one cared that a federal judge had been shot in the chest in his home. A little more than two months had passed, and not even a mention on the back page.

The FBI was still looking for me. They would keep the case open indefinitely. But they weren't tracking me anymore. Of this, I could be sure. The attempted assassination of the state's governor had to have them all occupied.

Which was good news for me. Bad news for poor Daniel.

My mouth went arid. All the tips I'd given the locals . . . for nothing. The one thing that could solve the case was me. If I went back.

No one would believe me. I had no proof. It'd be their word against mine, which wouldn't be so bad. But the involvement of higher-ups put the favor on their side. I'd either be shut down . . .

Or shut up for good. Forever-kind-of-good.

I closed my laptop and stood, staring out the window. The wind blew the curtains of Spanish moss clinging to the overhanging cypress trees. The little house I'd bought was built and used as a hunting cabin. Tucked into the boundary of the woods on one side, edging the bayou on the other. Two bedrooms, one bath, a cozy kitchen and dining combo area, and a good-sized living space. Perfect for me.

I already loved this little bayou town. Quiet. Serene. Here, everyone knew everyone. Except they didn't know me. But they would—the new me. The invented me.

First, I needed answers. I needed the truth about Daniel and this man.

And then I'd decide my course of action.

⚖️

"She hasn't called Mom in days. Even for Emily, that's odd." Hayden fingered the coffee cup in front of him.

Bella shifted across the table from him. She stared out the window of her kitchen toward the bayou. "If I had to guess, I'd say she was just off pouting."

"I'm used to that. But her not calling Mom for several days . . ." His mind wandered to every possible horrible situation, causing his gut to tighten.

The sun shone through the window, warming the room.

"I hate to mention this, but have you checked with Boyd?"

Hayden took another sip of coffee. Already cold. He grimaced. "Not yet. I really would rather not go down that road."

"I understand, but she might've told him where she was going."

"I know." He stood and ambled to the counter. "Did you hear the latest rumor?"

"What?" Bella's aqua eyes widened.

"MaryBeth is pregnant. At least, that's what she told their Realtor. That's why they're looking to buy a house."

Bella's mouth twisted. "Could be Emily found out about the baby and she's run off to nurse her wounds."

"Maybe. It's just not like her not to check in with Mom though." He poured his coffee, then returned to sit across from Bella. "Mom sympathizes with her. Takes her side. I think she'd want Mom to know so she wouldn't have to wallow alone."

"Unless her pride's hurt." She held up a finger to stop him. "Think about it, Hayden. Everyone in town knows she's been involved with Boyd. Now, MaryBeth and he are having a baby and buying a house. Everyone will soon know that the other woman has been dumped. That's hard on a person's pride."

"She brought it on herself." He let the coffee scald the sarcasm from his tongue.

"She did, but that doesn't mean her heart hasn't been trampled on and her ego smashed to smithereens." Bella frowned, indentations forming between her eyebrows.

"You think she's just off sulking?"

Bella shrugged. "Factor in her illness and who knows. I think you should at least ask Boyd. No, you don't like him, and you don't like having to ask him anything, but this is your little sister we're talking about. They might've had a fight and he knows where she could be."

Made sense. "I'll run by in the morning before he leaves for work."

Smiling, she lifted a single brow. "How's Ardy taking it? I bet not talking to Emily is making her nuts."

That was putting it mildly. "She calls me at least three or four times a day. Is all but demanding I eat supper with her every night, where she just mopes about."

Bella grinned. "See, that's another reason to find out where Emily is—the quicker she's back in town, the sooner your mom will stop pestering you so much."

"I hope." He glanced out the window. A breeze swayed the branches of the trees lining the side of Bella's property. Soon winter would be peeking her head around the corner. He liked winter.

"You know, Hayden, you should find a good lady and settle down. Grandchildren would *really* keep Ardy out of your hair."

He choked on the coffee. "We've been over this already. Let it go."

She grinned wider. "Nope. Not gonna let you off the hook so easily this time."

The imp. Not for the first time he wondered why he had never felt a spark of romantic interest for Bella. She was beautiful in a subtle way, had the best personality ever, and she loved his mother. Yet, he'd never felt any attraction toward her. Just a deep affection. Why couldn't he be attracted to her?

She snapped her fingers in front of his face. "Hello? Hayden? Anybody home?"

He met her stare dead-on. "Why did we never go out?"

Her face twisted and her gaze fell to the table.

What was with him? Had he just blurted his thoughts out loud? "I'm sorry, Bella. I was just thinking out loud."

"About not being interested in me?"

"I mean, I love you dearly now. But I'm talking about when I first met you. I was just wondering why I never thought of you in a romantic sense. I mean—"

"Shut up. You've shattered my ego enough as it is. Don't try to make up for it now, buddy." Bella's face reddened, but she flashed him a smile. "And you never were interested because then you couldn't be my best friend."

"But before you were my friend."

She shook her head. "We were destined to be friends, period. Anything else would've ruined our entire relationship."

He would've hated that. "Very true."

"Now that that's settled, don't think you can distract me from the subject at hand. Why aren't you dating anyone?"

Because he didn't find anyone who interested him that way but knew Bella wouldn't buy that. "I'm waiting on the right woman."

"You'll probably never find her if you aren't looking."

"I'm always looking." He grinned and lifted his cup. "What about you? Why aren't you dating anyone?"

That telltale blush of hers marched across her face. "Because I'm waiting on a knight in shining armor to come sweep me off my feet."

Hayden laughed, conjuring up the mental image. While amusing, he also felt a twinge of grief. Losing her friendship would hurt. Bad. "I don't think there are any knights hiding in Hopewell."

"You never know who might show up," she teased with her easy smile.

There was that.

⚖️

This was probably insane.

Rafe had reviewed the case until his brain hurt, not that it did any good. He still had nothing but questions.

After hours of driving in the bright October sun, there was no better time than now for answers.

He slipped out of his car and strode across the parking lot. The borrowed GPS had directed him right to the police department's front door. Adrenaline pushed him inside.

Welcome to Hopewell, Louisiana.

Excitement thrummed through him as he made his way to the counter splitting the reception area from the rest of the building. The stench of coffee left on a burner too long greeted him.

He couldn't stop himself from taking a mental inventory of the room. Leak-stained ceiling tiles . . . paint peeling off the cinder-block walls . . . cracked linoleum floor. The reek of stale cigarette smoke filtered through the recycled-air system, even though the sign over the counter clearly stated a no-smoking policy.

"Hayden Simpson, please." Rafe made direct eye contact with the uniformed officer perched behind the counter, even though the heat in the building suffocated him, cinching his tie until it felt like a noose. Maybe he should've foregone the bureau's acceptable dress code.

"May I ask what this is regarding?" The officer couldn't be more than twenty-two or three, but already lines wrinkled the corners of his eyes. His gaze traveled up and down Rafe's frame.

Reaching into his pocket, Rafe withdrew his badge and flashed it at the man.

His weighted eyes widened. "You're FBI?"

Rafe nodded and pocketed his badge. "I need to speak to Mr. Simpson. If you'll tell him I'm here . . ." Maybe this one lead would pan out.

It'd better—he had nothing else.

"He's not here."

He glanced at the clock on the wall—a few seconds away from four thirty. Was he out on a call? Rafe wasn't up-to-date on the policies and procedures of small-town law enforcement. "Will he be back in the office today?"

"Nope."

Rats! If only he'd been an hour or so earlier, he could've talked with Simpson. "Okay. I need to find a hotel. Can you make any suggestions?"

The officer laughed. "Agent, we only have one motel. It's right on Main Street. Hang a left out of the parking lot and go about a mile or so."

Rafe nodded. "Thanks. What time does Commissioner Simpson get here?"

The officer shrugged. "Depends. Oh, wait. Tomorrow's Wednesday. He has breakfast over at the diner at eight every Wednesday morning."

"And the diner would be where?"

"Pass the motel on your right, and the diner's just a block down. Can't miss it."

Rafe hoofed it back to his automobile. At least the suppressive heat from the station didn't dog him outside. He started the car and drove back to Main Street.

Large trees lined the road, their bare branches bowing. People walked their dogs along the sidewalk. He only saw two cars on the road.

He passed what he assumed was city hall. The stone front of the building looked as if it had weathered numerous storms over the years. Little grooves had formed in the stones as the years flew off the calendar, as well as chips and nicks, but dying kudzu covered most of the building's eyesores.

And he'd thought his new city was a mess. This place made Little Rock look like a vacation resort.

How a police commissioner of nowhere had anything to do with a case in the capital city of Arkansas was beyond Rafe, but he'd learned long ago not to make assumptions. Follow the trail of evidence . . . that's how cases were solved.

And never more important to solve one than now.

He followed the officer's directions until he saw the motel—it didn't look like it would even rate two stars, but what choice did he have?—and whipped into the parking lot. The vehicle bumped and rattled over a pothole large enough to hide a motorcycle. He rolled to a stop, praying he didn't have a flat tire, and stared at the building before him.

Slamming his car door, he headed into the motel's lobby, expecting to find roaches crawling up the wall.

It wasn't as bad as he'd imagined.

Rafe stood at the registration counter, waiting for the attendant to return. While he waited, he took stock of the motel's offerings. Carpet looked like it'd been replaced in the last couple of years. Counter didn't have scratches or grooves.

He glanced over his shoulder. Nice décor in the lobby—two wingback chairs and a love seat on an Oriental rug with a set of end tables, and a beautiful, if dark, matted photograph of the bayou framed over the catty-cornered-set couch.

Could be much worse.

"Thank you for waiting, sir." The young lady with bright blue eyes returned to her position, stuffed a can of disinfectant under the counter, wiped her hands on her jeans, and smiled. "Now, how can I help you?"

"I need a room, please." He knew the drill and pulled out his driver's license and credit card.

"Okay. For how long?" Her fingers flew over the computer's keyboard, her smile never waning.

"I'm not sure." He'd have to see what Hayden Simpson had to say before he could determine how much field investigation he'd have to conduct, could take several days or even weeks. "Can I book for three nights now and let you know if I need to extend?"

She chuckled. "Sure. It's not like we're going to have a rush on rooms." She took his credit card and swiped it while running through her spiel of the motel's fine amenities—a free continental breakfast, location of the ice machine, and pool hours.

"Thanks." He slipped the license and card back into his wallet.

"Here you go." She handed him an electronic key in a paper sleeve with his room number written inside. "My name's Daisy . . . if you need anything." She smiled wider, if that was even possible.

Heat marched up the back of his neck. "Uh, thanks." The unspoken invitation was there, but Rafe wouldn't take the offering. He'd crossed his moral turpitude line once and wasn't willing to go there again. Maybe he should just forget ever trying to become a SAC and become a monk.

He grabbed his stuff and headed to the end of the hall Daisy had pointed out. Once inside his room, he quickly unpacked his duffel, then opened his briefcase.

The room was standard motel fare, even though the décor was a bit higher standard than most. King bed that boasted a pillow-top, quilted cover. Plenty of pillows. Adequate computer desk, with a faux antique reading lamp. Flat-panel television. Another local area photograph framed on the wall.

At least the room's color scheme wasn't orange. Soothing blue and brown instead.

After setting up his laptop, he checked his e-mail, then typed up a quick notification to Hartlock that he'd arrived and sent it.

He laid back on the bed, staring out the window.

Hayden Simpson, how are you connected to my case?

⚖

Smiling, he reread the report. Initial numbers showed him leading. This was good. Very good. His advisors and managers were earning their generous salaries.

He flipped the page and stared at the smiling photo of himself—the one that screamed for people to trust him. They'd airbrushed his picture, removing all but the wrinkles at the corner of his eyes. Those, his advisor said, made him look wise and distinguished. Perhaps the expensive snake had been right. Looking at the ad now, he could see that persona coming out.

This was what he was born to do. If only his mother were still alive to see him now. She'd worked three jobs to put food on the table for him and his two brothers. Then later, to support her daughter-in-law and three grandsons. And for what? To put herself into an early grave?

The mesothelioma had taken a young man from three boys and a wife who needed him. Had the plant his brother worked for cared that they exposed him to asbestos? Did they bother to do anything for his sons or widow, financially or physically? Not hardly. After he died, his mother took in the surviving wife and three young boys. The family had taken the plant to court out of desperation. The company executives lied in the court proceedings, rendering a nonguilty verdict from the jury. After his mother died, his sister-in-law remarried and moved away. He never saw his nephews again. It was all the fault of that defense attorney . . . the one who'd swayed the jury not to hold the company responsible.

All he got out of the experience was disdain for the American justice system. What an oxymoron that was—nothing *just* about the legal system.

But he'd learned it wasn't about the truth. It was about playing the game.

He'd enjoyed playing through the vast majority of his career. Now he sat on the fringe of getting what he'd always secretly wanted.

He shook off his thoughts and glanced back at the ad waiting for his approval. It was just another step toward his dream. He was a chosen leader. Had been picked to lead people and cultivate ideals. No one could stand in his way now.

No one.

Chapter Seven

*"Trickery and treachery are the practices of fools
that have not wits enough to be honest."*

BENJAMIN FRANKLIN

His heart crashed to the porch.

MaryBeth stood in the doorway, her belted robe worn like a shield against him instead of the chilly fall morning. "Can I help you, Hayden?" From her tone, all in the Simpson household were personae non gratae with her.

"Is Boyd here? I need to speak to him for a moment."

"What's this about?" Suspicion knotted her brow.

"Official business."

She hesitated a moment before turning her head over her shoulder. "Boyd, honey, Hayden's here to see you." She nudged against the doorjamb.

Hayden didn't want to have this conversation in front of her. Boyd probably wouldn't be as forthcoming about knowing the whereabouts of his mistress with his wife standing right there.

Mistress and Emily . . . two words that should have never been in the same sentence together. Images of his little sister running around, sans her front tooth, in pigtails and ripped jeans filled his mind. He fought the groan. Dad would turn over in his grave. How badly Hayden had failed.

Boyd appeared behind MaryBeth wearing nothing but jeans and bed hair. "What can I do for you?"

"I'd like to ask you just a few questions." Hayden darted his gaze to MaryBeth, then back to Boyd. "Privately."

"Okay." Boyd planted a kiss on his wife's head as he maneuvered around her and stepped onto the porch, tugging a tee over his head.

She gave a little huff before backing into the house and shutting the front door.

The hint of burning leaves flitted on the breeze.

Hayden stepped off the porch and took a deep breath before speaking. "I hate to come here and ask, but do you have any idea where Emily could be? She's been missing for days."

Boyd gave a cough. "Why would I know?" He blew on his palms.

Hayden fought the urge to curl his hand into a fist. Was this idiot going to stand here and play dumb? "Boyd, I know about y'all's relationship." Everybody in Hopewell knew. Neither Boyd nor Emily had been discreet.

"That's over, man." He shot a glance to the front door. "Me and MaryBeth . . . we're having a baby."

"I heard. Congratulations." And condolences to MaryBeth. "But I'm wondering if you've talked with Emily."

"I just told you we were through."

Struggling to keep his breathing even, Hayden tried again. "I understand that. I was wondering when you told Emily it was over."

Boyd shrugged. "Dunno. Can't remember."

"As of four days ago, Emily was still under the impression you were leaving MaryBeth to marry her. She told me herself." And he still thought her naive in her belief.

"I never said I was gonna marry her, man."

If only he didn't wear the badge . . . Hayden would smack the smirk right off Boyd's acne-scarred face. "When did you tell her it was over? When you told her about the baby?"

"Yeah, I guess."

"Which was when, exactly?"

"A couple of days ago." Boyd cleared his throat. "Saturday evening, I guess."

Three days ago. "What. Did. You. Say. To. Her?"

Boyd glanced back at the front door again. "I told her MaryBeth was pregnant, so I had to try to make my marriage work."

"And what did she say?"

"She cried a little. Screamed a lot. Said no one was gonna make a fool outta her." Boyd grinned and shook his head.

"So she was upset?"

"Not really. More mad." He ran a hand over his hair standing up at odd angles. "I don't get it. I mean, I heard Marshall'd been nosing around her the past few weeks, so it wasn't like she cared about me anymore."

"Marshall?" No . . . couldn't be.

"Yeah, Marshall Abernathy."

Could his day get any worse? Hayden resisted the need to grind his teeth. "After you told Emily about the baby and calling off your relationship, what happened?"

"She left."

"Have you heard from her since? Any type of communication? Voice mail? Text?"

"Not me, but I'm pretty sure she's the one who messed up our car." Boyd stared at him through half-mast eyes. "We filed a report on it. You haven't found who did it yet."

"We're still investigating." Hayden caught MaryBeth spying out the window. "So, have you heard from Emily since you broke it off?" *Since you played around, having your cake and eating it too, no matter who got hurt?*

"Nope."

Hayden moved toward the stairs. "Let me know if you do, won't you?" The badge and his faith kept him from making mincemeat of the sorry excuse for a man.

"Sure. Hope you find your sister."

Wanting nothing more than to plow his fist into Boyd's face, Hayden stomped to his cruiser and slipped into the driver's seat. He gripped the steering wheel until his palms were raw.

God, where is she?

Day 73

What was I thinking? I had to be insane to have sought out a cop.

Then again, it could work in my favor. By all logic and reasoning, I should avoid law enforcement like the plague.

So far, I'd managed to keep the wolves at bay. Every source I utilized told me the same thing—I'd done it. I'd successfully gotten away from the *great hunters*. Not that I would ever think of them as anything like that again. But I couldn't get cocky. I still had to watch my every move to stay under the radar.

Yet I had a legitimate reason for being in this bayou town, and I would proceed to figure out why Daniel had kept such a secret. Even from me.

My luck held when I ran into the man I sought right in the middle of the city's diner. I'd been able to study him without addressing him at all. I watched how he interacted with the people in town and how they related to him. Everyone seemed to love him.

Very understandable. He seemed to be a charmer and quite handsome. Standing about six feet tall, his muscular build forced him to have a natural swagger. He wore his dark hair short and neat. Not even a hint of gray at the temples. But his eyes . . . wide and dark, they hinted at empathy and understanding. Drew people into their depths.

I'd bet the balance of my checking account he rocked at interrogations.

There was just something so honest and trustworthy about

him. My training taught me to read people. Experience made me good at it. And in my professional opinion, this man was a force of nature to be reckoned with.

And I needed to find out his connection to Daniel.

⚖️

Show time!

Rafe steered the car into the diner's parking lot. Early fall littered the sidewalks with the first leaves. The morning sun beat down on the city of Hopewell as he stretched out of the car. Taking a moment to utilize the opportunity, Rafe stared through the front windows, his gaze on the lookout for the telltale uniform. There, corner booth.

From his research he knew Hayden Simpson was thirty-six. The man sitting with a young woman looked physically fit—broad shoulders spread under his uniform shirt. The police commissioner smiled at something his companion said . . . an easygoing grin.

Rafe registered details about the young woman. She was very attractive, at least from what he could see of her profile. Light brownish hair cut in a straight line at the base of her neck. Her hands moved as she spoke. She threw her head back to laugh before she reached across the table to playfully slap Simpson's hand.

Very comfortable with one another. A great deal of affection for each other. Were they friends? Family? Lovers?

Shaking his head, Rafe forced his mind back to the urgent matter at hand. He didn't need to notice the woman at all. He needed to focus. Concentrate on the case. He had a lot riding on this case—like any chance of promotion. If he failed, Jackson would never give him a shot.

He reached into the console and withdrew the smaller-than-a-credit-card digital camera. Using the zoom, he took several photos of Hayden Simpson and the unidentified woman. He'd send them to Jackson and Hartlock later to run through the system.

Who knew what might come up?

Rafe punctuated his steps as he left the car, gravel crunching under his loafers, and entered the diner. The enticing aroma of bacon drifted over him. His stomach rumbled. He hesitated a moment, habitually taking note of the other people in the room. Counting Simpson and his lady, four patrons, plus a waitress and a short-order cook behind the grill.

He fingered the edge of the case folder under his arm. What was the connection? Time to find out. Silverware clattered against glass.

The element of surprise always worked in his favor. Rafe headed to the back corner booth.

The police commissioner and his lady friend both looked up as he stopped beside their table. Expectation hung in the lawman's eyes, while wariness marred the woman's greenish-blue orbs.

Rafe whipped out his badge. "Excuse me, Commissioner Simpson. I'm Rafe Baxter, FBI. So sorry to interrupt your breakfast, but I have a few questions for you."

⚖️

FBI?

Bella trembled as the badge shone under the diner's dirty lights. Her mouth went drier than the Spanish moss draping the trees outside her cabin.

Hayden offered his hand to the agent. "Hayden Simpson. Please join us." He stood and waved the agent to sit in the space he'd just vacated, then dropped into the seat beside her. She fumbled to scoot closer to the wall.

Bella's stomach threatened to reverse the pepper, onion, and cheese omelet she'd just devoured.

What had gone wrong? Where had she messed up?

"Please forgive my rudeness, Agent. This is Bella Miller." Hayden nudged her, all smiles and congeniality. Sometimes her best friend's extrovert tendencies and Southern hospitality drove her insane. This was one of those times.

Her insides turned to mush as her mind registered the man across the table from her. Nice-looking in an institutional type of way. Short, russet-brown, cropped hair. Bureau-issued suit. Broad shoulders and piercing, dark eyes. Yeah, very attractive, if you liked that type.

She didn't. She despised his type.

If only he didn't look as if he'd stepped off the cover of *GQ*.

Wait a minute . . . Rafe Baxter? It'd been many years, but . . . the memory stupefied her.

"Can I buy you a cup of coffee?" His eyes were sincere.

What did she have to lose? She was done with her training seminars, about to head back home but had some time to kill before her flight. And he was attractive. "Sure."

He held open the conference center's door. "I'm Rafe. Rafe Baxter." He smiled and her heart flipped. "Your seminar was very informative."

"Thank you." To be honest, she couldn't even remember what she'd lectured on. After six months of giving these sessions across the United States, they'd all started to run together. "I'm glad you enjoyed it."

Across the conference's campus, the light in the small coffee shop window glowed warmly against the bitter wind.

She pushed her balled hands into her jacket pockets and let him lead her across the courtyard.

A warm rush of air kissed her face as they entered the coffee shop. The aroma of freshly ground coffee welcomed her into its enticing fold. They placed their orders at the counter, then grabbed the table closest to the front window.

"So, you're an FBI agent?" She smiled as she warmed her hands against the disposable cup.

"Yes, ma'am." He took a short sip from his regular black coffee. "For almost four years."

"Do you like it?" She always wondered if the men she worked with honest-to-goodness enjoyed what they did, or if they did it because it was all they knew.

"I love it. This isn't just a job for me. It's my career." His brown eyes sparkled as he spoke, revealing gold flecks hiding in the irises. "It's all I've ever wanted to do."

"It's great that you love what you do." She understood.

"You're beautiful, do you know that?"

The alarm on her cell phone chimed, alerting her that she had to leave for the airport.

As much as she'd lacked for an adequate comeback then, he'd stolen her voice again today.

Hayden's elbow dug into her side. "Bella?"

"Ms. Miller." The agent offered his hand.

She shoved on a smile despite the discomfort cloaking her like a wool coat in August and shoved words past the lump in her throat. "Mister . . . Baxter, did you say?" She shook his hand, taking in his firm grip. He'd aged well. Extremely well.

"Yes, ma'am."

She wiped her palm on her jeans. The faint scent of his cologne permeated her space and did strange things to her pulse. How could she escape now?

"So, how can I help you, Agent Baxter?" Hayden reached for his coffee.

The agent cut his eyes to Bella, searing her to the spot, then glanced back to Hayden. "It's a private matter. Nothing to do with your capacity as police commissioner."

Baxter glanced at Bella again before directing his focus on Hayden. "I realize I've interrupted your time, but the questions I have are personal. About a cold case I'm working. I need your help."

Bella's throat tightened, and she forced her body not to tense. How much time did she have? If she left right now, she could grab Chubbers and her ready-to-go bag and be out of town within twenty minutes. She stared at Hayden from the corner of her eye.

Her best friend. How hurt would he be at her betrayal? Her lies? He was so honest . . . so full of integrity . . . so *good*. What would he think of her once he knew the ugly truth?

She was *so* going to be sick.

Instead she cleared her throat. "Why don't I catch up with you later, Hayden?" She nudged his side. She didn't have much time.

"Don't be silly." He focused on the agent. "Bella's like my sister—whatever you have to ask me that's personal, you can ask in front of her." He shrugged. "Since it's not police business, I'm going to tell her anyway."

She grabbed her purse. "I should go." Half an hour at most, then she'd be stuck.

No, she'd be dead.

Hayden didn't move, just laid a hand on her arm. "No, stay." He quirked a brow at the agent across the table.

Bella dared not move. Dared not breathe. Did the only thing she could—paid attention to every detail, every nuance of Agent Baxter. His body language wasn't defensive, nor was it predatory. Could it be . . . he didn't know?

"Okay." He pulled out an envelope from the folder he held and slid it onto the table. It was just starting to yellow, the edges stained dark.

She set her purse back in the booth beside her. Her heart slunk into her gut.

Hayden took the envelope from the agent, withdrawing a card of some sort from it. Bella never had been patient, but right now curiosity clogged her throat.

Hayden glanced at Agent Baxter. "Where did you get this?"

"At a crime scene."

"I don't understand." Hayden flipped over the envelope to study the front. "I don't know this person. Maybe he's an old friend of my parents." He stared at it again and frowned. "It's my mother's handwriting."

Bella fought the urge to yank it out of his hands. As it was, she could make out a card with blue bows as a border.

Baxter wore a scowl. "Seems strange you never met the man, yet he kept your birth announcement for more than thirty-six years."

"I don't know what to tell you."

She couldn't hold her tongue any longer. "What?"

Hayden handed her the card, still holding the envelope. The card dropped to the table.

Bella fisted her hands to avoid touching the card. No sense leaving fingerprints where the FBI could and would pull them.

Hayden gave her a funny look. "It's the announcement my parents sent out when I was born." He looked at Baxter. "And you say this was found at a crime scene?"

"Yes."

She scanned the card, standard birth announcement, then leaned back in the booth. Nothing wrong with it, as far as she could tell. Dare she believe she was okay?

"What kind of crime scene?" Hayden's voice cracked as he passed the envelope and card back across the table.

"The man who received your birth announcement was murdered three years ago." Baxter tapped the cardstock back into its envelope. "This was found on the floor near where he was shot to death."

Hayden let out a slow whistle. "I assure you, Agent Baxter, I've never met Daniel Tate before in my life."

Bella's blood stalled in her veins. This was her worst nightmare.

And her deadly mistake.

Chapter Eight

"Honesty is for the most part less profitable than dishonesty."
PLATO

Was he wrong and there was no connection?

No, Rafe's gut instincts had never been wrong before. He needed to just trust himself. Trust his training and experience. What had he observed?

Hayden Simpson had looked shocked and surprised. His body language reflected no knowledge of Daniel Tate.

Rafe paused in typing his update e-mail to ASAC Hartlock. He reached for his bottled water and took a sip.

Sure, people could and did deceive. Some were good actors. But without planning, without any warning . . . The case *was* three years old, so the visit had been completely unexpected. No way could Simpson have prepared his reaction.

Simpson had vowed to ask his mother about Tate tonight. His demeanor screamed innocence and no involvement. If that was true, what did it mean for the case?

Had this been, as Jackson had insinuated, a wild-goose chase? Had he just blown his chance to fit in?

The streetlights outside the motel flipped on. Dried leaves blew across the parking lot. His stomach rumbled, reminding him he'd not eaten since lunch. He should try the diner again. Looked like it was the only place close to grab a bite to eat. Maybe he'd see or hear something that could help him. Just what, he didn't know.

Yet.

What about Bella Miller? She had been stoic, unemotional. But there was something about her. Her obvious attractiveness aside, she looked somewhat familiar, but he just couldn't place from where. Maybe she just looked like someone he knew. The fullness of her face *did* remind him of Maddie. The intensity of her stare . . . and what exactly was her tie to Simpson? They seemed very cozy just to be friends, yet Rafe hadn't picked up any romantic energy between them. What was her story? Something about her seemed to pull him to her. He hadn't felt that way since . . . well, in a long time.

He had no business thinking about her in any way. Or any woman. He'd already broken his own code of conduct before and still hadn't made adequate restitution for his sin.

Rafe had to trust his instincts. Had learned to over the past decade. While he felt Simpson truly didn't know anything about the birth announcement and Tate, Rafe's gut still told him there was a connection here.

The one that could unravel everything.

After finishing the e-mail, attaching the digital photos he'd taken at the diner, then sending it into cyberspace, Rafe laid the photocopied contents of the case file out on the desk. The pictures of the suspect with the victim, Tate's bio as well as the suspect's, crime-scene photos, and reports of Hartlock and Devane.

He laid down the birth announcement last. Taking a step back, he glanced over the entire case documents. What wasn't he seeing? He rearranged everything, putting each item in chronological order as best he could.

What was it?

He lifted the photograph of the suspect, Remington Wyatt,

and stared. Something about her . . . Something about the tilt of her chin . . . no, the striking prominent cheekbones wasn't what hit him. He set the photo down on the bed again and stared into her amazing crystal-clear blue eyes.

Eyes that saw into his soul, even in a picture.

It unnerved him. Had he experienced a similar gut reaction to her when he'd met her before? He couldn't remember. It was years ago.

Before Georgia had died.

Rafe shook his head, clearing the painful memories, and lifted Remington's bio. She'd graduated magna cum laude in psychology from the University of Arkansas. Excelled in her field. The woman was smart. That she'd eluded the bureau for three years was nothing to sneeze at.

He glanced back at the snapshot of Tate and her taken mere months before the murder. Arms around each other, big smiles. Why would she kill him? It made no sense.

But neither did fleeing the scene of the crime if she was innocent.

The ringtone from *The Good, The Bad, and The Ugly* echoed off the hotel room's walls.

Dropping the picture back to the desk, he snagged the cell from his belt clip and flipped it open. "Baxter."

"Hey there." Despite the casual words, the tone of his best friend's voice told him something was wrong.

Very wrong.

Please, God, not Savannah. "Hey, Darren. What's new?"

"We're back at the hospital."

Just what he'd been afraid of. Rafe paced the small confines of the motel room. "What's the deal?"

"Looks like we'll have to move her surgery up a bit from what we'd anticipated."

Rafe froze, and his nerves tightened into a ball as he envisioned his goddaughter's cheery smile, so much like her mother's. "Why?"

"Apparently the valve replacement they used in the last surgery isn't lasting as long as they'd hoped."

Sweet Savannah, born with a heart-valve defect that would require a regularly set schedule of surgeries until she reached adulthood when the valves would stop growing. Only four, and she'd already undergone so many surgeries, yet she stayed sunny. The next replacement hadn't been slotted for another six months.

"Darren, I'm so sorry. When are they scheduling it?"

"Next Friday."

A little over a week away. Rafe's heart pounded like he'd just completed a workout. "Aw, man. I'll be there. What time?"

"It's at eight, but don't come back home for it."

"I won't let you go through this alone." His legs didn't feel strong enough to support him. Rafe sank to the chair. "I promised I'd always be there for you. And Savannah." Had made the vow to Georgia on her deathbed following a car accident not even a year after she'd had Savannah.

"I appreciate that, I do, but it's more important to us that you stay. You don't have seniority there and taking off . . . well, I just don't want you to do that."

"Doesn't matter. I'll come."

"Don't. I'm serious. Listen, I gotta go. Doctor's here to discuss pre-op stuff. I'll call you tonight and fill you in."

"Give Savannah a hug from me and tell her I love her." He snapped the phone shut, everything inside him tied into little knots—muscles . . . nerves . . . everything.

Rafe closed his eyes and let the painful memories break through the barrier he normally kept.

"Rafe." Georgia was slipping fast.

He should call Darren, but she grabbed his hand. "I know you love me." The light in her eyes was but a glimmer.

He couldn't form the words. Tears filled his eyes. "I've always loved you." But she never should have known. Ever.

She gave a pain-filled smile. "I know. So you have to promise me something."

His heart could break his ribs. "Anything."

"Watch over . . . Darren and Savannah. He'll . . . need you. They'll. Need. You."

Rafe ran a thumb over her knuckles before placing his lips there. "Shh. You're going to be okay."

"I'm dying, Rafe. You know . . . I know it. Darren . . . just won't . . . accept it."

He laid his head on the edge of the ICU bed. Mechanical noises surrounded them.

Her fingers found their way into his hair. "Please, Rafe. Promise . . . me."

He lifted his head and met the gaze of the woman he'd loved since high school. "I promise."

She smiled. "Thank you. Now . . . kiss me good-bye."

Rafe sank from the chair of the cheap motel room, his knees hitting the floor. He bowed his head and took his pain to the throne of his Father, once again begging for forgiveness.

⚖

"Are you sure you want me here?" Bella licked her bottom lip.

The moon climbed above the tree line. Stars studded the evening sky with their brilliant glow. October looked to blow out without much fanfare. Already some of the foliage had the start of beautiful orange and yellow.

Hayden twisted the steering wheel cover of the truck. "Yeah, I'm sure." He gazed out the windshield to his mother's house and narrowed his eyes. "Guess it's a good thing Emily isn't around, huh?"

"Have you heard from her yet?"

"No, and Boyd says he hasn't heard from her. If Mom doesn't hear from her by the end of the week, I'm going to put a BOLO out on her." He laid his head back on the headrest. "I don't need this right now."

Bella held her tongue, studying him. She loved him like the brother she never had and would do anything for him. That he was in this situation made her want to scream. That it was primarily her fault he faced this now scratched her conscience. If she could stop this train wreck, she would. But she couldn't, and that alone had her jumping out of her skin.

"Your folks ever do something that doesn't make sense?"

Bella swallowed. Hard. "Not that I recall." She smiled, hoping to lighten the moment. "But that doesn't mean they didn't have secrets. Everyone has skeletons in the closet." And she had a storeroom chock-full.

He grinned, but it didn't make it all the way to his eyes. He sighed, almost under his breath, and stared back at the house.

"You don't have to do this, you know." She fisted, flattened, then again fisted her hands in her lap. If she'd been honest with him from the beginning . . . "It was probably a friend of a friend or something."

"You're reaching."

The urge to throttle something—preferably Mr. FBI Hotshot—had her fisting her hands once more. The worry and pain he'd caused Hayden put a black hole in her chest. "More than likely, this is nothing. I wish you'd just drop it." Oh, how much she wished he'd just let this go.

"I have a feeling about this, Bella." He grimaced as he yanked the keys from the ignition and spun them on his index finger. "There's something to it. The FBI doesn't make trips like this without believing there's a connection to the case they're investigating. I wouldn't."

"Over a stupid birth announcement?"

"Which a man I've never met before kept for thirty-six years. That's unusual, wouldn't you say?" Hayden cocked his head and peered at her in the near dark.

She kept her face neutral. "I'm sure you've seen stranger things. Who knows why people keep the things they do?"

"For sentimental reasons, that's why." He ran a hand down his face. "My birth announcement was found at a crime scene. Come on, you gotta admit it's odd."

She shrugged, fighting to look casual. "Maybe it was on a desk and fell off whenever the murderer rushed by. Or maybe it was under an old filing cabinet or something, not even intended to be kept, and this person had just rearranged his furniture before getting murdered. There are a lot of logical explanations." *Please, buy one. Any one.*

He tossed her the same look she'd seen Emily give him. "And there are just as many other explanations. The one way to know for certain is to ask Mom."

Bella lost her appetite. "Ardy probably doesn't even remember. Some distant acquaintance she sent a birth announcement to so many years ago—you can't expect her to recall how she even met the man. If she even remembers him at all."

"Then it's no big deal, right? If she doesn't recall this Daniel Tate, then I can tell Agent Baxter I followed up and nothing came of it. Let him know this lead's a dead end." He shifted to face her. "I Googled him this afternoon. Bella, he was a federal judge."

Her heart skipped a beat. Two. Maybe three before her tongue loosened. "So? See, your mom doesn't know any federal judges." She forced a laugh. "I can't see her hanging out with any judge period."

"Thirty-six years ago, he wasn't a judge. He was a lawyer. In Little Rock, Arkansas."

Sweat slicked her palms. "Ardy's always telling everyone she's never even left the state of Louisiana."

"That's why I have to ask her about him."

"Even if she does remember, it doesn't mean anything. We're talking a long time ago." She pushed back the panic tightening its viselike grip on her chest.

"Are you implying I'm old?" A faint twinkle of humor lit up his eyes.

She grinned. Maybe if she could tease him into forgetting all about this, he'd let the matter go. "Well, just sayin' . . ."

"Come on. Let's get this over with." Hayden opened the truck door and hopped to the ground.

Apparently she had no such luck. She wasn't going to get out of this. Why hadn't she run as fast as she could as soon as she'd left the diner?

Because Hayden needed her.

If she still believed God would listen to her—or anyone, for that matter—she'd pray like crazy. But she'd learned her lesson the hard way. God didn't listen, or He did and just went ahead and did what He wanted regardless.

Bella slammed the truck door behind her and followed Hayden. She forced herself to put one foot in front of the other and walk up the cobblestone path, then up the stairs. Leaves crunched under her steps. Every beat of her heart was a nail in her coffin. She'd have to run soon, and the thought shook her to the core.

Ardy met them at the door, welcoming them both in a big hug. Her honey-colored hair was smoothed back into a bun, belying her fifty-something years. She wore a stained apron over a pair of jeans and a tee. "I thought maybe y'all had forgotten how to operate the truck doors." Her laughter filled the foyer as she shut the door. "Supper will be ready in a bit. Are y'all hungry?"

"I need to talk to you for a second." Hayden shifted his weight from one foot to the other, keeping his gaze on the floor.

The mouth-watering aroma of baking chicken and tomatoes filled the air, wrapping around Bella and welcoming her.

Bella held her breath.

Ardy froze, the dishrag dangling from her hands. "Emily?"

"No. I haven't heard anything from her. Have you?"

She shook her head. "No, but I ran errands today, so she could've called while I was out." Hope laced her words.

He gave a quick nod. "If we haven't heard from her by Friday, I'll file an official missing persons report."

Maybe it was time Bella searched for Emily herself. She couldn't stand to see Ardy and Hayden torn up over this. Finding Emily would be the least she could do for them. She owed them so much more.

She owed Hayden the truth.

"Mom, I need to talk to you about something else."

"Sure, honey." Ardy waltzed into the kitchen, her socked feet padding against the floor. "I need to finish the salad." She hovered over a cutting board littered with tomatoes and reached for a knife.

"Here, let me finish that." Bella stepped in place, taking the knife and chopping the tomatoes.

"Thanks, sweetie." Ardy smiled.

Why had she let herself fall in love with this family? Her affection for them had glued her mouth shut, holding all the secrets hostage inside.

She shifted the tomatoes on top of the salad, staring at Hayden as he leaned against the butcher-block counter. His face was drawn. She grabbed a cucumber and sliced.

"Mom, I need to know who Daniel Tate is."

Chapter Nine

"Everyone is like a moon, and has a dark side
which he never shows to anybody."
MARK TWAIN

The campaign was in full swing, and according to all reports, he was still in the lead. Had anyone expected anything less? Perhaps his opponent.

Never smart to underestimate a man of his intelligence and caliber.

Using the "smile of the people," as the state papers had dubbed his grin, he forced himself to shake hands with the preacher man, Reverend Something-Or-Other. He had no personal use for religion—it sure hadn't helped his mother, nor his brother. But in the political arena . . .

He'd also had to play that angle in the legal game. Draining, to be honest, to act like he had such faith when he could care less. Much like the field of science, the legal industry brought into focus a sharp sting of reality. There was no God . . . no divine being . . . nothing to intervene in issues of law. Everything was either black or white. Yes or no.

Until he'd had enough of legalities and saw a way he could make a difference. Little things could change the outcome of a case. A certain witness. A slight deviation in testimony.

Perception. It was all about perception.

Cameras clicked and bulbs flashed as he shook hands with the man of God. The man's aftershave was overpowering, almost gagging him. But it was worth it for the photo op. Tomorrow's paper would run with the photograph, which would increase his numbers with the conservatives of the state. His campaign manager had been begging him to do something like go to church, find religion . . . anything. This was enough. It was the best compromise he could muster.

He'd done nothing but compromise for years. Through college, law school, then at the bottom of the legal-system food chain. Continuing on through the federal system—all compromising his true self. What he wanted to stand for.

But now he was so close to being able to be himself. To stand up for the true victims, not the blood-sucking scum that got off because of technicalities. To right the wrongs that corporations got off scot-free because their attorneys referenced obscure cases that the brainless judges used for legal basis.

It was his time. Time to bring about change.

Time to be about *real* justice.

⚖️

Ardy's face paled until she looked albino. Her eyes widened, almost bugging out of her head. She swayed, then gripped the edge of the counter. Hayden moved for her, but Bella was faster.

Bella wrapped her arm around Ardy's waist. The look Hayden's best friend tossed him was nothing short of venomous. She led Mom to the kitchen table and lowered her into a chair before fetching a glass of water.

"Let it go," Bella hissed as she passed him with a glass on her way back to Mom.

If he had any doubt that Daniel Tate wasn't someone important in the past, it was gone now. Hayden hated seeing Ardy distressed, but he needed to know the truth. As a sworn officer of the law, he'd do anything he could to help with a murder case.

Even if that meant upsetting his mother.

He slipped onto a chair across the table. "Mom, you know who Daniel Tate is, right?"

She stared at Bella. "You promised you'd never tell him."

Bella's face turned red, and she cut her stare to him for a fraction of a second before dropping her eyes to the table. "I didn't say anything, Ardy."

His heart froze. Bella knew something but tried to get him to drop the matter? Told him it was no big deal? She wouldn't even lift her gaze.

"Mom, who is Daniel Tate?"

But she wouldn't address him. "Bella, if you didn't say anything . . . " Confusion cloaked her features.

Bella lifted her face. "Ask *him*."

As if he was the bad guy here.

His mother jerked focused on him. "Why do you want to know?"

Heat burned in his gut. "It involves a murder case, Mom." He scraped a hand over his face. "It's official, so I need you to tell me everything you know about Daniel Tate." He paused, letting his words sink in. "Now."

Mom's face paled. "A murder?"

"Yes. Daniel Tate was murdered."

Tears pooled in his mother's eyes. "Daniel's dead?"

He hadn't seen his mother this shocked and hurt since . . . well, since his father died. Something icy cold snaked around Hayden's heart. He leaned forward. "Mom?"

She held up a hand while covering her mouth with the other.

Bella threw him another pointed look.

He met her stare dead-on. What gave her the right? She knew . . . she *knew* what was going on and failed to tell him. Even after listening to him lament about having to ask his mother. What game was she playing? Bella was the one he shared all his secrets with and she him.

Wasn't she?

"Mom?"

She shook her head. "I can't believe Daniel's dead. And murdered? How? When?"

Empathy flew out the window. "I'm asking the questions here, Mom. Tell me the truth. Who was Daniel Tate to you?"

The oven timer buzzed. Bella shot out of her seat, snatched hot pads, took the casserole out of the oven, turned the oven off, then returned to her seat beside Mom. While the chicken smelled divine, his stomach knotted his appetite right out of play.

Mom cut a glance at Bella, then took in a shaky breath. "I need to start at the beginning for you to understand." Her eyes were weighted with . . . remorse? Guilt? Shame? "So bear with me, please."

Hayden leaned back in the chair and crossed his arms over his chest, his heart pounding to get out. "I'm listening."

"When we're young, we make mistakes." Mom licked her lips. "Back in my day, we called it stupidity of youth."

Fitting. Seemed to be what Emily suffered from.

"I'd just turned seventeen when several girlfriends and I decided it'd be a great adventure to go to N'Awlins for Mardi Gras."

Yeah, he'd done that trip himself. Hayden leaned forward, resting his elbows on the kitchen table. It'd do no good to rush his mother. She'd tell the story in her way, in her own good time.

"I was dating your dad then, of course, and he was none too happy about me going away for a week with just the girls." Her eyes glazed over as she remembered. "Worried about me like he always did."

Hayden smiled. Dad had been a worrywart of the worst kind. While annoying a couple of years ago, now it was only endearing.

"Despite his protests, I went anyway. I knew he planned to propose to me on Valentine's Day and wanted to have one last trip with my friends before I settled down."

Nothing wrong with that.

"We got to N'Awlins and checked in. One of my friends' father owned a hotel there, so we were staying in a big suite at no cost to us." She smiled, staring at nothing out the kitchen window into the dark void of night. "We were walking in high cotton, let me tell you. I'd never seen such a fine room. Had never been in a suite. It was a fantasy."

Mom paused, pinching her lips together until they turned white around the edges.

The cold infiltrated Hayden's spine. Patience tore free from the fabric of his being. "How does this relate to Daniel Tate?"

She focused on his face. "I met Daniel there. In N'Awlins. In our hotel, matter of fact." Her expression was emotionless, as was her voice.

"You met Daniel Tate?"

"Yes." Her gaze left his face, flitting out the window again. "Daniel was handsome, suave, but so down-to-earth. Friendly. A true gentleman." The corners of her mouth teased upward. "An *older* man at the ripe age of twenty."

Hayden wanted to scream for his mother to continue, but something inside held his tongue in place.

"Oh, he was brilliant and charming. On the path to be a big-time lawyer. He was going to make a difference in the world. Took me to supper. Opened doors for me. Blew me away with his quick wit and even quicker smile." Her own smile widened as she continued to stare into the darkness. "I was literally swept away by Daniel."

In that moment Hayden had a feeling where this was heading, and he didn't want to know.

Mom caught his glance and held it. Tears glimmered in her eyes. "I was young . . . stupid. I knew better, I did. But—" She shook her head and dropped her stare. "That's an excuse. I just—" She looked back at him, imploring him as she leaned forward in her chair. "I wanted to feel alive. For just once, just once in my life do what I felt like instead of what was right."

He *really* didn't want to hear this. "Mom . . ."

"I've only loved two men in my life—your father and Daniel Tate."

His pulse raced, echoing in his ears. "You . . . you . . ." His tongue refused to form the words. He couldn't find his voice with a highlighted route GPS.

Mom dropped her head into her hands. Her shoulders sagged, her bones disappearing. Bella scooted her chair closer and wrapped an arm across Mom's shoulders.

This was unreal. Unbelievable. "What are you saying?"

She jerked up her head, her eyes wide, and shrugged off Bella's arm. "I'm saying I had an affair with him. Do I need to spell it out for you?"

"No!" His throat closed. How was he supposed to accept that?

"It was a long time ago, Hayden." Bella's voice was an octave above a whisper.

He tossed her a glare. "Stay out of this, please."

She flinched, as if he'd slapped her. Maybe he shouldn't have used such a harsh tone, but right now he was shocked, surprised, and appalled all at once. And she'd *known*.

Mom sat straight, squaring her shoulders. "It's not something I'm proud of, but it's not something I regret either."

She didn't regret it? His tongue was two sizes too large.

"I know you can't understand, but that week was wonderful for me. I learned about life. About love. But mostly, I learned about myself."

He wanted to be sick.

"Daniel opened up a whole new world for me, one I'd never known existed. He showed me how to enjoy life."

"You were seventeen, Mom. A kid. A minor. He was an adult. What he did was wrong. And illegal." Hayden fisted his hands under the table. "He should've been arrested."

Mom smiled that soft smile of hers that she usually reserved for babies and weddings. "No, son. You don't understand. It wasn't like that. It wasn't ugly. Shameful. Nothing like that. It was beautiful. And I'd told him I was eighteen."

He *was* going to be sick.

"No." Disgust sat on his tongue like a bitter pill. How could she have done this to Dad?

Eyes filled once again with tears as Mom shook her head. "He gave me the greatest gift I could've ever imagined."

Hayden's heart stalled. A gift? This Tate took advantage of his mother. "What did Dad say when you came back?"

Her face paled.

"You never told him? Ever?" All these years? Dad was so noble . . . honest . . . respectable.

"I didn't want to hurt your father. I couldn't hurt him."

"But you were . . . *with* . . . someone else. How could you not tell him?"

Mom pressed her hand to her mouth. "I'd planned to tell him when I got back, I did."

"Then why didn't you?"

Tears seeped down her cheeks. "I couldn't. He proposed to me as soon as I came home."

"But you'd been with another man!"

"Yes, but I loved your father. Very much."

Hayden shoved to his feet, pushing the chair back so hard it slammed against the wall. "How can you say you loved him?" Every muscle in his body threatened to jump free of his skin. The sting of her betrayal burned to his heart.

"Because it's true."

"But there was Daniel."

"Yes, there was Daniel, who I also loved, although I didn't realize how much until months later."

His mother made no sense. He gripped the back of the chair.

"I loved your father with a love that continued to grow as the years passed, but I loved Daniel with a deep amount of gratitude."

Gratitude? How could she sit there and justify her actions and claim she was grateful? Had she lost her ever-loving mind?

Mom licked her lips. "You see, Hayden, I loved Daniel and was grateful to him because he gave me what I didn't even realize I wanted most in the world. A child. A son." Her eyes shimmered. "You."

What was it?

Rafe paced the worn carpet of the motel room, staring at the case documents sprawled over the little table and two chairs in front of the window. Through the crack between the curtains, he could make out the motel's marquee sign, announcing to all the world that rooms were available.

As if the place ever filled to capacity.

He lifted the plastic water bottle from the nightstand and took another drink. Man, if only Darren were here. His partner had always been the one to put the paper pieces of case puzzles together. But Darren was at the hospital with Savannah back in Tennessee.

And he was here in the boonies in a cheap motel with his gut protesting the Cajun-spiced gumbo he'd scarfed down at the diner. He took another long drink of water, still staring at the documents as if something would jump up at him.

Brring!

Rafe snatched the cell phone off the motel's desk. He glanced at the caller ID and grimaced. What did Maddie want? His sister only called when she wanted something. Maybe he should let it just go to voice mail. He wasn't in the mood.

Brring!

But it could be important. Could be about Riley.

He flipped it open. "Hello."

"Oh, Rafe." Sobs blasted against his ear.

His body stiffened. "What is it? What's wrong?" Without thought, his free hand curled into a fist until his nails dug into his palm.

He couldn't understand what she said. The sobs muffled out some of the words. "Got . . . letter . . . today."

"You got a letter today? Who from?"

More sobs.

"You have to calm down, Maddie. I can't understand you."

Sobs, then sniffles. "I got the letter today."

"What letter?" She was bawling like a baby over a letter? Rafe shook his head and moved back to stand before the case notes again. There had to be a clue here in the file. Something he was missing.

"The letter from the parole board. Simon Lancaster is up for parole. His hearing is coming up."

Rafe sank to the bed, the pictures and papers forgotten as he doubled over. The day he'd dreaded for years hit him square in the gut.

The drunk driver who'd killed his parents was up for parole.

Chapter Ten

"We must accept finite disappointment,
but we must never lose infinite hope."

DR. MARTIN LUTHER KING JR.

How was she going to explain how she knew about Ardy and Daniel?

Bella stared at Hayden, who'd stopped pacing when his mother dropped her little announcement. Now his gaze met hers. Disbelief and something she couldn't name sat deep in his dark orbs.

Gnarled fingers of fear snaked down her spine.

Right now, shock held him hostage. After he got all the details from his mother, Hayden would question how she knew. If only Ardy hadn't slipped up and let on that Bella knew.

What was she going to tell him?

Why did stupid Agent Rafe Baxter have to show up? Why was the FBI following up on Daniel's murder *now*? They'd let it drop for three years, just keeping the standard BOLO open. She'd come to terms that Daniel wouldn't have justice served on his murderers. She was alive because of that.

"You mean to tell me that Daniel Tate is my . . . father?" Hayden's muscles bulged as he gripped the back of the kitchen chair. His knuckles were stark against the maple stain.

The mood faded to dark as the night outside.

"Yes." Ardy motioned to the chair. "Sit down. I'll tell you everything."

Hayden slumped into the chair. "But you said Dad didn't know about Daniel."

"He didn't." Ardy smoothed imaginary wrinkles from her jeans.

"So . . ." He shook his head, eyes wide. "Dad believed I was his son, and you never told him the truth?"

Oh-my-stars. Bella chewed the inside of her bottom lip. If she could have figured out a way for Hayden to avoid this pain, she'd have done something. But no matter how she tossed it around in her mind, there was no easy resolution.

Never an easy answer.

"You have to understand, Hayden, that was a long time ago. Things were different back then."

"Lies and deception have been around since the Old Testament, Mom. What's changed?"

Ardy licked her lips. "You have every right to be upset. Just listen to what I'm trying to tell you, okay?"

Bella held her breath and studied her best friend. She loved Hayden dearly, but the man could be stubborn and ornery when pressed. This was going to be one of those times.

He crossed his arms over his chest. "Fine. I'll hear you out." But his expression screamed that his mind had already closed.

"Daniel and I had a love affair, but we both knew it wasn't a forever kind of love. Our lives were polar opposites. He was in college, already accepted into law school. He was going places— we both knew he wanted to change the world."

Bella continued to study Hayden. His stare was granite stone.

"He made no promises to me, nor I to him, and when the

week was over, we went our separate ways." Ardy ran long fingers through her bangs. "I was emotionally richer for having known Daniel."

Hayden snorted.

Tears welled in Ardy's eyes, but she gave a little shake of her head and continued. "I came back to Hopewell, knowing I was ready to begin my life with your father. He was happy that I'd at long last crossed the last threshold of commitment, and I accepted his marriage proposal."

"Having just come off an affair, how could you do that? Didn't you owe him the truth?" Hayden's jaw muscles popped. "How could you accept his marriage proposal without telling him about you and another man?"

"I didn't say I did the right thing, son. I knew I loved your father very much."

Hayden slammed his palms into his thighs. "Doesn't sound like you loved Dad all that much."

"But I did." Ardy's eyes were pools of shimmering glass. "I don't expect you to understand. I learned about me . . . my feelings. Knew that I loved your father and Daniel both. Both men had a place in my heart, just separate."

"Yeah, Dad for the long haul and this Daniel character just for fun."

The muscles surrounding Bella's spine tightened, and she struggled not to grind her teeth. This was *Daniel* that Hayden was dogging. The man who'd raised her since she was ten years old. The man who'd pushed her to follow her dreams. The man who'd loved her without reservation, even when she went through her rebellious stage. The man who'd taken a bullet because he refused to bend the rules of justice.

"It wasn't like that." Ardy's tone dropped a level. "I made my own decisions, and right or wrong, they were mine alone to make at the time." Her expression softened. "I loved your father deeply, Hayden. Until the day he died, we enjoyed an ideal marriage."

"But he never knew you had an affair. Never knew you let another man father what he thought was his son. How, exactly, is that ideal, Mother?"

The temperature in the room dropped by twenty degrees at least. Bella had never, ever heard Hayden use such a tone before—filled with such disgust and . . . hatred?—especially never directed at his mother.

Ardy squared her shoulders and glared at Hayden over the kitchen table. "I won't justify that question because I know you're hurting, but let me finish."

He sat back in the chair, not saying a word.

"Your father and I planned a perfect wedding, and it was one that every girl dreams about. Beautiful." Her gaze shot out the window. "And we had a special honeymoon. We were so happy. Blissful."

Hayden grunted.

"Two weeks later I found out I was pregnant."

"So you knew, beyond any doubt, that there was no way Dad could be my father?" Hayden's voice held such a hint of hope.

It all but broke Bella's heart. If only Hayden could have known Daniel, known what a remarkable man he was. If only he hadn't hero-worshipped George Simpson. If only . . .

"Yes. I knew."

"Did you think, even for a minute, about telling Dad the truth?"

"I did intend to tell him."

"So, why didn't you?"

"He found out I was pregnant before I could tell him. You have to remember, this was back before home pregnancy tests were so reliable. I had to go to the doctor and get the blood test. The nurse called the house to set up my prenatal appointment and George answered the phone."

"Still, you could have told him."

Bella ached for Hayden, so desperate to stand up for his father, yet so hurt by his mother's deception.

Ardy shook her head. "When I got home, George was beyond himself with excitement. He was over the moon . . . had already called his parents, his friends, and just about everybody else he ever thought of knowing." She pressed her lips together, then gave a quick jerk of her head. "There was no way I could tell him without hurting him to the core. And no way would I allow my indiscretion to embarrass him."

"So you just kept quiet?"

"I did."

"Dad didn't suspect? I mean, I would've been born before the due date, right?"

Ardy steepled her fingers over the kitchen table. "Again, that was back before obstetrics was down to such a fine science."

The Adam's apple in Hayden's throat bobbed. And again. "What about this Daniel person?"

Ardy dropped her gaze to the table and wound her arms around her middle. "I debated telling him. Argued with myself for months. Finally, I opted just to send him the birth announcement. If he figured it out, I'd deal with that. But at least my conscience was satisfied with that."

"Did he? Figure it out?"

"Yes. He called me the day he received the announcement." She frowned. "He knew at once and wanted to see you, be a part of your life."

Bella swallowed and clenched her hands together under the table. She hurt for Daniel . . . knowing how he'd always wanted children but had never gotten married. When she'd met Ardy, she understood.

"But?"

"But I still wouldn't allow anything to hurt George. You were *his* son and to have told him otherwise, well, it would have killed a part of him." Ardy shifted in her chair. "I refused to do that. And I convinced Daniel to agree with me."

"He never wanted to know me?"

Oh, Hayden. Bella yearned to tell him how much that would've meant to Daniel. How much he had to have loved Ardy to deny himself his own flesh and blood.

"I had to beg and plead with him to stay away, Hayden. Only because of that did he agree to stay out of your life. Our lives." Tears seeped from the corners of her eyes. "And now he's dead."

Fighting to keep her mouth shut, Bella studied Hayden. His granite expression had softened somewhat, and he chewed his bottom lip—a sure sign he was mulling over the facts.

"So he never had anything to do with me." He shook his head, then shifted his gaze from his mother to Bella. "How'd you know?"

Her stomach knotted into a ball.

Brring!

How cliché . . . to be saved by the bell, so to speak. It'd only buy her a few moments. She needed to think, fast.

Hayden snatched his cell from his belt. "Hayden Simpson."

She could tell him the truth, but right now he was still raw. Hurting. Shocked. He wouldn't understand. Wouldn't be willing to listen to her explanation. And unlike Ardy's admission, hers could put her life on the line.

"I see. When?" His entire body stiffened. "Where?"

Bella glanced at Ardy. How much would she volunteer when pushed?

"I'm on my way." Hayden snapped shut the phone and slipped it back into its holder. In a fluid motion he stood. "We've found Emily's car."

Ardy gasped. "Where?"

"Near Coon Lake." He held up his hands. "That's all I know right now." He turned and pushed the chair up to the table. His glance drifted over his mother and landed on Bella. "We'll finish our discussion later."

Her stomach slipped to her toes. Not only did she have to

worry about Emily, but she also had to think of an explanation to tell Hayden. One that wouldn't make him hate her.

One that would let her live.

$$\triangle\hspace{-0.3em}\mathbb{T}\hspace{-0.3em}\triangle$$

Simon Lancaster couldn't be up for parole. Not yet . . . not ever.

Rafe stared at the phone he still held. He wanted to scream in outrage like Maddie but couldn't. He couldn't think. Couldn't feel. He was numb.

In a very short time, he'd be allowed to speak at the parole hearing. To plead to the members of the board not to let out the man who'd killed two innocent people . . . two loving parents . . . two strong Christian missionaries.

Could he do it? Could he look across the room and see Simon Lancaster without the rage boiling under his skin? Would he be able to restrain himself when everything in him fought for taking matters into his own hands?

All through Lancaster's trial, he'd sat in the back of the room, clenching his jaw. The raw hatred that simmered inside him gave him migraines. Or was it his body's reaction to the constantly tensed muscles?

He couldn't do it again.

Lord, I know I don't deserve it, but please help me.

Images of his parents flitted across his mind like wisps of fog dancing over the bayou. Kind . . . gentle . . . every kid's ideal parents in their encouragement, love, and support. Giving his sisters and him boundaries, yet urging them to break free and fly to follow their dreams.

All that had been cut off when Simon Lancaster got behind the wheel of his oversized pickup truck after having several-too-many shots at the local bar. He'd run a stoplight and T-boned the Baxter's little compact, ending their lives in a single moment.

Rafe blinked away the memories and the tears. That wasn't 100 percent true. His mother had survived the impact. Made it to the hospital's emergency room in the back of an ambulance. She held on until Rafe arrived. Damaged spinal cord and multiple, massive internal injuries made her final words just a breath, but Rafe would never forget them.

"Faith, hope, love . . . son."

And then she was gone.

Rafe jammed the cell back into his belt clip and shoved himself up from the motel bed. He paced. He couldn't afford the memories and emotions at the moment. He had to concentrate on the case. Finish what he came here for and get back to Little Rock. Then he'd decide what to do about Lancaster's parole hearing.

He opened his laptop and signed on to the Internet. While he waited for it to load, he grabbed his water bottle and guzzled the no-longer-cold liquid. His thoughts were scattered. Too much going on in his mind. Darren. Savannah. Lancaster.

No, he had to focus. On the case. Nothing else.

His computer sounded the e-mail alert chime.

He accessed his e-mail account. Two junk e-mails, which he sent to the trash bin with one click, and one message from Hartlock.

> Will run photos through system and let you know if anything pops up. Alphonse said to tell you not to dally—if you don't find a connection to the case in the next day or so, he wants you to head back. Hang tough, buddy. If the answer's there, you'll find it. Good luck.

Rafe replied with a quick thanks, then shut his laptop. A connection in the next day or so? That was pushing it.

He arranged the copies of the case file back on the bed. Then rearranged them. He stood back, studying, committing everything to memory.

Sirens blasted outside.

He glanced at the clock on the nightstand—10:20 p.m. Crossing the room, he peered out the window into the darkness. Two police cruisers raced past the motel. Their tires zinged over the pavement.

His muscles responded with a twitch before he reminded himself why he was here. But . . . maybe, just maybe, if he followed them, he'd get to see Hayden Simpson in action. Maybe he'd gain some insight on the man.

He sure had nothing better to do than stay in the room and go stir crazy.

Rafe snatched his coat from the back of the chair and pulled his keys from his pocket. Maybe this was nothing.

But maybe he'd find something. Even if it was minor, it could be a break.

Lord knew he needed some kind of break.

Chapter Eleven

"Courage is resistance to fear,
mastery of fear—not absence of fear."

MARK TWAIN

"What does that mean . . . they found Emily's car?" Ardy paced the front windows of the Baxter ranch-style home, peering out on every pass.

"Just that. Her car was found." Bella inched to the edge of the couch. In the ten minutes since Hayden had left, every nerve in her body felt as if it sat outside her skin. None of them had wanted to eat, so she'd covered the casserole and stuck it in the refrigerator. Now her stomach twisted and turned like the dead leaves trapped in the bayou's wind.

"But what about Emily?" Ardy turned and began her next pass. If she kept up her pace, she'd wear a hole in the carpet.

"It doesn't mean anything. Emily could have left her car there." But Bella knew that was a reach. Emily was irresponsible and flighty, but that car was her pride and joy.

"Don't they know she has a disorder?" Ardy stopped pacing in front of Bella. "Do you think he'll ever forgive me?"

She knew right away who Ardy spoke of, even though the flip in topic of conversation came from out of the blue. "Sure.

In time." Bella swallowed the monument in her throat. "He's just got to have a little time to process everything." But if he forgave *her* was a whole other story, one that filled her chest with ice.

"I never expected to have to tell him." Ardy wrung her hands. "I hate that he despises me . . . and now, everything with Emily."

Bella stood, her own knees weak. "He doesn't despise you. He's just shocked. You took him by surprise is all." All because of that nosy agent Baxter and the FBI. She curled her hands at her side. "He'll come around." But she, on the other hand, would have to leave. Soon.

"I hope so." Ardy turned and paced again. "I wish we'd hear something about Emily. Coon Lake . . . what could she be doing out there?"

Crossing her arms over her midsection, Bella could imagine a scenario. One she wouldn't share with Ardy.

An isolated, wooded area surrounded the lake. A few straggling cabins sat along the edge. One or two piers marred the beautiful tranquility of Coon Lake. Teenagers would haunt the area to make out, but not on a Tuesday night. And definitely not now. Human presence there this time of year would be limited. A perfect place to dump a car.

And a body.

Bella shivered and glanced out the window. She didn't know what she expected to see in the darkness, but Ardy's pacing, and questions, wore thin on her nerves.

"I just can't stand the not knowing." Ardy pivoted and continued her march.

"Why don't I run out to Coon Lake and see what I can find?" She needed something to do anyway. Anything to keep her mind off the burning question Hayden would soon ask.

And if a worst-case scenario was out at the lake, she could be there for her best friend.

Ardy gave Bella a hug. "Would you mind?"

"Of course not." Bella squeezed Ardy back. She couldn't tell when she'd have to run without notice. She would so miss Ardy.

She released the woman she loved like a mother, blinking back the tears. "But I don't have my truck here."

"Take my car. Keys are on the floorboard."

Bella nodded and headed to the front door. "I'll call you as soon as I find out anything." She paused, wondering if Hayden's mother would be okay by herself. "As soon as I can."

"Thank you." Ardy hugged herself, returning to her self-appointed pace-race.

Bella let herself out the front door. The snap of chill wrapped around her like a vise, squeezing against her ribs. She quickened her steps to the old Honda sitting alone in the drive. Sure enough, keys waited on the floor mat under the steering wheel.

She slipped into the driver's seat and started the engine. A half-empty coffee cup sat in the console, filling the car with the hint of its stench. She blew on her hands as she rubbed them together before putting them on the wheel. Within seconds she backed onto the road and headed toward Coon Lake.

Maybe this was a mistake. After all, she didn't want to provide Hayden with an opportunity to question her until she had some idea of a response. But something inside, the instinct that said her friend needed her, screamed louder than her own discomfort.

She pressed the accelerator harder.

Darkness grew deeper than the ebony of wet ink. Bella trembled as she sped. Her thoughts spun faster than the tires on the road.

Was it only the car the police had found? Was there evidence of foul play in the vehicle? Where was Emily?

Bad news would push Hayden over the edge. He'd been thrust into an authority position with his sister, and their strained relationship had only worsened. Add to the fact that she'd been diagnosed as bipolar just over a year ago. As if it happened on Hayden's watch. Like it was all his fault she was bipolar. The situation ate at him all the time, and Bella had no way to help.

Well, not without giving herself up by revealing her training.

She turned onto the dirt road leading to the lake. Up ahead the flashing cruiser lights shocked the night. Her heart raced. The last time she'd had flashing lights disrupt a dark, calm night . . .

No, she refused to revisit those places she'd closed off inside her mind. And heart.

Bella parked the car behind Hayden's. Two cruisers sat at angles, blue lights going as well as headlights piercing the lakeside area.

Emily's car sat with its nose to the lake.

Exiting, she shoved her hands in the front pocket of her hoodie and picked her way carefully to the back of a cruiser. The fishy scent rolled off the lake with the fog. Hayden stood silhouetted by his headlights. His head ducked as he spoke with an officer.

"And get our tow truck out here. I want this car at the impound lot for our unit to go over tonight."

Most people who didn't know him well wouldn't be able to pick up the emotion in his voice, but Bella wasn't most people. She could detect the nuances of his tone. His posture. His mannerisms. And right now, Hayden was stressed to the point of exploding.

She took a step toward him, careful to stay away from Emily's car and any evidence.

"Bella? Bella Miller?"

The voice rooted her feet to the cold ground.

"Hi. I thought that was you." He stood beside her, smiling a crooked grin.

"Agent Baxter, what are you doing here?"

⚖️

After all this time, would Remington Wyatt resurface?

She wasn't that stupid. Couldn't be. She'd managed to stay hidden well for three years. No way would she stick her head out now.

Unless Rafe Baxter yanked her chain.

He stared at the data before him. Was it possible she'd been hiding right under their noses?

No, she wouldn't dare stay too close.

Yet, the system didn't lie. He'd executed the computer-generated age-progression photo for her from three years ago. Then this new one, and placed them side by side.

Couldn't tell about eye color—yet. Remington's cheekbones were more pronounced. Hair color and style was different, but that was always the first alteration someone on the run made.

As far as build, Remington was slighter, leaner. But who knew what changes had occurred over the last couple of years?

There were striking similarities, but the system hadn't marked them a match yet. What would he do if it did? Without hesitation, he knew.

He'd take her out, plain and simple. Just as he'd intended three years ago, had they found her.

Now, even more than before, he had to keep her quiet. He had more at stake now. Too much to lose.

Letting out a sigh, he reached for his private cell. He'd have to let the others know she was possibly back in play.

He leaned forward, his nose less than an inch away from his widescreen monitor.

If that's you, Remington, you should have stayed buried.

⚖️

Bella Miller's reception was colder than the wind whipping across the lake.

Rafe's training antennae shot to the moonless sky. "The police cars raced by the motel. I was up and bored, so . . ."

"So you just thought you'd follow them? That's odd." She narrowed her eyes. Even in the dim lighting, there was no mistaking the distrust.

Another gust came off the lake, this time pushing a fresh,

spicy scent teasingly under his nose. Bella Miller. Her perfume? Shampoo? Whatever it was, his gut reacted in a way it shouldn't.

He shook off the attraction. "Yeah. I've been accused of a lot worse than being odd before." He jerked his head toward Hayden and the officers huddled by a car. "What's going on?"

She toed something on the ground. "Nothing exciting, I'm afraid. Just an abandoned car."

But something in her tone . . . "An abandoned car warranted two police cars and the appearance of the police commissioner?"

"We're a small town, Agent. We take excitement where we can find it."

Maybe . . . but maybe not. "Have they identified the owner of the vehicle? Maybe I could help run some queries."

"They know." Her tone was sharp, snappish.

He waited for her to elaborate. After several long moments passed, he realized she wasn't going to offer more. "Is it someone important? Like the mayor or something?"

"No."

Her noncommittal responses reminded him of Riley.

"Well then, whose car is it?"

Bella let out what sounded an awful lot like a long-suffering sigh. "Hayden's little sister's."

Oh. That explained a lot. Like the number of responders. And Bella being here. He lowered his voice. "Is she missing?"

"Yes." Her answer was a whisper on the wind.

Rafe tried to imagine how he'd feel if he were in Simpson's shoes. While Maddie and Riley both tried his patience, he loved his sisters. If they were missing . . .

"Look, as you can imagine, this is personal to Hayden. I'm sure you mean well, but things are covered here."

Defensive or protective?

"Agent Baxter, Bella, what are you doing here?" Simpson's face was hidden in the shadows, so Rafe couldn't see his expression.

Bella turned to Simpson. "What'd you find?"

He ignored her and focused on Rafe. "Agent Baxter?"

Rafe forced a lightness he didn't feel into his voice. "I saw the cruisers from the motel. I was bored, what can I say? I thought I'd follow to see if I could be of any assistance."

"Appreciate your interest, but we have it under control." A polite *butt out*, but a dismissal all the same.

Rafe's face burned, but luckily the night hid the blush. "Well . . . okay." He started to turn, then stopped. No sense letting an opportunity get away. "By any chance, did you ask your mother about the birth certificate and Daniel Tate?"

Simpson stood ramrod straight. "I did."

A tangible tension stomped between them.

The hair on the back of Rafe's neck stood at attention. Years of honing his professional instinct kept his mouth shut. His case was about to get a hot lead. He just had to wait on it.

Simpson's face turned to Bella's. Something, Rafe couldn't distinguish what, passed between the two. An eternity later the police commissioner cleared his throat. "Daniel Tate was my biological father."

No verbal response came to Rafe. But a whole lot warred in his mind in that instant.

Had Hayden Simpson known this fact?

Was Hayden Simpson involved in Daniel Tate's murder?

If Simpson didn't know, had someone else, and were they the ones responsible for Tate's murder?

How did this information tie into Tate's murder?

"I didn't know until my mother told me tonight." Simpson's focus pinned to Rafe.

He needed time to think how to word his questions. But not allow too much time for Simpson to form planned responses. "I know you're busy right now. Why don't I come into your office first thing in the morning to discuss this?"

Simpson nodded. "I get in at eight."

"I'll see you then." Rafe jerked his head in Bella's direction. "Good night, Ms. Miller."

She didn't respond, but he didn't care. His feet carried him back to his car, yet his mind already plotted questions.

Adrenaline and excitement battled to claim the rate of his pulse as he got into his car.

He couldn't wait to report this to Jackson. Talk about getting something to go on. This was a primo lead. His new SAC had to respect his insight now.

He'd earned it.

Chapter Twelve

"Aim above morality. Be not simply good,
be good for something."
HENRY DAVID THOREAU

"What did you find?" Bella's question snapped Hayden from his mind-wandering.

The breeze coming off Coon Lake was nothing compared to the iciness in his chest. Where was his sister?

"Nothing. Her purse isn't there, the keys are gone . . . nothing." He'd been so hopeful to find something—anything—that would give an indication of where Emily went.

Bella cocked her head. "Any sign of foul play?"

His chest compressed. "We think there might be a blood drop on the driver's floorboard but can't say for sure until the crime techs check it out." He let out a long sigh. "Even if it is, doesn't mean it's fresh."

"Right." Her breath left a faint fog in the air between them. Fall was in full swing. She shifted her weight from one foot to the other, then back to the original.

"We'll know more once they go through the car." He could tell she was chilled by the way she hugged her arms over her chest, or maybe it was avoidance.

"Your mom's worried about Emily. Want me to call her?"

"Yeah. Since you two are so close and all, tell her I'll phone after the techs finish." The sarcasm rolled off his tongue. He didn't like how he acted, but at the moment, he didn't care. He glanced behind his cruiser and spied his mother's car. "You brought her car?"

"Yeah. I didn't have my truck." So she was just going to ignore his cutting remark . . .

"Bella, I need you to be honest with me. How did you know about Daniel Tate?"

Her face lifted. In the darkness he couldn't make out her expression, but her silence spoke volumes.

His heart sank. His best friend . . . even now, when the ugly truth had been bared on the rug for all to see, she still wouldn't tell him the truth.

Anger vied with betrayal for control of his heart. "Never mind." He shoved past her.

"Hayden, wait."

He spun around. "What? Are you ready to tell me the truth?"

"I knew because Ardy told me. But she made me promise not to tell you."

"Why?" He clenched and released his fists. "Didn't I deserve to know?"

She shook her head and reached for his arm. "It wasn't my decision to make."

"But you're *my* friend." He snatched free of her grip. "My best friend, or so I thought. Perhaps I was misinformed on that fact as well." His heart hammered.

"That's not fair. You know I'm your friend. But I gave my word to your mother."

"Why would you do that? This isn't some woman's thing. Isn't something unimportant. This is who I am. Or who I thought I was."

"You're still who you are, Hayden. You haven't changed." Her voice cracked.

"But why would you keep something so important from me, Bella? Why?" He ran his hand over his face. Nothing made sense. He still felt as shell-shocked as before. "Why couldn't you break your promise to my mother and tell me the truth? You owed me that."

"Maybe I should have . . . I don't know. I'm sorry."

He ached all over. "I just can't believe Mom . . . and then for you to keep her secret on top of everything."

"You need to forgive Ardy. Let it go."

He clenched his fists into tight balls. "Forgive? Let it go? Are you crazy? This is my life we're talking about here. *My* life."

"Isn't that what Christians do? Forgive? I'm pretty positive the Bible tells you to forgive."

He snorted. "You little hypocrite—telling me you're mad at God, then quoting Scripture to me and telling me what a Christian should do. What's your story, Bella?"

Even in the dark, he could make out the anger marching across her face. "I'm not the one who claims to be a Christian. I've pretty much laid it out that God and I aren't on speaking terms. You're the one who should practice what he preaches, Hayden Simpson."

She might have a point, but he didn't care. Not at the moment. "I can't talk about this right now." He nodded toward the tow truck ambling down the road, its diesel engine rumbling. "I have my job to do."

She nodded, then backed away. "I'll get your mom to run me back home when I take her car back." The pain in her voice was as clear as Emily's car sitting by the lake.

But he couldn't deal with her hurt feelings right now. Not when his own emotions were tied up in massive knots. "Good." He stomped toward the tow truck and his officers, leaving Bella standing alone.

"Hayden, techs are coming in early to go over the car." Officer Bob Travis waved his cell phone.

They'd only come in early because it was his sister. While the realization warmed him, it also made him think the men he worked with cared more for him than his best friend. After all, they would go out of their way to help him—Bella just kept secrets that were important to him. And for what?

As soon as the tow truck parked, his mother's car turned around and headed down the dirt road. Had Bella damaged their friendship beyond repair? He couldn't imagine *not* having her in his life. But he couldn't deal with the secrets. How many more was she keeping from him?

The driver of the tow truck stepped to the ground, clipboard in hand. "Who's signing?"

Hayden nodded and held out his hand. He scrawled his signature across the bottom of the page, then passed the clipboard back to the driver. "We need this in police impound."

"Yes, sir." The driver tossed the order into the truck and pressed a button, lowering the truck's rig.

"I'll follow in the car and see that the paperwork is processed ASAP," Bob said.

"I appreciate that." Hayden leaned against his cruiser and stared out over Coon Lake. What was he to do? He couldn't go back to his mother's, but he didn't want to go home either. His mind was too crowded—too many worries vying for top attention. Normally he'd run by Bella's and talk things through with her, but right now . . . not an option.

A car door slammed behind him. "Hayden Simpson, what's going on?"

He'd recognize that voice anywhere. Ashlee Wainwright, reporter for Hopewell's rag. Royal pain in the behind.

"I know you hear me."

He turned and watched Ashlee picking her steps toward him. "What do you want, Ashlee?"

She jutted her pointy chin toward the road. "Heard the call for a tow truck to come pull a car outta here. What's going on?"

He shrugged. "Just having an abandoned car towed." His gut tightened at the word *abandoned.*

"Really?" She stopped in front of him and popped her hands on her hips. "Just an abandoned car, huh? Not how I heard it on the scanner."

"What did you hear?" Possession of a police scanner by non-law enforcement personnel should be banned.

Ashlee smiled, revealing a row of perfect teeth that her momma worked overtime at the diner to afford. "C'mon, Hayden. Don't play coy with me." She batted those dark lashes of hers up at him.

He crossed his arms over his chest. "And you don't play cutesy with me."

"Fine." She narrowed her blue eyes. "Despite your buddies' attempts to keep her name out of the call out to you, I know it's Emily's car."

"And?"

"And . . . what did you find?"

"There's nothing to comment on at this time, Ashlee."

"Is she missing? Do you suspect foul play? Is this connected in any way to the vandalism on MaryBeth Keller's vehicle?"

Hayden stiffened and dropped his arms to his side. "We have no comment, Ms. Wainwright." He pivoted and marched to the cruiser's door.

"C'mon, Hayden. Give me something."

He reached for the door handle.

"You don't want to give the impression that you, as police commissioner, are covering up something just because it involves your sister, do you?"

Hayden froze, letting his arm fall. He swallowed once. Twice. A third time.

Ashlee was at his side in a moment. "I've heard a rumor that Marshall Abernathy is not only interested in law enforcement, namely your position, but has been seen with your sister as of late."

What did she know about it? He spun and glared. "When was he seen with Emily? Where?"

The moonlight shone on her widened eyes. "Is that important somehow? Are *you* asking *me* for information now?"

Pulling out a notebook from his pocket, Hayden lifted a pencil. "This is an official police investigation, Ms. Wainwright. I can have you brought into the station for questioning, if you'd prefer."

She stiffened.

"Look, just tell me what you know about Emily and Marshall, okay?"

"Give me something in return. A quote. A comment. Something. Anything."

Could she know something important? He gave a curt nod.

"Day before yesterday, Priscilla saw Emily get in Marshall's car at the diner."

His heart pounded. Monday—after her exchange with Boyd. "What time?"

"After the morning rush at the diner, but before lunchtime."

He scrawled down the info, then tucked the notebook back into his pocket. "Thanks."

"A comment, Hayden?"

What could he offer her? He licked his lips. "Yes, it was Emily's car we towed. She has been missing for four days. No further comment until the crime-scene unit can analyze the vehicle."

"Four days? But I just told you that—"

"Shh." Hayden held his fingers to his lips and smiled. Maybe—finally—something was giving him a break today.

Lord, please.

⚖️

This was too good.

Rafe struggled to concentrate on his notes and not show his reaction to Hayden Simpson's telling of his conversation with his mother last night. The tension rolling off the police commissioner as he sat behind his desk could have knocked Rafe over.

Daniel Tate's biological son—Rafe hadn't expected that one. Not in a million years. Now the implications and possibilities were whirring around in his head faster than a bullet fired from his handgun.

"So you can understand why I'm willing to do whatever possible to help you in your investigation." Simpson leaned back in the chair. The slight lines around his eyes seemed to have deepened overnight.

"You never had any contact with Judge Tate that you can recall? Ever?" If the judge was his father, surely there had to be some contact. A card . . . a phone call . . . a visit. After all, he'd kept Simpson's birth announcement.

The police commissioner shook his head. "Never. My mother said she had contact with him briefly after I was born."

The story was too incredible, if it was to be believed. Rafe studied Simpson's eyes, searching for emotion. He detected pain, betrayal, and shock, but not deception. "I'm sorry to keep asking, but it's just . . ."

"I know. It's hard to understand that I didn't know." Hayden ran his hand over his hair. "I'd think the same thing you're thinking right now. Matter of fact, if I were you, I'd be looking at me as a prime suspect."

Rafe didn't like poking and probing, especially when it caused someone upstanding and honest such obvious pain. At least Simpson understood it was the job and nothing personal. "I'll be honest, it's crossing my mind."

Hayden smiled. "And that's why I'm willing to do anything to help you with your investigation." The smile slipped from his face. "Someone murdered my f-father. I want to know who and why."

He didn't miss how Simpson had stumbled on the word. Rafe couldn't imagine how he'd feel if he'd found out his father wasn't who he'd believed him to be. It would affect everything he stood for.

On the other hand, if Simpson wasn't involved and had no information, then Rafe was back to square one. Not a thing. And his new boss would not be impressed that he'd garnered nothing on the case but cost the bureau money. "I hoped you had something, because there are no other leads."

"How about you let me look over the case file and see if something jumps out at me? Who knows, maybe I know something I'm not aware of."

Or he could be trying to find out what they knew. But Rafe didn't think so. "How about supper at the diner? We can review the notes then."

Simpson nodded. "Five thirty?"

Rafe pushed to his feet. "Sounds good. I'll see you then." He glanced over Hayden's head and stopped.

A framed photograph caught his attention. Very similar to the ones in the motel's lobby. But familiar in another way as well. From where?

Simpson stood and followed Rafe's focus. "Bella Miller took that. She's quite the local photographer."

Really? He wouldn't have pegged her for a photographer, but he could see her as an artist. Something about her kept pulling Rafe's attention. It was more than her looks—he couldn't figure it out. "It looks like the pictures in the motel lobby."

"They are. Bella has sold to almost all the business owners around here." Sadness tinged his words.

But just yesterday Simpson had claimed her as his best friend, his confidant. And she'd been at the lake last night. Something had changed between the two of them. What had happened? How serious?

Rafe met Simpson's gaze. "Speaking of Ms. Miller, will she be joining us for supper tonight? I'll make sure to get a table for three."

Hayden dropped his eye contact, just for a moment, and let out a small but noticeable sigh. "No, Bella won't be coming. It'll just be us two."

"Any word about your sister?"

A shake of the head, downcast eyes. "Our unit's still going over her car. We've confirmed it was blood we found on the floorboard, but that's it."

"I'm sorry, man. I'll be praying for her." The words were out before Rafe could stop them. Not that he was embarrassed by his faith—not in the least—but sometimes people took his statements the wrong way.

But Simpson's eyes widened and a smile followed. "Thanks. I appreciate that." Genuine. The man was a Christian as well.

Rafe hated causing him pain all the more. "I'll see you tonight." He turned and headed out of the police station.

He'd have to send Hartlock an update as soon as he got to the motel. This could buy him an extension from his new boss. He needed time—to work the case, to figure out what to do about Lancaster, for Savannah . . . He just needed a break all around.

And maybe, if he was lucky, he could figure out what it was about Bella Miller that kept snagging his attention.

⚖

Hayden rang the doorbell a second time. The musical trilling floated under the front door of Priscilla Barnett's. He'd already checked with the diner and knew she didn't have to work tonight. Did she go out? It was a few minutes shy of four thirty.

He reached for the doorbell again.

The front door swung open and a woman stood silhouetted in the backlit home. "What do you want? Some people are trying to get some rest."

Taking in her flannel pajamas, red nose, and mussed hair, Hayden took a step back. She must have a cold or something.

"I'm so sorry, Ms. Barnett." He took out his badge and flashed it. "I'm Hayden Simpson and I need to ask you a few questions."

She narrowed her eyes and studied the badge, then stared him down. "Make it quick." She sneezed into the crook of her arm.

No offer to step inside out of the early evening's chill. This woman wasn't in the mood to play. It was obvious she didn't feel well.

"Yes, ma'am. I received a report that you saw Emily Simpson with Marshall Abernathy on Monday morning."

"That's right." She sneezed again. "Wait a minute, I know who you are. You're Emily's brother, yes?"

He nodded.

"Yeah, she was talking about you to Marshall." Ms. Barnett leaned a little closer. "He didn't look none-too-happy about her mentioning you so often, in my opinion."

Hayden's gut tightened. "Why do you say that?"

"He kept frowning at her. Hushing her."

"Did they leave together?"

She shrugged. "It was near the end of my shift, so I can't say for certain, but they did walk out of the diner together."

He made notes in his notebook. "Anything else you can remember?"

"No." She covered a yawn with her hand. "Is something wrong?"

Hayden shut his notebook and smiled. "Thank you for the information, Ms. Barnett. Again, I'm sorry to have disturbed you." Without another word, he turned and headed back to the car.

So Emily had met with Marshall on Monday and they'd left the diner together. Where did she go from there? Where was she now?

Chapter Thirteen

"How much more grievous are the consequences
of anger than the causes of it."
Marcus Aurelius

He had too much to lose—his future career was on the line.

Now was not the time for Remington Wyatt to resurface. They had too much to lose. The timing could not be any worse.

Glancing back at the report on his desk, he wiped his palms against his right-down-the-center creased pants leg. Why now? After all this time . . . had the FBI agents not done their jobs before, or had Remington just gotten lazy?

They'd searched for her. He'd been there. He'd seen the reports. They'd looked high and low for her three years ago. As far as he knew, they randomly checked for her since, just to make sure there was no sign of her.

Clever girl. She'd found Tate's secret. Interesting that she didn't reveal it. He couldn't help but wonder why not. How and why had she kept silent all this time? He'd understood why she ran—her smartest move—but to never come back?

How had she hidden right under their noses? Was there a traitor in the bureau? Someone who'd let her stay hidden? Even helped her?

He'd have their badges.

He shoved to his feet, pacing the Oriental rug in his office. He hoped to move soon, but first he had to be sure Remington Wyatt didn't talk.

But now . . . now, when he was on the verge of getting everything he ever wanted, she slipped up and let herself be found?

Unacceptable.

He'd see to it that the boys cleaned up their mess at once. The one they should've handled three years ago.

He lifted the phone to make the call.

⚖️

Per Alphonse: Wrap things up and get back here.

Rafe stared at Hartlock's e-mail, rereading it for the twentieth time, then stared out the motel's window. How could his boss expect him to dive into the case by rushing? Or did Jackson *want* him to fail? Would make sense. Could they let him go if he messed up? If not, they'd have grounds for corporate to send him on his way. No secret Jackson didn't want him in Little Rock. Neither did Ed Major.

He clicked out of the mail program without replying and shut the laptop. Perhaps his supper with Simpson would render something else. Anything at this point would be a plus. He hadn't felt this frustrated over a case in a long time.

As he gathered the case documents and shoved them back in the folder, he couldn't help but wonder what Hartlock would think of him showing Simpson the file. He'd probably disapprove. But Rafe didn't have a choice—he was shooting in the dark and running out of time. And he was doing it all alone.

Man, he missed Darren. His partner had a way of seeing through the misdirections to the basic facts. Wait, make that his *former* partner. In a way, being away from Darren eased his guilt. Put some perspective in place.

Rafe ignored the emotions punching inside of him and strode to his car. He glanced down the block to the neon light flashing the announcement of the diner. The two-by-two strip of grass between the curb and the sidewalk was full of cardboard election signs. Walk or drive? It was only a block to the diner, and the evening weather held a hint of chill. Might clear his head and open his mind.

His cell rang before he'd even stepped off the motel's parking lot. He flipped it open. "Baxter."

"Hey, buddy." Darren's voice brought a smile to Rafe's face. Even in toughest times Darren's friendship had been a rock.

Sometimes that friendship was stronger than any other emotion. Rafe swallowed back the memories. "Hi, there." Darren's tone was too upbeat for there to be bad news about Savannah. "What's up? Why aren't you calling me from your cell?" He shoved the folder under his arm as he strode down the sidewalk.

"Just checking in with you. Forgot to charge mine, so I'm borrowing a friend's. Wanted to let you know the doctors said Savannah's doing great, all things considering. How's everything with you?" But something in Darren's tone . . . not Savannah, but he had something on his mind.

"On my way to speak to . . . a person of interest in this case. Might be a break." If he was lucky.

"That's great. Knew you'd fit right in. You're a good agent." The hesitation hung over the connection.

"What's wrong, Darren?" Just outside the diner Rafe paused, gripping the phone tighter. "I can tell by your voice something's off."

Darren gave a stilted chuckle. "You know me too well, my brother."

"So, what is it?"

"It's about your house."

"What about it?" Had he missed a call from the Realtor? Man, he hadn't even called her since he'd left Little Rock. He wasn't quite ready to have a legitimate offer on his house. He was still coming to terms with his move being permanent.

"Someone broke into it last night."

He felt like he'd been kicked in the gut. "What?" Why hadn't anyone called him?

"The police didn't have your cell number, so they had to find where you worked. They called the office a little bit ago, and Nick called me."

Why would someone break into his house? "There isn't anything there to steal. Was it a vagrant?"

"Maybe, but they vandalized the place."

Rafe slumped against the outer wall of the diner. "How bad?" He'd just hired painters to do a full interior touch-up after he moved out. Eleven hundred bucks down the drain if there was any vandalism in the house.

"Dunno. I'm getting a copy of the police report e-mailed to you as soon as they get it done."

Why did it all have to hit him at the same time? Sometimes, life just wasn't fair. "Thanks. I appreciate it."

"Don't sweat it, Rafe. I've got your back. I'll take care of it."

But Darren couldn't afford the time away from work and Savannah. "Once I get the police report and hear what my insurance says, I'll get somebody to oversee any repairs." Something else to handle. Maybe Maddie or Riley could pitch in . . .

"Savannah's supper just got delivered, so I gotta run. We're having, uh, mystery meat and veggies. I'll call you if I hear anything new."

"Thanks, Darren. Give Savannah a hug from me." He snapped the cell closed and slipped it into his pocket, then cast his eyes to the sky.

Am I being punished for my breaking a commandment?

Tires grated against asphalt.

Rafe opened his eyes to meet the confused look of Hayden Simpson stepping out from behind the wheel of a Hopewell Police Department cruiser.

The police commissioner cocked his head. "Everything okay?"

"Just asking for a little direction."

Grinning, Simpson ambled to the diner's door. "I hear ya. Been doing a lot of that myself lately."

Rafe followed Simpson as he made his way to the same table he'd occupied with Bella Miller. Must be his regular.

The delectable aroma of fried bell peppers assaulted Rafe's senses, causing his mouth to water while he continued following Simpson. Several of the diner guests called out to the police commissioner with a friendly wave as he wove through the group. It was obvious he was liked and respected by—

An older man in the corner narrowed his eyes as Simpson meandered to the corner booth. Pure venom shot from his glare at Simpson. His gaze then snagged on Rafe's for a moment before he returned his attention to the newspaper spread out on the table before him.

So, not everyone was wild about Hayden Simpson.

Rafe lowered to the bench across from Simpson. He motioned to the man with his chin. "Who's that?"

Simpson twisted to look, then turned back to Rafe. "Ah, that would be Caleb Montgomery, Hopewell city councilman."

No mistaking the animosity in his voice. "Why don't you tell me how you really feel?" He tented his hands over the cracked table.

"He just thinks he deserves special law-enforcement treatment because he's a city councilman is all." Simpson shrugged and motioned for the waitress. "And I disagree."

"I see." But was it more than that?

⚖

The aroma of grease and onions penetrated the diner and for the first time in a long time, almost turned Hayden's stomach.

Why did Caleb have to be here tonight of all nights? Why wasn't he at home, gorging himself on something his wife picked up and pretended she cooked herself? No, Hayden couldn't be that lucky. Caleb had to sit in the diner, glaring at him. Now the FBI agent would ask questions about his relationship with Caleb. The whole story about his contract being up would come out.

Hayden held his tongue while the waitress poured them large glasses of iced tea, took their orders, then shuffled away. He sipped the sweet liquid and then stared across the table at Baxter. Hayden could barely sit still with the anticipation tightening his muscles. "So, what do you have on the case?"

"Not a lot. You were my only fresh lead." Rafe slid a folder across the table. "But maybe you'll see something that will ring a bell or you'll recognize."

Doubtful, since he just learned about Daniel Tate last night, but Hayden couldn't deny the rush of excitement coursing through him.

The folder was creased in various areas, as if the FBI had viewed and reviewed the information several times over the years. He opened the file and his breath caught on the photo staring up at him.

It was like looking at himself at fifty-something years.

He'd never wondered how he'd look as an old man before. For some reason, in his mind, Hayden just assumed he'd look like a cross between him now and his dad. Boy, looking at this picture, he was dead wrong.

Or perhaps, dead right. He was the spitting image of Daniel Tate.

How had Dad never noticed that Hayden didn't resemble him at all? Hayden looked nothing like Mom. Didn't anybody notice?

He shook his head and flipped over the photo. The next was a picture of his—Daniel, about in his forties with a young teenager. A ceremony . . . ah, his swearing in as a judge. The somberness in Daniel Tate's face was offset by the pure joy in the girl's. Something about her smile . . .

"I'm sure this must be difficult for you." Rafe's voice broke in. "I'm sorry to have dumped everything on you at once."

Hayden turned to the next photo as he smiled. "It's hard, yes, but I'm glad I know the truth. At last." He dropped his focus back to the file.

Another picture of Tate and the girl, now a slight young woman with long, blonde hair and piercing blue eyes. This time the girl wore the serious expression.

Lifting the photo, Hayden waved it across the table so Rafe could see. "Who is this woman?"

"That's Tate's goddaughter, Remington Wyatt. He raised her." The agent took a sip of tea. Ice rattled against the glass. "That photo was taken eight or nine years ago, I guess. Right after she became a consultant for the FBI. She's a forensic psychologist. One of the best."

Hayden studied the photograph. The young lady was beautiful, no denying that, but there was also something else. Something vaguely familiar.

"She's also a suspect in Tate's murder."

No way. This woman? "Wow."

"Yeah. It's there in the file."

Hayden skimmed the information and case process, all the while feeling Rafe's burning attention. When the waitress appeared table-side with their plates, he welcomed the intrusion.

Hayden blessed the food for both of them, then began to eat. He took his time scanning the case details. The murder was clean . . . organized. No evidence left. Not a single tangible lead. A nightmare of a case. He reached the end of the file just before his last bite.

Already finished with his meal, Rafe sat with his arms crossed, staring at him. Hayden wiped his mouth and laid the napkin over his plate, then closed the file and slid it back across the table. "This is quite a case."

"Yes." Rafe waited until the waitress refilled their glasses and cleared their dirty plates before continuing. "Any thoughts?"

"The agents who handled the case—"

"Hartlock and Devane."

"Yes, them . . . they believe the goddaughter is a murder suspect?" Because there was something about her that made Hayden want to believe in her innocence. Made no sense why, but he just felt that way.

"They do."

Hayden leaned forward, letting the information wash over him. "And you? What do you think?"

Rafe let out a burst of breath. "I don't know." He shook his head. "She could have done it. She was trained enough to have done it. She fled the scene and hasn't been found since, even though the bureau's looked for her."

"But?" Hayden couldn't explain why he pushed the issue, but something nudged him to keep on.

"I don't know. There's no motive."

"Okay, I'll play devil's advocate. Case file said there was an emptied safe. She could've stolen something, right?"

"Why would she need to? According to everything I've read and uncovered, she had full access to all of Tate's finances and assets."

"So maybe what she needed was in the safe and she didn't have full access to it."

Rafe shook his head again. "Doesn't make sense. Why give her full access to everything, even name her beneficiary to everything, but not give her the combination to his safe? Seems out of character for him. At least as far as I can tell."

Hayden had run out of arguments for theft. "We both know people kill for only a few reasons: love, revenge, greed, or to protect themselves. If we've ruled out greed, what's the next angle? Love?"

"I think we can dismiss that altogether. They loved and respected each other like a parent-child relationship. Everyone said so."

Hayden thought about Emily. "What if she'd started seeing someone he hadn't approved of? After all, he was a federal judge. What if she started seeing a married man or a criminal? That would put them at odds with each other."

Rafe chuckled. "He disapproves of her boyfriend so she shoots him? I can't see that."

But Rafe hadn't heard all the details about Daniel. Like how he took advantage of a minor girl, then didn't man up. "He could've threatened to expose the boyfriend. Or cut her out of his will."

"She didn't need his money. She'd made some good investments and done well with her own income." Rafe tapped the folder. "She didn't take the money when she ran, and her balances right now are over seven hundred and fifty thousand dollars."

Hayden drained his tea. "So that leaves revenge and protecting herself."

"I can't see revenge. He'd been her legal guardian for years, put her through school, encouraged her. He was even the one who introduced her to the bureau. Revenge doesn't make sense."

No, it didn't. "We're down to protecting herself." But he hadn't any idea how that could be a motive.

Rafe popped his knuckles. "I'm not liking motive as self-preservation. There's no basis. Not in this case."

"So, there's no motive."

"No motive, which is why I don't see her as a viable suspect."

Hayden took a deep breath, his mind racing over the facts. "That leaves us with the burning question—if she didn't murder Daniel Tate, why did she run?"

Chapter Fourteen

"Life is an adventure in forgiveness."

NORMAN COUSINS

Every important aspect of his life had been documented, and Hayden was completely clueless.

Bella flipped through the file she'd kept hidden for the nearly three years she'd been in Hopewell. The photographs of Hayden smiled back at her—his football pictures, prom, his first car, bagging his first buck, his high school graduation . . . all snippets of his life that Daniel had stolen and harbored in his safe. Stacks of documents were woven in with the pictures: copies of report cards, immunization records, even a copy of Hayden's social security card.

At the bottom of the box were two envelopes. One was unsealed, filled with receipts to the private investigator Daniel had hired to acquire this invasion into Hayden's life. The other envelope was sealed and taped, with Hayden's name scrawled across the front in Daniel's chicken-scratch handwriting.

A letter to his son? Cashier's check for a secret inheritance?

How often over the years had she stared at that single envelope and fought the urge to rip it open? Curiosity wasn't her only motivation. Many times she'd felt the scratch from the claws of the green-eyed monster. Daniel had been *her* godfather . . . *her* parental figure . . . the person she loved and looked up to. She'd been the one there for him as he was sworn in as a federal judge . . . the one he took hunting and fishing . . . the one he'd named as his next of kin.

But Daniel was Hayden's biological father.

Why hadn't Daniel trusted her enough to tell her about Hayden? She wouldn't have betrayed him. Even now, she still kept his secrets.

She slammed the envelope back into the file and closed the flap. She stared out the window overlooking the bayou. Darkness had descended and filled the air.

Daniel's murderers were still free. No one was going to bring them down. Not unless she gave herself up and went public with what she knew.

Which would put her life in danger.

Chubbers nudged her with his nose. She smiled and absently stroked the Lab's head. As much as she hated to, she knew what she had to do. It was time. No, it was past time. This was something she should have done three years ago.

Bella grabbed her cell and opened the text-messaging feature. She sent a message to Hayden, asking him to come posthaste to her house, telling him it was important. When done, she tossed the phone onto the couch beside her. He might be too busy. He might ignore her. After all, he was furious with her.

The phone lit up. She accessed the incoming text message.

On way

Bella let out the breath she hadn't even realized she'd been holding and dropped the phone to the couch again. She set the file on the coffee table and stood, almost stepping on Chubbers. Her stomach coiled into a tight ball. The nightmare she'd been scared of facing for three years had come full circle and stared her in the face.

She could do this. For Hayden. For him, she'd swallow the panic. She'd endure his wrath at her. She would be there for him, no matter what.

But she didn't have to like it, and she was prepared to run if she had to. Her duffel was already in the truck, and she'd drop Chubbers at the kennel. The vet had Hayden's number in the event of emergency, so they'd call him when she didn't show up to pick up the dog. Despite anything he'd feel against her, he loved her dog.

Maybe, just maybe, she wouldn't have to run. It was possible Hayden could understand and help her get justice for Daniel without putting her life on the line.

Her steps trenched a path in the rug on the hardwood floors. Every ounce of peace she'd ever thought of having seeped into some locked-away vault inside of her. Once upon a time she'd have found strength and calmness in God, but she'd given up on that fairy tale years ago.

A good and loving God didn't let little girls' mommies die before they get to know them . . . didn't let daddies get shot in the chest in drive-bys . . . didn't let those little girls lose every person they ever loved.

Didn't put people in the position of having to lie just to live.

She shook her head and continued her pacing. Chubbers lay in his chair, his eyes following her frantic movements. Every now and again he'd whine.

Hayden would be furious with her for keeping everything from him, but would he be touched by Daniel's long-distance devotion? Would he realize what a good man Daniel had been? Oh, she'd been hurt when she realized the truth and that Daniel had kept such a secret from her, but as soon as she'd talked with Ardy, she understood. He kept his word to her. Being honorable, as usual.

Tires crunched the gravel of the driveway. Chubbers jumped from the chair and rushed to the door, placing his nose at the jamb. Bella's throat clogged—swallowing wasn't an option. Breathing would soon be an issue.

She let out a rush of air and shook her hands. Her focus stuck to the window as she concentrated on taking slow, deep breaths. *Bam! Bam! Bam!*

The door opened and Hayden stuck his head inside. "Bella?"

Forcing the smile that threatened to gag her, she nodded. "C'mon in."

He shut the door behind him and stepped into the living room, his hand on the dog's head. "What's up?" Hayden stood in the center of the room, a confused look hardening his expression.

"I need to tell you something. And show you." She motioned to the couch. "Have a seat." Her words sounded foreign to her own ears.

Chubbers jumped back into his chair, his gaze darting between Hayden and Bella. He let out a soft whine.

Hayden slumped onto the couch. He ran a hand over his hair. "What's going on?"

"It's about Daniel Tate." Just saying his name aloud choked her. She sat beside Hayden and reached for the file with shaking hands. "He didn't ignore you, Hayden."

Her best friend snorted. "Whatever." He pushed to his feet. "I don't have time to discuss this right now."

"Sit down, Hayden." Bella used the tone she hadn't called upon for three years.

He slumped back to the couch, his eyes widening.

"Here." She shoved the file into his lap before he could protest. "This is what Daniel Tate kept locked in his home safe. This." She motioned to the file he now held. "It's all about you." She pressed her lips together. Maybe that would keep her emotions from spilling into her words.

He pushed the file back toward the table. "I don't really want to—"

She jerked it back on his lap and slapped the flap back. "Look, Hayden. Just take a look."

He sighed and gazed down. His chiseled chin lost its severe stiffness as his hands lifted his Little League team photo.

Without a word, he flipped through picture after picture, copy after copy. What felt like an eternity later, he lifted eyes shimmering with moisture to Bella. "How?"

"There's something else." Her voice cracked and hitched as she handed him the envelope with his name. "I don't know what's inside, but it had to be very important to Daniel. His insistence that this be found in the safe was made with his dying breath."

Her heart held still as he took the envelope with trembling hands. At long last she'd know.

But Hayden didn't open it. Instead, he set it on top of the file and lifted his gaze to her face. "How do you have all this, Bella?"

Her mouth went as arid as the ground in July. Her mind scrambled but her conscience held its ground. "I knew Daniel Tate." She swallowed against a spitless mouth. "I loved him."

He narrowed his eyes. "How's that, exactly?"

"I need to tell you the truth about me, Hayden. About my past. About who I am."

Everything in her screamed to shut up and run, but she could no longer run. Now was the time to take a stand. And taking a stand meant telling the truth. "Daniel Tate was my guardian and godfather. He raised me from the age of ten, from the time my father was murdered."

"But . . ." His eyes widened. "You're Remington Wyatt."

⚖

He hung up the phone, trying to shake off the verbal bomb that had gone off in his ear. If he didn't want to end up on Jonathan's bad side again, he'd have to handle the situation at once. Already, the man was beyond furious.

He could understand—he was upset himself, but he wasn't ready to act without proof. And it was still inconclusive if this Bella Miller was, in fact, Remington Wyatt. He would not make another mistake. The one they'd made three years ago had haunted him.

And it was possibly back to wreck his life.

The situation would be resolved, once all the facts were known. Still, he couldn't help but wonder why, if this was Remington, she'd gone to Louisiana. Keeping a connection to Daniel could've exposed her a long time ago. So why would she do something that could've cost her her life?

Could still.

Bella's face faded to the palest he'd ever seen. Good thing she was already sitting because Hayden wasn't sure her legs would support her.

"You know who I really am?" Her voice warbled.

"Well, you kinda gave it away when you admitted he was your godfather and guardian."

She shook her head and trembled. "Agent Baxter didn't tell you that when he showed you the birth announcement? He never gave any details about Daniel's case?" Obvious fear circled her wide irises as she shot to her feet.

Chubbers jumped from his chair and moved to her side. He leaned against her leg, watching her.

Hayden grabbed her hand, keeping her in place. "No. But he showed me the full case file tonight." He tugged her. "Sit down."

Her eyes were still wide and she kept glancing at the doorway to the bedroom, then back to his face, then to the doorway again. Fight or flight.

"Bella . . ."

"But the FBI thinks I'm a suspect. And, Hayden, they'll kill me."

Kill her? What was she talking about? He pulled her back to the couch. "Bella, it's okay." Fear made her talk crazy. "I know you didn't kill Daniel—you couldn't, and Rafe doesn't think so either."

She sank to the couch. "Really?"

"Yes." He offered a smile. "Really."

"Back up and tell me what's in the file. What does Baxter say? Why didn't they ever follow up on—?"

Hayden held up his hands. "Whoa. Slow down."

She clamped her mouth shut.

"I have a few questions for you first, then I'll answer yours. Deal?"

She nodded.

"Why don't you tell me how you became Bella Miller? I mean, I didn't even recognize your picture." But now, from what he could remember from the photographs, he could see it as plain as day.

"You see what you want to see. I had injections to make my face fuller. I wear contacts to change the color of my eyes. I cut and colored my hair." She gave a slight smile. "And I put on thirty-five pounds, which is actually easy to do if you quit smoking."

Bella . . . smoking? He couldn't picture that.

She noticed his expression. "Yes, I used to smoke. I also used to drink coffee and would avoid any diet drink like the plague." Her smile widened. "I adore Dr. Pepper and I detest, I mean, truly detest, country music."

That's all she ever listened to. "But you—"

It was her turn to hold up her hand. "You're asking how I became Bella . . . I'm telling you." The smile slipped from her face. "That's how I didn't get caught—I changed everything that were markers for me." She rested her hand on Chubbers' head. "I even got a dog. I'm such a cat person."

She sat back on the couch, visibly more relaxed. "I got fake papers four or five different times, each from a different person, until my layers were tight. I bought vehicles and sold them to lay a fake trail. I opened bank accounts, closed them, then reopened them in different cities."

Accounts . . . "Money. How did you live?" It was one of the possibilities of motive.

She rolled her eyes. "Daniel taught me years ago to have several thousand dollars on hand in the event of an emergency." She ran a hand through her hair. "I never figured this would be the kind of emergency, but nevertheless the cash on hand saved me."

Made sense, but . . . "Why come here of all places?"

Bella tapped the file he'd placed on the coffee table. "Because Daniel's dying words to me were to get these papers out of his safe. Once I went through them, I realized he'd kept a secret from me. You."

"So you came here? For what? Why?"

She nodded. "I had to meet you. See what kind of person you were. I'd planned to give you the stuff, get to know you, then disappear again."

"But you didn't. Why?"

"It's hard to explain, but I felt an immediate connection to you. Almost as if Daniel tied us together, even if you had no clue who he was."

Hayden got that because he'd felt that instant connection to her too.

"Then . . . well, then I got to know you. And you became the best friend I never had before. I never had a lot of friends growing up. I was too focused on my career goals, so it was nice to have you."

Her honesty warmed his heart.

"But you never gave a hint that you weren't George Simpson's son. I even wondered if Ardy didn't suspect Daniel was your father, even though the resemblance is uncanny."

So he'd realized himself mere hours ago.

"One day I was at Ardy's, taking those pictures of the tractor she sold. I made a random comment about Daniel, and by her expression, I realized she knew the truth. I probed just a little more, and the whole story came rushing out." Bella licked her lips. "Your mom had kept that locked inside her for so long . . . it was eating her away."

It all made sense now. Not that it was right, but he understood. "And that's why you agreed to keep the secret."

She nodded. "That's why."

He glanced at the file. It was a lot to take in. Daniel Tate had kept very good, close tabs on him. By every indication had wanted to be a part of his life, but out of respect for Mom's wishes, hadn't. Hayden glanced back at Bella. "Daniel . . . did he ever marry? Have other kids? Do I have any half brothers or sisters?"

The corners of Bella's mouth drooped. "No. I think I cost him any chance of finding a woman and settling down." She squared her shoulders. "My mom died soon after I was born. Daniel and my father were partners in their own law firm. When I was ten, my father was killed in a drive-by shooting." Tears shimmered in her eyes.

She sniffed. "I didn't have any other family. Daniel was my godfather, so he used his position with the courts to rush the appointment of himself as my legal guardian. He raised me alone. Never married, so he never had any children. Except you."

"I'm sorry." He hadn't known. Hadn't even had a clue.

"It's okay. I loved Daniel very much."

That brought to mind his next question. "If you loved him, and you didn't kill him, why did you run?"

She stiffened. "Because I was there. I know who murdered Daniel, and they won't give up. Without proof, no one would've believed me, and they would've killed me." Bella pushed to her feet.

He stood as well. "You can't be serious. You have an inside track with the FBI. They would've believed you."

"The FBI wouldn't believe me, Hayden, because it was the FBI who murdered him."

Chapter Fifteen

"A true friend is one soul in two bodies."

ARISTOTLE

Rafe stared at the scanned police report on his laptop. The digital pictures Darren had been kind enough to run by the house and take were awful.

The vandals had messed up his hardwood floors as well as spray painted on the walls. Well, the walls they didn't punch holes in.

He enlarged the area of the spray-paint writing. What was that word? He tilted his head sideways . . .

Shoot!

Had to be teenagers. But man, what a pain to have to take care of. Especially when he couldn't take off and go there.

Maddie. He should've already called and asked her to take care of it, but he'd gotten sidetracked. He glanced at the clock—8:40 p.m. She'd be home on a Thursday night. He just dreaded the call. Not that he didn't love his sister, he did, but Maddie knew how to lay on a guilt trip something fierce.

He opened his cell and punched in her number. It rang twice before she answered. "Hey, Bubba."

"Hiya. How's everything going?"

A heavy pause filled the airway.

His gut tightened. "Maddie, what's wrong?"

"The parole board. They sent another letter. Inviting us to speak at Simon Lancaster's hearing."

The spicy jambalaya he'd eaten at the diner churned in his stomach. "What?"

"Yeah, I know. They're going to, wait, let me grab the letter and I'll read you that part."

He couldn't reply even if he wanted to.

"Mmm. Oh, here it is. They want to make sure they, quote, give us opportunity to speak at Simon Lancaster's hearing for or against his parole, unquote."

"Are you kidding me?" The words pushed past the massive rock lodged in his windpipe. "As if we'd even consider being there for his parole. Are they serious?"

"I know, right? It's crazy."

He leaned over the motel room's desk, dropping his head into his free hand. The void of his parents' deaths still left him numb and empty.

"It's gonna be okay, right, Bubba?" Maddie's voice was soft . . . faint . . . and desperate for reassurance. She hadn't called him Bubba in years.

"Yeah, sis, it's gonna be fine. We'll be okay, just like always." But the words scorched his tongue almost as bad as the cayenne pepper he had at supper.

She let out a long breath. "So, what's up?" Already she'd accepted his words and moved on.

"It seems my house was vandalized."

"Oh no."

"Yeah. I got the police report sent to me, and Darren went by and took some pictures. It ain't pretty."

"I'm sorry. What can I do?"

He ran a hand over his head, scratching his scalp. "I've called the insurance adjuster. He can just use the police report and photos and was going to make a quick inspection himself this afternoon. Could you please get in touch with the Realtor and have her set up people to perform repairs? Or ask Riley to do it?"

"I'll take care of it."

"Thanks, Maddie."

"Not a problem." She paused. "Have you heard from Riley the last day or so?"

Something about the way she asked stood the hair on the back of his neck at full attention. "No, why?"

"She and Garrison broke up."

Rafe cleared his throat. "That's a bad thing how?"

"Rafe, I know you didn't like him, but Riley did."

He scraped his face with his hand. "Well, I say good riddance. She could do much better."

"Yeah. I'm just worried about her. I think she really thought she was in love with him."

"He was a jerk."

"Yeah, well, the feeling was mutual. Riley said he always said he hated that she compared him to you, an agent."

Rafe knew the source of the jerk's attitude. "I can't help it he couldn't pass the entrance exam to get into the bureau's academy. You can't help stupid."

"Well, he must have had a bad case of sour grapes. Told Riley after meeting you, he was glad he didn't get in the FBI if the agents were all jerks like you."

Rafe chuckled. "Good thing she never told me that." He rubbed the aching spot in the back of his neck. "She'll get over the little dirtbag quick enough. She's young and cute, and I love her, but she has the attention span of a gnat. She'll move on."

"Yeah, you're probably right. And she said she was working on a big story."

His baby sister: wannabe Barbara Walters. "Listen, I need to call Darren and check on Savannah. Thanks again for taking care of the house thing." Rafe shut the cell and closed his eyes. He might've been able to comfort Maddie, but he was anything but peaceful about the Lancaster situation.

Hunching further over the desk, he began to pray. For his sisters . . . for Savannah and Darren . . . for Hayden Simpson . . . for himself.

The motel room's phone rang, vibrating the whole desk. Rafe jumped and snatched up the receiver. "Baxter."

"So serious."

Rafe swallowed. "ASAC Hartlock. To what do I owe the honor?" For the man to be calling him at night, it had to be serious.

"It's Lars, remember? I never did get into the whole last name bit. Anyway, just calling to check in. You didn't respond to my last e-mail, so I thought I'd just call you." A pregnant pause filled Rafe's ear. "So, have you made any progress?"

"Not really. I met with Simpson tonight and we had some discussion. Let me ask you something about Remington Wyatt."

"Go ahead."

"What did y'all think could be her motive for murdering Tate?"

"Could have been a lot of things, but primarily we thought money. The judge was a wealthy man, had a lot of investments and funds. His goddaughter was the sole beneficiary."

Which made Rafe even more curious. If what Simpson's mother told him was true, then Tate knew he had a son. Why would he cut his own flesh and blood out of his vast wealth? Rafe would have to do some digging to get an idea on that one.

Hartlock continued. "His estate is estimated in the hundreds of thousands. Not bad, considering our economy. Why do you ask?"

It didn't make sense. "If she murdered him for money, why didn't she stick around to claim it?"

"Because the security guard saw her."

Rafe pulled the initial reports and scanned the details. "Back up for a minute. Who sounded the alarm? The alarm company reported the panic code came from the front door keypad."

Hartlock hesitated. "We'll never know for sure, but it's possible they were arguing in another area of the house and he pressed the button for the silent alarm."

"If you're arguing with someone, pull a gun on him, you aren't going to allow him to push a panic button, then go to another room before you shoot him." It wasn't logical. "But for the sake of argument, let's say that did happen. So she saw him push the button, lets him get to his office, then shoots him. Minutes later the security guard arrives. What is she doing from the time she shoots Tate until the guard gets there?"

"Robbing the safe? It was cleaned out, remember?"

Rafe shook his head. "We have no proof of that. Tate himself could have emptied its contents a long time ago for all we know."

"But she could have done it that night. He could have had bearer bonds in there that she's been living off of for three years."

"Okay, still for argument's sake—she cleaned out the safe after she shot her godfather. Now, the guard comes knocking at the door. If she's the murderer, why does she answer the door?"

"Because the guard would've broken it down."

Rafe chuckled. "I'm looking at the report of the guard. Do you think he could've broken down that door?"

Hartlock gave a snort. "Not at all, but those guards do have a set of emergency keys, so he could've unlocked the door."

"All right. Say she opens the door because she doesn't want him to come barging in. She tells him Tate's been shot and to get an ambulance."

"She uses that time to sneak out the back door and disappears."

"The file shows the security guard reported Wyatt was in her socks when she opened the door."

"So?" Now Hartlock sounded annoyed. Because he didn't do his best job? Didn't follow up on some things?

"Why would she still be in her socks? If she had time between shooting Tate and letting the guard inside to clean out the safe, and by then having made the decision to run, why didn't she take the time to put on shoes?"

"What're you getting at, Rafe?"

"I don't think she killed him. She had no motive, and while the scene is clean of forensic evidence, if she's the murderer, she was sloppy. Everything we have on her disputes that she'd be so unorganized."

"Crime of passion, maybe." But Hartlock didn't sound as sure of himself anymore.

"Forensically, too clean for an unplanned murder."

A long silence settled heavy over the line before Hartlock spoke again. "Where are you going with this?"

"I think someone else shot him. She was there and tried to help, but Tate died and the killer got away."

"If she was innocent, why'd she run? She's one of our own, in a way . . . Why didn't she come to us? Why hasn't she come in since?"

And that was the one point for which Rafe had no plausible explanation.

"What do you mean the FBI killed Daniel Tate?" Hayden's face turned red.

Bella let the dark secret spill out of her. "Just what I said. The two men who murdered Daniel were FBI agents."

"Are you sure?"

Was he serious? "Of course I'm sure. I was there." She trembled as the memory slipped out of her well-guarded vault and tugged on her heart.

He blinked, then let out a rush of air. "Let's back up. Tell me what happened."

With her heartbeat increasing, she relived the most painful night of her life. When the tears threatened to swallow the words, she paused, then continued. A final sob tore from her as she finished.

Hayden's face was slack in shock. "And that's why you ran?"

She nodded. "I knew if they found me, they'd kill me. Don't you see? It wasn't just the agents—there was someone else, someone pretty powerful, involved. How could they allow me to live and tell everyone—anyone—what I know?" She shivered. "I have no clue how high up the corruption goes. I couldn't expose myself unless I knew. I still can't."

The chirping of Hayden's cell phone broke the strained silence hovering in Bella's living room.

He snatched the phone from his waist, his attention never wavering off Bella. "Hayden Simpson."

She inched to the edge of the couch. Would he believe her? If Rafe Baxter didn't think she was a murderer . . .

"I see. Are you willing to release her into my custody?" Hayden's voice came out strained.

Her heart raced. Was someone talking about her? Oh no— she couldn't go into anyone's custody, even Hayden's. They would be after her as soon as she blipped on their radar.

"Can you fax me the paperwork?" Hayden locked stares with Bella. "I'm assisting the FBI with an investigation here and it'd be difficult for me to leave right now."

If he was telling someone about assisting, they weren't talking about her. Then what? She mouthed a name at Hayden, "Emily?"

He gave a snap of a nod. "I understand. I appreciate it, I do." He glanced at his watch. "If I leave within thirty minutes, I can be there before ten. Is that okay with you?"

What a relief! Emily had been found. Was she at a hospital? Releasing into his custody? She couldn't be badly hurt.

"Thank you." Hayden replaced the phone to his hip.

Bella stood. "Well?"

"Seems Emily's been found. She's at the Calcasieu Parish sheriff's."

"Is she okay?"

He gave a grunt. "She was arrested."

"For what?"

"She tried to steal a car."

What? "I don't understand."

"Neither do I. The sheriff said they found her breaking into a car from their local rental business. She said she was just trying to get back to Hopewell, that she was just *borrowing* the car."

"What about her abandoned car? Where has she been?"

"She refused to give them any more details than that. Just my name and phone number. Oh, and she mentioned several times, quite loudly, I'm told, that I was the police commissioner." He shook his head. "The council's going to love hearing this. I can just see my contract renewal shredding."

Bella squeezed his forearm, her heart bleeding for him. "It's going to be okay, Hayden. It will."

He shrugged her off. "I guess I'll need to call Mom and let her know. I don't want her to keep on worrying."

"Want to call her from here?"

"No. On second thought, I'll wait until I know more and have Emily with me."

Bella swallowed. "Would you like me to go with you?"

He paused. "I appreciate it, but no. I think it's time Emily and I had a long discussion and got some things straight."

"I understand."

Hayden headed for the door, then strode back and grabbed the file. "We haven't finished this discussion."

She nodded, not trusting herself to speak. What could she say?

"You stay here, okay?"

That despite her secrets he still knew her so well should've unnerved her. Instead it saddened her. She nodded again.

Hayden shifted the file from one hand to the other. "No nodding, Bella. I want your word. Promise me you'll stay put."

If he only realized what he was asking her . . . to put her life on the line. Put herself in danger.

"Bella!"

"Fine. I'll be here when you get back." He was about on her nerves.

"Promise."

"I promise." Surprisingly she didn't choke on the vow.

Chapter Sixteen

"Stupidity is a talent for misconception."
EDGAR ALLEN POE

Lars gripped the phone tighter. "You're positive?"

"Yes. I wouldn't make the call otherwise." A beat passed over the cellular connection. "You know what must be done."

"Yes, sir."

"And you'll take care of it this time?"

Lars squirmed. "Yes, sir. Consider it done."

"Very good. Let me know when the situation has been handled."

The connection went dead in his hand. He slipped the cell into his pocket, considering his options.

He had none.

Jack strolled into view. Lars waved him over.

"What's up?"

Lars glanced around and lowered his voice. "It's her."

His partner narrowed his eyes and his voice as well. "Who?"

"Bella Miller. In that Louisiana hick town. She's Remington Wyatt."

Jack slumped into the chair behind his desk. "Seriously?"

2

Lars nodded. "And we've been assigned to take care of the little problem we left lingering three years ago."

"He knows?" Jack's eyes widened.

"Just got off the phone with him." And Lars didn't want to talk to him again until Remington Wyatt was out of the picture. Once and for all.

Jack let out a sigh. "What's the plan?"

"First off I need to make arrangements to follow up with our newbie Rafe." Lars pointed at his partner. "You don't look so hot, Jack. I think you might be coming down with the flu. I hear it's gonna be horrible this season."

Coughing behind his hand, Jack nodded. "I do feel a bit feverish."

Lars gave a slight grin. "I'll make my arrangements. You do what you have to in order to get some sick time. I'll pick you up tonight. Be packed and ready to go by seven."

And soon, their little problem would be all gone and they could take their early retirement plan with no fears, no hitches.

Last night had been long, and Hayden was exhausted. He and Emily had gone at it for the better part of Thursday night, on into the wee hours of the morning, until he'd gotten the truth out of her. Now he sat at his desk, desperate for about four hours' more sleep, trying to pay attention to Bella.

"So, let me get this straight: Emily went with Marshall Abernathy on Monday after breakfast to run some errands, as he put it."

Hayden nodded, squinting against the bright morning sun sneaking past the window blinds.

"He drives her to Sulphur, where he picks up a boat he'd special ordered."

Again, Hayden nodded.

"Then they go to a bar where Marshall proceeds to get plastered."

"According to Emily, he said he couldn't drink in Hopewell because it would kill the council's consideration of him for my position, which Caleb Montgomery has apparently already promised him." Hayden shifted in his seat. "You and I both know how some of the council members are."

"Super religious." Bella crossed her arms.

"Yeah."

"Okay. He gets rip-roaring drunk and then refuses to give Emily the car keys. He rents them a room at the local motel."

"Separate rooms, so says Emily."

"And Tuesday morning rolls around." Bella opens her hands into the air.

"Emily says she banged on his motel room around ten in the morning." Hayden needed an aspirin. "But he didn't answer the door. She called and had them ring his room, but he didn't answer. Around noon he came out."

"And they went out to lunch at some dive there."

"Yep." And that's as far as he'd gotten in telling Bella the story his sister had told him.

She shook her head. "What did she say they talked about? I mean, I don't get it."

"According to Em, he was consoling her about her breakup with Boyd. He said he understood how she felt. That he'd been hurt in a similar way and wanted to help her."

"How, exactly, could he do that?"

Oh, Bella was gonna love this one. "Well, from what Em says, he told her that the best way to get Boyd and MaryBeth back was to get married." Hayden sneered, ignoring the painful pulsating at his temples. "And Marshall's such a great guy, he volunteered to sacrifice his freedom to help her out."

"You *have* to be kidding me. Please tell me you're making this up just to get my mind off everything else."

"I wish I were." Oh, how he wished that were the case.

"Don't tell me Emily fell for such a line of—"

"She said she told him she'd have to think about it."

Bella snorted. "Why would he want to marry her?"

"The council thinks married men are more settled."

"You have got to be kidding me."

"I'm dead serious. They've hinted that to me several times over the last few months. A family unit. I mean, they push the whole *family man* thing hard."

"That's crazy."

He nodded, then regretted it as pain shot through his temples. "And if she married him, well, I couldn't very well speak out against my brother-in-law, now could I?"

"Oh, this is insane."

"It gets better." Or worse, depending upon how one viewed it. "He told her it would not only get Boyd and MaryBeth back, but it would clear her of vandalizing MaryBeth's car."

"How on earth did he figure that?"

"His reasoning is that if she was in love with Marshall and planning to run off and get married, why would she care if MaryBeth was pregnant and she and Boyd were looking for a house?"

Bella leaned back in the chair. "You know, warped as it is, I can see how he'd come up with that."

"Scary, isn't it?" He couldn't put it off any longer. Hayden reached into his top drawer and pulled out a bottle of aspirin. He popped the top, flipped three tablets in his mouth, and chased them down with the coffee that had now chilled. He grimaced and shoved the bottle back in the drawer. "So while she was thinking about it, he suggested they look at wedding rings, just in case."

"Oh, that's dirty pool." Bella crossed her arms over her chest.

"Yep. Taking a young woman into a jewelry store. That's low, even for Marshall." He reached for the coffee cup out of habit, then remembered it was cold and set the cup back on the desk. "They killed time until it was night again. He took her to a nice restaurant this time, probably to butter her up. Again, he got drunk."

"So he couldn't drive home again."

"Right. Only this time he didn't get them separate rooms. Em said when she complained, he told her if they were going to be married, they might as well save the money."

"Please tell me she didn't—"

Hayden shook his head. "She waited in the bathroom until he passed out, then took his credit card and went to the office and got her own room."

Bella grinned. "Good for her."

"So the next morning, Wednesday, Em went through the whole thing again, trying to get him up, all that. Same as day before, he doesn't show until noon."

"What'd he say about her having a separate room?"

"He never knew, according to Em. She played like she'd slept in the room but he'd passed out so didn't remember anything."

"Smart girl."

Hayden pinched the bridge of his nose, trying to stop the splitting pain. "So this time Em told him she wanted to come back home. She couldn't think about getting married without talking to Mom."

"And what'd Marshall say?" Bella stood and moved behind him. Her cold fingers soothed his temples.

He closed his eyes and leaned his head back. "He didn't like it but said he understood. Then he told her he needed to run one more errand while they were so close to Moss Bluff."

"Let me guess, she agreed?" Bella continued rubbing small circles with just enough pressure to hurt, but in a good way.

"Yep." The lack of common sense his sister showed drove him up the wall. Or maybe he needed to get her another appointment with her shrink and up the dosage on her medication or something. "But when they got to Moss Bluff, he took her to a camp of a friend of his. It was a party."

"Oh no." She pushed harder on his temples.

"Yeah. Em says she told him she wanted to leave after he'd had a couple of drinks. She didn't want to get caught with him being too drunk to drive again."

"Probably the smartest thing she did."

"He got angry and was showing off in front of his friends."

Bella's hands stilled. "What did he do?"

"He told her if she wanted to go so badly, she could just hoof it outta there."

"And her response?" She moved back to her chair.

The pounding had lessened. "Thanks. Well, she thought he was bluffing, so she grabbed her purse and headed for the door. She thought he'd come running after her."

"But he didn't."

"No, he didn't. And she had no idea where she was."

Bella slapped her hand on the desk. "Why didn't she call?"

He cringed at the noise. "Her cell phone was dead. She didn't have her charger in her purse. She'd left it in her car, which she left at Coon Lake when Marshall asked her to go with him."

"That was two days ago, Hayden."

"Yep. She says Wednesday night, she found a motel and got a room. Funny thing, she still had Marshall's credit card so that's how she paid the bill."

"Why didn't she call you?"

"I haven't a clue." He'd given up trying to figure out his sister. "She said she called him yesterday from the motel and he promised to come get her."

"But he didn't."

"Bingo. She tried to use his card again, but it was over the limit, so they denied it. By this time she says it was late and businesses were closed and she had nowhere to go, so she figured she'd *borrow* a rental car and come home."

"Surely she couldn't believe that was okay."

"With Em, who knows? She thinks the world revolves around her. All she knew was that she was tired, hungry, and sleepy. She honest-to-heavens thought I could make everything go away if I only talked to the sheriff's office."

Bella patted his hand. "I'm sorry. What does the sheriff's office say?"

"If she'll pay for the scratches on the rental, they've convinced the company not to press charges."

"So this *can* all go away."

"But I don't think I'm going to tell her that." He caught Bella's look. "The longer I keep bailing her out, the more trouble she'll let herself get into. She needs to learn how to do the right thing."

"Really? You want to teach her a lesson right now?"

"I have to, Bella. The thought of what *could* have happened to her terrifies me."

She scrunched her nose. "I understand, kinda."

"Thanks." He sat up and propped his elbows on his desk. "Now, let's talk about you, Remington Wyatt."

⚖️

Why would she run? Why?

Rafe slammed his palm against the desk. It shook, bumping against the motel room's wall. He glared at the e-mail.

Am coming to you to assist. Be there tonight.

Great. Hartlock would show up and take over the case. It made Rafe want to scream. He was the one who had found the clue in the first place. He was the one who begged Jackson to let him come to Hopewell for follow-up. He was the one who uncovered Simpson's connection to Tate. But Hartlock would get the credit for anything uncovered.

It wasn't fair. He needed to make progress and get something going before Hartlock showed up. A solid lead, a new direction . . . that would prove to Jackson he could handle this case and didn't need a babysitter.

As he flipped through the case file, nothing new struck him. Lowering his head into his hands, Rafe grabbed the hair at his temples and pulled. Why couldn't he figure this out?

The tune from *The Good, the Bad, and the Ugly* rang out.

Savannah? Rafe snatched up his cell and flipped it open. "Hey, Darren." He held his breath, praying his goddaughter was okay.

"Hiya. How's all in swampland?"

Rafe let out a rush of air. "Not so much swampy. How's all back home?"

"We're doing well. Savannah's doctors are very pleased with how she's doing. They don't think there'll be any issue or delay with the upcoming surgery."

Unlike two before in which she got an infection that had delayed the surgery to the point where she almost went into cardiac arrest. "That's great. I'm happy."

"Yeah, us too. Maddie handling the house repairs?"

"Yep. She's getting in touch with the Realtor to get everything set up." He shook his head. "Guess that means another month the house won't sell."

"Well, I have some news about that. The police have arrested the guy who vandalized the place."

"Who?" If it was some kid he'd busted . . .

"It wasn't a kid like they thought. Guy is thirty-one."

And did *that* to his house? "Who?"

"Foster. Garrison Foster. I'm guessing you don't know him."

"I do know him. That's Riley's ex-boyfriend."

"Well . . . that explains a lot. Then I'm safe to assume you do want to press charges?"

"Oh yeah. I do." The snot. To break in and vandalize his house—all because he and Riley had broken up and he resented that Rafe was an FBI agent? Talk about issues.

"You okay, buddy?"

He shook off his irritation. "It's this case. Kicking my butt."

"Tell me."

Rafe laid out the details as he knew them. He ended his monologue with the news of Hartlock being on his way. "So I need a break on this before he gets here, and he'll be here tonight." Rafe slammed the folder closed and shoved it to the edge of the table.

"This Hayden Simpson . . . you believe him? That he didn't have any idea about Tate being his father?"

Considering the man's reactions and such . . . "Yeah, I do."

"This woman . . . Bella Miller . . . What's your take on her?"

At just the mention of her name, Rafe's gut tightened. "I can't get a read on her. She's an enigma to me."

"Bet that's making you crazy, eh?" Snickering sounded over the phone. "What does she look like? Is she attractive?"

Maybe that was what infuriated him about her. That he couldn't get a handle on her like he did most people. "Yeah, she's attractive." Gut-pulling attractive, but he wasn't going to go there. He'd learned his lesson about women who were in it for the long haul and the heartache they caused. "Tell me you have some insight. A germ of an idea I can follow up on to get a lead."

Darren laughed. "Miss me, do you? Don't answer that." More chuckling. "Give me a second."

Rafe stood and stretched. He grabbed his water bottle and took a long swig, then made strides across the motel room.

"What about Simpson's mother?"

"What about her?"

"Have you spoken with her?"

"No."

"I think you should. You might get more info out of her than her son. She was, after all, keeping secrets from him."

Why hadn't he thought of that? How was he ever going to get in line for a promotion by not working the details?

Maybe Nick had been wrong, and he wasn't that good.

Chapter Seventeen

"Be courteous to all, but intimate with few, and let those few be
well tried before you give them your confidence."
GEORGE WASHINGTON

Bella had hoped Hayden would let the subject drop. At least for a couple more days while he concentrated on Emily and her issues. It wasn't fair that Agent Baxter had shown up and destroyed her life. She loved Hopewell and Hayden and Ardy and Emily—she didn't want to have to leave. She had nowhere else to go.

Leaning across the desk, she batted her eyes at Hayden. "Wouldn't you rather I go find you some decent coffee?"

He chuckled. "As much as I crave some strong java, you've put me off long enough." He waved her away. "And stop that silly blinking at me. My head already hurts, and you're making it worse."

"Fine." She leaned back in the chair. "But first, I need to know you aren't going to tell Agent Baxter who I am."

"He's going to figure it out. He has pictures of you, Bella. Remington. You know what I mean. He'll put it together."

"You didn't. You saw the picture of me as Remington, right?"

He nodded.

"Did you recognize me?"

"No, but I should have." A hint of a blush tinted his cheeks. "I knew there was something familiar about her. You."

"Uh-huh. Yeah. Sure. Right." She grinned and waggled her brows. "You know me better than any FBI agent, and you didn't recognize me. I think I'm pretty safe." She tilted her head. "Amazing what a little Botox and extra pounds can do when combined with hair dye and tinted contacts, isn't it?"

The blush darkened across Hayden's cheekbones. "I would've figured it out. And Rafe Baxter will eventually." He narrowed his eyes. "He seems to notice a lot about you already."

"Don't be silly." Her heart skipped a beat. "And he won't figure anything out unless you make him look twice at Bella Miller."

"It doesn't matter. He's a good guy. He won't come after you." Hayden pled with his voice. "I think he'll be able to help you."

She shook her head, her heartbeat echoing in her ears. "I can't take that chance." She crossed her arms over her chest. "So I need you to promise me you won't reveal who I am to Agent Baxter."

"I won't lie to him. I can't."

Once upon a time, she wouldn't have been able to lie convincingly either. Those days were gone. Yet another reason to hate the agents who'd murdered Daniel. "Okay, but promise you won't volunteer the information, and you won't do something stupid to draw attention to me."

"I promise."

Bella relaxed her shoulders. "Okay. So, what do you want to know that I haven't already told you?"

Hayden frowned, then winced. "The murderers . . . corruption in the FBI . . . why my—Daniel Tate was killed. Come on, let's get it all out in the open. We can figure out the answers together."

Her heart snagged. It was time, though. Time to get the truth off her chest. Time to figure out who all was involved. Time to stop running and see justice served.

She let out a sigh. "As I told you, Agents Lars Hartlock and Jack Devane were the ones who shot Daniel."

"Which one?"

She shrugged. "I honestly don't know. I couldn't see into the office. One of them." Her stomach hurt. "If I had to make an educated guess, I'd say Hartlock probably pulled the trigger."

Images of Hartlock's scowl, the lack of compassion he seemed to have toward many, his arrogance, his determination . . . she shuddered. "Yeah, between those two, I'd bet Hartlock actually shot Daniel."

"You mentioned something about one of Daniel's cases being the reason. Do you know anything more?"

The memory slammed against her. "Daniel said government witnesses had come to him after a trial and confessed the FBI pressured and bullied them to fabricate their testimonies."

Hayden's brows lowered into a unibrow, the wrinkles on his forehead digging deeper. "And you have no idea which trial?"

As if she hadn't tried to figure it out. "I Googled and searched as best I could but came up empty. The last two cases presented in Daniel's court were mortgage- and investment-fraud cases. I couldn't find a connection. Well, not just using public resources so my probing would stay undetected." She'd searched several times over the years and had never been able to figure anything out.

"White-collar cases are hardly ones that would provoke murder."

But for Daniel . . . "Actually, I just realized it doesn't matter the crime at all. It's that Daniel learned the FBI had coerced witnesses into lying on the stand. That would be enough motive for them to kill him."

Hayden nodded. "They wouldn't want anybody questioning their tactics. And if they were proven in the wrong, it would kill their careers."

How high did the cover-up go? Was the Assistant Special Agent in Charge in on this? The SAC? One or both of them had to be. No way could Lars and Jack have come up with such elaborate schemes on their own, despite their years in the bureau.

Oh-my-stars—how many other cases had these agents messed with? If they could and would tamper with witnesses on one case, why not others? The numbers could be staggering. And what could legally happen to those cases now if the corruption were exposed?

Her body stiffened. Her life was more in danger now than ever before. If they thought they'd gotten away with murder, then found out she was alive *and* talking . . . well, she'd be taken out in a flick.

"Bella?"

She jerked her attention back to the present. To Hayden. She swallowed. "We need to find out who all is involved. When Lars was talking to Daniel, he said someone high up knew about this. This could be bigger and further reaching than I ever imagined."

"So where do we begin?"

"His last cases." She sprang to her feet and moved around his desk to hover over his shoulder. "Google Daniel and find the link to where his last trials are listed. We'll start there and move backward." She tapped her nails on his desk. "It won't raise red flags for a cop to look at trial details online."

Hayden shrugged off her hand. "I can do this myself. Why don't you go find me that decent cup of coffee you mentioned?"

And now that he knew she was Remington, she could drink some too. At least when they were alone.

Like manna from heaven.

Hanging up the phone, he worked to control his breathing. Everything would be handled soon. As long as the agents cleaned up their own mess, everything would be fine. No one would be the wiser.

Once he won the election, he'd make sure to put Hartlock and Devane firmly in his back pocket. Just in case. It never hurt to own FBI agents.

Hartlock had assured him Remington Wyatt would be taken care of by Monday morning. Just a weekend, and he could breathe freely again.

With the election just weeks away, he couldn't afford to take a chance she'd resurface. And heaven forbid she started talking. If she did, he could kiss his political career good-bye. Not to mention the legal mess he'd be tangled in.

He glanced down at his notes. The National Cancer Society wanted him to speak at their luncheon next week. Apparently the news that his brother had died twenty-three years ago from mesothelioma made him the most attractive candidate to them.

It seemed like only yesterday . . .

"Dude, you have a call. A woman." His buddy jerked his thumb over his shoulder, motioning to the pay phone in the law school dorm's hallway.

His stomach burned as he made his way. He dragged his feet against the scuffed floor. There was only one woman who would call him. He avoided eye contact with the other law school students lingering in the hall.

The bile seared the back of his throat. He grabbed the receiver lying faceup on top of the phone. "Hello?"

His mother's voice cracked on his name, and he knew.

His chest tightened as he swallowed the grief sitting bitter on his tongue.

"It's Vernon." Her sobs nearly ripped his heart to shreds. "Honey, he passed on early this morning."

Passed on? He died. Laid in a hospital bed while the disease ate his insides away. Sat helpless as no one could or would help him. Dead. His brother was dead.

And he couldn't just accept that. Someone had failed. Someone was responsible. And he intended to see that he paid.

"Honey, I need you to come home. Your family needs you."

His sister-in-law . . . Vernon's young sons—they wouldn't make it alone.

The finality of his brother's death cut him to his very core.

Staring off into space, he couldn't help wondering, as he did so often these days, where his nephews were, what kind of men they'd grown up to be, if they had families of their own. He'd hired private investigators to no avail. His sister-in-law had divorced the man she married after Vernon died, and there was no trail of her to be found.

Nothing but dead ends and disappointments.

He'd lost his family needlessly. His brother. His nephews. Even his mother had died soon after Vernon, letting the grief consume her.

He shook himself back to focus on the present. On winning the election. On having Remington Wyatt taken care of once and for all.

⚖️

Rafe checked the clock again—a little after lunch. Surely Mrs. Simpson would be home. He'd done his research and knew she didn't work outside the home. He really needed to speak with her without Hayden present.

He climbed the steps of the porch and took a deep breath. He exhaled and rang the doorbell.

Seconds later the door swung open.

Rafe didn't know what he'd been expecting, but Ardy Simpson was nothing like he'd imagined. From his investigation he knew she was in her early to mid-fifties. She didn't look it.

Her honey-colored hair hung below her shoulders. Her eyes were bright against smooth skin. She smiled wide. "Hello. May I help you?"

"Mrs. Simpson?" He found his voice as he flashed his badge. "I'm Agent Rafe Baxter. I'd like to ask you a few questions, if I might."

The smile slunk off her face. "This is about Daniel's murder."

"Yes, ma'am."

She opened the door and waved him inside. "Come on in and have a seat." She shut the front door behind him and led the way into an open-plan living-dining room. Her lithe form eased onto an overstuffed chair.

Rafe took a seat on the couch adjacent to Mrs. Simpson. He pulled out a notebook and pen. "I'm sorry to have been the one to bring the news to Hayden."

Her smile was not nearly as welcoming as when she'd opened the door. "I understand." She smoothed her jeans and picked at imaginary lint. "How can I help you?"

No offer of something to drink. So much for Southern hospitality when it was apparent she wanted him out of her home as soon as possible. He could relate. "I need to ask you about how you knew Daniel Tate."

"I thought Hayden had already told you this."

"He did, but I need to hear you tell me."

Ardy Simpson nodded, then launched into her history as Hayden had already relayed. Her voice choked on emotion several times, and he felt like a heel for making her admit her transgressions yet again. Still, he had a job to do.

"After Tate received the birth announcement, he called you, at which time you were able to convince him not to have any future contact with you or his son, correct?"

"Yes." She glanced to the floor, then met his stare.

But not the whole truth. "Did you have any other contact after that?"

"Once." Her voice cracked. "Daniel came to Hopewell to see for himself that Hayden and I were happy and taken care of."

So there *was* something she didn't tell Hayden. Or Hayden had kept from him. "What happened when Tate came to town? Did you see him?"

She nodded. "He cried when he held Hayden. I didn't think he'd keep his word to stay out of our lives." Tears made her eyes even brighter.

Rafe's chest tightened as sympathy rose for the victim he'd never met. He could very easily imagine the pain these two had endured because of their lack of good judgment.

"I gave him my word I'd contact him if I ever needed him." Her eyes lost focus as she stared blankly into nothingness. "I actually thought about calling him after George died."

"Why didn't you?" Maybe the star-crossed lovers could have found some measure of happiness after all these years.

Ardy smiled and met his gaze. "Because I didn't know if Daniel had fallen in love, married, had his own family. I couldn't disrupt his life. He respected my wishes and kept out of my life." Her tone had dropped to barely above a whisper. "It's selfish of me, but I couldn't stand knowing he'd found someone. I know, I had George and a love-filled marriage, so it seems silly, but . . ."

Images of Georgia flitted across Rafe's mind. How many times had he wished he didn't know she'd had a happy marriage and a beautiful baby? His throat thickened. "No, I understand completely."

"Do you? I wonder if a man as young as yourself can." She narrowed her eyes and studied him. "Perhaps you can."

"Age is not a prerequisite to lost or forbidden love, Mrs. Simpson." But that had been before he found Christ. Before he made the choice to follow Jesus.

A meaningful pause hung low and heavy in the spacious living space.

"Well said, Agent Baxter." She stood. "Can I get you a cup of coffee or something to drink?"

"Coffee would be nice." He stood as well.

"Follow me. Friends normally sit in the kitchen with me."

So he'd moved up from the agent she couldn't wait to get rid of to a friend invited into her kitchen. The pain of unrequited love made strange bedfellows indeed.

"This won't take but a minute to brew." She filled the pot with water. "Have a seat at the bar."

As instructed, Rafe dropped to the barstool. The kitchen was much cheerier. Brighter. A framed photograph hung over the kitchen table. A family portrait.

Rafe stood and moved in front of the picture. There was no resemblance between George Simpson and Hayden. Had the man ever noticed? Especially since the daughter carried strong traits of her father.

"No."

He spun and cocked his head at Ardy.

The corners of her mouth turned slightly upward. "George never had a clue that Hayden wasn't his son. He never knew he had any reason to suspect otherwise." She turned back to the coffeepot.

Rafe returned to the barstool. "I heard your daughter was found safe and sound. I'm glad for you."

"Me too. If only she and Hayden could get past their differences."

"Differences?"

"Well, ever since George died, Hayden has tried to act as a parent to Emily. She doesn't take well to that."

Rafe grinned. "I can imagine." Riley had been a handful since their parents' accident. Thank goodness she was an adult. He nodded at the photograph on the wall. "She's a beautiful girl."

"Thank you." Ardy winked, then reached for the pot. "Coffee's ready. How do you take yours?"

"Black."

She slid his cup to him, then added sugar and cream to her own. "I can't drink it like that. Hayden drinks it black as well."

Apparently Rafe and the police commissioner had a lot in common. More than he'd imagined. He took a sip. Hot and strong, just the way he liked it. "Well, as long as you drink it. There's just something about a person who doesn't drink coffee. I can't make myself trust 'em."

"Oh, that's a shame."

He set the cup down. "Why's that?"

"Bella doesn't drink coffee at all." Ardy peered at him over the rim. "I'm assuming you know Bella."

The flavor turned bitter on his tongue. "I've met her."

Ardy arched her left brow. "And?"

"And what?" He shrugged, hoping he looked disinterested. "She's Hayden's best friend, right?"

"Yes, they're best friends."

"Well, then." He took another sip of coffee.

"Interesting."

His chest was tighter than the Tennessee Volunteers' defensive line. "What?"

"You're attracted to her. Is she attracted as well?" She leaned on the bar, resting her chin in her hands.

"I-I . . . I don't know what you're talking about." Oh, mercy . . . he hadn't stuttered in years. Now he sounded like some lame boy with a crush.

"Oh, you've got it bad." Ardy straightened, her eyes widening. "Don't worry. Your secret is safe with me." She winked. "I love Bella as if she were my own daughter. You couldn't do better."

Great. If he argued with Mrs. Simpson, she'd think he was just denying to save himself embarrassment. Now what was he going to do?

Especially when she was dead-on.

"And she's very trustworthy. She's known about Daniel being Hayden's father almost since she moved here and never said a word."

"You told her? You must trust her a lot."

"Oh, I do trust her. But I didn't tell her. She already knew."

Rafe stiffened. "How did she know?"

Ardy cocked her head to the side. "You know, I don't really recall. It's been a long time since we had that conversation." She shrugged. "I asked Bella not to say anything to Hayden—begged, more like it—and she didn't. Not even a hint, which was why he was so shocked when I told him."

Now what was he going to do with this information?

Chapter Eighteen

"Honesty is the first chapter in the book of wisdom."
THOMAS JEFFERSON

"What else don't I know about the real you?" Hayden leaned back in the kitchen chair and stared at Bella over his coffee cup.

She pointed the spatula she held at him. "I told you . . . I love coffee and Dr. Pepper and I really, really miss smoking. You cannot believe how much I miss smoking." Even three years later, she could taste the menthol in the back of her throat. "You know how people say you get better taste buds and sense of smell after you quit smoking? That's a lie."

"Really?"

"Yeah. Big, fat, hairy lie." She turned to check on the biscuits in the oven, nearly tripping over the dog. "Chubbers, go lie down."

The black Lab ambled to the back door and plopped on his rug.

"And I miss my cat something fierce." The long-ignored yearning seared her chest. "So many times I wanted to call and find out where Whiskers ended up. Who had found her and where she is."

Hayden shook his head. "I would've never taken you for a cat person."

People didn't own cats—they owned their humans. Bella flipped the sizzling bacon. "I love cats."

Chubbers lifted his head from his paws.

She laughed. "I love you too, Chubs." She grinned at Hayden. "I swear, that dog understands English."

"He's smart. What else?"

She pulled the bacon from the pan and set it across paper towels. "Well, I used to be a vegetarian." She flipped another piece of bacon. "Obviously, I had to get over that."

"I find it fascinating you had me so completely fooled."

She pulled the biscuits from the oven and turned it off. "Hayden, I didn't set out to fool you or anyone for fun. I didn't have a choice. I had to change everything so I could get away." All her life, from her father to Daniel, she'd been raised to respect the truth. Her heart ached with having to live so many lies just to stay alive. The reality didn't ease the adjustment to her moral compass.

"I know. And we're going to figure everything out so you can be free to be yourself from now on."

"I hope so." She carried the plates to the table and dropped to a chair across from Hayden. "I wish I'd been able to find more of Daniel's cases. I only got the last five he presided over."

"We'll figure it out." Hayden bent his head, softly said a prayer, then met her gaze. "Since we're being honest now, would you tell me why you're mad at God?"

She figured he'd get around to the subject of religion. Just hadn't expected it quite so soon. She took a sip of coffee, savoring the much-missed flavor. "My mother died very soon after I was born. From complications of pneumonia."

"I'm so sorry."

"I never knew her to miss her." Even looking at photos of her mother hadn't tugged on any heartstrings. "My father is a different story."

He'd taught her everything—to cook, shoot a gun, thread a needle, dress her dolls, and change the oil in his truck. He let her watch scary movies and encouraged her to read everything she could get her hands on.

Hayden wiped his mouth and took a drink of coffee. "He died when you were how old?"

"Ten."

"What happened?"

She set down the biscuit she'd taken a bite from, her appetite gone. "He was coming out of the office he shared with Daniel and was shot in a drive-by. The police never caught the shooter." And her life had been ripped to shreds.

Her first true taste of injustice.

Wasn't it because of this injustice that she went into the field she did? That she acted on Daniel's suggestion that she hire out to the FBI? How ironic that the ones who paid her salary were now after her.

"I'm sorry, Bella."

"He was a good man. Daniel had met him when Dad was right out of law school. They met on a golf course, if you can believe that." She wiped away the tears misting her vision. "Daniel invited him into his private practice before Dad even took the bar exam."

Hayden set his napkin on top of his plate.

She did the same, although she'd barely touched her breakfast. "He took Dad under his wing. Helped him in the industry. Taught him the way around the courts." She smiled as memories rolled through her mind. "Neither of them ever missed anything of mine. Ballet recitals. First crushes. Concerts."

Taking another sip of coffee, she stared out over the bayou. "When Dad died, Daniel never hesitated. He'd been my godfather all my life. He was the only family I had. It was never a question of if I'd live with him and if he would become my guardian." She shrugged. "He got all the paperwork done and it was legal within months."

"I hate to keep saying I'm sorry, but that's all I can think of. I truly hurt for you." Hayden flashed her a gentle smile.

She smiled back. "It's okay. But losing Daniel to such a violent crime too . . . well, now you can understand why I'm mad at God." That was putting it mildly. All these years later and she was still so angry.

"But you know Scripture so well. You must've had a Christian upbringing."

"Yes. My father was a very religious man. After he died, Daniel tried to keep up a Christian home. It just didn't work. I was angry, he didn't know what he was doing—before long, he just gave up." She remembered the feeling. "I don't blame him. I was relieved when he did. I never wanted to disappoint Daniel, but it was all an act."

"But if you were raised as a Christian, you know that—"

She stood and lifted her plate. "Please don't try to preach to me now, Hayden. I know the Bible. I don't deny there's a God. I don't argue the point. I'm mad at Him. That's my personal business, okay?"

He grabbed his plate and put it in the sink. "Fine. But I'm going to be praying for you, no matter what you say."

She shook her head. "Knock yourself out." She rinsed the dishes and handed them to Hayden, who put them in the dishwasher. "Just keep your prayers to yourself."

Shutting the dishwasher door, he grabbed a rag and wiped his hands. "Well then, let's see those cases. We should be able to get a lead."

Good. He'd let the matter drop. She led the way to the living room, grabbed the papers he'd brought. "None of these ring any bells. Daniel never talked about any of them."

He grabbed the file and sat on the couch, flipping through the pages. "Okay, let's start on the last ones for the month before his murder. You take these three." He passed her pages. "And I'll take these two. Let's find out if those agents were involved in either case. If not, I think we can eliminate them." He reached for his iPad, rattling off his login information so she could also get into the legal database system.

She sat at her computer desk and began searching. Using Hayden's login ensured no red flags would be raised that would put her in danger. There were limited documents, but the dockets of each trial were a matter of public record. That would contain the pretrial motions, including the witness lists. If Lars or Jack were involved with the case, they would be listed as potential witnesses.

Ten minutes garnered the government's witness list for the first case. FBI agents were listed, but not Lars Hartlock or Jack Devane. Dead end. She began her hunt on the second trial.

What if they didn't find anything? Where would they go if they couldn't find a connection in Daniel's last cases—go back further? No, that wasn't right. It had to be a recent trial. Unless the witness who came to Daniel waited a long time to tell him. She ran her fingers through her hair, tightening the strands in her hand and tugging.

The government's witness list from the second case came up on the computer screen. Bella leaned forward and chewed on her bottom lip. Scanning . . . reading . . . all the way to the end. Nope, no Hartlock or Devane.

She cleared the information and started the search on the third one. This was going nowhere. They wouldn't find any connection. If it'd been this easy, she would have thought to do it years ago.

Bella was more than a little embarrassed she hadn't considered stealing Hayden's login information years ago and doing this. Maybe that was a good thing—she hadn't turned into a full-fledged criminal. She smiled to herself. Not yet.

"I found it. Both agents were on the witness list for this trial."

She spun and faced Hayden, her heart hammering so hard it hurt her ribs. Could they really be on the right track? After all this time, would justice finally be served for Daniel?

⚖

"Sorry I didn't call last night. We got into town later than I'd anticipated." Hartlock peered over the top of the diner's laminated menu. "By the time we got settled in the motel and grabbed something to eat, I didn't want to disturb you."

"No problem." Rafe worked to sip on his coffee without his displeasure being easy to read.

Devane shifted in his chair. "What's good here?"

Rafe shrugged. "It's all good." Good, but a little spicy. Maybe the agents would get upset stomachs and head back to Little Rock. He swallowed. That was mean, even if he was only teasing. Kinda.

"Might watch out for the spices. Has a little bit of a kick."

"Thanks." Devane concentrated back on the menu.

The young waitress sashayed back to their table with a pot of coffee. "You boys ready to order?" She smiled a little too long at Rafe, the obvious youngster of the trio.

They placed their orders, Devane ordering enough to feed all three of them. The waitress left, then tense silence hung as heavy as the bacon grease in the gravy.

"So," Hartlock began, "anything new?"

Rafe took a sip of hot coffee. "Yes, I solved the whole thing since I heard from you yesterday." He forced a chuckle. "Did you get any hits with the photos?"

"No. We showed them to all the old security guards at Daniel's subdivision. And to the students who clerked for Daniel. And to the interns in the courthouse. No one recognized Hayden Simpson at all."

Devane shook his head. "You might be right and the man didn't know Tate was his father."

"I believe he didn't have a clue." That was the truth.

Hartlock cleared his throat. "What about this Bella Miller?"

Rafe clenched his hand under the table, curling it into a tight fist. "She's Simpson's best friend."

"What do you think she knows?"

Shrugging, Rafe relaxed his hand and reached for his cup. "She moved here a couple of years ago, is younger than Simpson, so she really has no ties to the area or its history. Or the Simpsons."

Although she knew about Tate being Simpson's father before Mrs. Simpson told her, and there was no explanation for that, Rafe didn't want to bring that fact to the table just yet. Not until he figured out how she knew.

The waitress delivering their meals broke Hartlock's study of Rafe. The smell of the sausage nearly turned his stomach, but he smiled at the waitress as he thanked her. When she left, Rafe bowed his head and offered up grace, then lifted his eyes to meet the ASAC's stare.

"You into all that religion stuff?"

Rafe paused in unwrapping his silverware, his muscles tensing. "I'm a Christian, yes."

"How's that work in this profession?" Devane poured salt and pepper over his scrambled eggs.

"What do you mean?" Rafe asked.

Devane swallowed, then took a gulp of coffee. "Christians aren't supposed to lie or cuss or anything, right?"

Rafe nodded.

"As an agent, how do you get around all that?" Devane shoved a forkful of sunny-side up fried eggs and scattered southern hash browns into his mouth.

The man ate with such relish it was almost hard to be disgusted. Hard, but not impossible.

"As agents, we're called to an even higher standard than other people. Just like Christians hold themselves to a higher moral standard than nonbelievers." Which is why Rafe knew he'd been such a sinner to have loved Georgia, even though he'd fallen in love with her before he'd given his life to God. Of course, he found it extremely ironic that Georgia was the one who'd led him to Jesus.

"You really think that?" Hartlock paused in his precise cutting and eating of his pancakes, snatching Rafe's attention.

"I do." Something nudged against Rafe's conscience. "Don't you?"

Hartlock shrugged and rolled his eyes. "Wouldn't know. I'm not into all that religion stuff."

That explained a lot. Rafe refrained from going into a salvation sermon. This wasn't the time, wasn't the place, and Hartlock most definitely wasn't open to the conversation.

"I'll need to talk with this Hayden myself." Hartlock switched subjects so quickly, it took Rafe a moment to recover.

"Certainly. Won't be a problem. But it is a weekend." Hartlock never did explain why he couldn't wait until Monday. Did they think Rafe was down here on vacation or something?

"I like the element of surprise, don't you?" Using Rafe's own words . . . did Alphonse tell Hartlock everything?

"When it's something to surprise, yeah, I do." He managed to swallow a bite of toast despite the strained conversation.

Devane, on the other hand, didn't seem to have a problem as he finished off his biscuits and gravy in a large bite, then noisily ran his tongue over his teeth. "I'm anxious to meet Daniel Tate's son."

"You have to remember Simpson's not exactly thrilled over the revelation. He had quite a shock. He adored the man who raised him, the man he believed to be his father." Rafe forced his expression to remain neutral.

"Of course," Devane replied.

Hartlock shoved his plate toward the center of the table. "If you don't mind, I'd like to hold my impression until after I've met the man."

"Understandable." Rafe finished his coffee. What would Hartlock think about Rafe sharing the file with Simpson?

Probably wouldn't be too happy. More than likely, he'd be furious and write up Rafe.

"You didn't mention to him that more agents were coming,

did you?" Hartlock's eyes were barely narrowed, but enough for Rafe to get the point.

"No." But two could play his game. "Did you want me to?"

Hartlock hesitated, just long enough for the hairs on the back of Rafe's neck to notice. "Of course not."

Rafe forced the smile as he motioned to the waitress for the check. "Good. Very good."

"Do you have any idea where Hayden is today?"

"Could be at home. I doubt he's at the station."

The waitress handed Rafe the check. Hartlock took it out of his hand. "I'll put it on my expense account." His smile was colder than the last sip of coffee in Rafe's cup.

"Thanks." Rafe struggled to his feet. He shoved the chair back up to the table, scraping the legs against the time-worn floor, and led the way out of the diner.

The wind gusted as the three agents exited. Leaves danced across the parking lot, flipping and twirling.

"And Bella Miller. I'll want to speak with her as well." Hartlock crossed his arms over his chest. "You wouldn't happen to know where I could find her today, would you?"

Rafe's mouth went drier than the brown leaves littering the curb. "No."

Hartlock nodded. "I'm looking forward to meeting her."

What was Hartlock's interest in Bella? Those hairs on the back of Rafe's neck rose to full attention.

Chapter Nineteen

*"He that would live in peace and at ease must
not speak all he knows or all he sees."*

Benjamin Franklin

"Which case?" Bella abandoned her desk to perch on the arm of the couch, looking over Hayden's shoulder to his iPad.

"The conspiracy and wire fraud one." Hayden enlarged the text. "A case against a mortgage firm. Nine indicted. All settled but two—the owner of the company and one of the managers."

Bella tapped her fingers on the edge of the couch, waiting for Hayden to get to the next page of details.

Chubbers nudged her hand. She rubbed between his ears like he loved.

"The manager's trial was before Daniel. Both Devane and Hartlock were the agents of record, as well as being on the witness list."

"And the owner of the company?"

"His trial date was set for after the manager's." Hayden flicked his wrist to access the next page. "Ended up being transferred to another judge after Daniel's murder."

She slumped down to the cushion, crowding Hayden. "What's the manager's name?"

"Cason Moore."

"And the government won, right?"

"Yeah. Jury trial. Not guilty of mortgage fraud, but of wire fraud. And conspiracy." He moved to another page. "All of the ones who took a plea bargain and became government witnesses testified against Moore, except for one of the ladies."

"How'd she manage to get out of testifying?"

"She died."

Bella sat up straight. "Was she murdered?"

"No. Cancer. Had been sick with it for years."

"Oh." She bit back her disappointment. "So this Cason Moore was found guilty. What did Daniel sentence him to?" She bit her lip while Hayden looked up the answer.

"Four months in federal prison camp."

"A weekend." She leaned back against the couch.

"Excuse me?"

Bella chuckled. "Anything you count in months in a fed camp is called a weekend by the inmates." She leaned forward again. "Let me guess, those others who turned into government witnesses got deals with no prison time?"

"Actually," he paused as he forwarded to another page, "one of their witnesses, the comptroller, a Mark Dossey, got a year and a day."

"So he could be out in seven months. That's really strange for one of the government's witnesses to serve more time than a defendant who went to trial."

Hayden looked up from the iPad to shoot her a quizzical look. "Really strange?"

"Yeah. That's normally one of the enticing factors to turn government witness—less prison time than if you go to trial." It didn't make sense. Unless . . . "Did Daniel sentence the government witness?" Her mind raced across other possible explanations while Hayden searched.

"Daniel sentenced everyone in the case with the exception of the owner because his trial was held after Daniel's murder."

Daniel was fair if nothing else. For him to have sentenced a government witness to a harsher sentence than a defendant found guilty by a jury . . . "He didn't believe the witness." Bella jumped to her feet. "That's the only reason why Daniel would give him a tougher sentence than Moore. He didn't believe this Dossey character on the stand."

Hayden tapped a few more times on his device, then set it on the coffee table. "What exactly does that mean? If he thought a witness was lying . . . that's perjury."

"Only if the person on the stand is caught in a lie." She paced, swinging her arms. It helped her think.

"Want me to order the transcript?"

"Yeah—no. It doesn't matter. This is the case. I know it. Daniel's sentencing discrepancy is enough for me."

"Okay, so this is the case. What now?"

She sank onto the chair. "I don't know. I can't think." Her mind went in a gazillion different directions at the moment.

Hayden stood and stretched. "How about a fresh pot of coffee to help get the old brain cells kicking?"

"Yes, please." She stared absently out the window as Hayden went to the kitchen.

It made sense. But she needed to be able to prove it all. Otherwise Hartlock and Devane would dispute her eyewitness account. She was a suspect. The evidence she'd have to have must be indisputable.

She'd have to find the witness who'd come to Daniel. But after his murder, would he or she be willing to tell the truth? He would have to.

Hayden returned with two cups of coffee.

"We need a list of everyone who actually testified at Moore's trial." She accepted the cup.

Wonderful, blissful coffee.

"Okay." Hayden returned to his seat on the couch. He set

down the cup and lifted the iPad. "Let me see what I can find out."

Bella warmed her hands on the mug as she continued slowly pacing. And thinking. She turned to Hayden. "Were there any other agents on the case?"

"Give me a second."

How high did this go? ASAC? SAC? If they were involved at all with the witness prepping, then they almost had to be in on this.

"Hartlock and Devane were the only agents."

She ran her finger along the lip of the cup. "Is there any notation who their supervisor was on the case?"

"Hang on."

Did everything have to take forever?

"Alphonse Jackson."

Disappointment bittered the coffee on her tongue. He'd been the one she reported to when she did her freelance for the FBI. She liked him. Had entertained the thought several times to call him and tell him what she'd witnessed.

Man, was she glad now she hadn't followed through on that idea.

"Who's he?" Hayden took a sip.

"The SAC of the Little Rock office."

"You know him?"

"Yes. And I like him. Well, I did." If he was the super on the case and Hartlock and Devane had threatened witnesses into lying . . . well, then it was almost proof he was at least aware of their tactics. It broke her heart.

Chubbers bounded off his chair and rushed to the front door. He growled low in his throat and barked twice.

Hayden shoved to his feet and joined her at the window. Two cars pulled up the driveway. They both recognized the man who stepped from the first car. "Looks like Agent Rafe Baxter has come to visit."

Her blood froze as she saw the two men who got out of the unmarked bureau vehicle.

"I don't know who those guys are." Hayden spared her a glance.

"I do." Her knees gave out, and she sagged against Hayden. "Those are Agents Lars Hartlock and Jack Devane."

⚖

"What do you want me to do?" Hayden supported Bella, who would have fallen had he not grabbed her.

Her face was paler than white, and her eyes wider than he'd ever seen.

"Bella."

She didn't move. Didn't blink. She stared out the window with the same expression.

Terror.

They had no time. He shook her and raised his voice. "Bella."

She jerked, then met his stare.

"Think fast. What do you want to do?"

"Run. I have to run." She moved out of his grasp as if she could walk on water. "I have a bag already packed. I have another identity. I'll disappear in less than thirty minutes." She was in the hallway to the bedroom before he caught her.

"You can't run. Rafe knows you're here." He glanced over his shoulder. "Your truck is parked out front."

She trembled. He pulled her against his chest. *Lord, show me what to do.* Men's voices drew nearer. Chubbers alternated between barking and growling.

And it came to him what to do. "Shower."

"What?" Her eyes held more focus.

"Get in the bathroom and turn on the shower. On hot. So steam will seep out under the door." He ushered her to the bathroom. "I'll tell them you're in the shower because you're not feeling well. I'm taking care of you."

"Hayden . . ."

He left the bedroom door open and shoved her in the bathroom. "Do as I tell you. Shower. Don't turn it off or come out until I tell you it's clear." He hesitated, then placed a kiss on her forehead. "You can trust me. I'll take care of this." He pulled the door closed and turned back to the living room.

A loud knock rapped against the front door. Chubbers barked like he wanted to rip out someone's throat.

Maybe that wasn't such a bad idea.

"Hello?" Rafe's voice sounded from the porch.

"Chubbers, quiet."

The dog immediately stopped barking but stayed in an alert stance. For a woman who claimed to be a cat person, Bella had sure trained her dog well.

Hayden stuck his iPad in the desk drawer with the paperwork he'd brought. He turned off her computer monitor before cracking open the front door. "Agent Baxter. What a surprise."

"Wasn't so hard to track you down." Rafe's gaze shot over Hayden's shoulder. "Is everything okay?"

"I'm here checking on Bella."

One of the men behind him cleared his throat. Loudly.

Rafe pivoted, motioning to the men hovering on the porch. "Hayden Simpson, these are colleagues of mine. With the FBI. Assistant Special Agent in Charge Lars Hartlock and Agent Jack Devane. They're interested in speaking with you."

He nodded at the two men, taking in their intense and probing study of him but keeping the door cracked somewhat as a shield. "Agents." He looked back at Rafe. "I would ask y'all in, but Bella isn't feeling well. She's come down with something, and I'm just here to make her some chicken noodle soup." Now he'd have to make her soup, just so he won't have lied to the FBI. That was, after all, a federal offense.

Then again, did it even matter when they were murderers?

"Oh. Is she okay?" Genuine concern draped over Rafe's face.

Hayden swallowed a grin. Was it possible the agent was smitten with Bella? How would he feel about being attracted to the woman he sought in his case? "Uh, she's fine. Probably just a cold, but she's been running a fever since early this morning." He glanced back at the two agents. "We're just hoping it's not the flu. It *is* the season."

"We really would like to speak with her," Agent—which one? Had to be Hartlock as he had the creepiest look—interjected.

Rafe's jaw dropped. Just for a moment, but Hayden caught it. Rafe had no idea they'd wanted to question Bella.

Hayden straightened and tapped his outer thigh. Chubbers was at his side in protective stance in a moment, a growl low in his throat. "Why?"

"It's regarding an official FBI investigation." Hartlock crossed his arms over his chest, making his biceps jump under his taut long-sleeved Henley.

Baloney! Hayden knew what was really going on—they were here to get a look at her and see if she was Remington.

Lord, give me strength.

These were the men who'd murdered his biological father. Had shot Daniel Tate down in cold blood. *God, please give me strength. A lot.*

He put on a fake smile. "Well, I'm sorry to inconvenience you, but you'll have to come back in a day or so. She's in the shower right now and will most likely go straight to bed when she gets out. I told her I'd wake her in a few hours to see if she'd like to eat."

"So you're just gonna hang out while she sleeps?" The tone and expression of Hartlock grated against Hayden's nerves. "She your girlfriend or something?"

What nerve and rudeness. How'd this man become an ASAC? He had the personality of a pit bull. He patted his thigh again. Chubbers moved against him, a growl rumbling in the pit of his chest.

"I'm hanging out with the dog." He resisted the burning urge to laugh at Hartlock's wide eyes.

"Is it yours?"

"Chubbers here?" He reached down and rubbed the Lab's head. Remington had been a cat person. Bella was a dog person. "I wish. No, he is Bella's pride and joy. She loves this boy as if he were her baby. She raised him from a puppy. He just tolerates me."

"I'm sorry she's ill." Rafe nodded toward the hallway behind Hayden.

He glanced over his shoulder. Just as he'd thought, the chilly air from the October morning had seeped through the open front door, and steam puffed out from the bathroom like a charge of miniature Casper the friendly ghosts. "I'll let her know you dropped by."

"We also need to ask you a few questions, Commissioner Simpson." Hartlock was relentless.

Hayden widened his stance and squared his shoulders. Posturing.

By the slight shifting, Hartlock recognized the boundary had been set.

"Well, Agent, I can appreciate that, but I'm not on duty right now. We may be small here in Hopewell, but we do give the police officers days off. This weekend is my time off. And as I've already told you, I'm helping out a sick friend."

"We just have a few—"

Hayden held up his hand. "She'll be needing my help soon, so I really can't talk right now. Why don't y'all come by my office on Monday morning when I'm back at work? Say, about nine o'clock? You can ask me all those questions you have, and we'll have a right nice chat. How's that?" He laid the accent on thick, resisting the strong urge to really go redneck on the arrogant agent.

"We're sorry to have bothered y'all." Rafe took a step backward. "Tell Ms. Miller we hope she feels better."

"I will." Hayden met Rafe's gaze. A world of understanding passed between them, and Hayden caught the unspoken message loud and clear.

Hartlock passed him a business card. "In case you get a moment before Monday." He pointed at Hayden who slipped it into his jeans pocket. "My cell number is written on the back. Call me anytime."

Hayden gave a final nod in Rafe's direction, then shut the door. He let out a heavy sigh.

One set of footsteps echoed down the stairs. A second set. A moment passed. Hayden put an eye to the peephole.

"Lars, are you coming?" Devane waited at the bottom of the stairs.

The agent continued to stare at the front door. A minute jumped off the clock. Finally footfalls clunked down the steps.

Hayden dared to breathe again but continued watching through the peephole. Just to make sure Hartlock didn't sneak out and let Devane drive away. He wouldn't put anything past the jerk.

Car doors slammed in unison. Engines revved. Tires crunched on dead leaves and dry ground.

"Are they gone?"

He jumped and spun. "I thought I told you not to come out until I let you know the coast was clear?"

Bella shrugged. "I never was good at following orders." She jutted her chin toward the bayou. "They gone?"

He glanced out the window. The second car's tires hit the road. "Yep."

She plopped onto the couch. "That was close. What did they want?"

"To talk to me. And you."

"You, I can understand. Why me?"

He shook his head, gauging the fear creeping back into her eyes. "I have a meeting with them in my office on Monday at nine. Guess we'll know then."

She stood again, grabbing the back of the couch. What little color had restored to her face dissipated like the steam filtering through the house. "They've figured it out. I need to get out of here. Now. No one around me is safe. I have to go."

"I don't think that's a good idea." He moved closer to her, in case she crashed again. "Not right now."

"Hayden, they didn't come here to ask questions. They came to kill me. Don't you get that?" Her voice raised several octaves.

No doubt Hartlock would take a shot if he could. "I do. And I understand why you're scared. Trust me, after seeing Hartlock in person, I get it. But I don't think they're sure you're Remington."

"How do you figure?"

"Well, for one, they didn't tell Rafe who they think you are. I could tell. He's clueless." And attracted to Bella, but Hayden would keep that tidbit to himself for the time being.

She snorted. "You know him that well now, huh? Known him all of what, three or four days?"

"I *am* trained in analyzing body language, you know."

Bella laughed. "So am I. Extensively and exhaustively."

"But you didn't see him, so you wouldn't be able to tell."

She shrugged, but at least her posture was more relaxed. She still kept her position in the hallway, clutching the back of the couch.

"And hearing that Chubbers was your pride and joy confused him."

"I bet it did. It was well known back then that I had a lot of disdain for dogs." She glanced at her Lab, leaning up against her leg. "Sorry, boy. Just saying how it used to be. I love you."

His tail wagged in response.

"Hartlock's not positive, which is why he came here. He wanted to see you . . . talk to you. Find out if you are Remington."

"I can't stay hidden in the shower forever."

"No, but maybe you can stay hidden long enough for us to figure out who all is involved in their murder conspiracy."

She chewed on her bottom lip.

"If you make a move now, I think you'd be putting yourself in more danger. He'll be expecting Remington to run."

She smiled. "Hayden, I *am* Remington, you know."

"I know." But she'd always be Bella to him.

Chapter Twenty

*"All life is an experiment. The more
experiments you make, the better."*

RALPH WALDO EMERSON

Why were Hartlock and Devane so bound and determined to meet with Bella Miller? It didn't make any
sense. Hartlock seemed more intent on talking with her
than interviewing Hayden Simpson.

Rafe stared at the case information sprawled out on the motel
bed. *What am I missing?*

Back up to the beginning. Okay . . . what had he uncovered about the case during his short stay in Hopewell? Hayden
Simpson was Daniel Tate's son, but Hayden hadn't known that
until he'd been told this past week. Rafe wouldn't believe otherwise—the man showed every sign of surprise and not a single
deception marker. What else?

Rafe's talk with Ardy Simpson had been enlightening. Bella
had known Simpson was Tate's son. How?

Was it possible Hartlock and Devane were aware not only
that Bella had known, but *how* she knew? How could they know
something he hadn't any idea how to explain?

Rafe scrubbed his scalp. Why couldn't he figure this out? He went back over his personal notes. His impressions. Mrs. Simpson's impressions of his unexplained feelings for Bella.

That stopped him cold.

Aw, who was he kidding? He was very attracted and very interested in her. Her quiet strength seemed to call to him. There was something about her on a very deep, almost spiritual level that pulled him to her. But he wanted—no, needed—to see her and get to know her better.

And he couldn't explain why he felt the way he did. He'd also never had such a strong, out-of-the-blue pull to anyone. Not even to Georgia.

Rafe waited for the guilt to assault him. It didn't. For the first time since becoming a Christian, when he thought of Georgia, the guilt didn't cloak him.

God, have I done enough? Am I truly forgiven?

The loud notes of *The Good, the Bad, and the Ugly* theme song filled the room.

He grabbed his cell and flipped it open. "Hey, Darren. What's up?"

"You sound odd. Everything okay?"

"Yeah. Was just praying." It was so nice to be able to just be himself without guarding every word he spoke.

"It's going that badly?" Darren chuckled.

"Yes. No. I don't know." He sat on the edge of the bed, staring at the papers of the file flung on the bed with no rhyme or reason. "The ASAC and another agent are here. Arrived in town last night."

"On a weekend? Wow, did you catch a break?"

"I'm not real sure what their game is."

"No score, eh?"

"Not that I can figure out."

"How'd the talk with Simpson's mother go?"

"Pretty good. Discovered a couple of things I didn't know."

"Like?"

Rafe smiled, loving that he could fall back into the same routine. "Tate came here once after Simpson was born."

"You think there's any connection?"

Rafe stared at his handwritten notes. "I can't see how there's any tie. Unless someone saw Tate, but still . . . there's no connection."

"What else did you find out from Mrs. Simpson?"

"That Bella Miller knew Simpson was Tate's son."

"How?"

"Don't know. Mrs. Simpson didn't know either."

"Was Miller attempting to blackmail the mother?"

Rafe laughed. "Not hardly. She agreed to keep quiet about Simpson's paternity and did so for the past few years."

"This is the woman you can't get a read on, right?"

"Right." But he needed to. Desperately. If God was leading him to her, then he needed to get everything about her figured out.

A heavy sigh sounded.

That caught Rafe by surprise. "Darren? Is everything okay?"

"You're attracted to this woman, aren't you?"

Rafe swallowed. "Yeah, so? It won't affect my ability to work the case."

Silence.

"Darren?"

"Maybe it's best that we have this conversation on the phone and not in person."

Rafe's heart skipped a beat. "What are you talking about?"

"Are you going to destroy your chance of happiness with this woman like all the other ones you've been interested in before?"

He opened his mouth, then snapped it shut. He'd only dated a few women in the past several years. None of them lasted more than a few months. He just couldn't forgive himself for having loved Georgia. "What are you talking about?"

"She's gone, Rafe. We both have to accept that and move on. I can't because of Savannah, but you can."

Rafe went cold. "What are you saying?"

"It's time we talked about Georgia, don't you think?"

His muscles tensed without his intention. "I don't know what you're implying, Darren."

"Come on, buddy, don't insult me like this. We both know you were in love with Georgia. Were from the first time you met her."

Heart racing, Rafe let out a whoosh of air. "You knew?"

Darren chuckled, but the sound was foreign, lacking humor. "Of course I knew. I'm not blind. Or stupid."

"You have to believe me, there was never a single time—"

"I said not to insult me. I know there was never anything going on between y'all. I trusted Georgia with my heart . . . my love. I've always trusted you with my life."

Rafe's vision blurred.

"I knew neither of you would ever betray me."

"I'm sorry, man." If he'd have been able to choose not to love her, he would have. It sure would have made his life a lot easier.

"Don't apologize. Georgia inspired love in everyone." Darren's voice was thick with emotion. "Remember how passionate she was when she found Jesus?"

Rafe smiled at the memory.

"Darren, Rafe . . . y'all have to understand. Our lives have purpose. Meaning. We aren't just here by some fluke. God's been orchestrating our lives from before we were born."

Her smile . . . her enthusiasm—she hadn't stopped until both Rafe and Darren had followed her to church and met with the pastor.

"She loved life and people." Darren sniffed. "But she's gone, and you have to move on. She wouldn't want you to miss out on love, Rafe. She loved you too. Not like you loved her, but you know what I mean."

His response got stuck on the roof of his mouth.

"I've watched you subconsciously measure every woman you ever dated against Georgia. It's not fair. Not to them. Not to you."

Did he? He didn't think so, but maybe . . . "I—"

"Don't argue. I've seen you do it time and again. Don't mess this one up. Let Georgia go."

"Darren, I—"

"I'm tired of watching you ruin the possibility of perfectly good relationships."

Guilt, his faithful old friend, returned to torment him. "But I coveted another man's wife. I broke one of the Ten Commandments."

Darren sucked in air, hissing over the phone. "That's what your problem is? That you loved a woman who was vibrant and passionate and loving?"

"She was your wife." The words cut him. But this time he didn't feel like blood gushed from his heart.

"Yes, but she was your friend first. And you fell in love with her before we got married."

"That makes it okay?"

Darren chuckled. "I'm not a Bible scholar or anything, but I'm pretty certain God isn't holding your emotions against you."

Yet . . .

"Rafe, you honored our marriage. You never disrespected me or Georgia's and my marriage, right?"

His tongue felt thicker than Riley's gravy. "No. Never." He could barely whisper.

"So why would you think God is keeping score?"

"But the commandment says—"

"I know what it says, but you controlled yourself. You never acted on your love, except for being there for Savannah and me even more."

"Still . . . I asked for forgiveness, but I couldn't stop loving her. I couldn't turn away from her. From loving her."

"Pray about it. I honestly don't think God's angry you loved her. You need to stop beating yourself up, pal."

"I feel so unworthy of God's love because I broke this commandment." The truth scraped across Rafe's chest.

"Man, we're all unworthy of God's love and mercy. All of us are such sinners. But guess what? His grace is enough. For me." A heavy pause echoed silently over the phone connection. "And it's enough for you, Rafe. He forgave you the moment you asked. You just have to forgive yourself."

Darren's words were a balm to Rafe's raw wound.

"Think about what I said. Just consider everything."

Rafe dropped his gaze to the crime-scene photos. "Okay. I will."

Darren heaved a sigh. "Now, on to more promising things. Savannah's team of doctors said she's doing extremely well, and they're all set for the surgery."

How his partner could switch gears so quickly . . . "That's great. I miss her." And he did. So much.

"She misses you. Says she's coloring you a picture for your new house."

"Can't wait to see it." Rafe smiled and stared at the picture on the motel room wall. The nature scene's composition was quite unique. Dark.

"I can't thank you enough for transferring . . ."

But Rafe wasn't listening any longer. He snatched up the crime-scene photo. The one on the wall in Tate's office. He held the snapshot close to his face, studying the framed photograph that hid Tate's safe.

His gaze danced to the picture hanging on the motel room wall. Back to the photograph. Back to the picture. Back to the photograph.

"Rafe? Are you still there, buddy?"

"I'll have to call you back." He shut his phone and let it drop from his fingers.

Could it be?

The picture. The photograph.

Yes, he was positive. No mistaking the dark tone. The unique contrast. The play of natural light.

Bella Miller had taken the framed picture hanging in Daniel Tate's office.

⚖

"Do you think it's likely the SAC was involved?" Hayden asked.

Chewing her bottom lip, Bella curled her feet under her on the couch. "If he wasn't involved, he had to at least be aware." That fact broke her heart. Alphonse Jackson, while reserved and cautious, had always impressed her as a man of integrity. A man of honor. To find out he had anything to do with Daniel's death . . . Well, it turned her stomach.

Hayden shifted on the couch to stare at her. He studied her for a moment before replying. "Is it possible he wasn't aware?"

As much as she'd like that to be so, she just couldn't see it. "Hartlock's the ASAC. I don't see how he could act independently of Jackson." Alphonse was many things, to be sure, but stupid wasn't one of them.

"I think you need to talk to Rafe Baxter. I think you can trust him."

Cold wound its tentacles around her chest. "I can't. I don't know how deep and wide this corruption runs. That would put my life in danger. And yours now, Hayden. They already assume you're protecting me." Now she had put her best friend, the man she loved like a brother, in the crosshairs of corrupt FBI agents who'd already resorted to murder to keep their secrets safe.

"I trust him."

"With your life?" She shivered.

"Yes." He grabbed the afghan from the back of the couch and wrapped it over her lap. "Think about it, Bella. If he was in on it, he would know you're Remington. And if he knew for fact you were Remington, he'd have already acted. Sound logical?"

"Yeah." But she didn't want to be logical. What if she put her trust in the wrong people and Hayden or Ardy or Emily got hurt? Once upon a time she'd trusted Hartlock and Devane, and look what happened to Daniel.

"And he's perfect to talk to. He's new to that office, so he doesn't have any loyalties to anyone there. Matter-of-fact, they treat him as an outsider."

She narrowed her eyes. "How do you know that?"

"He told me."

"You've gotten awful chummy with him. Do you think that's wise?"

Hayden straightened. "Are you kidding me?"

"I'm just saying . . . maybe he's in cahoots with Hartlock and Devane and his assignment was to befriend you to get closer to me, to the truth. Now that he's pretty certain who I am, he called in reinforcers. Namely, Hartlock, to do his dirty work." Like put a big, fat bullet in her head.

Face paling, Hayden stilled. "That could be. I did think it odd that he shared the case notes with me." He shook his head. "And that would explain his interest in you. How could I have misread him?"

Her pulse spiked. "What do you mean his *interest* in me?" She hadn't been able to avoid noticing his mere *presence* when he was in a room. The intensity of his eyes. The smell of his cologne. His intelligence. His easy smile. His muscular frame . . . No, she would not go there. Not now and not with an FBI agent, for pity's sakes.

"I can't believe I didn't think of this. I thought he was interested in you. Like a man to a woman." Still wearing a grave expression, Hayden inched to the edge of the couch. "I even thought it comical that he seemed attracted to the woman he sought in relation to his case."

Hayden thought Rafe was attracted to her? She licked her lips and sat up too. "Wait a minute. Let's talk about this. What made you think he was attracted to me?"

Her head felt as if someone had shoved wads of cotton between her ears. Every time she'd been around Rafe she had felt strange things. She'd chucked it up to nervousness that he'd figure out who she was. What if she'd been wrong? What if she felt like she did because—oh-my-stars—she was attracted to him?

"Just the way he looks at you, like he's trying to get inside your head. How he says your name . . . softer than his regular tone." He smiled. "The way he seems to be overly cautious around you. Almost like he's scared to scare you off."

Her tongue refused to obey. Words wouldn't form. This was bad, very bad. If she was attracted to him, and he to her . . . this could not end well. There would only be heartbreak because no matter how attracted they were, *they* could never be.

"I was actually a little jealous. That you might find him attractive and things would advance, and I'd lose my best friend."

She smiled. "Hay, you're always going to be my best friend. No matter what."

He slumped back against the couch. "I can't believe I misread him. I'd been so sure."

Rafe Baxter was a handsome man. Strong. Determined. For a moment Bella allowed herself to wonder what it would be like to be in his arms. To have him look at her with passion.

"I'm sorry." Hayden snapped her back to reality. "But what if we could trust him?"

"What?"

"If we could trust Rafe, would you tell him the truth? Let him help you?"

Could she allow herself to be so vulnerable? Put her life and the lives of those she loved at risk? She didn't know.

"Bella?"

"I honestly don't know. It would be hard to trust anyone with that badge."

"Fair enough. But I do think we should figure out which side he's leaning toward on the fence he's straddling."

"How do you intend to do that?"

Hayden shrugged. "Not a clue."

She didn't have another plan, and despite her confusion over Rafe, she didn't have many options left. Not that would keep

Hayden and his family safe. "Why can't I just run?" But she lacked conviction even as she said the words.

He didn't buy it either. "You know you can't. Isn't it time that somebody pay for killing Daniel?"

Her stomach tightened as if she'd been punched.

"Look, we'll figure this out together. You'll stay safe."

Physically, perhaps. But what about her heart? Would it remain unscathed?

Chapter Twenty-One

"Don't go around saying the world owes you a living.
The world owes you nothing. It was here first."
MARK TWAIN

"Thanks for letting me come by, Bella." Emily hung her jacket on one of the coat hooks in the entryway.

"No problem." Bella nodded toward the kitchen. "I was just about to put on a fresh pot of coffee. If you'll excuse me." She winked at Hayden, then left.

He motioned his sister into the living room. "So, what's this about?" He couldn't help but be wary.

She perched on the arm of the couch and licked her lips. "Marshall."

Great. Now what? "Okay. What about Marshall?"

"He's jockeying for your job." Her eyes were wide as she blinked.

Like he didn't know? "Yes, I'm aware."

Her bottom lip quivered ever-so-slightly. "No, you don't understand. He said there's one particular councilman who is talking to the others to get them to replace you." Her eyes filled with tears. "I'm so sorry, Hayden. I was mad at you because you were right—Boyd *was* just using me."

Oh no. He recognized the tears for what they were: sympathy grabbers. He uncrossed his legs. "What did you do, Emily?"

Tears streamed down her face. "I didn't mean to do anything that would hurt you. I really didn't."

He clenched his jaw. "Just tell me . . . what did you do?"

"I-I told Marshall you knew I keyed MaryBeth's car and didn't do anything."

He managed not to groan aloud, but it was hard. Very hard. "Why would you say that, Em?"

The tears kept flowing but Hayden wasn't fazed. He'd become immune to his sister's dramatic tactics. "I didn't mean to. It just slipped out."

"How does a lie *just slip out*?"

She dug a tissue out of her purse and dabbed at her eyes, then blew her nose. "He was talking about how he wanted your job and how he'd be so much better at it." She blew her nose again, most unladylike. "I was angry with you because you'd been right about Boyd, so I wanted to get back at you. But I promise, I didn't know he'd call that councilman."

Great. Now Montgomery would have some ammunition on him. Even though it was untrue, there was no way for Hayden to prove that. There was only one way to at least save part of his reputation. "So you did key MaryBeth's car?"

Emily nodded. "I was so angry. Boyd had lied to me . . . led me to believe he was leaving that fat pig to marry me. Then I found out she was pregnant! He'd told me they weren't even sleeping together anymore." New tears made tracks down her face.

"She was . . . is his wife." He straightened. No sense having the old argument. She wouldn't listen and this particular one was a moot point now anyway. "I need you to come to the station with me."

She wadded the tissue into a ball. "Why? Are you going to do something to stop Marshall?"

"I don't think I can untell the lie you told, but I do have a job to do."

"So, what now?" She stood and grabbed her purse. "Do I give a statement or what?" She didn't get it.

"Emily, I have to officially charge you with vandalism."

She froze, shock drying up her tears. "W-what?"

"You vandalized MaryBeth's car. She filed a police report with my office. You just admitted to me that you are the one who did it. I have to charge you."

"You're my brother, Hayden Simpson."

He shook his head. "You'd prefer the lie you told Marshall be true?" He dug in his pocket for his keys. "Sorry, Em, you know better."

"But I'm your sister!"

"As if you care. Emily, you don't respect me or my position." He headed to the door. "You've made that abundantly clear." He stopped in the entryway and shook his key chain. "Bella! Bella!"

She appeared in the walkway. "I'm right here, stop yelling. What's up?"

"I'm taking Em to the station."

Bella met them at the door. "Why?" She glanced at his sister's tear-streaked face and put her arm around Emily, but asked him, "What's wrong?"

Oh, she couldn't feel sorry for Emily. "She told Marshall I knew she'd keyed MaryBeth's car and did nothing. And she *did* key the car. So I'm charging her with the vandalism and am taking her to the station for her statement."

Bella released Emily. "You did what? Oh, Em, how could you?"

Emily lowered her head and pulled the tissue to her face again. Hayden sighed. This poor-pitiful-Emily routine was getting old.

"Look at me." Bella's voice left no mistaking she wasn't playing. "That was a mean and horrid thing you did. You like to use the sister-card to your benefit, but you conveniently forget

Hayden's your brother." She shook her head. "You have no idea how much he does for you. How he goes out of his way to give you the benefit of the doubt. And how do you repay him? Like this?"

"I said I was sorry." She wouldn't even meet Bella's stare.

"Are you, Emily?" Bella put her hands on her hips. "Look at me when I'm talking to you." She sounded so much like his mother it took him aback. Very scary.

Emily raised her head and glared at Bella. "Who do you think you are, talking to me like that?" With her face twisted, she took a step forward, invading Bella's personal space. "You are nobody. Nothing."

"Emily!" He couldn't believe the venom in her voice.

Bella held up her hand. She cocked her head to the side, staring deep into Emily's face. A long moment passed.

Emily took a step back. "What?"

"How long?" Bella's voice was barely audible.

"I don't know what you're talking about." Emily took another step back and turned away from Bella.

"Yes, you do." The sternness was back in Bella's voice, but not the harsh edge. "How long?"

He'd had enough. "What are you talking about?"

Bella stared at Emily, who remained still and silent. She sighed. "Emily's not taking her medication."

"How do you know?" And then he remembered Remington Wyatt was a forensic psychologist. She had training in mental illnesses and could probably detect if a patient had stopped taking such medications. He spun and faced his sister. "Emily!"

She shrugged. "It's no big deal. I'm fine. Don't need that stuff anyway."

"You're bipolar. Not exactly a cold that resolves itself." Bella's hands were fisted on her hips. "If you stop taking your medication, you can mentally nosedive."

How could she have put her health at risk? Hayden nodded to Bella and mouthed the word "thanks" before easing his arm around his sister's shoulders. Emily trembled. "Come on. We'll get this all straightened out."

He opened the door and led her down the stairs to his car. After he secured her in the passenger's seat, he grabbed his cell and called Emily's psychiatrist. If there was ever a time for an emergency weekend appointment, this was it.

⚖️

She couldn't just have appeared from nowhere.

Rafe let his fingers fly over the keyboard of his laptop. He could find nothing on Bella before three years ago. She'd come to Hopewell from Lake Charles, Louisiana. She'd lived at a rental house for six months there and had good bank references and a driver's license. No work record. No credit cards. Nothing.

He took a drink of water, keeping his eyes on the computer screen. No further data available. What exactly did that mean?

And before Lake Charles? Not a single thing. It was as if she'd just appeared as a thirty-two-year-old. No background, no history.

She'd apparently been a photographer before then for Daniel Tate to have had one of her prints framed and in his home office.

He'd used every one of the bureau resources to find some record of her. As a photographer. As a woman. Nothing. She wasn't a member of any of the photography organizations. No record of her having a tax-identification number to sell her work independently. No mention of her in any Louisiana publication.

How could there be nothing on her past? Her childhood or teenage years or even her college days? Surely, something had to be somewhere.

He had a call into the landlady of her rental house in Lake Charles. That was the only thing he had to go on. *If* someone called him back.

His cell phone chirped. He flipped it open. "Baxter."

"Rafe."

He gripped the cell tighter. "Hartlock."

"Listen, Jack and I are going to do a little sightseeing around the area. Maybe grab a real meal, not from the hick diner. Might check out some of the area nightlife offerings."

A long pause. "Uh, okay."

"Just didn't want you to get worried if you tried to catch us at the motel and didn't know where we were."

But didn't want to invite him along. Not that he'd go, but it would've been nice to have had the courtesy extended. "Thanks for letting me know."

"Don't wait up for us, Dad." Hartlock laughed, sounding foreign and very fake. "We'll see you in the morning."

"Okay." He closed the phone and set it on the desk. Hartlock sure was acting oddly. Very odd.

Perhaps their rudeness was more than that. A covert operation, maybe?

Rafe stood and stretched, chuckling at himself. He must have watched too much television lately. He'd never been a conspiracy theorist before. Still grinning, he glanced out the motel room window. Hartlock's car wasn't in the lot.

He opened the door and stepped out, looking up and down the single row of motel-room parking. No sign of the car.

Rafe stepped back inside the motel room and shut the door. Rafe and Devane had already left when they called. And he couldn't figure out why Hartlock had wanted to talk with Bella so badly. Hartlock had almost asked to talk to Simpson as an afterthought. Didn't make sense, and things that didn't make sense bugged Rafe. A lot.

Adding in that he couldn't uncover background information on Bella, and his unease crept higher and higher.

Even an Internet search for a website on Bella had garnered him nothing. Everybody had a website these days, especially when they had something to sell like photograph prints. He couldn't even find a listing for her on the top three social media outlets. These days, that was practically unheard of.

Everything about this reeked: not being able to find out any-thing on Bella, Hartlock's attitude and actions, the gut feeling making his stomach hurt.

He shut his laptop, grabbed his car keys, and headed out of the motel. He had to get out of the room or go insane. Leaves sat lodged at the connection of windshield vent and engine. The wind cut through his pullover, chilling him deeper than he ever remembered.

Rafe slipped behind the steering wheel, put the car in gear, and headed onto Main Street, no particular destination in mind. He passed the diner and didn't see any cars he recognized. He kept on and passed the little grocery store and community center. On the left, he spied Simpson's cruiser parked outside of the police station.

Thought he was off work for the weekend?

Not really considering much of anything, Rafe turned into the police station's lot and parked. What was he doing? He had no business checking up on Simpson. Maybe the man forgot something personal in his office. Maybe he was called in for an emergency issue. Regardless of the reason, it wasn't Rafe's busi-ness. He cranked the car again and reached for the gearshift—

His cell phone's ring startled him. He kept the car in Park and opened his phone. "Baxter."

"This is Mrs. Cox. You left me a message?" The older lady's voice cracked over a nasal wheeze.

"Yes, ma'am. As I stated on your voice mail, I'm Rafe Baxter with the FBI. We're doing a standard investigation on a Bella Miller. She listed you as a reference."

"This is about Bella? You need to speak up, son."

Rafe spoke louder. "I'm with the FBI. Bella Miller listed you as a reference. Can you tell me your experience with her?"

"Yes, she lived here for a couple of months."

He ran his thumbnail against the steering wheel. "And what was your impression, Mrs. Cox?"

"Of Bella?"

"Yes, ma'am."

"A good girl. Nice."

"Do you happen to know where she worked while she lived in your rental house?"

"Work, you say? Bella didn't work."

Rafe gripped the steering wheel. "She didn't work? How did she pay her bills? I mean, do you know?"

"Who did you say you were again, son?" The elderly lady's voice sharpened.

"Rafe Baxter with the FBI."

"Well, you sure don't know diddly, Mr. Baxter."

It was agent but whatever. "What do you mean?"

"Bella didn't have to work."

Color him confused. "She didn't?"

"No, sir. She had plenty of insurance money."

Now he was really confused. "Insurance money?" He hated to sound like a parrot, but this woman's information matched nothing of what he knew of Bella.

"Yes. From the fire."

Fire? Maybe they weren't talking about the same person. "About how old was Bella, Mrs. Cox?"

"Late twenties, early thirties, bless her heart."

Age fit. "What did she look like?"

"She's about the same height as my great-niece. About five six or seven, I guess." The woman coughed, phlegm rattling over the connection. "With light brown hair. Such pretty reddish highlights. And she had the most unusual eyes I've ever seen. Seafoam green."

Definitely the same person. Those eyes were unique. But the fire? "What can you tell me about the fire that Bella received insurance payment from? Anything you can share would be most helpful."

"Well, poor thing, had her house burn down. That's what took his life." The woman coughed again. "And although she never said it, bless her heart, it was so painful for her to talk about, I'm betting she got a life insurance payment as well."

She had totally lost Rafe. Now she wasn't making a lick of sense. "Her house burned down? Did she happen to say where that was?"

"No, I don't believe she did. She just told me she moved to Lake Charles to start totally over. Poor thing, she didn't have but maybe one box of personal stuff she was able to save from the fire." Mrs. Cox coughed. Then again. "She wasn't even able to save a single photograph. It still breaks my heart."

"What did you mean by *took his life*?"

"Well, I'm talking about her husband, of course. Left that poor young woman a widow."

He laid his head on the steering wheel and turned off the engine. Every muscle in his body tensed tighter than a bowstring.

Bella had been married?

Chapter Twenty-Two

"Try not to become a man of success,
but rather try to become a man of value."
ALBERT EINSTEIN

Woof! Woof! Woof!

Bella set down her bowl of popcorn on the coffee table and pushed to standing, careful not to get her feet twisted up in the blanket. The moonless night surrounded her cabin in darkness, pressing in on all sides. Masking. Smothering. She padded across the living room hardwoods, making her way to the back of the house where Chubbers continued to bark and growl. No mistaking his *there's-someone-out-there-Mom* bark.

She made her way down the hallway lit only with the flickering that crept around the corner from the television. Chubbers growled and his nails tapped against her bedroom window. Goose bumps pimpled her arms. Her heartbeat kicked into overdrive.

Entering the bedroom, she kept to the walls, using the shadows as cover. "What is it, boy? What's out there?" she whispered.

The dog barely turned his head. He kept his focus out the large bay window, ears matching his hackles standing at full alert.

Bella dropped to her hands and knees and crawled to join him at the window. The motion-detector security light blazed, throwing shots of light into the bowels of void in the backyard. She laid a hand on the dog's back and followed his line of sight.

Up against the bayou's edge . . . was that someone moving or wind shoving the tree limbs?

Chubbers growled again from deep within his chest. His muscles tightened under Bella's touch.

"What do you see, boy?" she whispered again, keeping her eyes trained into the black night.

Movement. Definitely not a tree. Human. Silhouetted in the shadows.

Bella scrambled on her hands and knees to her bed. She shoved her hand between the mattress and box springs, grabbed the butt of her 9mm, and jerked the handgun into her lap. Quickly she checked the magazine, then slid one into the chamber. Loaded.

Her pulse echoed inside her head. She forced herself to concentrate on her breathing. In. Out. Slow. Steady. In. Out.

This was the moment she'd been dreading for three years. They'd found her and were here to silence her forever.

So much for Hayden's theory about Rafe Baxter. And just when she'd thought . . . no, she should have never let her guard down, even in her own mind. *This* was the reason why.

Hayden!

With a trembling hand, she grabbed the cordless phone from the nightstand. Nothing. No dial tone. No buzzing. Nothing.

She clicked the Off and On button several times. Still nothing.

Her heart jackhammered her chest. The phone line had to have been cut. Stupid her, she'd left her cell in the living room.

Wait a minute. Hayden had left his iPad. It was on the nightstand.

She pulled it onto her lap, turned it on, registered it was connected to her wireless router, then opened the website that would let her text from the Internet. Keeping a tight hold of her gun with one hand, she used the other to type in Hayden's cell phone number and then wrote her frantic message:

Someone is in backyard. Come. Hurry.

She sent the message, then opened Safari to connect with the Hopewell police department.

Chubbers went crazy! He jumped against the window, growling and barking like she had never seen before. He snarled and lunged again, hitting the glass.

Bella dropped the iPad and gripped the gun tight. She dropped flat on her belly and slid across the smooth wood floor toward the window and Chubbers.

An inch, maybe two.

She could practically hear the blood rushing to her brain.

Another inch. Using her legs to propel herself.

Her heartbeat rammed inside her.

A little farther. Pushing herself.

A bead of sweat heated her upper lip. She swiped her upper pajama sleeve against her face.

Socks slid against wood. An inch. Another. Three. Four.

Psing! Psing!

Everything exploded at once. The glass shattered, spilling onto the floor with tings and pings. She ducked and covered her head. Chubbers yelped midbark. A thud sounded just before another spray of bullets.

Psing!

Bullets whizzed over her head so close she could feel the wind. She lifted her head just a fraction and glanced toward the window.

Chubbers lay in a still heap on the floor. Her heart stuttered, then froze. Chubbers? Movement stirred outside.

She couldn't hear anything over the pounding of her own heart and the racing of her pulse. The metallic stench of fear—*her* fear—filled the room and turned her stomach.

No! She would not go down like this.

Bella rolled onto her back, used her heels for traction, and shoved herself toward the window. Grasping the 9mm with both hands, she extended her arms over her head and squeezed the trigger.

She barely felt the recoil as the gunshot filled her ears.

Pop! Pop!

Again she pulled the trigger. And again. And again.

Incoming fire ceased.

She kicked herself beside the still form of her dog. Rolling over, she propped up on her elbows and fired off another shot. And another.

Then nothing but silence.

No gunshots. No movement in the yard. And her dog lay as still as the night was dark. Even her own heartbeat had hushed.

Trembling gone, she reached over and laid a hand across Chubbers's chest. Slow rise and fall. So he was breathing. She withdrew her hand, now wet. Wet? She stared at the red moisture coating her palm.

Her dog had been shot and lay bleeding. Her breath quickened as silent tears burned tracks down her cheeks.

She needed to get help and needed it now. Her entire body shuddered and shook.

Leaves crunched in the yard.

God, if You're still listening, please help me. Please, God.

⚖️

"Thanks for letting me know, Mom. I'm glad to hear Em's safe. Text me her room number so I can call in the morning and check up on her." Hayden finished the phone call and placed the receiver on its base on the corner of his desk.

The night officers ambled up and down the station's halls, the aroma of coffee brewing chased them. Voices, then laughter.

Hayden grabbed the report off the printer, scanned the information, then scrawled his signature across the bottom. With a sigh, he walked it across the main floor and dropped it in the head night officer's box.

Emily had given her official statement and been charged with petty vandalism. She would be held responsible for the damage of MaryBeth's car.

His sister had also been admitted into the hospital. Mental ward.

He cringed at the words but had long ago learned that the term encompassed all patients with varying stages of mental illness: depression, anxiety, dementia, psychotic disorders, and yes, bipolar.

At least at the hospital, his sister was safe and would again be given the medication and proper dosage to help her function as normally as possible with her illness. It was all he could ask for . . . a start.

But the end of a very long day for him. He stretched and headed back to his office. A glance at the clock on his computer told him the diner would already be closed. He'd have to grab a sandwich at home to keep the hunger pains at bay. The tortilla soup Bella and he had made hadn't meant for him to stay up so late.

Pathetic, really, to plan to be in bed before ten on a Saturday night. Maybe Bella was right and he should get out more. He'd never find someone to spend his life with if he didn't bother to look.

He retrieved his cell phone off the charger. The buzz of the intercom startled him. "Hayden, you still back there?" the front desk sergeant's voice filled the room.

Now he'd get pulled into work tonight when he didn't feel like it. Not to mention he wasn't even on duty.

Contract renewal. And because of Emily's stunt, he'd have to do all he could just to keep his job. He turned away from his cell phone and pressed the intercom button on the desk. "Yes. What is it?"

"There's someone here to see you, sir. Says he saw your car and needs to ask you a question."

"Who is it?"

"An FBI agent. Rafe Baxter."

Hayden sighed. "Sure, send him back." He'd already committed a felony by lying to the FBI agents about Bella being sick. Why not just compile his crime?

Lord, help me.

He remained standing until the agent appeared. "Agent Baxter, what can I do for you tonight?"

Rafe smiled and extended his hand. "Sorry for dropping by so late. I was out for a drive when I got some information I needed to run by you. I saw your car was here and took a chance."

Hayden shook his hand and then motioned for him to have a seat. He took his seat behind the desk and leaned back in the chair. He could only pray he looked calm, cool, and collected. "It's been a long day, so what can I help you with?"

"It's about Bella Miller."

Big surprise. "What about her?"

"Do you know anything about her past? Before she showed up here in Hopewell?" Rafe sat on the edge of the chair.

Hayden shook his head. How was he supposed to answer these questions? The truth? He couldn't do that to her. But he could answer based on *Bella*, not Remington. "Not really. I mean, she told me she'd moved to Hopewell to start over in life."

"Do you know why she wanted to start over?"

"No. I asked her once and she implied she had a bad relationship." He shrugged. "Over the years it wasn't important to bring up again." He studied the expression in the agent's face. "Why do you want to know?"

Rafe held up a finger. "I just heard from her landlady in Lake Charles, where she lived prior to Hopewell. Did you know that?"

"Why are you looking into Bella's past at all? She has nothing to do with your case." Maybe she'd been right and he *did* know she was Remington. But if that were true, why hadn't he gone after her yet?

"Actually, she does." Rafe scrutinized Hayden.

Here it came—the facts. Was Hayden prepared to commit another felony in lying to protect his best friend? A lie they'd most likely charge him for?

Lord, what do I say? I need to protect Bella, but I can't lie. Guide my words, God. Please.

The agent leaned forward, his expression one of animation. "One of the photographs of the crime scene reveals a framed print of a nature shot. It was covering Tate's wall safe. I'm positive Bella Miller took that photograph, which means she had to know Tate prior to her moving here."

Hayden forced himself not to react, but how could she have been so careless?

Zuzz!

His cell phone vibrated on the filing cabinet beside the desk, indicating an incoming text message. Hayden waved it off—just Mom texting Emily's hospital room number as he'd requested.

He shrugged at Rafe. "Perhaps not. Maybe Daniel just bought the picture because he liked it. My mother buys art created by artists she's never met all the time."

Rafe leaned back. The old chair creaked against the weight. "Well, I thought it was at least something to look into. You know, following every lead no matter how obscure. So I talked with her landlady in Lake Charles."

If it wasn't in Little Rock, maybe Agent Baxter was going down a rabbit trail. Bella hadn't said anything about Lake Charles.

"A Mrs. Cox. Nice elderly lady. Rented her guest cottage to Bella for almost a year. She remembered Bella quite well. Spoke very highly of her."

That had to be good, right? Where was Rafe going with this? Hayden did his best to look bored. He needed to call Bella and warn her. As soon as he learned everything the FBI knew. "Well, that's nice, I guess."

"It would be except that she called Bella a widow."

Hayden slumped in his chair. "A what?" He hadn't expected that one.

"Widow." Rafe leaned back in his own chair. "As in, had a husband who died." He crossed his arms over his chest. "Apparently, according to Mrs. Cox, he perished in a fire. For which Bella received insurance money for not only the house that burned down, but for her husband's death." He dropped his arms and leaned forward again. "Tell me the truth, Hayden Simpson: Is Bella Miller a widow?"

Wow, Hayden had no idea Bella had such an amazing imagination. What a backstory she'd created. But her story put him in a bad situation now.

"Hayden? Has Bella been married?"

Lord, forgive me for the deliberate mislead. "I honestly don't know. She's never told me, but I've never asked about her past romantic relationships."

"She's your best friend. How could you not?" Rafe wore the most shocked expression. Just wait until he found out Bella was Remington. He'd go through the roof.

Hayden pushed the chair out from the desk. "I guess I assumed it was none of my business. *Correctly* assumed. If Bella wants me to know about her past relationships, she'll tell me." He stood. "Maybe that's what she meant by the fresh start she needed when she moved to Hopewell." He reached for his cell from the filing cabinet.

Rafe stood as well, bewilderment reflecting in his eyes. "Maybe. I still think she'd tell her best friend." The dig was implied—she didn't consider Hayden a close enough friend to tell him about her past.

It was all Hayden could do not to laugh in the agent's face. If Rafe Baxter only knew the enormity of the secret Bella had shared with him. "I don't know. Who can try to understand why women do what they do?"

Rafe chuckled, even if it did sound forced. "There is that."

Speaking of confusing women, he needed to write down Emily's hospital room number. He clicked on the envelope icon on his cell and then selected the Read option.

Hayden had to read the message three times before the meaning sunk in. He broke out into a sweat.

"I've got to get to Bella's right now." He reached for his holster and wrapped the belt around his waist.

"What?" Rafe went still.

"Someone's in her backyard."

And he'd almost bet his badge that it was someone after Remington Wyatt.

Chapter Twenty-Three

*"The fear of death follows the fear of life. A man
who lives fully is prepared to die at any time."*
Mark Twain

Bella made it into the hidden panel she'd built in her
closet before the front door crashed in. She secured the
entry, panting.

Oh-my-stars. This was it. She was going to die.

Her pulse throbbed throughout her body. She steadied her
breathing, forcing herself to relax. She wiped one palm free of
sweat, then the other. Her hands trembled as she gripped the
butt of the 9mm tighter.

Footsteps stomped on the cold, wood floor. In the entry. In
the living room. Scraping and thundering.

She pressed her back against the hidden wall and silently
adjusted herself to the peephole she'd installed.

Thuds . . . thumps—they were tearing up her living room.

Her cell phone chimed from the living room. Her heart
caught in her throat. It chimed again. After a pause, a third time.
Was it Hayden?

Bella shifted slightly, just enough so she could see Chubbers
on the floor. She'd wanted to move her brave dog but couldn't.

There was no space in the tiny hidey-hole she'd created. Undetectable unless you looked at the plans, the two-by-four area was just enough space for her and the bag she kept ready to go.

But her stomach ached so badly at having to leave poor Chubbers out there, dying. Alone. With *them*. Her silent tears continued to fall.

Masculine grunts sounded. More heavy footfalls squashed across the floor, coming from the kitchen and dining areas. Clattering of pots crashing to the floor. The smashing of glass rebounded through the cabin.

She pressed her lips together. Her china hutch? A window? How long could this go on? Why hadn't Hayden responded to her text?

God, I know I've been difficult. I know I've screamed at and turned my back on You. But if You really love me like Scripture says, and You're listening, I really, really need some divine intervention. They're going to kill me.

She let out a slow breath. *Oh, and God, please take care of Chubbers. Please don't let him die because of me.*

"Where is she?" Footsteps thundered down the hall.

Bella bit her bottom lip. Lars Hartlock. She had known it all along. Had told Hayden. And she'd been right.

Her left leg cramped, but she couldn't chance changing position. Not now. They were too close.

The footfalls pounded into the guest room she used as an office. Bangs echoed as furniture overturned . . . scraped against the wall . . . clattered to the floor.

She gritted her teeth. *Hayden, where are you?* Why hadn't the cavalry shown up with sirens squalling and lights flashing?

"Have you found her?" Hartlock asked from just outside her bedroom.

She held her breath.

"No. Not a sign." Devane's emotionless voice found its way down her spine, rendering her unable to breathe.

"She couldn't have gotten out." Hartlock's words were accompanied by footsteps into the bedroom.

Bella concentrated on breathing through her nostrils and stared out the peephole. She adjusted her grip on the gun as Hartlock moved into view, followed by Devane. They wore ski masks, but she knew who they were. Her heart responded by skidding and stuttering.

They approached the blown-out window. Devane squatted beside Chubbers. "We got the dog." He stood and pushed a toe against Chubbers's head. "Some guard dog, huh? He warned her we were out there."

Tears blurred her vision. She should just storm out of her hiding place and blast both men to kingdom come. They'd killed Chubbers, just like they'd killed Daniel. She reached for the handle—

"This is where she was when she returned fire." Hartlock kicked the empty shell casings. They clattered against the wood planks as they rolled. "9mm. She's here—armed and aware. Find her."

Oh, she was armed and aware all right. And tired of running and hiding and lying to people she loved. Tired of losing people she loved.

She wanted her life back. Now was her chance.

Bella reached for the hiding place's handle again. The metal was cold and clammy against her palm.

⚖️

Rafe's gut cinched as he sat in the front seat beside Simpson, racing to Bella Miller's cabin. The strobe light atop the cruiser sliced the darkness of the night. Rafe's heart beat in time to the flashing.

Simpson's call to Bella had gone unanswered. To which he swore was highly unusual.

Simpson's white knuckles were stark against the black of the steering wheel. He flexed, then tightened his grip. Over and over again.

"Surely she gets intruders quite often, right? She's out in the middle of the swamp." Rafe considered Simpson's expression—pure worry.

"It's a bayou, and no."

"It's probably somebody out hunting."

Simpson spared him a glare. "In the dark? Game and Fish frown upon spotlighting down here."

"Right." He was just trying not to panic. "Fishing? Frog hunting?"

Simpson shook his head. "No and no." He gunned the engine. "It's your buddies Hartlock and Devane."

"Whoa! Where'd that come from?" Although, he didn't know where the agents were and they'd been acting suspiciously. "Why would they be in Bella Miller's backyard?"

"Did you tell them about the photograph in Daniel's office? The one you're positive Bella took?"

"No."

Simpson glanced at him before returning his focus to the road. "Why not?"

"I didn't have a chance." Actually, he did, but he hadn't wanted to share with them. He still wasn't quite sure why he had such a strange gut instinct about those two agents. But he'd learned a long time ago not to ignore his instincts.

"Is that the only reason?"

"Where are you going with this? If you have a solid reason for accusing two FBI agents, one of whom is an Assistant Special Agent in Charge, then by all means, tell me." Maybe Simpson had picked up on something he'd missed.

"You've gone over the case. Hartlock and Devane missed my birth announcement." Simpson jerked the wheel. The cruiser flew down the dirt road, dipping and bobbing as potholes pounded at the tires. "I read the notes. Looked to me like they weren't really trying to solve the case."

Rafe didn't think they tried really hard either. "So what are you saying?"

"Why is that? Such a high-profile case . . . why didn't they pull out all the stops to solve it?"

Maybe that was the thing that bugged Rafe the most. "Because there was an attempt on the Arkansas governor right after Tate was murdered. Hartlock and Devane were reassigned to that case."

"And that was solved, I assume?"

"Yeah."

"So why didn't they come back to Daniel's murder and give it their full attention? They didn't, did they?"

No, but—

Simpson turned into Bella's driveway. Her truck sat alone outside the cabin. Hayden jumped from the car, gun and flashlight in hand. Rafe drew his own gun and raced behind the police commissioner.

They charged up the steps to the porch only to find the front door busted in.

No hunter or fisherman could be responsible for this. Rafe's mind tripped over possible scenarios . . . not a single one was good. His insides turned into spaghetti.

He followed Simpson into the house, his service handgun comfortable in his right hand and his flashlight held tight in his left.

In the piercing light from their flashlights, Rafe could make out the chaos of the living room. Couch overturned. Chairs on their sides. Television broken on the floor. Popcorn crunched under his steps.

Not daring to think about what could be waiting for them, Rafe kept on Simpson's back as his cover man and ignored the urge to rush through the house until he found Bella.

Rafe nodded at Simpson's silent direction to check the kitchen. He crossed-stepped into the kitchen, gun in firing position. Pots and pans littered the floor. Ceramic shards coated the counters. But not a sign of an intruder. All clear.

He pushed open the pantry door and flashed his beam of light inside. A creak was the only response. All clear.

A woman's quiet sobbing reached him. His heart jumped in response, and he rushed from the kitchen, down the hall, and into the master bedroom. He skidded to a stop in the doorway and holstered his gun and flashlight, taking in the scene.

The room had a single lamp burning, casting odd shadows on the wall as wind seeped into the room from a hole in the wall where a window had once been. Simpson paced the bedroom with a cell stuck against his ear.

Bella Miller sat on the floor, her dog's head in her lap, with tears streaking down her face as she stroked the dog's head with a trembling hand. She sniffed and wiped her face on her shirt sleeve, then went back to holding a T-shirt on the dog's torso.

Never before had the urge to run to a woman and hold her taken hold of Rafe. He nearly acted on the impulse until she glanced up at him. "What is he doing here?" She barked the question at Simpson but glared at him.

Rafe couldn't remember the last time he'd felt a woman's wrath with just a single look. No mistaking this, Bella Miller would rip his head off if she could.

Simpson slipped his cell into his pocket. "The vet's on his way. So is a crime-scene unit." He squatted in front of her, withdrawing his notebook. "Bella, Agent Baxter was in my office with me when your text came in."

Rafe would have to be stupid to have missed the emphasis Simpson placed on his second sentence to Bella. A world of discussion passed between the two of them as they held a silent conversation in his presence.

It made him uncomfortable. And more than a little jealous. But more than that, it piqued his curiosity. Why did she have such animosity toward him?

"Why don't you tell me what happened?" Simpson asked.

"I was watching a movie in the living room when Chubbers

let me know someone was out back. I came to check it out, then they started shooting at me. They hit him when they shot the window out. Where is that vet?" She kept running her fingers through the dog's fur with one hand and readjusting the bloody shirt on the dog's wound with the other.

"On his way. Then what happened?" Simpson spoke softly.

"I grabbed my gun and fired back."

Feisty. Rafe took in the empty casings scattered over the floor. She did more than just fire back. There were at least five or six rounds spent. She'd meant business. He knelt and inspected the casings. The little lady packed a 9mm. Interesting.

"How many were there?" Hayden asked as he held a pencil over his notebook.

"Two." She was sure. Confident.

"What happened next?"

"Then it got really quiet. I hid in the closet. They busted down the door and I could hear them wrecking the house." Bella sniffled, then she jutted out her chin and squared her shoulders. She kept her hands on the dog. "Why isn't the vet here yet?"

"He's on his way. About the two men . . . did you see them?"

She paused, then nodded. "From the closet."

Rafe clenched and unclenched his fists.

"Can you recognize them?"

"They wore masks."

The cowards. Rafe ground his teeth.

"Okay, Bella, then what?"

"I heard them looking for me, then I heard you coming in."

Hayden finished scribbling on his notebook and slipped it back into his pocket. "The crime scene unit will try to get some forensic evidence. I'll have a unit out back to collect as well."

Bella glared at Rafe. "So, again, why is *he* with you?"

⚖

"He was with me the whole time." Hayden leaned to her until his mouth was at her ear. His breath was hot against her neck. "No way could he have been involved."

Rafe paced, staring at her as if she were a bug under a microscope. She didn't miss the frown he wore, either.

Energy zipped through her, making her muscles tense and bounce. She turned her mouth to Hayden's ear. "It was Hartlock and Devane. I recognized their voices." Again. The memory of hearing them when they shot Daniel sent little tremors throughout her body.

Hayden plopped onto the floor beside her, wrapped his arm around her shoulders, and pulled her into him. "He was with me, not here. I told you, he's one of the good guys."

The agent looked like anything but a good guy at the moment. Dark and brooding, yes. Good guy? No.

"Maybe his assignment was to distract you while Hartlock and Devane took me out." She kept stroking Chubbers's head. The poor dog was unconscious. Probably for the best. If the vet didn't hurry up . . .

Hayden glanced at the agent, then back at her. "Do you really think that?" he whispered.

She shrugged.

Rafe continued to pace and frown.

Sirens shattered the silence.

"Agent Baxter, would you please go meet backup and fill them in on the situation?"

He hesitated, then nodded at Hayden and left the room.

"Where's the stupid vet?" She buried her fingers in Chubbers's thick fur. The T-shirt over his wound was nearly saturated. Her heart broke all over again as she fought against the tears.

"He'll be here as soon as he can." Hayden stood. "Why don't you let me take you to Mom's for the night? She'd love to have you, and I'd feel better knowing you were safe."

And put Ardy in danger? No way. "This is my home. I'm not letting them chase me out." She shook her head, which made her a bit dizzy, but she wouldn't let Hayden know. "They won't run me out of my home again."

"Then I'll camp out on your couch."

"No." She was a big girl, and she would do this on her own. She'd been in charge of her own safety for over three years now, and she'd keep looking out for herself. "I'll be fine by myself."

"Come on . . . don't be so ornery."

She tugged at her sleeves. "I don't need a babysitter." She turned the shirt on Chubbers's wound. "And you shouldn't have brought *him* here. You're getting awfully chummy with the good agent."

"You'll have to make a decision about trusting him sooner rather than later, Bella."

"Why's that?" Her energy waned.

"Because in the crime-scene photos, he recognized the picture on Daniel's wall as one you took."

The picture . . . oh, no. How could she have been so stupid? Her blood went cold.

"So he deduced it was possible you might have known Daniel before you moved here, so he started doing a little digging into your background."

Adrenaline crash was the least of her worries at the moment. She tightened her hold on the dog. "What'd he find out?" she whispered.

Hayden crossed his arms over his chest. "I'd be amused if there hadn't just been an attempt on your life."

"What?" She could grab her bag and just disappear into the night. Hayden wouldn't turn her in. He wouldn't tell them who she was.

"It seems, Ms. Miller, that you are a widow, having lost your husband in a fire."

Oh no. "I had to tell a landlady that so she'd rent me a cottage."

"And apparently, she remembers you quite well. Poor, young widow, living off insurance money."

This was too much at the moment. Suddenly, just lifting her hand to stroke Chubbers's head took more energy than she had. "Help me up."

Hayden gave her his hand, then jerked her to her feet. She wobbled until he wrapped his arm around her waist, steadying her. "You okay?"

"Yeah." She planted her feet and held on to Hayden's arm until she didn't feel quite so dizzy. "I can deal with that. How much more did he learn? Did he get anything beyond Lake Charles?"

"I don't know. That's all that he shared with me." Hayden shook his head as voices from the porch rose. "But you need to make up your mind what you're going to do soon."

Shuffling against the floors rang out.

"I think you can trust him," Hayden whispered.

But could she?

Chapter Twenty-Four

*"All I have seen teaches me to trust
the creator for all I have not seen."*
RALPH WALDO EMERSON

Hayden froze. Something must be seriously wrong for Bella to show up at his house on a Sunday morning before eight. He should have ignored her arguments last night that she would be okay at her house alone, but she was one determined woman. She'd even threatened him if he didn't leave.

He practically begged her to go stay with his mom, but she refused. Adamantly. When Bella made up her mind, there was no changing it. She hadn't budged on the issue, assuring both he and Rafe that she had a firearm and knew how to use it. Hard to argue with a woman toting a gun.

The hint of freshly turned dirt carried in the wind. Overcast, the sun hid behind clouds not dark enough to be daunting. He waited on the front porch while Bella parked.

Was it Chubbers? The vet had taken him to his office and performed surgery. Last night the vet said the surgery had been successful. Had Chubbers taken an unexpected turn for the worse?

Bella stepped out of the Jeep and Hayden nearly fell over. She wore a dress. In the three years he'd known her, he had never seen her in a dress. She looked beautiful, but he still found himself speechless as she approached him.

"Good morning." Her voice carried a hint of uncertainty.

"Morning." He nodded at her. "Don't you look pretty. What's the occasion?"

She stopped at the foot of the stairs. "I thought I'd go to church with you this morning, if that's okay."

The boards of the porch became glued to his feet. "Uh, yeah." Every beat of his heart lifted hope into his chest.

She flashed him a crooked smile as she joined him. "I guess you want to know why, huh?"

"If you want to share with the class, yeah." He grinned back at her. Pure joy surged through him. *Oh, God, I pray You've called her back into Your fold.*

She leaned against the stair railing, a tinge of blush decorating her face. "Well, last night, I actually talked to God. A little." She frowned. "Kinda."

He wanted to laugh but settled on a smile. "And because you kinda talked to God, you're going to church?"

Her nose wrinkled. "Is that silly?"

"Not at all." As long as she was open to God's pulling on her heart. "Sounds logical to me."

"Don't think this means I'm not angry with Him anymore. I am. But . . . well, I just thought it'd be a good idea to go to church with you. See if He had something else He wanted to tell me, you know?"

He resisted the impulse to fall on his knees. "Yeah, I know." He nudged her with his shoulder. "Let's head out, then." He pulled the keys from his pocket and nodded toward his Jeep. "Have you checked on Chubbers this morning?"

She followed him to the driveway. "I did. The vet said he had a peaceful night and actually ate a little this morning. I plan to go visit him this afternoon."

"Glad to hear it. Mom and I are going to visit Emily after church. Want to come?" He pressed the button and both door locks clicked.

Bella slipped into the passenger's seat. "I think maybe it'd be better for just you and Ardy for the first visit."

She was probably right. He started the engine and put it in Reverse. He didn't want to do anything to offend Bella right now while going back to church, but he still had a job to do and the crime-scene unit would need direction. "I hate to bring this up, but I need to know if you want me to officially question Hartlock and Devane about last night."

"What good would it do, Hayden? They aren't going to admit anything. It'd be my word against theirs, and I'd have to give a reason to accuse them, which would reveal who I am." She fiddled with the seat belt. "As usual."

"But you can identify them without revealing you're Remington."

"How?" She twisted to face him. "Bella has never met them, so how would I recognize their voices? Remember, they wore masks."

"I forgot." The fact that they were disguised was in the report he'd taken. He just wanted so desperately to help her. "But I can question them unofficially."

"And say what?" She shrugged and played with the seat belt again. "If you do, it will only confirm who I am and open me up to even more trouble."

"Bella, if they were shooting at you last night, they must know who you are already."

"I know," she whispered.

He hated that she was in such danger. He turned into the church parking lot. "I think you should just tell Agent Baxter everything."

"I still don't know if I can trust him." She let out a long breath. "I want to, I really do, but I can't put myself at further risk. Or others I care about." The way her voice trailed off at the end . . .

"You aren't thinking about running again, are you?"

Her silence spoke volumes.

"Bella, you can't keep running from this. They found you. They'll find you again." He parked the Jeep, leaned over, and grabbed her shoulder, turning her slightly to face him. "I won't lose my best friend. We have to figure something out."

She smiled at him, but there was no happiness in her expression. "Maybe I should ask Rafe out and see if he's interested in me, or interested in killing me." She opened the door and slammed it closed.

Great. *Now* she decided to employ that wicked sense of humor of hers.

Well, the roof of the church hadn't come crashing down as she entered, so maybe she was safe.

But Bella almost hyperventilated. It'd been a long, *long* time since she'd darkened the door of any church.

She forced a smile at Hayden who hovered beside her like a guardian. He was such a good friend—sensing her discomfort and never leaving her side. Just what she needed. So many of the townsfolk attended the services, people crowding around her. They meant well, but she needed space. Needed to breathe.

She followed him to the third pew from the front on the right and sat beside him. Her heart clamored as organ music filled the sanctuary. She closed her eyes.

His hand gripped hers and squeezed. Reassurance washed over her. She cut her gaze at him and smiled, then squeezed his hand back.

The choir filled the loft behind the altar. The opening words of a song thundered throughout the church. The song was unfamiliar to her, but it wasn't like any of the praise music from her youth. Upbeat, the tune had people standing and clapping. The congregation lifted their voices to join the choir.

"How great is our God, sing with me. How great is our God, and all will see how great, how great is our God."

Hayden stood and sang. His clear baritone voice rang out clear. It was beautiful.

Chill-bumps crept across Bella's arms. She slowly rose to her feet with the others. She closed her eyes and let herself sway to the music.

The words of the hymn seemed to seep right into her soul, warming and comforting her. A great sense of belonging surrounded her, but she didn't feel pressured or pushed. And her breathing came surprisingly easy.

The last notes of the song hung in the air like the sweet breath of a cherub. She opened her eyes and followed suit with everyone else as they sat.

The preacher took his place behind the podium. He opened with a prayer of thanksgiving. Bella mentally went through the prayer with him. Little sparks of recognition zinged through her as she did.

"Amen." She lifted her head.

Two ladies sang a beautiful version of "Amazing Grace" before the preacher made the weekly announcements. He opened his Bible and began reading from the book of Luke. Chapter 15, to be exact.

The parable of the prodigal son.

She inched to the edge of the pew, a strange sensation settling over her. Although the fall day had turned quite chilly, heat waves rolled over Bella.

"'He was lost and is found.'" The preacher's words emblazed over her heart.

Oh, God, is that me to You? I've been lost and You've found me?

"'You are always with me, and everything I have is yours.'"

Heat scorched her cheeks. Breathing became difficult again, labored and heavy as if a lead weight sat on her chest.

The choir began a new song. Bella stood and rushed down the aisle and out the front door. The cool breeze soothed her burning skin. She gulped in air.

The door clicked behind her.

"Are you okay?" Hayden's hand on her shoulder nearly seared her.

She jumped. "Sorry."

He peered into her face. "Wow, your face is really red. Are you all right?"

"I don't know. I was fine one moment, then couldn't breathe the next." She sucked in more of the chilly air, as if it could cool the burning inside her.

"Let me take you home." He took hold of her elbow and led her to the Jeep.

She let him lead her. "My truck's at your place, silly."

"Well, then we'll see how you're feeling once we get to my house." He opened the passenger's door and helped her inside.

The cabin of the Jeep was comfortingly cold. Hayden opened the driver's door. "I'll get the heat on in a second."

"Please don't. The cold feels good."

He narrowed his eyes at her. "Do you have a fever?" He reached his palm toward her forehead.

She gently slapped it away. "Stop mothering me." She laughed. "I don't know what's going on with me."

He backed out of the parking space and steered toward the main road. "I'm worried about you. There's a lot going on right now. Hey, did you get a flu shot this year?"

She laid her head back against the seat. "Stop being a nervous nilly. I'm fine. Just stressed."

"I'm sure." The blinker ticked as he waited to turn. "So, how did you like the service?"

Opening one eye to peer at him, she grinned. "It was fine. I liked the music."

"I found it interesting the sermon's subject today was on the prodigal son."

"I'm sure you did."

"Didn't you find it . . . ironic?"

She let out a long breath and turned her head to look out the window. "I suppose it was ironic." Or that God had as wicked a sense of humor as she did. "Or pure coincidence."

Hayden shook his head. "You know I don't believe in coincidence. Everything has a reason."

Despite having heard him make the statement many times in the past, this time rubbed her wrong. She sat upright and crossed her arms over her chest. "Tell me the reason why my mother died. Why my father died. Why Daniel was shot by two FBI agents who've gotten away with his murder and are now here to kill me. Give me a reason for any of that."

"Bella, come—"

"No, I really want to know. Give me one good reason." She gripped her upper arms until they hurt.

"I never said we'd know the reasons. I just said there was a reason for everything. We may never know the reason why some things happen."

"That's nothing but a platitude. I'm tired of hearing excuses."

"I don't know, Bella. All I do know is I believe with everything I am that there are reasons—good ones—for why everything happens."

"And you're okay with not knowing? Just accepting?"

He nodded. "I am."

"And that's where I'm not." She undid her seat belt as soon as Hayden pulled into his driveway. "Thanks for letting me go. I'm feeling better now." She jumped from the Jeep and made strides toward her truck.

"Bella, wait." Hayden was beside her in a flash.

Stupid shoes—the heels sunk in the gravel, preventing her quick getaway. "I'm okay, Hayden."

"Wait a second. I don't want you to leave angry."

She stopped and smiled, resting her palm against his cheek. "I'm not angry with you. I'm just angry and need to work it out on my own." She planted a soft kiss on his jaw. "Okay?"

"Are you sure you don't want to stay at Mom's? Or I'm more than happy to crash on your couch."

"I said I'm fine. It's broad daylight. Let it be."

He studied her for a moment. "All right, but call me later." He planted a kiss on the top of her head. "And drive carefully."

She chuckled as he opened her truck door. "Yes, Dad."

"Brat."

She pulled the door shut and turned the engine over. If she hurried, she could pick up a quick lunch at the diner before the church crowd swarmed.

Once again she was overwhelmed with gratitude for Hayden's friendship. She would not put him or his mother or his sister in harm's way.

Period.

⚖️

Rafe waited until Devane had finished eating before he motioned the waitress for the check.

"And that little bar just outside of town, what was it called, Jack? The Gator's Gap or something? Anyway, it was a real hoot." Hartlock took a swig of his coffee. "We had a good time, didn't we, Jack?"

Devane nodded.

The waitress dropped off the check. Hartlock snatched it away with a grin. "Remember, my expense account is already set up."

Why was the man being so overtly friendly? Chattering almost too much. It sent warnings off all over Rafe. Like he was establishing an alibi for last night.

Rafe smiled across the table to the ASAC. "Gator's Gap, huh? Never heard of it."

Hartlock's smile looked more like the baring of teeth. "Probably because it's a bar. You religious types don't hang out in them very often, right?"

Which was probably why they'd chosen that exact place. "I've been known to visit a sports bar or two." But not often . . . not since a drunk driver had killed his parents.

"Really?" Hartlock handed his credit card off to the waitress as she rushed by. "Hmm. Didn't know y'all would ever dare to visit such an establishment."

"You don't know very much about Christians, do you? We're normal people, you know. Just saved by the grace of God." Just like Darren had recently reminded him.

Hartlock's eyes widened and he gave a slow nod. "Yeah. Okay." He winked at the waitress as she returned with his card, receipt, and a pen. He scrawled his name and thanked her before standing. "We were out pretty late last night. I think a nap's in order."

Ditching him again. "That's fine. I've got some calls to make, so I'll see you back at the motel later."

"Calls?" Hartlock cocked his head. "On the case?"

Curious? Rafe smiled. "No. Personal ones." He nodded toward the cashier. "I'm going to grab a root beer to take back to the motel with me. The vending machine doesn't carry them. Do you want something?"

"Just a bed and a pillow." Hartlock laughed and clapped Rafe's shoulder. "See you later, then."

Rafe sat on a barstool and waited on the waitress to get a chance to check on him. He eyed the pies sitting under glass. That pecan made his mouth water. Maybe he should get a piece to take back and enjoy with the root beer.

The waitress swept by, taking his to-go order, then rushing on. Townsfolk began filing into the diner. Church must have let out. Several people pressed around the bar area.

Rafe stood, letting a lady have his seat, and moved toward the cash register. The waitress ran up and down the length of the counter, pouring coffee and taking orders.

He smelled the perfume first—just a hint. Rafe froze as he sensed her arrival beside him. The waitress stopped in front of her. "Hey, Bella. Your order's about to come up."

"Thanks." Bella shifted and spied him beside her. She backed up a step and let the smile slip off her face. "Hello, Agent Baxter."

"Miss Miller. How are you today?"

Red dotted her cheeks. "I'm okay. Thank you for asking." The blush crept deeper. "And thank you for helping Hayden last night. I appreciate the boards over the hole in the wall."

"You're most welcome." He tried not to grin too wide. He really made her uncomfortable, and that shouldn't excite him, but it did. Yet he didn't know if her discomfort was due to his being an FBI agent or because she found him as attractive as he found her. He shook his head. "Don't you look pretty?"

Her face flushed as she gestured to her dress. "I had to dress up for church." Her forehead wrinkled into a frown.

"Well, you look really nice." His thoughts were discombobulated. "How's your dog?"

"Doing well. Vet said he rested comfortably through the night. I should be able to bring him home Wednesday or Thursday." She smiled, and it held no hint of anything other than her happiness.

Perhaps he should ask her about being a widow. A wait person dropped a tray behind them. Dishes clattered to the floor, breaking.

Bella jumped, then steadied herself against the counter. A busboy appeared with a broom.

No, Rafe decided, he couldn't ask her about being a widow. Not here. Not now.

He gave himself permission to appreciate Bella's long legs shown beneath the hem of her dress. She had killer legs that tapered down to delicate ankles. He swallowed and focused on the waitress approaching him. "Here you go, sir. One slice of pecan pie and one root beer. Sorry for the wait." She handed him a ticket.

He paid the bill and turned to go. "It was nice seeing you, Miss Miller."

She smiled wider, and he nearly fell over backward from the sheer force of her unusual beauty. "You know, there's a pretty good restaurant right outside of town. They're open on Sunday nights." She cleared her throat, the blush coating her entire face.

Heat crept up his own face. "Are you asking me out to dinner, Miss Miller?"

"Y-yes, I suppose I am." She pressed her lips together and avoided eye contact. She rocked a little as she shot glances at him.

"I'd like that." And it didn't even surprise him how much he meant that. "How about I pick you up?"

"Great. Six?"

"I'll see you then." He headed out of the diner, his stomach doing strange things.

He'd walked over from the motel, so he set out on foot, his mind reeling right along with the leaves in the wind. She'd asked him out on a date. It'd been a long time since he'd had a date. And he couldn't remember the last time he was excited about one.

If he was going to be completely honest with himself, he'd admit he was very excited about this date.

Probably more than he should be.

Chapter Twenty-Five

"The only abnormality is the incapacity to love."
ANAIS NIN

"What do you mean, *you failed?*" He twisted the flyer until the glossy paper was no more than an overpriced wad. He tossed it into the trash can beside his desk. His campaign treasurer would have a fit.

"She had a dog that alerted her. She shot at us." The ASAC's voice rose an octave on the last sentence.

"Hartlock, you're an FBI agent. Aren't you trained to dodge bullets?" How dare this moron ruin his afternoon with a report of failure? It was one woman . . . how hard could it be to take care of her?

"Yes, sir. We're just going to have to plan a little more carefully. We won't make this mistake again."

When had the agent turned into a pansy? He didn't remember Hartlock being so meek. Had he mellowed so much as he aged? Or was the enticement of retirement making the agent go soft? Either way, it was unacceptable. He cleared his throat. "You assured me she would be handled this weekend."

"Yes, sir. And everything will be."

He glanced out the window of his study. Leaves swam in the gentle Arkansas breeze. "It's Sunday afternoon, Hartlock. The weekend's almost over." Did the imbecile expect him to take care of everything? He sighed. He'd always been the brains and Hartlock the brawn. And Devane? Well, Devane wasn't much of any use. Never had been.

"Yes, sir. We're working on a plan to conclude everything tonight."

"Very well." What else could he say? "See that it's all handled and call me." If it wasn't, he'd have to hire someone more competent to finish the job. Then take care of Hartlock and Devane, and he'd have yet another loose end to get rid of.

"I will."

He hated loose ends. If these two agents would just do their job, they could retire in peace and he could win the election without fear of exposure. "And Hartlock?"

"Yes, sir?"

"Don't disappoint me again."

⚖

It was official—she'd totally lost her mind.

Bella shifted through hanger after hanger of shirts, discarding most as soon as she held them up to her chest. Some hangers made their way back onto the rod. Others dropped to the closet floor.

Wrong cut. Wrong color. Ugly. Why had she bought that? Too big. Too little. Was there anything in her closet she could wear on her *date* tonight?

What had she been thinking to ask Rafe Baxter out? On a date. She hadn't seriously considered Hayden's suggestion because it was ludicrous. But then she'd seen Baxter in the diner—alone and handsome, and he'd been so helpful and polite last night, despite her rudeness. Hayden's thoughts about him being attracted to her had prompted her to open her mouth without thinking everything through.

She should have her head examined.

Hayden was wrong—the man wasn't attracted to her. He thought her a widow, for pity's sake. Which brought up a whole other mess. What was she going to tell him when he asked her about that?

If she stuck with the widow story, once she gave him a name of her supposedly dearly-departed, it wouldn't take much for him to do a little searching and learn she lied. She'd have to think of something to tell him. Anything but the truth, no matter what Hayden said. She didn't think she could ever trust someone in the FBI. Especially when they hung out with Hartlock and Devane.

So why did she care so much about what she wore?

Bella jerked a royal blue sweater off the hanger, tugged it over her head, and stepped back into her bedroom. She evaluated the outfit in the mirror in the corner. Not bad. The blue brought out her peaches-and-cream skin tone. She groaned. There she went again, thinking she had to care about what she looked like for this *date*.

Turning, she stopped at the plywood sheets covering where the bay window used to be. She would have to remember to call her insurance agent in the morning. She wasn't quite sure if her policy covered damage done by crazy FBI agents trying to kill her. At least Hayden had said he'd rush the police report.

Maybe she should call Rafe and tell him she wasn't feeling well. A relapse of whatever she had on Saturday when he'd shown up on her doorstep with Hartlock and Devane.

Oh no . . . what if he brought those two out this evening?

She leaned against the door frame. Had she really been so stupid?

Her cell chirped. She jumped and snatched her purse off the bed. The phone chirped again while she felt around for it. "Hello."

"Hey, Bella. Whatcha doing?" Hayden sounded more chipper than he had a right to be. His stupid suggestion was what had gotten her into this mess in the first place.

"Planning your demise." She plopped across the bed, staring up at the ceiling fan.

Hayden chuckled. "What'd I do now?"

It was hard to stay angry at Hayden when he was in such a good mood. She grinned to herself. "I have a date tonight."

"How's that my fault?" Surprise lilted his voice. "Wait a minute . . . you have a date?"

She took a moment's pleasure over the fact that she'd shocked him, albeit briefly. "Don't sound so surprised. I mean, sheesh, it's entirely possible I get asked on dates all the time. For all you know, I could be turning down a date every single day."

"Do you?"

"No, but I could."

"Stop avoiding the question, Bella. Who are you going out with tonight?"

She grinned. If only she could see his face right now. "Rafe Baxter."

"W-whhaatt? When? How'd this happen?"

Bella chuckled. "I ran by the diner to grab a sandwich and he was there. I remembered what you said."

"That I think he likes you?"

"Yes. What, are we in junior high again?" She snorted. "Let's just say that after getting shot at last night, I realized you're right."

"I am?"

She laughed. "Yeah, well, don't get used to it."

"What, exactly, am I right about this time?"

"That I need to know if I can trust him. I know for a fact I can't trust Hartlock and Devane. It's time to figure out which side Baxter leans toward—the truth, or the corrupt." It surprised her a bit to realize she actually cared what Rafe Baxter thought.

"Smart idea, if I do say so myself."

"Yeah, whatever." She rolled onto her stomach, propping up on her elbows. "Of course, now I have no idea what I'm going to do about the whole widow thing."

"Well, that's part of why you need to see if you can trust him. Then you could just tell him the truth."

Yeah, well, there was that. But there was also the tightening of her stomach. What if she *could* trust him? How would she feel about him? It would almost be easier for her if Rafe turned out to be as corrupt as Hartlock and Devane.

Almost, but not quite.

⚖️

Rafe checked his reflection again, all the while admonishing himself for acting like a boy with a crush. His heart thundered. He hadn't felt this way since . . .

He ran a hand over his freshly shaven face. He never figured Darren knew how he'd felt about Georgia. He'd been shocked enough to learn she'd known, never once thinking Darren could be aware of his love for her. But love Georgia, Rafe had. With all his heart. And that's why he'd respected Darren's and her marriage. Anyone with eyes could see how the two adored one another.

On the other hand, just seeing them together all the time almost ripped Rafe's heart out. Yet, he'd remained best friends with Darren, allowing salt to be ground into his open, gaping wound constantly.

When she'd led both Darren and him down the winding path of Christianity, he'd realized loving her as he did, wanting her, was wrong. He'd tried to stop loving her. Tried to turn away. He never could. And that ate him up inside.

But Darren's words, his confidence that God understood— could it be he truly was forgiven? Free to move on and fall in love with someone else? Someone like . . .

Bella Miller.

Rafe noticed the time. He grabbed his keys and headed out of the motel room. The evening October air held more chill than he'd expected, and he hadn't even brought a Windbreaker.

He'd cleaned out his car earlier in the afternoon, so the hint of new-car air freshener welcomed him. He set the thermostat to hot and activated the defroster before slipping the car in Reverse. At least it'd be comfortable when Bella got in.

Rafe's pulse spiked as he drove the ten minutes to her house. So close to town, yet so isolated. A log cabin nestled against the bayou wasn't what he'd have imagined her to own, but it fit her. She was very much the nature type: outdoorsy and full of life. The type of woman he found most attractive.

Nerves bunched his muscles as he clamored up the steps of her porch. He took a deep breath before knocking on the door.

It opened with a creak, and she filled the doorway.

Bella left him speechless. Her brown hair with reddish streaks looked as if it'd been kissed by the sun. Her skin still glowed with the fading shades of a tan. No makeup marred her natural beauty. Her welcoming smile warmed him faster than any car heater.

"Hi." She sounded almost as breathless as he felt. She wore a bright blue sweater that brought out the blue in her amazing seafoam eyes.

"You look beautiful." The words escaped before he could stop them. Heat marched across his face. He forced a smile.

Pink dotted her cheeks. "Thank you." She turned and grabbed a purse, slinging the strap over her shoulder. "Are you ready?"

He waited while she locked the door, then motioned for her to precede him down the porch steps. "How's your dog?"

"Good. The vet says he'll recover without any permanent damage."

He opened the passenger door for her. "That's good." She didn't realize how important having the dog was to her safety.

Had the dog not alerted her to the men in the backyard last night
. . . well, the situation could've had a much different outcome.

And she could have been hurt or worse. That thought turned
his blood to ice.

Rafe shut the door behind her, then went to the driver's side
and slipped behind the steering wheel. He cranked the engine,
then looked at Bella. He couldn't help noticing how perfect she
looked in his car. "Um, you'll have to give me directions."

She smiled and rattled off a quick route that would take him
right outside city limits. He'd passed the restaurant she named
on his way into town. A steak house. His stomach rumbled. Not
that he hadn't enjoyed the diner's plate specials, but the thought
of a thick porterhouse made his mouth water.

"So, how long have you been in the FBI?" She shifted in her
seat to better face him.

"Just a little more than ten years." But some days, it felt like
so much longer than a decade. Some cases just wore him out,
wore him down.

"What made you want to become an agent?"

He glanced at her face, gauging her interest. Her eyes
were wide and alert, her eyebrows slightly raised. "My parents
were stateside missionaries. They were all about defending the
rights of those who couldn't defend themselves." He shrugged,
pleased that talking about his parents didn't rip his chest out any
longer. "I guess their moral code rubbed off on me."

She smiled. "They must be very proud of you."

His chest squeezed. "They're dead now."

"Oh, I'm so sorry." Her eyes widened more, and her lips
parted slightly.

"Thanks." He swallowed down the lump caught in his
throat. "They were hit by a drunk driver years ago." Which was
why the jerk was up for parole. He'd served half his sentence
already. Funny it didn't seem so long ago.

The ache in Rafe still threatened to suffocate him at times.

She licked her lips as an uncomfortable silence filled the air.

He probably shouldn't have discussed something so depressing on the first fifteen minutes of their date.

"I know how much it hurts to lose someone you love." She reached over and squeezed his hand. "The ache lessens over time, but it never goes all the way away."

Her husband?

Even Rafe knew discussing a dead spouse was inappropriate etiquette on a first date. Yet he wanted to know everything about Bella Miller, even about the man who'd stolen her heart. He wanted to know what made her tick . . . what she loved . . . .what grabbed her.

He turned into the parking lot of the restaurant. She withdrew her hand from his and reached for the purse she'd set on the floorboard. He pulled the car under the awning and rushed to the passenger side, but the valet had already opened her door. He handed his keys to the valet, then escorted her inside.

Just the simple touch of his hand to the small of her back sent sparks of electricity up his arm.

The enticing aroma of sizzling onions and beef slammed against him as soon as they entered the restaurant. Rafe's stomach surged. The hostess sat them at a table off in a corner. The candle on the table flickered, casting intimate shadows on the walls.

Almost immediately a wait person brought a basket of bread and two glasses of water, then whisked away as if he'd never been there. Very unobtrusive.

He cleared his throat. "Would you like me to bless the food, or do you prefer to do the honors?"

Her face scrunched as she shook her head. "You go ahead."

He stuttered for a moment, then bowed his head. "Father God, we thank You for the food we're about to receive and ask that You use it for the nourishment of our body and our bodies to Your service. In Jesus' name we pray, amen."

Rafe opened his eyes to find Bella studying him, an odd expression darkening her beautiful face. Did he say something wrong? Maybe she prayed in a certain way or something? She'd told him earlier that she'd been to church, so she was surely a Christian. He'd have to find out for certain.

They perused the menus and almost as soon as they'd made their selections, the waiter appeared, introduced himself, then took their orders before rushing away.

She smiled at Rafe as she grabbed a roll and spread butter on the inside. "Do you have any brothers or sisters?"

He returned the grin. "Two younger sisters: Maddie and Riley."

"Your face just lit up. Y'all must be very close."

"We are." Warmth spread up from his stomach. "We got even closer after Mom and Dad were killed. The only good thing that came out of the ordeal."

"I'm sorry. I keep bringing up painful things for you."

Rafe sensed a wall bricking up. "No, don't be. I'm fine. I like talking with you."

"What do your sisters do?" She took a bite of the bread.

"Well, Maddie is an animal cruelty investigator."

"That's interesting." She leaned closer. "How does that work?"

"She's a freelance investigator. When the local ASPCA gets a complaint or the police department, Maddie's called in to go check things out. If she finds an animal that's been abused, she gets law enforcement to step in."

"That's really interesting."

He grinned as he took a sip of water. "She likes it."

"And your other sister—Riley?"

"The baby. Spoiled rotten." He couldn't help widening his grin. "Riley's a reporter."

"As in news reporter?"

"As in aspires-to-be-Diane-Sawyer reporter."

Bella matched his grin before snagging another roll. "Ah, an investigative journalist?"

Riley would like that. "Yeah, I guess so."

"Is she any good? As a reporter?"

He shrugged. "She's covered a couple of stories in the local papers. Seems to be making a name for herself."

The waiter appeared with their salads, served, grated fresh Parmesan over the chilled china bowls, and then disappeared.

They enjoyed the salad, then Bella pushed her empty bowl to the side. "So, you've been with the FBI for over a decade. Do you enjoy it?"

"For the most part." That was the honest truth. "Like when we solve a kidnapping case and reunite a child with the parents, it's a pleasure to do my job. Or when we solve a case that's been heart wrenching for a family and can help bring them closure, it's worth it."

"What about your partner?" She took a sip of water. "The FBI utilizes partners, don't they?"

"We do, but I just got transferred to the Little Rock office. I haven't been assigned a partner yet." And he wasn't really all that anxious to get one. No one could compare to Darren, and Rafe didn't look forward to being put in that situation.

She sat up straight and took another sip of water. "Really?"

He chuckled, pleased more than he would admit that she showed such genuine interest in him. "The bureau is doing some restructuring and rebudgeting. They're trying to level out the number of agents per office. The Memphis office was one agent heavy and the Little Rock office was one short."

Her eyes widened. "They transferred you?"

"I volunteered." He struggled to keep the smile in place while the waiter removed the empty bowls.

She picked up the conversation as soon as the waiter left. "Why would you do that? Were you unhappy?"

"Not at all." He took a drink of his water, carefully considering his response. "Most of the team in the Memphis office have been there for a couple of decades. My partner was actually the one who would've been transferred."

"So, why are you in Little Rock?"

"Darren has a daughter, my goddaughter, who has a heart condition. All her doctors are in Memphis."

She blinked once . . . twice, then she smiled so softly, sending his heart to racing. "That's really sweet. You're a good man, Rafe Baxter."

Her words sent waves of heat up the back of his neck and released a swarm of butterflies into his stomach.

The waiter returned with their entrées, but Rafe couldn't stop staring at Bella. Praise from her did some mighty strange things to him.

And he liked it. A lot.

Chapter Twenty-Six

*"Most of the change we think we see in life is due
to truths being in and out of favor."*

ROBERT FROST

"So you know all of my ugly history now . . . what about you?" He sliced into his humongous steak.

Bella stared at Rafe. She'd hoped to pick his brain while offering up no intel on herself but knew that was nearly impossible. She still hadn't a clue how much to tell him but found herself inclined to trust him. "Well, I've passed thirty, my parents died when I was a child, and I have no siblings." All true.

"I'm sorry." He was so sweet and sincere. And handsome as all get-out, as Ardy would say.

"Don't be." She grinned and shook pepper on her pasta. "You know, we'll have to stop apologizing to each other all the time." She took a bite, which melted in her mouth. The alfredo sauce was perfect: creamy, savory, blended to the ideal consistency.

"Sounds like a plan to me." His smile sent heat to her toes. "Tell me the rest of the Bella Miller story."

He was such a charmer as he slipped a bite into his mouth. She'd have to be careful not to spill everything when he flashed that killer smile. "I like being outdoors, love my friends and my dog, enjoy reading mysteries with humor, and love watching movies." She winked, enjoying the flirting. "How's that for my singles ad?" It'd been so long since she'd flirted with any man . . . sadly, so long that she couldn't even remember the last time.

That smile of his should come with a warning to all women on the planet.

"I like long walks on the beach and want world peace." He spoke in a falsetto, then chuckled. "Seriously, I do like walks and hikes, my friends and family, and watching movies. Reading?" He grimaced as he wiped his mouth with the linen napkin. "Not so much."

"How can you not love reading? It's wonderful. An excursion, an adventure . . . an escape from reality." She adored reading and had a hard time grasping anyone not loving it.

"An escape from reality, huh?" He grinned around his fork.

"Hey, we all need them from time to time." So many of her favorite novels had been what kept her going as she ran. Sometimes those familiar characters were her only friends. Time to change the subject. "So, have you ever been married?"

"Nope. Not even close." His eyes turned darker. "How about you?"

Here she was—at the crossroads. Should she trust him? Could she? As charming and handsome as he was, she just wasn't sure.

"Well, no. I've never even been close." She leaned forward and lowered her voice. "But I've told someone I'd been married so I could get a perfect rental house."

His brows formed a single unibrow. "What do you mean?"

"I found a perfect rental cottage from an elderly widow. She didn't really want a single person living right behind her house for fear of parties and such. So I lied and said I was a widow so she wouldn't turn down my application." It was the truth. Kinda. "Does that make me a horrible person?" She swallowed the last bite of pasta, relishing the taste.

"That doesn't make you a horrible person." He swiped his mouth with a napkin. "So, what do you do? For a living, I mean?"

A ton of bricks landed on her chest. They'd been getting along so well—she'd been inching toward opening up to him and telling him everything. And now . . . he was going to play dumb, was he? Well, two could play that game. She was, after all, on this date for one reason—to find out if she could trust him. She had no business thinking or feeling anything outside of her goal.

She gritted her teeth. "You don't know?"

He hesitated. Took a quick breath. Then smiled. "Well, I *am* an FBI agent, trained to detect things. You're a photographer."

She laid her fork and knife across her plate, keeping her expression as well as her tone neutral. "Then why did you ask?"

His charming smile abandoned him, but a hint of a blush spread across his cheeks. "I guess I wanted to know your story. What drew you to become a photographer . . . what you like to photograph . . . things like that."

"Oh." Quick on his feet, she'd have to give him that. Or was he being honest? She couldn't tell. "I've always looked at the world a bit differently. I see things in an alternate light than most people, I suppose." She pushed her plate forward and took a sip of water. "I just capture with the camera what I see, the way I see things."

"You take beautiful photographs. While stills, the sense of movement in the pictures grab you."

"Thanks. That's the goal." Speaking of . . . her focus shifted back to the task at hand. *Let's see if you'll lie to me.* Turnabout was fair play. "You've seen my work?"

He nodded. "At the motel."

"Ah. I forgot about those. That series is titled 'Changes.' It was one of my favorites." She ran a finger along the lip of the glass. Why not throw open the door wide? See if he crossed the threshold. "Have you seen any others of mine?"

"In Hayden's office."

She smiled. "The bayou ones? That's one of our favorite fishing spots." She'd taken the same shot during different types of weather—raining, sunny, a rare instance of sleet. In each of the pictures, the color scheme was totally different. The end result of the three photos was something she was truly proud of.

"They are beautiful."

The waiter interrupted to whisk away their plates and drop off dessert menus. She perused the offerings, despite being full. Perhaps Hayden was right and Rafe was a good guy and worthy of trust.

"I've seen another print of yours." His voice came out thicker, deeper.

She shut the menu. "Which one?"

"There was one hanging in Daniel Tate's home office." He went still. Studying her. Analyzing her every reaction.

Bella kept her expression in check. He didn't hold back anything. He'd effectively bounced the ball back in her court. While she'd been testing his trustworthiness, had he been testing hers? She took a deep breath. "You're quite sure it was one of mine?"

"Almost positive. I'm no expert, but the way you photograph—dark in composition, dense, but moving—it's a unique style."

"Interesting." What else could she say? He'd picked up on what made her portraits individual, and she couldn't deny the style was her unadvertised trademark.

He frowned. "That's a noncommittal response if I ever heard one." He straightened and crossed his arms over his chest.

She mirrored his movements. "I'm sorry, am I missing something?"

"I also saw one of your photographs hanging in Ardy Simpson's dining room." He paused, scrutinizing her so deeply she had to clench her leg muscles not to flinch. "I saw it when she told me you knew about Daniel Tate being Hayden's father before she told anyone."

Blindsided! She steeled her reaction. Ardy hadn't said a

word about talking with Rafe, so Bella hadn't even a hint of warning. She had no time to prepare an answer, appropriate or otherwise.

"No response to that either, Miss Miller?" His voice had an unfamiliar edge. His tone was colder, sharper, harsher.

The waiter chose that moment to return to the table to take their dessert orders. Bella smiled at him as sweetly as possible. "Nothing for me, thank you." She glanced back at her date. "I've had quite enough."

⚖️

"Where is she?" Lars Hartlock shone the flashlight on his partner and glared.

Jack shrugged. "I don't know. Her truck is still here."

"I thought I told you to watch her and inform me immediately if she left." He kept the beam on Jack's face. "She's not here."

"I said I didn't know. I got here almost two hours ago, just like you told me, and there's been no activity. Nothing. No one's come by, no one's left. Her truck hasn't moved. There hasn't been anything to report to you."

Was Jack really so stupid, or had he just gotten lazier the closer he got to retirement? "Was she in the house when you got here?"

"I didn't exactly walk up to the door and knock, Lars. I really don't know."

He turned off his flashlight. "Well, we'd better figure out where she is and when she's coming home, because we have orders to have this done before tomorrow morning." No way would he admit to failing again. That outcome wouldn't be good for his health.

"I checked the tap we have on Hayden Simpson's cell. Heard him arguing with Bella Miller when she refused to go stay with a friend. She's alone. Even her dog is still at the vet."

Lars kicked the ground with his toe. "Good. Stupid dog. Thought we'd killed it." They should've already killed Remington, like three years ago, but that was beside the point. He would ensure it was handled tonight.

"Apparently not. According to Hayden's phone call with her, the vet said the dog will be able to go home in a few more days."

Another reason to strike tonight. The gods seemed to be smiling down on them, making the path easy. If only he knew where she was.

"Well then, she should be returning." Lars leaned against the tree at the edge of the woods adjacent to the bayou. He nodded toward her cabin. "We'll just wait on her to come back home."

⚖️

He'd blown it but good.

Rafe signed the check, slipped his credit card back into his wallet, and waited for Bella to return. She'd excused herself to the ladies' room a good ten minutes ago, and he hadn't seen sight of her since.

He groaned. He'd pushed her too hard. She'd volunteered about the widow thing with no direct probing. Was it the truth? He didn't know, but Rafe was inclined to give her the benefit of the doubt.

What he did know was he had feelings for Bella Miller. Feelings that had nothing to do with the Daniel Tate case and everything to do with him personally.

And he'd blown any romantic chance he had with her by backing her against a wall on a case she probably had nothing to do with. Yet every bit of evidence pointed to her being involved, or being aware of something, in the case. It infuriated him that he couldn't figure it out. It annoyed him even more that he'd gotten his emotions tangled up with a woman who had anything to do with one of his cases.

Maybe he just had bad luck, period.

Bella appeared beside the table. She didn't bother to sit. Her expression was unreadable. "I think I'd like to go home now. I'm not feeling very well." Her voice came out stiff and her tone stilted.

If he'd been holding out on a slight hope, her cold shoulder killed that. He pushed to his feet. "Okay."

She turned and stomped out of the restaurant. He almost had to speed-walk to keep up. One thing he'd learned well from Maddie and Riley—a woman ticked marches. The smartest thing he could do would be to keep his mouth shut.

He handed the valet ticket to the young man, then stood beside Bella, keeping his trap closed even though he warred between wanting to apologize and wanting to defend himself and wanting to do his job. Raindrops pelted the asphalt.

The valet returned with his car. Before he could open the passenger door for Bella, she jumped inside, slamming the door behind her. He tipped the valet, then got behind the wheel.

An uneasy and heavy silence filled the car's cabin. Only the hum of the engine sounded.

Scenario after scenario rushed through Rafe's mind—none of them with a good outcome for him. Why did this have to be so hard?

The wisdom of keeping his mouth shut lost out to the nervous thrumming of his pulse. "Look, I'm sorry. I didn't mean to imply anything. I'm just stating the facts."

She didn't reply, just stared out the window into the dark night.

"This *is* my job, Bella. I'm not asking you questions to try to make things difficult for you. I'm just trying to solve a case."

She made a muffled sound. Was that a snort?

"Your work being in Tate's home office? Yeah, that could be a coincidence, I suppose." Even though he didn't believe in coincidences. "But Ardy Simpson told me you knew about Tate being Hayden's father." He cut his eyes to her, then back to the road. "And that fact links you directly to my case."

She jerked in the seat to face him. "So you go on a date with me to pump me for information?" Her glare was nothing short of lethal. "That's a real low blow, even for an FBI agent."

Another slight against the bureau—what did she have against them?

"No. I honestly didn't mean to interrogate you on our date. I'd just been working on the case and . . ."

"And what? You thought you would just take advantage of the situation?" She leaned as he took a sharp right. "How do you think that makes me feel? That you would press me for information on your case *on our date.*"

"It isn't like that, Bella." His stomach roiled with the steak he'd enjoyed half an hour ago. "I didn't intend to ask you about the case."

"But you just couldn't help yourself, is that it? The road to hades is paved with good intentions, Rafe Baxter."

Words left him as he steered down her drive. He'd give up on the romantic angle, but he still had an ongoing investigation he was working. "Perhaps I went about this the wrong way, but I do still need an explanation of how you knew about Tate and Hayden." He stopped in front of her house, put the car in Park, and stared at her.

Even in the dimness of her security light on the porch and the orange glow of the dashboard lights, there was no mistaking the fury lining her face. "You know what, Mr. FBI? If you want to interrogate me, I'd suggest you contact me during daylight hours in a professional setting." She opened the door, stomped on the gravel, then slammed the car shut for a second time.

Bella marched up the stairs, shoved a key into the lock, and disappeared without so much as a glance back at him.

Dare he follow her? Bang on the door and apologize? Demand she answer his questions?

Barely a minute passed before the porch lights went out, plunging the bayou into darkness, save for his headlights.

Guess that answered his question. If he stayed on her porch all night, she probably would ignore him.

He sped back to the motel, debating how to best approach her tomorrow. He didn't have a choice—he had to question her and get answers in relation to his case.

Seeing about dating was a whole other problem. Maybe he would call Maddie and get some advice. Scratch that—if his sister thought he was interested in a woman, she'd hound him with questions. He'd do better to call Darren.

Alone in his room he shucked out of the slacks, trading them for jeans, and sat at the desk. He opened his laptop and accessed his e-mail program. Not that he expected anything—he'd been reporting in to the ASAC and, unfortunately, Hartlock was in a room across the motel's parking lot.

He clicked through the spam folder, deleting all twenty-eight pieces of junk mail. If he cashed in all the monies he'd *inherited*, he could retire in style. And take care of all of Savannah's medical bills.

Rafe shook his head and went back to his in-box. He ignored the one from Riley—it'd only be a guilt trip. Then he bypassed the e-mails from two of his hunting buddies because he saw the attachment indicator. Probably showing off pictures of their first bucks of bow season.

He hovered the mouse over the next message as he read the return e-mail address: a.jackson@fbi.gov. He slowly opened the e-mail.

Baxter, ASAC Hartlock will arrive tomorrow morning to assist you in the case. Check with him before going any further.

He double-checked the date the e-mail was sent—this afternoon. Chills drilled into his spine as the enormity of the e-mail hit him. If Hartlock wasn't supposed to show up until Monday, why had he arrived on Friday? What had he and Devane been up to this weekend?

Hartlock's interest in Bella . . . the attack on her house . . .

No, that was ridiculous. Hartlock had never met Bella. This was all confusing. He just had Bella on his brain. Yet . . .

Everything sure seemed coincidental all of a sudden. And Rafe didn't believe in coincidences.

He snatched his keys and cell phone from the desk and shut his laptop. It didn't matter how ticked off Bella Miller was, he was going to get some answers.

And he would get them right now.

Chapter Twenty-Seven

"Keep cool; anger is not an argument."
DANIEL WEBSTER

Stupid, stupid, stupid. Bella repeated the mental bashing she'd been giving herself since she walked in the house, flipping on every light she passed. She'd be glad when Chubbers was home. Something about coming home to an empty house just made her even more depressed than a ruined date.

How could she have been so stupid? Despite his looks and charm, Rafe Baxter was just like the other FBI agents: crooked and untrustworthy.

Well, he wasn't necessarily crooked—at least not that she could prove just yet, but she sure wouldn't trust him with anything as important as her life.

A moment of conscience sidled against her as she acknowledged the main reason she'd gotten him to ask her out was to see if she could trust him.

Guess she'd found that out.

She kicked off her shoes, swapped her pants and sweater for sweats, and shoved her socked feet into her lambskin slippers. All comfy, she should have been in a better mood, but she wasn't.

Still berating herself for almost trusting Rafe, she shuffled down the hall and into the kitchen. So what if it was almost ten o'clock? She needed coffee.

Once she'd set the pot, Bella headed back to the living room and flipped on the television. After reading the online guide, she turned the set back off. Nothing grabbed her interest.

The enticing aroma of fresh brewed java filtered through the house. Just the smell calmed her frayed nerves and took the edge off her anger.

She headed to the kitchen, grabbing her cell from her purse as she passed the entryway. Hayden was going to get an earful tonight. Trust Rafe Baxter?—ha, that was a joke. She'd have to figure out some way to explain what Ardy had told him.

Or she could run again.

Her finger froze over Hayden's number on her cell. If she decided to disappear, it'd be better just to go. Everything in her wanted to stay. Maybe Hayden was right and it was time to get justice for Daniel. He'd waited three years already.

Yes, it was time she took a stand. Right, wrong, or indifferent, she wouldn't run again. She'd stand and fight. Try to stay alive while seeing justice served. And if Rafe Baxter stood in her way with Hartlock and Devane . . . well, she'd just have to deal with her raging feelings for him.

If only he didn't appeal to her so much. If she could ignore the quickening of her traitorous heart every time she saw him. If she could pretend he didn't make her stomach do backflips with that velvety voice of his. If he didn't look at her like he could see into the very depths of her being.

Bella sighed and pressed the button on her cell. Hayden would come over, and they could decide what she was going to do.

Thump! Thump!

The wooden frame around the kitchen window facing the bayou shook.

Whaa—?

In a split second, she registered the sound: bullets hitting her house.

Not again.

Bella dove to the floor behind the island. The cell phone flew out of her hand and clattered across the wood floor. The battery skidded out of sight. Her heart thundered, but she shoved fear aside. On all fours, she crawled to the pantry where she kept her shotgun.

Ping! Ping! Ping!

Those were coming from the side of the house, closer to the guest room than the front door. Whoever was shooting outside, they weren't that great of a shot. Or they were too far away. She hoped for the latter as she slammed two shells into the shotgun. Her hands were steady as she chambered the rounds.

She opened the panel for the breaker box and turned off the main switch. The house plummeted into darkness.

Bella held the shotgun and inched out of the pantry. All of her senses went into overdrive—she could see every shadow cast by the moonlight, hear every snap of a twig broken in the yard, smell even the stench of her own fear. The pounding of her pulse thudded inside her head as she crept forward into the kitchen.

Not another bullet hit. No echo of a gunshot split the eerily silent bayou. Her mouth went as dry as the Spanish moss veiling the cypress trees outside.

She pressed her back against the wall and sidestepped to the living room, darting her focus between staring out the windows into the darkness and listening for any sounds. One step, two step, pause. Listen. Look.

A step. Two. Three. Look. Listen.

Step, again. Again. Again. Was that a shadow in the front yard? She gripped the shotgun tighter. No, only the wind shifting the limbs of an old live oak.

Another step. Two. Listen. Look.

Step. Step. Was that someone stepping on leaves?

Crunch. Snap. Crunch.

Definitely someone creeping around outside.

Bella slumped silently to the floor and scooted into the living room, positioning herself behind the couch. She would use it for cover.

Creak.

The loose bottom stair. She'd been meaning to fix it for months but hadn't gotten around to it. Now she knew someone climbed the porch stairs.

Tap. Tap.

From her bedroom. Someone trying to get in the back door?

Her chest hurt. Every nerve of hers was at attention. Footfalls on the bottom of the staircase pushed her into action. She propped the shotgun against the back of the couch, aiming at the front door.

Her heart pumped blood through its chambers at record speed. The pressure in her eyes thumped in sync with her pounding heart. The only sound she could hear was the blood thudding in her eardrums.

Bam! Bam! Bam!

The one at the front of the house rammed against the door. Her heart faltered as she glimpsed a silhouette of a gun in his hand.

She flinched.

He used a pin-light, affording her a brief glimpse of the man at the front. A sliver of metal clutched in his hand, glistened against the burst of light. His gun shimmered again in the moonlight.

Pinching her eyes shut, Bella willed herself to be strong . . . and her aim to be steady. For Daniel. For herself.

I am come that they might have life.

Her gaze darted around in the darkness. It wasn't his voice she'd just heard. Whose? She shook her head. Her mind had played a trick on her.

I am the good shepherd: the good shepherd giveth his life for the sheep.

She shook her head again. Now she was hearing things. Her mind failed to grasp reality as it unraveled, unnerving her. Couldn't she get a break? Just one?

The image of Hayden tiptoed across her mind. His firmness of faith. As quick as the flicker of light shooting across the room, a steadying calm pressed against her.

God, is that You?

She waited a moment. No one answered. It was official— she'd been scared out of her mind. Her eyes sought the figure at the front door.

I am the door: by me if any man enter in, he shall be saved, and shall go in and out, and find pasture.

She froze, then recognized the lead in her chest. She thought of this morning's sermon—the prodigal son. *She* was the prodigal son. It was time to stop being childish. Stop holding grudges. She'd ignored justice for Daniel, so how could she be mad at God for not intervening against Hartlock and Devane? It was time to return to her Father.

Oh, God, I'm so sorry. I've ignored You, hated You. I'm so, so sorry. Please forgive me.

Pounding at the front door. She steadied the barrel of the shotgun.

More banging from the back of the house. Hartlock and Devane . . . they'd split up, dividing and conquering.

She trembled.

Dear God, help me.

The front door crashed in with a thud.

She fingered the trigger of the shotgun as she took aim.

A boom sounded from her bedroom. Footsteps, running . . . behind her . . . coming to her. "She's got you in sights!"

She squeezed the trigger. Pain covered her left shoulder. Her eyes closed. The warm blanket of darkness wrapped around her.

⚖

Rafe fired another shot at the armed figure on Bella's porch.

This time the silhouette slammed against the door. It turned, then raced into the house. Rafe gave chase, gun and flashlight in position, fairly certain he'd hit him. The gravel slowed him down as he raced to the porch steps. He steadied his footing, then entered the house.

He shone his flashlight into the kitchen. Nothing. Into the living room.

He froze.

Bella lay sprawled on the floor. A shotgun sat beside her. Blood seeped out from under her body.

Rafe's body tensed until he ached.

Training dictated he follow the shooter. He rushed into the master bedroom. He aimed his flashlight just in time to illuminate two figures hitting the woods.

Ignoring his training Rafe rushed back to the living room. He shoved his handgun into his waistband, then knelt beside Bella, surveying her injury as best he could. She'd taken a shot to the left shoulder. He couldn't be sure how bad she'd been hit with just the light from his flashlight.

Oh, God, please help me.

He yanked his cell from his hip and punched in 911. Quickly and concisely, he informed the dispatcher who he was and relayed the situation, adding in the request that Commissioner Simpson be notified immediately. He closed his cell and turned his attention back to Bella.

A metallic smell permeated the room—blood. Bella's blood. His gut clenched, nearly doubling him over. The blood still seeped from her shoulder. He'd taken emergency first aid during training, but it'd been a long time since he'd had to use any medical knowledge. He cast the flashlight's beam around the room. What could he use for pressure to stop the bleeding? There—one of those lace things on the coffee table.

He snatched it from the table, folded it, and then pressed it against the front of her shoulder, where the blood seemed to come from. *Lord, please send help.*

Uncertainty washed over him, lasting for what seemed like forever.

He pulled her into his lap, keeping pressure on her wound with one hand and cradling her head in the crook of his other arm.

Rafe checked her pulse. Strong and steady. Should she be unconscious from a shot in the shoulder? He'd been shot in the gut and never lost consciousness. What if the bullet had gone downward and hit her heart?

No, her pulse wouldn't be so strong if she'd been hit in the heart.

Sirens screeched against the night.

Thank You, God. Get them here quickly. Please.

Blinding lights flashed up the drive. The squall of the sirens was deafening. Rafe welcomed both. *Thank You. Thank You.*

Simpson broke through the doorway first, gun in firing position. "Bella!"

"Here, Simpson." Rafe waved his flashlight toward the door. "She's been hit."

"How bad?" Simpson didn't wait for a response as he spouted directions to the paramedics. He grabbed Rafe and pulled him away as two EMTs rushed to Bella's side.

"I think it's an in-and-out." Rafe stared at her pale face under the artificial lights. He suddenly didn't feel so hot. "I don't know how much blood she lost."

"Get me some lights on in here. Check the breakers—box is in the kitchen pantry." Simpson pulled him to the porch where officers huddled, awaiting instructions. "Tell me what happened."

The cold, fresh air cleared his mind. Rafe sucked it in, then let it out in a rush. "I heard a shotgun blast as I pulled up. From my headlights I saw a figure at the front door. He had a gun. I jumped out of the car and identified myself as an FBI officer, then fired my weapon."

"Did you hit him?"

"I don't know. He ran into the house. I followed. Saw Bella unconscious on the floor. The intruder joined another, and they ran out the back of the house, into the woods." He shivered.

"Did you follow?"

"No. I went back into the living room to evaluate Bella's condition."

The house suddenly flooded with light.

"Bob, you and the others go check out the woods." Simpson nodded at the officers, then led Rafe back inside. "Did you recognize them?"

He shook his head, his gut burning while his body felt like it'd been dunked in ice water. "I didn't get a good look."

"Can you recall anything about them? Something?" Desperation clung to Simpson's voice. "Anything?"

Rafe searched his memory. There was something vaguely familiar about the figure at the door, but he couldn't place what. "I'm sorry, I can't."

"Excuse us." The paramedics rolled the stretcher to the front door. Bella lay still, but she had color in her face, even if her lips were still paler than normal.

"How bad?" Simpson asked.

"It's a clean one, Commissioner. Nothing major was hit that we can tell—no organs, no tissue damage."

"Then why was she unconscious?"

"Shock. Fainted. She'll be fine."

"Hayden," she whispered, opening her eyes and holding out her hand.

"Hey, you." He leaned over and took her hand. "Felt like you needed a little excitement in your life?"

She probably wasn't in the mood to see Rafe right now, so he took a step back, out of her line of vision.

She gave the police commissioner a weak grin, then grimaced. "Don't make me laugh. It hurts."

Simpson planted a kiss on her forehead, and Rafe had to clench his hands not to push him away from her.

"Hay, it was them." Her voice was weak but firm.

"Are you positive? Did you see them?"

"I'm sure. I saw him at the front door. It was Devane. And he doesn't do a thing without Hartlock."

Rafe froze, sure he'd misheard her. He took a step forward, standing right behind Simpson.

Bella's gaze drew to him. Her eyes widened and fear danced in them. She looked back at Simpson. "Oh-my-stars. Why is *he* here?"

Chapter Twenty-Eight

"We are punished by our sins, not for them."

ELBERT HUBBARD

"You got hit!" Lars closed the motel room's drapes, his focus on Jack's forearm. A stain of red grew into a large circle.

Jack shucked off his coat and sweatshirt. The outer edge of his skin was gone, as if something had rubbed off the top layer. Something had: a bullet. A bullet fired by a fellow agent.

"Let me look at it." Lars removed his coat as well and reached for his partner's arm. He inspected the area. "Just a graze. Nothing more." He let out a sigh. "A bandage will cover it all."

"Stings like the dickens." Jack wobbled on his feet.

Lars grabbed the chair from the front table and moved it beside the lavatory. He eased Jack to sitting. "Once I get it cleaned up, you'll be good as new." They couldn't stand for Jack to get an infection. That would prompt questions they couldn't answer.

"I can't believe Rafe shot me."

"He didn't know it was you, thank goodness. I'm just grateful he was far enough away that he couldn't get a kill shot on you, buddy." Lars cringed to think how he'd have cleaned up *that* mess.

"I saw her go down. Good shot, Lars."

"Yeah, but I don't know how accurate I was. Everything happened so fast." He saw her take aim at Jack, yelled . . . she shifted at the same time he fired . . . Rafe shot at the same time, clipping Jack. And then they'd run.

Rafe hadn't followed them. He defied the standard bureau training and had not given chase. It was a rookie mistake, but Baxter was no rookie. Why hadn't he come after them? Had he recognized Jack? No, if he'd recognized him, he wouldn't have shot him. Or would he?

Lars finished cleaning the glorified brush burn, added a good slathering of antibiotic cream, then covered the wound with a sterile bandage. He shook two ibuprofen tablets out for Jack, then handed him a glass of tap water. "Take this. It'll help with the soreness."

Jack did as told, as always. He made his way to his bed and sprawled on his back. "You can't imagine how much this stings."

Lars gritted his teeth to keep the retort sitting on the tip of his tongue from being spoken. He'd been shot—really shot, where he had to have surgery—and hadn't complained about the pain once. That was what made him strong. Made him an asset.

Like his ability to follow orders. He'd been well compensated over the years to *advise* witnesses in certain cases. The special team's conviction rate sat at the all-time highest ever: 98.7 percent. Now that the boss was poised to win the election, the benefits would continue to flow down.

As long as Remington Wyatt didn't resurface.

Lars knew he'd hit her. He'd seen her slump to the floor. But where had he shot her? He'd been aiming for the heart, but he had to yell at Jack.

Rafe would know. Lars needed to find out how much the new agent knew already. It was highly possible that he was as dangerous as Remington "Bella Miller" Wyatt. Even more, potentially.

And if he was . . . well, that was bad luck for Rafe Baxter. But first Lars needed to know if he'd taken care of Remington for good.

⚖️

He had to have heard her wrong. "Did she say she recognized the man at the front door as Jack Devane? As in, FBI Agent Devane?" Rafe still couldn't believe it. None of it made any sense. He either had to have heard wrong, or she'd been mistaken.

Simpson shot him an incredulous look, shook his head, then motioned for one of the officers. "Bob, please get someone to the hospital pronto. I want a guard outside of Bella Miller's room at all times. No one outside of medical staff and me is allowed in her room." He glanced at Rafe. "No one, no matter what kind of badge he flashes. Understood?"

"Yes, sir." The man turned and hustled to a cruiser.

Rafe crossed his arms. "I don't understand—"

Simpson held up a hand. "I'll talk with you in a minute. For now, just hang tight." He turned and directed various teams.

The crime-scene unit arrived, following the directions of the commissioner as some entered the home while others tromped about in the back.

An officer hesitated mere steps away from Simpson. He spied the man and waved him forward. "What is it?"

"Sir, we found one shoe print in the dirt, but the wind is working against us."

"Get the CSU on it immediately."

"Yes, sir."

Simpson turned back to Rafe. "Are you positive you hit the man at the front door?"

"I'm not 100 percent sure, but I think so. He jerked like he'd been hit."

Simpson lifted a radio to his mouth. "Bob, at the hospital, check out the emergency room for anyone with a gunshot wound."

Static crackled over the electronic device. "Yes, sir. Arriving now, just behind the ambulance."

"Copy that." He glared at Rafe.

"What?" Rafe didn't like the man's attitude toward him. "I don't understand."

"Come with me." Simpson led the way outside and to his cruiser. He pointed at the passenger side as he sat behind the steering wheel.

Rafe shut the door behind him. "Why don't you tell me what's going on?"

"I'll ask the questions here. This is my crime scene. It's not your jurisdiction." Simpson's face was stone.

The man was worried about Bella, that had to be why he came across so brazen to a federal officer. Rafe would let it slide . . . this time. He gave a curt nod.

"What were you doing here tonight?"

Rafe stared out into the darkness.

"Agent Baxter, I asked why you were here. I expect an answer."

He glared at Simpson. "I'd been on a date with Bella and we had a . . . miscommunication. I came back to try to straighten it out."

"What was this *miscommunication* regarding?"

He liked Simpson, he really did. Respected the local lawman. But Simpson's probing wasn't endearing him to Rafe.

"Agent Baxter, I would strongly advise you to answer my questions now, or we'll go to the station and you can call some uppity lawyer to be present for your questioning."

"You do remember I'm a federal officer, yes?"

The muscles in Simpson's jaw tightened. "I remember, but you were the first to arrive on a crime scene in which a woman was shot." He rested his hand on the butt of his handgun. "And

I'm beginning to wonder why you're refusing to answer simple questions regarding your presence at my crime scene."

Rafe checked his anger. If the tables were turned, he'd be the same way. He let out a long breath. "Bella thought I'd used our date to pump her for information about the Tate case."

"Did you?"

"Kind of. It wasn't my intention per se, but the topic came up and I asked the questions. She got mad and demanded I take her home. I did. She didn't give me a chance to apologize or explain when we got here. She stomped inside and turned off the porch light."

Simpson chuckled. Rafe shot him a scowl. Simpson cleared his throat. "Sorry. Typical Bella when she's ticked. Go on."

"I got back to the motel and realized I'd really done nothing wrong. Sure, I shouldn't have pushed while on a date, but I should've questioned her regarding her connection to my case before I agreed to go out with her on a social level." Social level? How about falling-for-her involvement?

"Her connection to your case?" Simpson didn't miss a thing.

How much to tell him? Sure, he was a police commissioner, but he also had personal ties to the case. What if Rafe had been wrong all along and Simpson was involved in Tate's murder? He studied the man—his eyes were serious, his expression intense. No, Rafe hadn't been wrong. Every bit of training, experience, and instinct assured him Simpson wasn't involved. "Did you know Bella knew about Tate being your father before your mother told her?"

"What? Perhaps you're mistaken." But Simpson didn't look shocked. And he hadn't answered the question.

Just as sure as he was that Simpson wasn't involved with Tate's murder, Rafe knew this information wasn't new to Simpson. "Wish I were, but I'm not."

"Who told you such nonsense?" Not a trace of surprise, just pure defensiveness. Or was that protectiveness?

"Your mother."

The guilt on Simpson's face lingered, settling in the crevices. He remained silent, but Rafe detected the awareness.

"What, no comment to that, Commissioner Simpson? That just ties Bella Miller even tighter into my case. A photograph she took hung in Daniel Tate's private study. She knew about your link to Tate before you did." Rafe shifted in the seat. "I have to wonder, which is why I came back tonight . . . to question her. But I think you already know all the answers I'm seeking. You just haven't shared."

"It's not my place." Simpson shook his head. "But you're getting away from the subject at hand. You arrived here to talk with Bella. What did you see?"

"I've already told you." This was getting old. Simpson might have a crime scene on his hands, but so did Rafe. "Now, what isn't your place to tell? I think it's time you brought me up to speed on what you know about your *father* and Bella Miller."

Simpson's hesitation was so slight, anyone with lesser powers of observation would have missed it. Rafe, however, was a master at observing and interpreting reactions. With his emphasis on the word *father*, he'd scored a direct hit.

"I think it's best if you talk to Bella directly."

"By all means, yes. Would you like to escort me to the hospital, or would you prefer I follow in my own car?"

"I need to check in with a couple of my men and get things wrapped up here. It might be a while."

Rafe reached for the door handle. "Then I'll just wait in my car."

Once alone in his car, his anger defused. He turned on the dome light, withdrew the copy of the file he kept in the car, and flipped through it. The photograph in Tate's home office. He considered Bella's knowing about Tate and Simpson. He stopped on the picture of Remington Wyatt and Tate. The tilt of her head as she smiled at him. The sharpness of those unique blue eyes.

Rafe's body jumped. He closed his eyes and conjured up the image of Bella tonight . . . so angry with him she could've laid him out with a look from her unique eyes.

He studied the photo. Closed his eyes and imagined Bella.

The picture on Tate's wall . . . the pictures in the motel and Simpson's office.

Bella. Remington.

She knew about Tate being Simpson's father.

Bella. Remington. Bella . . . Remington.

They were one and the same.

⚖️

Boy-hidey, did she ever feel woozy.

Bella stared at the IV bag hanging next to her hospital bed. Whatever stuff they were giving her had to be a controlled substance. If street drugs had the same effect, no wonder there were so many users out there. This was the best feeling ever.

Ever.

A nurse swept into the room, leaving the door ajar. Bella could make out a man in uniform in the hall. Police uniform. She smiled.

"How're you feeling?" the perky, blonde nurse asked.

"Groovy." She lifted a hand—it looked like it had a tail with the movement—and pointed to the officer. "He loves me and keeps me safe."

The nurse chuckled and patted Bella's right shoulder. "You're going to be just fine, Ms. Miller." She typed on the computer at Bella's bedside, then gave her a final pat. "The doctor will be in to talk with you shortly. Buzz me if you need anything."

Bella smiled, watching the white tail follow the nurse from the room. Contentedness filled her chest.

Hey, God. Thanks for saving my butt back there. Wait a minute, should she say *butt* when talking to God? Probably not. *I really*

am sorry for being so pissy toward You. I guess You understand, right?
She probably shouldn't use the word *pissy* either. *Anyway, I just wanted to say thanks and let You know I wasn't calling on You just so You'd save me. I really am sorry.*

She rolled her head to the left and stared at her shoulder. It was so much bigger than her right one. Wasn't it? She turned her head back to the right, inspected her shoulder, then compared it to her left. Yep, left one definitely bigger.

And whiter.

Snorting back a chuckle, she grinned. She'd been shot in the left shoulder, so there were bandages covering that. Lots of bandages. Made her kinda look like the Hunchback of Notre Dame. She'd always hated that story. Was creepy.

The door swung open and a man in a white, flapping coat drifted to her bedside. "How're you feeling, Miss Miller?"

"Just groovy." She smiled wide at the blonde nurse who'd followed the doctor into her room.

He chuckled. "Good. I'm Dr. Benton." He clicked the mouse on the computer beside her. "Your stats all look great. The bullet did nominal damage to your shoulder. We've got you packed and stitched up, so you should heal with minimal scarring. You shouldn't have any issues from this at all in the future, except maybe a little scar tissue. But that won't be for five or ten years down the road."

Did she care about anything he was saying? Nope. As long as the dope stayed in the bag and dripped into her veins, she could care less.

Wow, so this was how addicts felt. No wonder children were abandoned, places robbed, others hurt. To keep this feeling, well, Bella would do just about anything.

"I'll check on you in the morning, but if you need anything, Nurse Cheryl will be here all night. Just push the call button on your remote." As quickly as he'd entered, Dr. Whatever-his-name-was whooshed out of the room.

The nurse typed on the computer. The tapping of the keys sounded like tiny hammers. Bella grinned as she imagined itty-bitty elves tapping away on little toys.

"I'll be back to check on you later." Nurse Cheryl nodded. "You get some rest." She turned off the light as she left the room.

Yeah. Rest. Bella's eyelids were getting heavy, now that she thought about it. She closed her eyes. Kaleidoscopes of reds, blues, purples, and oranges dotted in her mind's eye, floating around with no rhyme or reason. No specific pattern, just a hodgepodge smorgasbord of colors and designs. She floated on clouds. Weightless.

Her eyes shot open. What was that?

Bella lay very still. What had woken her up? A sound? She concentrated on nothing but the sounds around her.

The hum of the computer's fan. The faint buzz of the IV machine. Voices in the hall. Male voices. One she recognized clearly.

"I understand . . . Officer." Muffled voices. ". . . fifteen-minute break." Shifting. Phones ringing. Female voices in the background. "Just fifteen minutes, though." Hospital public address system paging some doctor. "I have to report back in, so don't be late."

Her tongue grew double in size. What was Hartlock doing in the hall? Who was he talking to about a break?

The door creaked open. Bella blinked, fighting to focus. Her heartbeat drowned out the buzzing and hum as a silhouette squeezed through the crack in the door.

Rubber-soled shoes squeaked on the waxed floors as the shadowed figure made his way to her bed.

She clenched her hands, her right thumb pressing the call button. Pain shot out from her left shoulder down her arm.

Hartlock stood over her bed. "It's been a long time, Remington. You should've stayed hidden."

A buzz boomed in the room from a speaker on the wall. "Yes, Miss. Miller?"

Nurse Cheryl!

"Help! Help me!"

Hartlock grabbed the pillow and shoved it over her face. She twisted her head right, then left. Shook. Kicked. Used her right hand to claw at him.

He kept pressure on the pillow.

She couldn't breathe. Oh-my-stars, he was going to kill her right here in the hospital!

"Who are you? What are you doing?" Nurse Cheryl's voice reached Bella just as darkness threatened to welcome her. "Security!"

The pressure disappeared.

"Oomph." *Thump. Thud.*

Bella shoved the pillow aside just in time to catch a white-coated Hartlock shoving out of the room. Nurse Cheryl lay sprawled on the floor.

"Oh-my-stars, are you okay?" Bella tried to sit up. Dizziness swayed her.

The nurse wobbled to her feet. "I'm fine. Are you okay?"

The room swarmed with people before Bella could reply. Lights flooded. Bella squinted against the brightness. All at once, people talked, asked questions—the ruckus hurt her head.

"What happened?"

"Who was that?"

"Page Dr. Benton."

"Why did you leave your post?"

"Did he mess with her IV?"

People coming and going. Footsteps. Movements. All crowding her.

"Was he trying to suffocate her?"

"The policeman guarding the door . . . he just collapsed. We need a doctor, stat."

Bella covered her eyes with her right forearm. People poked and prodded her. The activity around her pressed on her as tangible as Hartlock had held the pillow over her face. She couldn't take any more. She screamed.

The room went silent.

She let out a slow breath.

"What's going on in here?" Hayden's soothing voice filled the room.

She opened her eyes and locked gazes with her best friend. Only then did the tears come. Sobs shook her as Hayden rushed to sit on the edge of the bed and pull her into his arms. Like a father comforting a child after a bad dream, he petted her head and rocked her.

Bella didn't care. She was scared, plain and simple. Hartlock had made three attempts on her life now. She had to do something, or he'd kill her.

Looking over Hayden's shoulder, she spied Rafe Baxter in the doorway. His expression was soft yet concerned. Intense.

Her heart leapt into the back of her throat. She didn't have a choice anymore. Hartlock wouldn't stop until she was dead. She had to trust him. Had to take the chance.

She pulled back from Hayden and rested against the pillows he situated behind her.

"Everybody, out." Hayden turned from her to address everyone still hovering in the room. "I said, everyone out of here."

Bella licked her lips and held Rafe's gaze. "Agent Baxter, I think it's time I answered your questions."

He slowly approached. "I think that's a very good idea, Ms. Wyatt. Or would you prefer I call you Remington?"

Chapter Twenty-Nine

*"Character is higher than intellect. A great soul will
be strong to live as well as think."*
RALPH WALDO EMERSON

"And I haven't a clue how deep the corruption goes, but to get away with murdering a federal judge, I'd say whoever's calling the shots with Hartlock and Devane has to be pretty high on the food chain." She finished telling him the whole story and laid her head back against the pillows.

Rafe could only stare at her, a bit in awe. This woman had single-handedly evaded not only a very cunning ASAC, but also a bureau-wide search. Her story was incredible, which made it hard to believe, but because it was so, that's why he did.

"She's not making this up," Hayden interjected.

"I know."

The hospital had calmed down after the excitement. Barely any sounds infiltrated the double-guarded room. Only the nurses' hourly checks interrupted the wee hours. Rafe didn't like hospitals. They reminded him of when his parents died, when Georgia died, and every time little Savannah had another heart surgery.

"We figured out which case links Daniel to Hartlock and Devane. We just didn't have the resources to follow up and see who else was involved." Considering what she'd been through tonight, Remington's voice came out surprisingly steady.

"I can." He'd have to be discreet. Maybe he could get Darren to help. Scratch that—Savannah's surgery was scheduled for Friday. Rafe would have to go it alone.

"If we could just find the witnesses that came forward to Daniel, confessing Hartlock and Devane had made them lie . . ."

Hayden stood. "I'm going to interview the nurses and check on my officer." He kissed Remington's forehead. "I'll get that file for you and be back in a bit." He met Rafe's stare. "Don't leave her alone. Wait until I come back."

Rafe nodded.

"I'm sorry for being such a snot earlier tonight. I just didn't know if I could trust you or not." She smiled.

"And you know now?"

"Not really, but I don't have much of a choice, now do I?"

At least she was honest. He chuckled, then sobered. "You've put me in quite a sticky situation." If he played this wrong, any chance he ever had of promotion would be gone. Possibly, even his job as an agent could be in jeopardy.

"I know, and I'm sorry."

"You realize you can't stay hidden now, right? You can't pretend to be Bella Miller any longer. You have to come back to Little Rock and tell the truth."

"Who do you think will believe me, Rafe? If we can't find those witnesses, it's my word against Hartlock's and Devane's. I fled a murder scene. And if Jackson's in on this, he'll make sure no one believes a word I say. I have no proof." She hit her hospital bed with her fist. "Don't you think if I had proof I would've given it up to see my godfather's murderer punished? I hated walking away and letting Hartlock and Devane and whoever their boss is get away with Daniel's murder."

"I don't think Jackson's in on it. He sent me an e-mail today that Hartlock would be here tomorrow. If he was involved, I don't think he'd have sent me the message."

"Unless he was setting the groundwork to cover for his agents. So it would be documented that Hartlock didn't arrive until Monday, so my murder would be unrelated."

That was a reach, but considering everything that'd happened, it was possible. "We have to do something." But what, he didn't know. He could protect her, of that he was certain. He'd keep her safe.

"We?" She shook her head. "It's still my word against theirs." She held up her hand. "Even if you speak up for me, you weren't there. They were. They were the agents handling the case."

But Hartlock had made a mistake tonight. "It's not just your word anymore. Hartlock spoke to the officer on duty here. That officer can recognize him."

"That officer might not live. I heard the nurses talking while the doctor was working on him. They think he's been given something. Even if he lives, he'll probably be in a coma. Not able to confirm anything."

"We won't know that until Simpson gets back." But what if she was right? "Security cameras."

"What about them?"

"Hospitals have them. We can probably find Hartlock on one. That would back up your story."

She slumped back against the pillows. "Or he could say he'd found me and was coming to arrest me."

He let out a sigh.

"Look, I've had three years to run every possible scenario— they can twist and turn almost anything to their advantage. Without any proof at all, I'm the one who ran. I won't be believed, and you know it."

She was right, of course, which made him all the more irritated. "The bullets recovered from your house. They can be matched to Hartlock's gun."

She laughed. "Do you really think he'd be stupid enough to use his service firearm? He had to use a throwaway."

He hated this.

"As long as Jackson's still the SAC, I can't risk coming in." She took a sip of water from the cup on the tray beside the bed.

Nick. "How about coming in to a different SAC? Mine in Memphis? I can assure you, Nick Hagar is as clean as they come."

"Will he believe me?" Her eyes were wide.

"If you're with me, yes. He trusts my judgment and instincts."

Her gaze flitted over his face, as if she was searching, debating. "Okay."

He didn't know if the emotion rolling through his gut was relief or not, but his heart skidded as he realized she'd at last put her trust in him. "Once I get the file you and Simpson dug up, I can get a couple of agents from Memphis to start looking into things."

Her brow furrowed.

"Don't worry. These are guys I trust with my life."

"It's just going to take me a while to really trust agents. No slight against you or anything."

"I understand." He'd be leery too.

"Nurse Cheryl!" She sat upright.

"Who? What?"

"Hartlock knocked her down when he ran from my room. Maybe she can identify him. We need to let Hayden know so he'll be sure to question her."

"I will. You just sit tight."

"Rafe! Don't leave me." Panic hung in her expression as well as her voice. The way she said his name . . . like a breath. Well, it did some mighty odd things to his insides.

"I'm not. Just sticking my head out the door to talk with the officers there. Okay?"

She nodded. He told the officer to tell Simpson about a nurse named Cheryl, then returned to Remington's bedside. "Any idea when they'll release you?"

"Doctor said he'd see me in the morning. Guess I'll know more then." She shifted on the bed. "It doesn't really hurt."

"It will. Tomorrow, it'll be sore as all get-out."

"You've been shot?"

"Twice." And neither time had been a walk in the park. "Want to compare scars?" He grinned, hoping the teasing would break some of the tension.

"I think you'd win." She yawned. "Sorry."

"Am I boring you?" He laughed.

"I'm just so tired."

That was his cue. He stood. "You need to get some rest."

She bolted upright in the bed and grabbed his arm. "You can't leave me alone." The terror in her voice came through loud and clear.

He held her hand. "I wasn't. I was just going to sit outside the door." He squeezed her knuckles. "I won't let anyone hurt you. Never again."

She flashed him a weak smile. "Just stay in here. Do you mind?"

He pulled the chair closer to the bed and sat. "Not at all. I'll be right here. You get some shut-eye."

"Thanks." Already sleep thickened her voice. She snuggled down in the hospital bed.

Rafe stood and pulled the blanket up around her shoulders. She murmured softly. Strange sensations shivered in his gut. He stared down at her, taking in her delicate features.

With her eyes closed, her lashes looked longer and darker. He could make out little freckles across the bridge of her nose, just like Riley had. "A dusting of fairy kisses," his mother used to say.

With a sigh, he sat and studied Remington. In sleep, she looked as angelic as Savannah.

Lord, please help me keep her safe. Lead me to do what's best for her. Please.

No longer able to resist, Rafe leaned over and planted a feathery kiss on her temple. The scent of her shampoo filled his senses. He breathed her in, letting the heat wash over him. He returned to his watch in the chair beside her.

If Hartlock, Devane, Jackson, or anyone else wanted to harm her, they'd have to come through him first.

⚖️

His officer might not make it. His best friend had endured three attempts on her life. His sister was under mental evaluation. And the father he'd adored all his life wasn't really his father. Hayden decided it just wasn't his week.

He headed back down the hospital wing, two folders tucked tightly under his arm. One contained the information on the Cason Moore case that linked Daniel Tate to Hartlock and Devane. The other contained photographs of Hartlock and Devane for him to show Nurse Cheryl, who'd been more than willing to pick the man who'd flattened her out of a picture lineup.

The two officers he left guarding Bella's room still sat at the ready in the hall. They'd better—after what happened to the last officer, everyone was on full alert and in pairs.

Bob Travis rounded the nurses' station. "I have two officers sitting in a conference room with nurse Cheryl Lee and the hospital attorney and chief of staff. If you'd like, I can do the photo lineup."

Hayden handed him the file. "Thanks, Bob. I appreciate it."

"No problem, Commish." He took the folder and headed down the hall, another officer by his side.

If Hartlock was in this hospital waiting for another chance at Bella or any of the Hopewell police officers, he was in for a rude awakening.

Hayden headed to Bella's room. He nodded at the two officers, then eased the door open and silently slipped inside.

He froze at the sight before him.

Bella lay sleeping peacefully. Rafe sat in the chair beside her bed, facing the bed, holding her right hand. His head rested on the bed beside her.

Tranquil.

It was a couple scene if ever Hayden had seen one. He didn't know what to think. She was his best friend, but at the moment Hayden felt like an intruder. He took a step back to leave.

Rafe's head shot up and he twisted, hand on the butt of his holstered gun.

"It's just me," Hayden whispered, moving toward them. He nodded at Bella. "How's she doing?"

"Good. Finally sleeping." Rafe eased his hand from her grip. She mumbled in her sleep. Rafe smoothed her blanket.

The intimacy slammed against Hayden. He held out the folder. "Here's the case Bella and I found that Daniel presided over and Hartlock and Devane were witnesses."

Rafe took the folder and flipped through the notes. "And this was the only one you could find that involved the three of them?"

Hayden nodded. "For the six months prior to Daniel's murder."

"I'll get some of my buddies in the Memphis office to look into this. No one in Little Rock will have any idea things are being checked."

"Good. And talk to the government witnesses. Two of them talked to Daniel, which is what got him killed."

"Don't worry, the Memphis agents are good."

Hayden waved toward Bella. "She needs whatever security we can provide her."

"She's agreed to go with me to my SAC in the Memphis office."

Hayden's heart sunk to his toes. "When?"

"As soon as the doctor releases her. There's no sense in staying around." Rafe turned from her. "Did you talk with that nurse Remington mentioned? Cheryl?"

His calling her Remington made it all real. That he was losing his best friend. "Uh, yes. We're conducting a photograph lineup right now."

"Good. If we can get a corroboration of it being Hartlock, it'll make my job that much easier." Rafe turned back to her and took her hand. His thumb rubbed her knuckles. "And that'll keep her safe."

Hayden struggled not to be jealous. Bella was too wonderful not to eventually have someone in her life other than him. He just thought the transition would be slower . . . that he'd have time to adjust to her having another man in her life and heart.

"I'll stay with her."

Rafe lifted his head. "I'm okay. I told her I'd stay."

Hayden moved closer to the bed. "It's going to be a long night. Why don't you grab a cup of coffee and stretch a little? I'll stay with her in case she wakes up." He needed privacy to say some of the things he needed to say to her.

"Coffee does sound good." Rafe released her hand and inched back. "Can I get you a cup?"

"No, but thanks."

"I'll be back in a few minutes." Rafe headed to the door.

"Take your time."

The whoosh of the door indicated they were alone. Hayden sat in the chair and took Bella's hand. *Dear God, help me give her peace for the journey she needs to take. Don't let my own wants come out and influence her.* "Bella, honey."

Her eyelids fluttered open. She blinked, then focused on his face. "What's wrong?" She struggled to sit.

"Nothing's wrong. I just need to talk to you for a minute."

"Okay." She managed to get in a semi-sitting position.

"You know I love you, right?"

"Yeah." She frowned. "Hay, you're scaring me. What's wrong?"

"Nothing." He forced his emotions to remain in check. *God, help me get my point out right.* "I just wanted to tell you I'm glad you decided to trust Rafe."

"Really?"

"Yeah. I told you he was a good guy."

She grinned and relaxed. "You woke me up just to be able to say you told me so?"

He smiled and squeezed her hand. "Well, that too, but not only that." He inhaled deeply, held the air in his lungs for a long moment, then slowing released. "I wanted to tell you that I want you to be happy." *Lord, please help her understand.*

"What're you talking about?"

"With Rafe. In Memphis. Or Little Rock. Or wherever." Far away from him.

"I don't understand."

He kissed her hand. "You're going to leave Hopewell, and me. And I want you to know that it's okay."

"Oh, Hay . . ."

"I'm serious. Once you don't need to hide out here anymore, you'll need to get on with your life. Using your education, your degree. It'd be a waste for you not to, once everything's cleared up."

"Are you trying to get rid of me?" Tears pooled in her eyes.

"Not at all. But I wanted you to know that you'll always be my best friend, and no matter where you go, you won't get rid of me."

She smiled and opened her right arm. He stepped in and gave her a hug.

"I love you, Hayden Simpson. And you'll always be my best friend too."

Except that he wouldn't.

Chapter Thirty

"Take away love and our earth is a tomb."
ROBERT BROWNING

Buzzzzzz!

Rafe bolted upright in bed. Disorientation clogged his head. Then he remembered. He slapped the alarm on the motel room's nightstand and pulled himself to sitting. He ran a hand over his face, then scrubbed his head. Morning had come entirely too soon.

The coffee from the maker in the room was less than appealing, but a cup of black coffee, along with a hot shower, helped Rafe feel a little more human and a little less like a bear. His cell chimed.

"Baxter."

"Well, imagine that." Nick's deep baritone boomed over the line. "Better be you since that's who I called."

"Thanks for calling me back."

"What'd you expect after the voice mail you left me last night? Excuse me, early this morning." The Memphis SAC cleared his throat. "You were rather cryptic."

"I'm sorry about that." Rafe had left the message after he left the hospital and after he'd read the notes on the Moore case.

"So, what's this all about?"

Rafe took a deep breath. "I'm working a cold case that has . . . I believe . . . well, there's no other way to say it, dirty agents involved."

A thundering pause. "Did you say *dirty agents*?"

"Yes, sir. One of them is the ASAC. And I'm talking to you about this because I'm not sure if the SAC is involved or not."

"Maybe you'd better back up and start at the beginning."

"Yes, sir." Rafe relayed the entire story, including all the details. He used the file for reference to make sure he didn't miss anything.

"I can't believe . . ."

Rafe remained silent, letting his former boss work things out.

"We can always go straight to main justice in DC."

He could hear the hesitation in Nick's voice. "But?"

"But that's a long process. If I'm getting what you're saying, this girl's in danger until every person involved is put away."

Leave it to Nick to cut right to the heart of the matter. "Right."

"Have you looked into that case you found linking the judge to the dirty agents?"

"Not yet. Just got it last night. I don't have anyone in the Little Rock office I can trust yet."

"Fax the details to my personal fax number. I'll get a couple of boys to look into it from here."

"Thanks, Nick. I really appreciate it."

"You seem to have gotten yourself into a fix over there. Guess it wouldn't do me any good to say I told you so, huh?"

He knew Nick wouldn't let it pass. "No. We both know why I'm here."

"Apparently, for more than one reason."

"Yeah." Rafe studied the photograph of Remington. How had he missed that she was Bella? Now that he knew, he could clearly see it was the same person. "And you're okay with me bringing the witness in to the Memphis office? It won't cause problems?"

"Oh, it'll cause some problems, but if Alphonse Jackson isn't involved, he'll understand. And if he is . . . well, we won't care what he thinks at that point."

"I'm grateful to you, man." Rafe released the tension in his shoulders. "I don't know when she'll be released from the hospital, but I'll call you before we head in."

"Fax me that info ASAP. We'll start on that."

"On its way as soon as I get off the phone. Thanks again."

Nick grunted before disconnecting the call.

Rafe glanced out the window across the parking lot. Hartlock's car was parked in front of their motel room. He shrugged off the urge to storm over there and beat on the door, just to see if he'd hit Devane. The hospital reported no gunshot wounds in the ER last night. Rafe shook his head. He'd been so sure he'd hit him.

He grabbed the Cason Moore file and his jacket, then rushed out the door and strode to the motel's office. A chilly fog-like density hovered low.

A blast of forced heat slammed him when he opened the office door. Daisy was on duty, allowing him to use the fax machine at no charge, even though it was long distance and against policy, as she was quick to point out. Still no sign of life from Hartlock and Devane's room. Their car still sat unmoved outside. It didn't matter—they'd get what they deserved. Rafe got behind the wheel of his car, then headed to the hospital.

Simpson met him as soon as Rafe stepped off the elevator on the hospital floor. "We're about to bring in Hartlock as a suspect in the attack on Bella." His eyes shone with excitement. "The nurse picked him out of a photo lineup. We just got all the paperwork."

Rafe wasn't entirely sure what the proper protocol was when bringing in an FBI agent for questioning regarding an assault, but he was pretty sure it'd be better if he went with the police commissioner. Just in case. "Mind if I tag along?"

Simpson smiled and nodded. "Hoped you would be interested in joining us."

"What about Remington?"

"Two of my men are guarding her and the hospital security is on full alert. I told her we were going to pick up Hartlock. She's relieved."

He'd like to at least say hello to her before he left, just to see for himself that she was okay this morning, but Simpson stepped into the elevator and jabbed the button to the lobby. "You can ride with me. Two other units are following us. I have a car already on-site, just to make sure they don't leave before we get there."

"I didn't notice any activity when I left the motel." Rafe followed Simpson from the elevator.

"Good. I don't want him getting away." Simpson slipped inside the cruiser before Rafe could even open the passenger door.

Dare he call Jackson? If he didn't and Jackson was clean, Rafe's head would be on the chopping block. To not give the SAC a heads-up when the ASAC was being brought in for questioning? Yeah, Rafe could kiss any hope of a promotion good-bye.

On the other hand, if Jackson was involved, calling him in advance would give him time to warn Hartlock. It was a catch-22 in the worst kind of way.

Or the best opportunity.

Rafe pulled out his cell phone and flipped it open. "Simpson, I need to call Jackson and tell him we're about to pick up Hartlock."

"What are you doing? He'll warn him."

Rafe nodded. "If he does, then we know for a fact he's involved in all this. Don't you see? This is one safe way to learn if we can trust him about Remington's story."

One slight measure he'd use to help keep her safe.

⚖

Why hadn't Hayden called her yet? And where was Rafe?

Bella sat on the edge of the hospital bed. She'd already taken a shower, having been set free of the IV after the bag of antibiotics had emptied. The morning nurse assured her the doctor would be by any minute for his morning rounds.

She planned to be discharged soon. No matter what Dr. Benton said, she wasn't going to stay in the hospital any longer. She felt fine. Her shoulder was pretty sore, but Rafe had already warned her about that.

Rafe.

He had haunted her dreams during the early morning hours. Bits and pieces of images: his smile, those smoldering eyes of his, the set of his jaw, the broadness of his shoulders. She'd faded in and out of reality and dreamland, never really sure which was which. The result was her road map eyes and restless irritation.

The hospital door swung open and Ardy rushed to her side. "Oh, honey. I'm so sorry. Hayden just told me about you this morning." She smoothed Bella's hair. "I can't believe you were shot. I already gave my son a good talking-to for not telling me about this last night. I could've stayed with you. And then to have to go through such a brouhaha to get in your room . . ." She stood back and stared at Bella's bandaged shoulder. "Oh, honey. I just can't believe this."

"It hardly hurts anymore." Hayden probably hadn't told Ardy earlier to save Bella from this overzealous attention. She'd have to remember to hug him for it later.

"But shot?!" Ardy shook her head. "I just don't know what Hopewell's coming to. Shot, in your own home."

"I'm going to be fine."

"Hayden said they have a suspect and will be picking him up this morning. Have you heard if they've done that yet?"

Ah, so that's why he'd told Ardy . . . so she could babysit Bella while Hayden picked up Hartlock. Sneaky man that he was. "I haven't heard."

The door whooshed open before Ardy could further comment. The doctor, with a new nurse trailing him, went straight to the computer at her bedside. "Good morning."

Click-click-click. "Looks like you had an uneventful rest of the night after your excitement."

"Yes."

Click. Click. Tap. Tap. Tap. "Your stats are good. Bloodwork from this morning gives no indication of infection."

Tap-tap-tap. Tap. Tap. "Everything looks great." He finally turned from the computer and addressed her. "Let's take a look, shall we?" He faced Ardy.

The nurse scooted Ardy toward the door. "You'll be allowed back in after the doctor completes his exam."

Dr. Benton eased the bandage back, then peered over the rim of his glasses. He secured the bandage back in place, then did the same thing on the back of her shoulder. "Well, Miss Miller, everything looks like it should. How're you feeling?" He pushed his glasses up to the bridge of his nose.

"Fine. Ready to go home."

"Are you sure? You might prefer staying another night."

"No. Please. I'd really like to go home."

He scribbled on a pad of paper the nurse passed him. "Well, it seems you have a ride home, so you're free to leave." He handed the nurse the papers, then patted Bella's right hand. "The nurse will bring you the discharge papers and your prescriptions. If you have any problems, call your family doctor."

"Thank you."

He nodded and left, the nurse on his heels.

Bella stepped to the floor. A sensation of wooziness caused her to sway. Ardy rushed to her side and balanced her. "Honey, should I call that doctor back?"

"No. I'm fine. It's a side effect of the pain medications." She straightened, giving her equilibrium a chance to right itself. "I'm being discharged. I wonder where my clothes are."

"You just sit down. I'll find your clothes." Ardy helped her sit in the chair Rafe and Hayden had taken turns occupying throughout most of last night. She shuffled into the bathroom, making odd noises.

Bella rested her head against the side of the bed, more tired than she'd realized. But she wasn't going to stay here.

"I found these, but no shirt." Ardy laid the sweatpants on the foot of the bed. "Your shoes are right here. Don't see any socks."

"I have my socks on." They would've had to cut her shirt and bra off to treat her wound. Lovely. She stood, wobbling again. "Can you help me get the pants on?"

"Sure, hon. No problem."

Between the two of them, Bella had her sweatpants, socks, and shoes on when the nurse arrived with her discharge papers and prescriptions. She went over the wound care instructions, then handed the paperwork to Ardy before staring back at Bella. "Let me get you a shirt. We have plenty of scrubs left around here."

"Thank you." Bella stared at the clock on the wall.

Ten o'clock. Plenty of time for Hayden and the other officers to make it to the motel. Maybe she'd hear something soon.

And where was Rafe?

⚖️

Bam! Bam! Bam!

"Police, open up!" Hayden kept his hand on the butt of his gun. "Agents Hartlock and Devane, Hopewell Police. Open the door."

No response.

Hayden knocked again, even harder than before. "Agents Hartlock and Devane?"

Silence save for the shifting of nervous police officers.

Hayden nodded at the officer who held a master room key, given to them by the young woman named Daisy at the front desk. He inserted the key and turned the knob, then pushed in the door and flattened himself against the wall.

Rafe moved past Hayden and marched into the empty room. "They're gone."

Officers checked the small bathroom area, then returned to Hayden. "Nothing."

"But their car is still outside." Hayden glanced around the parking lot. "Bob, take two men and walk to the diner. See if they're out having breakfast." He nodded at the rookie officer just hired three months ago. "Call in a BOLO on both agents."

Rafe exited the bathroom area, carrying a trash can. "Look here."

Hayden glanced inside to find wadded papers, but at the bottom, gauze with dried blood. "Devane?"

"I *knew* I'd hit him."

"Hey," Hayden hollered after the cop he'd just spoken to.

The rookie faced him. "Yes, sir?"

"Get the crime-scene kit. There are some items here to be bagged for evidence." And he'd have to take photographs and preserve as much as possible in the event this went to trial. "Everyone else, vacate the room immediately."

Hayden couldn't deny the adrenaline pumping through his veins as he ordered his men about, collecting evidence and documenting. He turned back to Rafe. "We don't have a warrant on the vehicle, but I've called in a request for that, given what we've found here. We should get that back soon."

Rafe nodded, his face grave as he stared at the car.

"What?"

"I just now noticed the car's plates." He pointed.

Hayden looked. Rental car plates. Not good. Hartlock and Devane were covering their tracks.

"Have you heard from your men on foot?" Rafe's voice sounded lighter than normal. "Have they found Hartlock or Devane yet?"

Hayden radioed to Bob Travis. "Any sign of them?" He deliberately didn't say names or other identifying words on the off chance the agents had access to a scanner and were monitoring.

"No, sir. No one at the diner has seen them either."

Hayden let out a sigh. "Head on back, then. Keep an eye out on your way back. Over."

"Copy that. Out."

Hayden turned back to Rafe. "Not a sign. I guess we don't know for certain now if your SAC tried to warn them or not."

"True. That could be why they're staying away. However, they were gone long before I called Jackson, and they left their car then. Something's up." Rafe rubbed his jaw.

"What're you thinking?"

"Where'd they go on foot, and why?"

Hayden shrugged. Then his blood went cold as he locked stares with Rafe.

They both spoke at the same time—

"Bella!"

"Remington!"

Chapter Thirty-One

"All our dreams can come true,
if we have the courage to pursue them."
WALT DISNEY

If anything happened to Remington . . .

Rafe gripped the car door handle tight as Simpson spun the cruiser into the hospital's parking lot. The tires barely stopped rolling outside of the emergency entrance and Rafe's shoes hit the pavement.

He jogged down the hall, opted for the stairs over the elevator, and raced up flight after flight of steps. He wasn't even out of breath as he spilled out of the staircase onto the hospital ward. He eased down the hall. No guards sat outside her room. His heart pounded as he pushed open Remington's door.

"Hey . . ."

No one was inside. The bed had been stripped. The computer on the bedside table had a blank screen.

Rafe backtracked to the nurses' station. Hayden strode off the elevator and met him at the counter. "She's not in her room. Your officers aren't there."

Hayden nodded. "I know. They checked in a few minutes ago. Bella's been discharged and left. The officers are following her."

The knot in his gut loosened just a bit. "How did she get home? She was in no condition to drive, and her truck wasn't here."

"My mother is driving her."

Rafe shoved aside the feeling that Simpson had set all this in motion to keep him away from her, which was ridiculous. He was just being overly suspicious.

"I have security here still on high alert, with Hartlock and Devane's photos distributed. They shouldn't know she's been released."

Unless they'd been watching. FBI agents were trained in covert operations. The same training could be applied in this situation. After all, Hartlock and Devane had managed not to arouse any suspicion of wrongdoing for all this time.

Rafe's cell phone rang. "Baxter."

"We've uncovered some interesting information about the Moore case I think you'll be most interested in seeing. What's a good fax number?"

"Hang on, Nick." He got the police department's fax number from Simpson, then passed it along to Nick. "Thanks. I really appreciate it, man."

"Keep me updated. And stay safe."

Rafe shut the phone. "He's faxing some important information to me at the station now. Mind if we head that way?"

"Let's go." Simpson led the way to the elevator. "I'll call Mom and tell her not to be alarmed at the officers out front."

"Ask her how Remington's feeling." He didn't care if Simpson read into the comment whatever he would. He couldn't bear not to know how she was.

Simpson flashed a small, sad smile. "I will." He placed his cell to his ear as they exited the elevator.

What was that about? Didn't matter. He crossed the lobby

and headed to his car, Simpson's footsteps and muffled voice trailing. Instinct told Rafe something was about to blow wide open with his case. Anticipation had him speeding down the road in minutes.

He waited for Simpson outside the police station a good five minutes before the commissioner whipped into the parking lot.

Simpson's face wore a scowl as he swung open the station door.

What was up with him? Rafe followed, about to demand an explanation, when two men met Simpson in the main room.

"We've been waiting on you, Commissioner Simpson," the first man said. Wait a minute . . . Rafe recognized him from the diner.

"Should have called if you wanted to visit, Councilman." Simpson motioned toward his office and nodded at Rafe. "Your fax should be in there."

"Who is that, and why is he receiving a fax at a public official's office?" the councilman asked.

Rafe ignored everyone and strode purposefully to Simpson's office. The men's loud voices followed. Rafe shut the door and grabbed the pages off the fax machine. He slumped into the chair in front of the desk. His eyes scanned Nick's notes faster than his mind could process.

Cason Moore case changed the unwritten custom of government witnesses receiving less of a sentence than noncooperating witnesses. In Judge Tate's confidential notes, he states he believed the government hadn't proven their case, with the exception of two witnesses. His notes further state one of those witnesses had contacted Tate's clerk, requesting a meeting. That notation is the last in the file. It was dated the week prior to Tate's murder. The only two agents who assisted the US attorney's office with case preparation were Lars Hartlock and Jack Devane. They worked the investigation and case for nearly two years prior to the trial. Because of their successful conviction rate on the case, Hartlock was promoted to ASAC in his office. That position had been vacant for several years. Former ASAC retired.

Swallowing, Rafe considered the implications. The case smacked of all kinds of legal maneuvering, the complete repercussions well over his head. He flipped to the second page of the fax.

Everything I've looked at gives me no indication that Jackson was involved, nor knew anything about this. From what I gathered, Hartlock and Devane worked exclusively with the US attorney's office. Could Hartlock's motive been the promotion?

Very likely, Hartlock needed the promotion. Maybe he paid off Devane. But if Jackson wasn't involved, who was? Remington had been adamant in her retelling of what she overheard the night Tate had been murdered. He'd threatened to report the agents, and they'd informed him they were acting on orders of *higher-ups.*

Could they have been bluffing Tate? It didn't make sense why they would. They were going to kill him, why lie?

Could Remington have been mistaken? She was upset, heard people she trusted kill her father figure . . . maybe she misheard. It happened all the time to people in such stressful situations. He, himself, had seen witnesses fall apart because their minds had created an alternative to what they'd really seen or heard.

But Remington was a forensic psychologist. And she was adamant. Very adamant.

So who did that leave? If Jackson wasn't involved . . .

Simpson swung the door open and slammed it shut behind him. His face was Razorback red. His chest rose and fell quicker than normal, and he pushed out air through his nostrils.

"What's going on?"

Simpson paced the small space behind his desk. "I should've seen it coming."

"What're you talking about?"

"See that man with the councilman?" Simpson nodded out the glass window of his office.

Rafe stood and glanced. A younger man, probably in his late twenties, maybe early thirties, with dark hair and needing a shave, spoke to one of the officers in the main room. Rafe turned back to Simpson. "Yeah, what about him?"

"That's Marshall Abernathy."

"The guy your sister went off with?"

"Yeah. The one who wants my job."

Rafe kept his mouth shut and sat back down. Simpson would get the information out when and how he wanted, in his own time.

The commissioner made another short stride before yanking out his chair from under his desk and plopping down. "Seems my sister not only told Marshall I knew about her vandalizing someone's car—which I didn't—but she also told him I'd been skimming money from the office."

Rafe still kept his mouth shut. Maddie and Riley drove him nuts at times, but they'd never, ever messed with his career. Not like this.

"He, of course, took it straight to the city council and told them." Simpson flicked a wrist toward the two men. "So the good councilman, Caleb Montgomery there, told the others on the council that he'd personally oversee an audit.

"I don't have time for this mess." Simpson scraped a hand down his face. "And now, since the nice officers at the front desk know we answer to the city council, when Montgomery and Abernathy questioned where I was, the officers were only too happy to inform them I was bringing in an FBI agent for questioning regarding an assault on my best friend."

Rafe knew what Simpson wasn't saying—the implication was that he'd been using taxpayers' money and resources for his personal use. Rafe had heard the talk when he'd first gotten into Hopewell and asked around about Hayden Simpson. His contract was almost up and the city council was the sole decision maker on whether or not to renew.

"Lord, I sure could use some direction. My life's going way off track here." Simpson pinched the bridge of his nose. "I can use all the divine guidance You can spare."

"Amen," Rafe whispered. "Amen."

⚖️

This was his last chance.

Lars waited on the side of the road while Devane snored in the backseat of his car. It was regrettable that they'd had to leave the rental in the motel parking lot. Some things just couldn't be helped.

It was already Monday, and he'd avoided *the call* twice already. He couldn't think about what would happen if he didn't take care of Remington. Lars decided the best thing would be to just have her disappear so the locals would think she was missing. If there wasn't a body, it'd be hard to prove there was a murder.

He'd been waiting in the car for almost half an hour, with no sign of her yet. The woman driving Remington had pulled the car up to the front entrance of the hospital when he left. What could be keeping them? He blew on his hands, despite the heater keeping the car's cabin a comfortable temperature.

His cell vibrated in his front pocket. No way! Talk about a coincidence. He jerked the phone out and checked the caller ID. His boss. What?

"Hello, Alphonse. What a surprise."

"I got an interesting call from Agent Baxter a bit ago."

Rafe Baxter was quickly turning into a pain in Lars's side. "Really? I haven't been able to sit down with him just yet. I don't—"

"What is this business about you assaulting a woman in a hospital?"

Lars's mind couldn't process a lie fast enough. Remington wouldn't have identified him. She had as much at stake as he did. "I-I—"

"Assaulting a woman?" Alphonse's voice drummed against Lars's head.

"Sir, I don't know—"

"A witness picked you out of a photo lineup. What are you doing, Hartlock?" Alphonse's tone raised two octaves. "You were supposed to assist Baxter on the Tate case. Now he calls and informs me that the local police are picking you up for questioning. What is going on?"

Lars's tongue filled his mouth. "Sir, it's all a misunderstanding. I'll have it straightened out this afternoon."

"I don't know what's going on down there, but you'd better get it cleared up and get your butt back to the office by morning." With each word, Alphonse had gotten louder.

"Yes, sir."

"And bring Baxter back with you. I want you both in my office first thing in the morning. No excuses."

"Yes, sir." Unless he killed Rafe first.

Which suddenly seemed like his only solution.

⚖️

The sky streaked overcast, cloaking the bayou in gloom. Bella closed her eyes and rested her cheek against the headrest.

She loved Ardy dearly, but Bella would be so glad to get home and relax in silence. Ardy had kept up a stream of meaningless conversation the entire trip from the hospital to the pharmacy to now. Bella's ears hurt and her head throbbed. All she needed was her bed and silence.

Emphasis on the silence.

"I can stay and help you." Ardy turned off the main road. Asphalt merged into freshly grated gravel.

"No." Bella forced a smile. "Really, I'm fine." Especially since Hayden had probably already picked up Hartlock. Exhaustion tugged her down. "I'm going to take my pain medication and sleep." Now that she didn't have to worry about Hartlock and Devane coming to kill her, she'd sleep deeply. It'd been a long, long time since she'd been able to do that.

"Are you sure, hon?"

The car fishtailed on the gravel. Ardy took her foot off the accelerator and corrected the path. "I don't mind staying one little bit. I could catch up on your laundry for you. Cook you some nice soup."

Bella clutched the white bag of her medications. "Thank you, but no." She pinched her eyes closed, the bumpiness of driving over the gravel causing a minor bout of nausea.

Wham!

She slammed against the car door. Her eyes shot open, taking in everything but hardly registering anything.

Another car plowed into the driver's side of the car. Everything slowed down in Bella's realm of reality.

The force flung Ardy sideways, her temple smacked her window, then her head bounced back against the headrest.

Tires slid on the loose gravel. Grinding screeched so loud it made the fillings in her molars rattle.

The stop came so suddenly the car rocked right, then left, then right. Then nothing. Stillness.

Gravel dust clouded the air and burned Bella's eyes. She blinked rapidly. A buzz rang in her ears. The pain shooting out from her injured shoulder caused her to grind her teeth. *Oh-my-stars, the pain!*

She released her seat belt, then looked across the console. "Ardy? Ardy!"

Hayden's mother groaned in response. At least she was alive.

Bella grasped the door handle and pushed to open the door.

She needed to process what had happened. Everything was fuzzy in her mind. An accident . . . they'd been in an accident.

A rough hand grabbed her left forearm.

Pain kicked her in the teeth as she dropped to her knees. She forced herself to focus, even as she felt herself falling into darkness.

Lars Hartlock smiled down at her, but she couldn't react.

Already, darkness opened its smothering arms to her.

Chapter Thirty-Two

"Excellence is not a skill. It is an attitude."

RALPH MARSTON

"Excuse me, sir!" The rookie officer barged into Simpson's office.

Rafe startled, then folded the fax pages and slipped them into his pocket. He sat on the edge of the desk.

"Yes?" Simpson glanced up, already his face looked like it could drag the floor. "What is it now?"

The rookie's expression was grave. "I'm sorry to interrupt, sir, but there's been a car accident." He squirmed. "It's your mother, sir."

Simpson jumped to his feet. His chair shot out behind him from the force, crashing into the wall. "Where?"

"Old Promises Lane. First responders have already been dispatched. Officers are on the way." The rookie ducked out of the office.

Rafe's chest constricted.

Simpson grabbed his car keys, but Rafe snatched them away. "She was driving Remington home. Come on. I'll drive."

Simpson followed him out of the station and into the car. Rafe jammed the keys into the ignition.

"Dear Lord, please watch over them." Simpson's voice came out shaky. "Please, God, let them be okay."

"Amen." Rafe gunned the cruiser out of the parking lot, tires squealing as they raced toward Bella's street.

"I should have warned Mom about the gravel. They just graded it yesterday." Simpson shook his head. "We've begged the parish to pave that road because it can be so dangerous, but they won't do anything. They say there isn't enough traffic to justify the expense."

"Stop beating yourself up." Rafe's palms slicked the steering wheel. "You don't know what happened yet."

The sun hid behind dark, ominous clouds. A sign? *Lord, please let them be okay.*

He took a sharp turn, and a fire truck came into view. Rafe's heart dropped to his stomach. The Simpson car was T-boned, pushed almost into the ditch. The driver's door completely caved into the cabin. The passenger's door stood open.

Simpson jumped out of the cruiser before Rafe could get it into Park. He bypassed the two police cars and ran straight for the ambulance. Rafe raced to catch up.

Ardy Simpson lay on a stretcher in the back of the ambulance, an EMT dabbing at a cut on her forehead with wet gauze. Rafe took a quick evaluation. No gushing blood. Nobody having to administer CPR.

"Mom!" Simpson rushed to her side. "Are you okay? What happened?"

"The car came out of nowhere." She propped up on her elbows. "I hit my head."

The EMT finished bandaging and met Simpson's questioning stare. "She'll need a couple of stitches, and they'll check her for a concussion at the hospital. We've already radioed it in."

One of the officers waved for Simpson's attention. "We can't find the driver of the other car. We ran the plates and it's registered as a federal vehicle."

Simpson turned back to his mother. "Where's Bella?"

"She's missing. They're supposedly looking for her, but I don't know if they believed me 100 percent when I told them another person was in the car."

Hartlock and Devane.

Rafe went cold to the depths of his spirit. "Stay with your mom. I'll find her."

He went to the squad car parked with its lights still blinking and approached the officer leaning against the door. "Do you have any idea where the passenger of Mrs. Simpson might have gone?"

The sergeant pushed off the vehicle. "Who are you and why is this any of your business?" Arrogance oozed off the man like mud between toes.

Rafe flashed his badge and put an edge to his voice. "I'll ask one more time—do you have any idea where Mrs. Simpson's passenger might have disappeared to?"

The officer stood at attention. "I'm sorry, sir. I didn't realize—"

"Just answer my question."

"Best we can tell so far, there were two people, we're guessing men based upon the size of the shoeprints, in the car that hit Mrs. Simpson's. Both of those prints are beside Mrs. Simpson's passenger door. There's a bit of scuff markings, as if something of about 130 or so pounds was dragged into the ditch there." He pointed as he spoke. "We lose the tracks there in the grass, going to the woods around the bayou."

"How many officers have been dispatched to search?"

"Every available man is out there. All four of them."

Four? Was he serious? Rafe shook his head. Not bothering to respond, he took off into the woods. *Oh, God, keep her safe until I can find her. Please.*

⚖

It felt like her head had been packed with gauze.

Bella pushed to sitting and blinked. Again. And again. Nothing came into focus. Where was she? It was cold. She could smell fish. Fish and dirt. And—

"Well, well, well . . . it's about time you came to."

She trembled at Hartlock's cold, heartless voice. She forced her eyes to stay open. Where was he? His voice had come from behind her, but his footsteps . . . in leaves . . . crunched to her right side. She turned her head that way. "What do you want, Hartlock?"

He laughed, more in front of her. She blinked again. "Remington Wyatt. All this time, you were just a state away."

A fuzzy blob shifted in front of her. She flinched. *Hey, God . . . it's me again. I need Your help something really bad now.*

Hartlock laughed again, then his voice dropped even colder. "You've made my life very miserable."

She jerked backward as someone yanked the hair on the back of her head. Hard.

"Very miserable." Hartlock's breath scorched the side of her neck.

Bella shuddered. He released her hair with a push to her head.

She ran her right hand over her eyes, but she touched cloth instead. She tugged it free from her face. Bella glanced around, fighting for her bearings. She knew this area—this was the woods across the street from her home.

Hartlock and Devane hovered over her. Over her. *God, please help me. I don't want to die like this. Please, God, help me.*

"How have I made your life miserable, huh? I haven't chased you. Tried to kill you." She stood, wobbly, but on her own feet. "You murdered Daniel. In cold blood."

Hartlock's eyes widened. "Well, there's the spunk of the Remington I used to know. I wondered if you'd turned mushy while you hid like a coward."

She lunged for him.

He gave her left shoulder a hard shove that sent her reeling. She landed on the hard, cold ground with a thud. He snorted. "Oh, you've been a thorn in my side ever since Rafe knocked you loose of the bushes."

She stood again, watching as Hartlock paced. Devane held a gun, but it wasn't aimed at her. Devane looked to favor his right arm. His shooting hand, as she recalled.

"You should have stayed hidden. But no . . . you had to come out of the woodwork, didn't you?"

"You murdered a federal judge."

Hartlock smiled. "I did. Daniel was too self-righteous for his own good. All that religion stuff he believed."

Her stomach acid bubbled in the back of her throat. She checked on Devane from the corner of her eye. He barely looked awake. His grip on the gun, weak and limp.

"Doesn't matter. I've spent enough time on you already." Hartlock gave a jerk of his head toward Devane.

"Why didn't you just kill me back there after you hit us? No witnesses. You'd get away clean."

He shook his head. "We both know it's better if you just up and disappear."

"You left the car. What about that?"

He smiled, sending chills all over her. "Poor Jack here . . . he'll be found wandering in the woods later. He was in an accident and became disoriented."

And there'd be no proof that she'd met with any foul play. At least, not by him. "Who's pulling your chain, Hartlock? Who's threatening you?" She turned, angling herself adjacent to the space between the two FBI agents. Devane still looked uninterested and dazed.

Hartlock lifted his lip and sneered. "What's it to you?"

She gave a flash of her teeth as she inched forward. "Maybe I want to send him a thank-you card. I like seeing *you* squirm like a worm on a hook."

He reared back his hand and slapped her across the face. The sting and heat cut deep. The coppery taste of blood rested on her tongue.

"Don't be cute with me. Jonathan wants you dead as much as I do. Even more, which is hard to believe."

Devane straightened for a moment, then relaxed.

Jonathan Busch, United States Attorney.

Of course. It all made sense. How the high-profile cases he won put him in line for his political aspirations. His race for the governor's seat was practically a shoe-in, so the papers implied.

She angled a little more, leaning over to spit blood to the ground. *Oh-my-stars that hurt.* She wiped her mouth with the back of her hand. "You make me sick, Hartlock. You took an oath. You're supposed to enforce the law, not be judge, jury, and executioner." She shifted closer.

"What do you think we've been doing, Remington? We've been making sure the guilty don't get off on technicalities or some such nonsense. Keeping those violent criminals behind bars, keeping people safe in their own homes."

"What did Cason Moore do that was so violent?" She turned and moved a bit closer to Devane, who really looked like he'd been drugged. "That's the case you murdered Daniel over, right?"

"That case was personal to Jonathan."

"Personal?" She moved another inch or so.

"None of your business." Hartlock's eyes narrowed.

She recognized the look. Now or never. *God, please give me strength.*

Bella gritted her teeth and lunged into Devane. Her injured shoulder made contact with his chest, shooting hot pain throughout her body.

He dropped the gun as he fell. She grabbed for it as did Hartlock. Her hand wrapped around the waffle-patterned grip. She brought it up quickly, slamming it into Hartlock's temple. He grunted as he dropped to all fours.

Devane was up faster than she'd imagined. He tackled her. She landed on her back with him on top of her. His hand tightened on her wrist. She twisted and kicked, trying to wrestle away.

Pop! The gun vibrated her hand as heat spread over her chest.

Rafe's muscles locked at the sound of the gunshot. His breath got trapped in his lungs, scorching.

Then he reacted.

He blew out air, grabbed his gun, and sprinted in the direction he'd heard the shot fired from. *God, please don't let it have been her. Please, God. Please.*

His thighs burned as he ran faster and faster over the uneven terrain. Dodging the tree on the left. Ducking under limbs. Sidestepping the stump on the right. Jumping over the small shrub.

Then he saw her.

Remington stood, a bloody circle on her shirt. She held a gun on a trembling Hartlock, kneeling in front of her with his fingers laced behind his head. Devane lay facedown on the ground. Unmoving. An exit wound leaking blood.

"Remington?" Rafe inched closer to her.

She looked at him, tears streaming down her face. "He murdered Daniel."

"I know." He kept his voice low, soothing, as if he were comforting a frightened child. In a way, he was.

"Rafe, help me. She shot Jack." Hartlock turned to him.

She shoved the gun to his forehead.

"Hartlock, shut up." *Lord, don't let her pull the trigger. She'll never be able to live with herself later.* He walked right beside her. "Don't do it. He's not worth it."

The tears kept flowing. "I didn't mean to kill Devane. We were wrestling for the gun."

"I know."

"She shot him in cold blood."

She pushed the barrel of the gun harder, digging the end into Hartlock's flesh. "You would know, wouldn't you? You murdered Daniel."

Rafe holstered his handgun. He could easily disarm her, but he might accidently hurt her in the process. "Remington . . . Bella."

"He tried to kill me."

"I know. But we've got him now. You got him." He laid his hand on her arm, sliding it slowly down until his hand covered hers holding the gun. "You got him. He'll pay for Daniel's murder."

She released the gun and turned into his chest, openly sobbing. *Thank You, Lord.*

Chapter Thirty-Three

"The best proof of love is trust."
JOYCE BROTHERS

There were two things she knew for certain: one, ripping out stitches after surgery sucked sour apples, and two, she could never be Bella Miller again.

Remington sat on the examining table in the emergency room—again. At least the pain in her shoulder had subsided. Then again, with as much pain medication as they'd pumped into her, it shouldn't hurt. Ever.

The door eased open and Hayden stuck his head inside. "Hey, you."

"How's Ardy?"

He grinned and sat beside her on the table. "Good. Swapping recipes with the nurses."

Remington chuckled. "Is she gonna have more stitches than me?"

"Probably. They're going to keep her overnight for observation."

She nodded. "I'm just really thankful she's okay."

"Me too." He took her hand in his and held it. "I heard you were going to Little Rock with Rafe in the morning."

"Yeah. I'm going to talk with the FBI. Give them my official statement."

"Are you okay with that?"

She shrugged, not really sure how she felt. "Rafe's SAC from Tennessee is meeting us there. I'm just ready for it to all be over."

"I bet." He squeezed her hand. "I'll take care of Chubbers for you."

"Thanks." And she hoped to be able to track down Whiskers back in Little Rock. She'd love to see her furry face again.

"Hey, the council offered to renew my contract. And give me a raise."

"Wow, how'd that come about?"

He waggled his eyebrows. "Apparently, when you assist the FBI in solving a major case, you get major kudos."

Remington laughed. "I'm happy for you. Proud of you too."

"Ditto that." Hayden squeezed her hand again. "You done good, kiddo. Brought down the bad guys and made the right choice in the end."

She rocked against him. "I guess. I feel bad about shooting Devane. I didn't really mean to."

"I know. It was an accident."

Yeah, but . . . "Hayden?"

"What?"

"I really wanted to shoot Hartlock. I mean, *really* wanted to shoot him."

"But you didn't."

How could she explain? "I couldn't."

He lifted her hand and kissed her knuckles. "Of course not. You're not like him. Not a killer."

"No, you don't understand. I wanted to pull that trigger."

"So why didn't you?"

He was really gonna think she was nuts. "Don't laugh."

Hayden drew an invisible *X* on his chest and grinned. "I wouldn't."

She nudged him. "Seriously."

"Okay. What?"

"I think God stopped me." She refused to blink, her scrutiny ready to record any change in his expression.

His eyes widened and his mouth formed an *O*.

"I knew you'd think I was nuts."

"No. I don't. I believe you."

"You do?"

He nodded.

"Why?"

Chuckling, he shook his head. "I tell you that I believe you, and you ask me why. Because, silly girl, I've been praying for God to talk to you, talk some sense into you."

"You have?"

"Yep. So I figured He was working on you when you showed up Sunday to go to church with me."

Interesting. Very interesting.

She felt Hayden's stare. "What?"

"So, you two are talking again?" The hope in his eyes made her laugh.

"Let's say we're clearing some of the air between us and leave it at that. For now." But inside, her spirit to God's, she knew she was coming home.

Hayden's grin could split his face. "I have something for you."

She sat straighter. "I hope it's chocolate."

He laughed. "No. I hope it'll be something better." He handed her a folded piece of yellow, lined legal paper.

Her hand trembled as she took it. "What is it?"

"The letter from Daniel."

Even as she craved to devour every word, she pushed the letter back to him. "It's to you. Not me."

"I've read it. Many times." He dropped it back into her lap as he stood. "You should read it." He planted a kiss on her temple, then turned and left.

She stared at the folded paper in her hands. Her heart

pounded. She'd shot Devane. Hartlock had been arrested. Two men responsible for Daniel's murder had been caught.

But not the main culprit. Not the one who set everything in motion. He was still free.

Her hands trembled with the letter. She couldn't read this. Not now. Not yet.

Soon.

⚖️

There were just times that Rafe truly loved his job. This was one of them.

He leaned against the back wall of the Peabody Hotel in downtown Little Rock, blending in with the crowd. Good turn-out. Every local media outlet was represented on the front row from the podium, microphones and cameras at the ready.

This day had been a long time coming. Well, a week and a half since returning from Hopewell felt like a long time, but they'd needed every hour to conclude all the research and gather all the evidence. Now they had everything. Even Hartlock's signed confession.

Rafe checked his watch, then glanced across the room to see Alphonse Jackson looming. Opposite Jackson, on the other side of the room, Nick Hagar grinned. Rafe returned the smile.

Applause thundered, nearly rattling the ornately curtained windows as the favored candidate for Arkansas governor took the stage. A preelection convention. A last bid to get free media exposure. A last chance to snatch a few votes from anyone still left undecided.

A prime opportunity for the FBI.

The expected future governor began speaking into the booming microphone. Showtime!

Rafe paid no attention to the man's words as he wove his way through the crowd. He caught the motions of both Jackson and Hagar in his peripheral vision. They were all moving in for the kill.

Reaching to his belt under his jacket, Rafe pulled out his handcuffs and had them ready. He made it to the stage.

A large security officer stopped Rafe with a hand to his chest. Rafe smiled and badged the man, who had no choice but to let him through. Rafe climbed the stairs and crossed the stage, Jackson and Hagar blocking the exits.

The man stopped speaking and wore a look of pure confusion. It almost made Rafe laugh. Instead, he withdrew his handcuffs and spoke at an angle that the microphone could pick up his words.

"Jonathan Busch, you're under arrest for the murder of Judge Daniel Tate, conspiracy, witness tampering, and terrorist activity."

His reading of the rest of the Miranda rights was lost in the clicking of cameras, murmuring of the crowd, and the clanking of the scales of justice coming into balance.

⚖️

Remington sat on the end of the pier, the breeze pushing over the bayou. The paper danced in her hand. With unexpectedly trembling fingers, she unfolded the letter and read . . .

Dear Hayden,

You don't know me, but I'm your father, and I've loved you from the moment I knew about you. I never had the chance to know you, not face-to-face, but I've watched you grow into a strong, faithful man. You are kind, gentle, merciful, and wise. I take no credit for any of these admirable traits. Your mother and her husband loved you and taught you well.

You are my son, but I've only been able to love you from afar. Oh, how I wish I could have raised you, but your mother insisted otherwise and I felt obligated to respect her choices. But know that I loved you very much and wanted to be a part of your life. Also, please don't think I've missed out on the honor and pleasure of being a parent. While the reason was tragic and heartbreaking, circumstances (or perhaps fate?) allowed me to raise my goddaughter, Remington Wyatt.

Now, since I've passed on, I'm certain she will come looking for you when she finds these documents. Of that, I'm positive. (Once you meet her and get to know her, you'll understand.) My hope is the two of you will hit it off upon meeting and will grow to love one another as you should have had the chance while growing up. You need to understand some things about her, son.

She's smart and funny and generous. Her goodness makes her glow from the inside out. She comes across as tough as nails, and she is that, but she's also pensive and considerate, warm and giving. You won't find a better woman anywhere in the world. Matter-of-fact, she reminds me a lot of your mother.

Remington will be upset when she meets you, as I never told her about you. Your mother asked me not to, and I would grant Ardith anything. So Remington will be hurt and feel betrayed. You owe me nothing, Hayden, but I beg of you, please, don't judge her too harshly. She's had to endure a lot of tragedy in her life, and she was raised by this single old curmudgeon.

While you are my son—my flesh and blood, and I love you, Remington has been my heart. She has brightened my life by walking into a room. Lifted my spirit with her smile. Touched my soul with a hug. Every ounce of goodness I ever possessed was gained from her. Each honorable and good thing I ever did was because of her. She made me a better judge . . . a better man . . . a better person just by being with her.

So I ask you to take the time to get to know her. I guarantee you'll come to love her as I did. And when you do, will you please share with her how much being in her life meant to me? That I can't imagine what my life would have been like without her bright light in my world? That every single day of my life, she blessed me in ways I can't even begin to describe?

But most of all, I'm without a shadow of a doubt positive her father would have been as proud of her as I've always been. If nothing else, please grant this dead man's request and let her know that.

I love you, Hayden . . . and wish I could've gotten to know you better. My prayer is that you and Remington will make things right in your generation that Ardith and I messed up in ours.

Your father,

Daniel Tate

Epilogue

It's no surprise that he pled out." Rafe handed her the rest of the pages on the prior bad acts of Jonathan Busch. "Hard to imagine a man playing for our team throwing the game." He shook his head. "He'll stay in prison for the rest of his life."

But Remington had stopped listening. Her breathing became labored. Her attention was stuck on the page Rafe had just handed her.

"What's wrong?"

"This can't be right."

"What?" He sat beside her. "What can't be right?"

She pointed to the last paragraph. "This says two drug users alleged Busch hired them to kill the defense attorney of the factory his family filed a wrongful-death suit against."

"Maybe yes, maybe no. That was more than twenty years ago. Guess that was one of his first crimes. Personal, since it was his brother who died from mesothelioma. Busch has done much worse since then."

"Rafe, look at the name."

"Wesson Wyatt." He looked at her. "I don't recognize the name."

Tears burned her eyes. "That's my father. We thought he was shot in a drive-by." She dropped her gaze back to the paper. "Busch had him killed because Daddy won the case."

Fresh grief hit her from nowhere. Sobs choked her until she released their fury. Rafe's arms wrapped around her as she cried. She balled the fabric of his shirt in her fist.

The pain ebbed slowly as Rafe held her in his strong, warm embrace. At least now she knew the truth of what had happened to her father. His killer would spend the rest of his life in prison. It wouldn't bring her father back, but it really did help ease the ache she'd carried around for over two decades.

All cried out, she looked up at Rafe. "I'm sorry. It's just . . ." She shrugged, not even knowing what to say.

With his thumb, he wiped away her tears. Her skin blazed where he touched. Her breath froze in her chest.

Never breaking eye contact, Rafe took possession of her mouth with his own.

Remington's limbs went limp. She leaned into the kiss, into Rafe, and let his most gentle embrace ease her residual grief and pain. The kiss was soft and sweet, with just a hint of underlying passion, and over way too soon for her liking.

Rafe smiled and pulled farther back. He swept her bottom lip with his thumb while he chewed his own bottom lip. "We're going to take this slow."

She smiled back, still struggling to regain control of her erratic breathing. "Are we now?"

He nodded. "Oh, yes ma'am. We're going to take it very slow." He swept a feathery kiss over her lips. "And savor every moment."

Dear Reader:

I've so enjoyed sharing this first book of the Justice Seekers with you. The story idea came to me as I sat in a federal courtroom for months listening to trials. As I listened and watched, I noticed how in every profession, even those within the justice system, there were good and bad people. After witnessing a rather extremely difficult cross-examination, I asked myself what would make someone turn away from a core belief. At that point, the premise for *Injustice For All* was born, and I couldn't rest until I wrote the story. At one time or another, we all feel like we've been treated unjustly. Whether it's perceived or accurate, each of us have walked down such an emotional road. This is the place I dug into to write this story.

While researching for this book, my own faith was tested many times over. Getting to know Rafe and Remington/Bella and their multiple flaws was great fun for me, even as I worked on the issue of forgiveness myself. So many, many times I've felt I was unworthy of God's forgiveness, so I was able to write Rafe's angst from my own heart. Part of Remington's spiritual journey was also mine. I thank you for letting me share it with you and hope the message challenges you to examine your own core beliefs. After reading this book, if you've felt led to give your life to Christ, please contact me immediately so I may send you a special gift.

I hope you've enjoyed traveling through this story with me and will return to learn more about Riley, Rafe's stubborn little sister.

As a reader myself, I love hearing from other readers. Please visit me at www.robincaroll.com and drop me a line, or write to me at PO Box 242091, Little Rock, AR, 72223. I invite you to join my newsletter group and sign my guestbook. I look forward to hearing from you.

Blessings,

Robin Caroll

Discussion Questions

1. Rafe was willing to sacrifice his career for his best friend and goddaughter. Has someone ever made a personal sacrifice for you? Describe how it made you feel.

2. Remington turned from her faith after the death of her father. Have you ever experienced a time when you were tempted to ignore your faith? Describe how you reconciled yourself.

3. Because she was scared, Remington ran. How do you handle fear? What does Scripture tell us about fear? (See Psalm 27:1 and Isaiah 41:10.)

4. Remington re-created herself to stay alive. Have you ever wished you could? Describe why or why not.

5. Rafe felt like he had to "earn" God's forgiveness for perceived past sins. What does Scripture teach us about God's forgiveness? (See Matthew 6:14, Acts 2:38, and Colossians 3:13.)

6. Hayden felt betrayed by Bella, his best friend. Have you ever felt betrayed by a friend? Describe how you felt and how you handled the situation.

7. Rafe carried the burden of guilt for having been in love with his best friend's wife. Do you believe who you love is a choice? Discuss your answer.

8. Hayden was very quick to judge both his mother and his sister. Do you think he was justified? Why or why not? (See Matthew 7:1 and Luke 6:37.)

9. At first Bella didn't trust Rafe because of her past experiences. Have you ever had to overcome an issue with trust because of past experiences? How did you deal with the emotions? Discuss any Scripture that offered you peace during this time.

10. Which character did you most relate to and why? The least?